Meri Strikes Back

Meri Strikes Back

M. APOSTOLINA

Simon Pulse
New York London Toronto Sydney

SIMON PULSE

An imprint of Simon & Schuster Children's Publishing Division
1230 Avenue of the Americas, New York, NY 10020
Copyright © 2006 by Cafegogo, Inc.
All rights reserved, including the right of reproduction
in whole or in part in any form.
SIMON PULSE and colophon are registered
trademarks of Simon & Schuster, Inc.
Designed by Tom Daly
The text of this book was set in Weiss.
Manufactured in the United States of America
First Simon Pulse edition July 2006
2 4 6 8 10 9 7 5 3 1
Library of Congress Control Number 2005930536
ISBN-13: 978-1-4169-1163-0
ISBN-10: 1-4169-1163-4

For Jane

Acknowledgments

With thanks and gratitude to Jason Agard,
who gave encouragement and advice
when I needed it most; Christine Beirne,
for all her continued support
(and her spanikopita); Kristy "Scandalous" Scanlan,
who cheered me on during the final stretch;
Demanda Maraschino, for simply being s-o-o-o-o
Demanda; and Bradley Inners, who broke up my days,
made me laugh, and bought Grey Goose.

And once again, many thanks to Jennifer DeChiara,
Frederick Levy, and Julia Richardson—
and everyone at Simon & Schuster—
for letting Meri run amok.

Meri Strikes Back

October 14

Dear Diary:

I had a nightmare last night. The sun rose, my alarm clock sprang to life, I slapped it silent—just like I do every morning—then I gazed at the two sleeping figures next to me. Here I was, I thought, at Alpha Beta Delta, the most prestigious sorority ever at Rumson River University in North Carolina. And there was Keith Ryder (my love, my sweet, my everything!) sleeping in my bed. I heard a slight moan. Coming up from beneath the covers was Rags, Keith's cute-as-a-button floppy-eared mutt. He stretched his limbs, yawned. I gently petted his head.

"Hey, Rags, how's it hangin'?"

He glared at me and sniffed, "That's not funny. You know I've been snipped. I swear to God they cheaped out on the Novocain. I felt every single solitary excruciating second."

Okay, this was a dream, and anything can happen in dreams—dogs talk, so I guess cats and birds do too—but I was still surprised.

"And while I have your ear," he continued, "I'd like my water bowl filled twice a day. At least. And less rawhide. It plugs me up. Oh, and no more table scraps, 'kay? I mean, would it kill you to make one more pork chop?"

In the blink of an eye, I was in the shower—just like that—

washing and shampooing for the day. Then I slung my bookbag over my shoulder and made my way across the campus to my first class. *This is going to be a great day*, I thought. After all, I had only recently brought down Meri Sugarman, the former president of Alpha Beta Delta.

I was nearing the Polk Academic Building, where my first class, Masterpieces of Western Lit I, is held, when a shivery breeze quivered past. *Brr.* I reached for my sweater. It wasn't there. In fact, nothing was there. I was naked. I'm not saying I "felt" naked. I. Was. Naked. Really-really naked. Bare-assed without-a-stitch-of-clothing naked. I closed my eyes and cursed myself. Why, oh why did I forget to put my clothes on this morning? Stupid-stupid-stupid. *Maybe*, I thought, *if I run behind a bush, or crouch behind a parked car, no one will see me. Quick, do something!*

I opened my eyes—and nearly screamed. Several students were rushing past (the second bell had rung, so classes were just about to start), and it took me a few moments to realize that none of them seemed to notice that I wasn't wearing any clothes. In fact, a few students even gave me a casual wave, including Doreen Buchnar, a pretty, if potty-mouthed, girl from New York City who's head cheerleader for RU's football team.

"Hey, Cindy, what's up? Beautiful fucking day, huh?" And then she moved on.

I cautiously held out my arms, I looked at my body. Yep, I was still *au naturel*, as the French say. I had to laugh. See, I'm definitely not the sort of girl who wears short-short skirts, or flirty blouses with plunging necklines (a cowl neck or polo collar is more my speed), and while I know that a lot of guys think it's really "hawt" when girls wear low-rise jeans with their thongs peeking out, I'd rather die than be caught in something like that. But there I was. Naked. Really and truly naked. And I didn't care. In fact, I felt free.

Wheeee! Why should I be late for class? I thought. *Who needs clothes?*

Without a care in the world, I strolled into Masterpieces of Western Lit I and took my seat. Professor Scott began his lecture on *The Odyssey*, an epic Greek poem about Odysseus, who returns to his kingdom after a long absence and tries to reassert himself as king. Then I heard cruel, snickering laughter. I looked up— and my heart skipped a beat. Meri was sitting on Professor Scott's desk, her legs demurely crossed, and she was pointing right at me. Suddenly, everyone in the class was laughing, even Professor Scott. Oh my God, they could see me—they knew I was naked. The laughter echoed and swirled around me, and I heard voices, too.

"She's not as flat as I thought she'd be," and "Eeeow, she's got an outtie," and "Naked or clothed, her hair's still tragic."

I ran. In an instant I was on the Great Lawn of the campus, bolting past students playing Hacky Sack, still more making out on blankets, while covering my breasts with one hand, my nether regions with the other. Horse whistles and derisive catcalls followed in my wake. Then I tripped, I fell—*boom!*—right on top of Bud Finger. Oh, why Bud Finger? Why did I have to be on top of him? Naked? Being sensible—even in my dream—I immediately jumped back up. But he grabbed my hand.

"Ooo, Cindy," he said with a loopy grin. "I like that you don't shave down there. Never shave."

I screamed, kicked him away, and kept running. *Somehow*, I thought, *I'll make it back to my room at Alpha Beta Delta, whip open my closet, and put some clothes on.* Then I shrieked. Sharp fingernails dug into my back. I was twirled around. There was Meri, right before me, in all her cool perfection; her makeup flawless as always, her gray-blue eyes luminous and piercing, her lips shiny and moist, her lustrous black hair whipping in the wind. She almost looked like one of those too-perfect Pantene Pro-V shampoo models, but this was Meri, after all, so I knew she wasn't going to tell me about the virtues of Hydrating Therapy Color or Multi-Dimensional Shine Glossing Serum. When she finally did speak, she spoke softly, delicately. "Have a nice trip, see you next . . ."

I should have guessed the next part. Her arms jutted out, knocking me backward. I was falling, but I wasn't falling to the ground, I was falling off a fifty-story skyscraper. I screamed, my limbs desperately flailed. I lunged and tried to grab hold of the building—or a window, or a ledge—but no luck. Instead, during my speedy descent, I saw Meri in every other window. As I fell faster, the windows seemed to come alive as one window, like one of those flip books that animate a drawing or a photograph. It was the same action over and over. Meri was smiling complacently, running her hands through her lustrous raven hair, flipping it back, and whispering breathily, "Cindy's my little bow-wow. Bow-wow. Bow-wow. Woof woof. Grrr."

I looked away. It was too horrible. When I opened my eyes, I saw the ground rushing up toward me. I was about to go *splat* on the hard cement. I closed my eyes again, braced myself. *Ka-boom.* I felt all icy and tingly. I wasn't flattened. I was wet. I was in the ocean. I struggled to swim to the surface. My head popped up. All around me, as far as the eye could see, was water, just water, and headed right toward me, the biggest wave I'd ever seen. There was nowhere to go, it was right upon me. I'd survived being naked, being groped by Bud Finger, and being pushed off a skyscraper by Meri, but now I was about to be pulverized by a super-gigantic wave.

My eyes opened. I was in bed. I turned to my side and saw Keith sleeping next to me, and beneath the covers, Rags stretched out, yawned.

"Rags?" I softly asked.

Rags didn't answer, thank God, so I knew my dream was over. Keith stirred.

"Hey, morning," he said, giving me a smile, his (left) eye twinkling. Wow. What the heck is this super-cute star quarterback for RU's football team doing with me? In my bed? He's been the sweetest surprise of my life. I never really thought any decent guy would ever be into me, much less this dreamy, blue-eyed, dark-haired dreamboat (with a six-pack!) (ha!). I'm not saying I'm a complete loser or anything, but let's get real, I'm hardly *Maxim* material. My younger sister, Lisa, once helpfully explained, "You're plain, and that's, like, totally okay, because plain girls make pretty girls look even prettier. Like *moi*." But see, Keith went through his pretty-girl phase all through high school and into college, and of course they all assumed he was just this dim-bulb Ken doll, good for banging and not much else, given the way he looks and the fact that he plays football. When he met me he thought I was "really hot" (I'm not sure I believe him on that one), but more important, he thought I was smart, and he never thought a smart girl would ever be into him. At least that's what he told me, and I'm going with it. He also used to be Meri's boyfriend, but I don't want to go there. That's all in the past. Meri is gone. And yet my mind keeps spinning back to her. How can it not?

Meri. Beautiful, glamorous, seemingly perfect Meri. Her reign of terror was legendary. Blackmail. Extortion. Humiliation. Under Meri, Alpha Beta Delta was a House of Horrors, held to the increasingly deranged and drug-fueled whims of both Meri and Gloria Daily, her fiercely loyal vice president. But I fought back. No, I wasn't the prettiest sorority girl around, and I was very insecure (I still am. I guess I'll always be battling my low self-esteem. And my hair. I can never get it just right. When I die, I hope they don't lay me out. I really don't want to meet my maker with a cowlick). But my "plainness" worked to my advantage. No one ever seems to notice what a "plain girl" is up to. With help from my friends, I boldly exposed Meri's illegal activities: the wire-tapping, the money siphoned from supposedly "charitable" sorority events, the cruel attempts to demean Keith by planting drugs and gay porno mags in his football locker. Oh, and so much more. And guess what? My efforts paid off. Meri was exposed. And Meri ran. The last time I saw her was just yesterday, in Vegas, where she desperately attempted to escape from the police with Gloria Daily, her partner in crime. Meri's still running, and so is Gloria, though as a nice Vegas police detective assured me, "Not for long." Let's hope so.

Downstairs, Keith joined me and a few of the other sorority girls for breakfast, including Shanna-Francine, a sweetly chubby-cheeked, frizzy-haired senior who "played dumb" when Meri was president of Alpha Beta Delta. It was all part of her strategy to fly under the radar as far as Meri was concerned, and it worked. She didn't just fool Meri, she fooled the entire school. But now, with Meri gone, Shanna-Francine can be, well, Shanna-Francine—a cheerfully giggly brainiac—and even though a lot of the girls thought I should be president of Alpha Beta Delta given my efforts to expose and drive out Meri, I put my vote behind Shanna-Francine. She was elected in a landslide.

It's a big responsibility for her, and it's not one I would want. She has to completely remake Alpha Beta Delta from top to bottom as a respectable sorority, given all the negative publicity generated by Meri's downfall. In fact, come December 15, Shanna-Francine and all the girls from Alpha Beta Delta have to appear before Sigma Gamma Lambada, the national intersorority governing council in Vero Beach, Florida, that oversees and grants exclusive memberships to tons of college sororities nationwide. Sigma Gamma Lambada's president, Sister Nellie Oliverez, has already called Shanna-Francine and told her that Alpha Beta Delta is on "thin ice." Either we prove Alpha Beta Delta is a newly respectable sorority by December 15, or that's it, we lose our membership. And if that happens, then RU will no longer allow us to be a sorority. We'll cease to exist. That would be so sad, especially since we all went to so much trouble to get rid of the bad apples in our group, namely Meri (and Gloria, too!).

But I have faith in Shanna-Francine. She's got all sorts of new ideas. She'll be doing a complete overhaul on everything—our bylaws, our activities, our charity events. She even plans to make the house "politically appropriate," which sounds an awful lot like "politically correct" to me, but Shanna-Francine says it's different.

After kissing Keith good-bye, I was on my way to my first class, joined by Patty Camp, one of the nicest girls I've met at RU—we were dorm roomies before I moved into Alpha Beta Delta—and yes, she's what you might call "large" or "plump," but Patty is happy to just say, "I'm fat. Who's kidding who?" She's also determined to become the world's most helpful psychologist. She's practically got the entire DSM-IV, a clinical handbook of psychological disorders, completely memorized, so when I told her about my dream, she was eager to analyze it.

"Fascinating," she said between bites of her morning Dunkin' Donut (she was carrying a box with six, which she claimed she would share with her Psych 101 classmates, but I somehow doubted the donuts would last that long). "So let's see. The fact that you were naked means that you're feeling exposed, that you're scared of being your 'authentic self.' You follow?"

I guess that makes sense. Naked. Exposed. It's kind of obvious, actually, which is a bit depressing when you think about it. Even my dreams are ordinary. Still, I was interested to hear what she had to say about Meri.

"Oh, that wasn't Meri at all," she said, taking a huge bite from her second Dunkin' Donut. Then she said something that sounded sort of like: "Hugger begun err mmmgurrr."

"What?"

"Sorry," she said, swallowing, wiping her mouth with the sleeve of her blouse. "Meri in your dream wasn't Meri at all. Okay? She was just a symbolic stand-in for all your repressed doubts and fears."

I had to think about that a moment. Meri sure seemed like Meri in my dream; she looked like Meri, she behaved like Meri.

"And that big wave," she continued with authority. "Pure routine. Nothing to worry about. That's symbolic too. You're overwhelmed by a big wave, ergo, you're overwhelmed by your emotions. Get it? It fits in perfectly, given all the troubles you're having with your deeply buried fears and doubts."

Wow. I was shocked by how easy my dream was to evaluate, which is a testament to Patty's skills as a budding psychologist. I had to laugh, too. She was prattling on, saying the most insightful things, while donut crumbles and sugar dust dribbled from her mouth and stuck all over her blouse. Patty has problems, and she'll be the first to tell you about them. "I'm borderline," she once told me. "And I also have rapid cycling mixed with cyclothymic disorder, which can cause manic or sometimes major depressive episodes. I'm actually a fascinating case study." Yet she's absolutely determined to better herself and help better those around her too. She even has a boyfriend these days, Jesse "Pigboy" Washington, a gargantuan black football player who plays with Keith on RU's team, and happily, he doesn't seem to mind that Patty's a big girl. In fact, I think he kind of likes it. Just last night, when we were all celebrating the demise of Meri and playing music and dancing, he grabbed her around the waist and shouted, "Daaaaaayum! Check out that gadong-a-dong-dong. Weeeeerk it!"

Patty squealed. So sweet. Still, she wants to lose weight, and after analyzing my dream, she told me all about the new Karl Lagerfeld Diet that she's on. If you ask me, it sounds kind of disgusting. She has to eat things like horse meat, and calf's liver with strawberries, and consume scary-sounding "protein sachets" five times a day.

"He has a wonderful recipe for tuna and blackberry mousse," she gushed. "And look at me. I'm already losing weight. Can't you tell?"

I was about to ask her if Dunkin' Donuts were on Karl's regimen, but then I thought, *Why be a killjoy?* I couldn't tell if she'd really lost any weight, she looked the same to me, but I said, "You look fantastic." And you know what? I wasn't lying. With her hair out of kilter, her makeup hastily applied—she always has bright red lipstick stains on her front teeth—and her loose, ill-fitting clothes splotched with food and coffee stains, I thought, Patty is Patty, and that's a pretty fantastic thing to be. She was off in another direction to her class, but before she left, she had a reminder for me.

"Remember, Cyn, Meri's gone. The high-alert is over. Now you can come into your own. It's so exciting. And don't worry. Your anxieties will decrease if you allow your authentic self to come through."

Then she was gone, leaving a trail of Dunkin' Donut crumbs and sugar dust in her wake, and I was left wondering, *What is the "authentic" Cindy?* Which I guess sort of raises the question, What is the "inauthentic" Cindy? After I took my seat in my Masterpieces of Western Lit I class, I was half-listening to the lecture on *The Myth of Sisyphus* and half-pondering my authentic self. I began listing. My authentic self is one or more of the following:

1. Being a good student (even though I'm thinking of changing my major from literature to something else, but it's not even the middle of my freshman year yet, so I have time)

2. Being a good daughter (I think I have that one pretty much locked up)

3. Being Keith's girlfriend (my love, my sweet, my every-thing!)

4. Being a good sister (that one's been really-really hard lately, given that Lisa's become a one-hit-wonder pop star—she calls herself "Lissa," just "Lissa." Her semidirty dance song, "Tune My Motor Up," is still getting lots of air-play. But even without that, she's always been prettier than me, and way more popular. It's hard being compared to her all the time, especially since she's a whole three years younger than me! It's so not fair)

5. Just plain Cindy B. (But what is that, anyway?)

I looked over my list. I didn't know which one to choose, or how many. My cell phone trilled. I had a text message. Furtively, since I'm well aware of the ban on cell phone use in classrooms at RU, I propped up a textbook, carefully flipped open my phone, and read the text: "luv u! u rawk!" My heart swelled. It was Keith. I quickly sent him a text back: "luv u 2! u rawk more!" I felt myself blush all over, and that's when I knew. My authentic self is Number 3: "Being Keith's girlfriend." Woo-hoo! And I don't care if that's retro or not feminist enough, or whatever, it's how I feel. I was on a cloud as I strolled out of class. Professor Scott tapped me on the shoulder and cleared his throat.

"Miss Bixby? We need to talk."

Uh-oh. I took a seat opposite Professor Scott's desk. He closed the door firmly and stepped toward me. He did not look pleased. But then Professor Scott hardly ever looks pleased, or even vaguely happy. He's such a serious, literary-type person—he has brown elbow patches on his jacket, and I'll bet he smokes a pipe, and he's always frowning (so much so on one side that at first I thought he had palsy), but I couldn't imagine what I had done wrong. Then he let the bomb drop. Using a cell phone for conversations or texting during class time is forbidden at RU, and he said he felt obligated to report me. I must have looked really sad or something—and I was, though more miffed than anything—because he reached out and placed his hand on mine, and with a surprisingly soft and caring voice said, "Cindy, it's just not like you. And *The Myth of Sisyphus* is such an important piece of literature, and so applicable to your life, too. Aren't you searching for meaning?"

He had me there. I guess I am searching for meaning, or self-meaning, or my authentic self, like Patty says. Professor Scott kept talking about the importance of Camus' philosophy: We should all strive to derive meaning from our own existence, and learn that mere hope for meaning can sometimes be enough, even in the face of insurmountable obstacles—like the kind Sisyphus himself faces when he's forced to push that rock up the hill. I've actually read it twice before, but I didn't want to come off like a smart-ass, because I was still hoping he wouldn't report me. Then he clutched my hand tighter, leaned in close—his face was right up to mine—and spoke in a really low and gravelly voice.

"Think about it, Cindy. Who knows where you'll find meaning?"

Oh my God. I could smell it. Professor Scott was wearing Paris Hilton's men's cologne, and before you ask how I know that, just take a whiff of any semi-dorky would-be "playa" on campus. They all think they'll "score" by wearing it, and I don't know why, since it smells like Dad's stinky old deodorant stick, and I only know what that smells like because Lisa once double-dared me to take a big sniff of his balled-up workout T-shirt that she'd pulled from the hamper one day (I did it, but only on the condition that she smell his underwear next, and she agreed) (she went back on her word) (of course) (sometimes I really hate Lisa). I thought, *Does Professor Scott think he's a "playa"? Isn't he a little long in the tooth for that sort of thing?* (He's in his late thirties!) And why, I wondered, was he holding my hand so tightly? And why was he smiling at me in kind of an eerie, skeevy way?

And then I knew. Holy crap. I hated that I knew. Professor. Scott. Was. Flirting. With. Me. I honestly don't know how I got out of that classroom. It's all a blur to me now. I promised to turn off my cell phone in class from now on, of course, and told him that, yes, *Sisyphus* was "really important," but all I could think about was the sticky, clammy sweat on my hand from where his hand touched mine. I ran-walked down the hall and straight into the ladies' room and all but scalded my hand with hot water. I wanted to disinfect it entirely. I'm in bed now. I've taken a shower. I'm clean.

Keith is off at some secret kegger tonight. I wish he were here. Maybe I should have gone, but I'm over all the drinking that Keith likes to do. "Let's get tra-a-a-a-shed!" is something he and his football buddies are always shouting out. Okay, it's fun to do once in a while, but not all the time, and besides, keggers are illegal at RU now. We have Meri to thank for that. Ever since me and Keith and Lindsay and Shanna-Francine and Patty and Bud and Pigboy exposed her, the university decided to clamp down hard. No more keggers, no more drinking on campus, nothing. There's actually all sorts of new rules and regulations, and I can't be caught breaking any of them because that would hurt Alpha Beta Delta's chances of renewing our sorority membership. Maybe it's silly that I'm so concerned about that, but I worked really hard to get into Alpha Beta Delta and meet new friends and turn my life around after being such a loser in high school (and junior high) (and elementary school). Sometimes it feels like Alpha Beta Delta is my second family; they accept me as me, no questions asked. Maybe

I should just go to bed, but for some reason I'm still thinking about Meri. I have to keep reminding myself, Meri is gone. Patty's right, the high-alert is over. If I'm thinking about Meri, it's only because I'm not dealing with my own repressed fears and doubts. The real Meri is not in my life anymore. That much I know for sure.

October 15

Dear Diary:

Shanna-Francine is off and running! She convened a special meeting with all the girls at Alpha Beta Delta this afternoon to outline her initial plans to transform the house. We were gathered on the porch in back, and there was lemonade (and some really good sugar cookies, too), along with new Alpha Beta Delta embossed notebooks that Shanna-Francine had specially made for us to write notes in.

"In the eighteenth century, the original intent of sororities was to assist girls in becoming 'socialized,'" she cheerfully announced. "And that's what we're going to do. We're going to be a shining example to everyone on campus of what it means to be socially appropriate."

"Appropriate." There was that word again. "Politically appropriate," "Socially appropriate." I wasn't sure where this was going, and she could probably sense we were all a bit confused, but she pressed on.

"For example, forget about 'rushing.' We'll no longer 'rush' our new members. Instead, we'll 'recruit' them. And instead of going through 'pledging,' the new recruits will be put through 'New Member Development.'"

Okay, I was now officially confused. I raised my hand and asked,

"So we're just renaming everything? What's the point?"

Shanna-Francine was thrilled to answer my question. You could tell that she'd really put some thought into this. To her, renaming sorority activities was merely one step, but it was an important one, since words like "rushing" and "pledging" have "inappropriate" and "sexist" connotations. If we were going to set an example to the entire university, she explained, and prove our worthiness to the intersorority governing council in December, then we had to demonstrate our respect for gender, color, and class, and actively display our devotion to the plight of the disenfranchised.

I was listening, of course, but I also had to discreetly elbow Lindsay Cunningham once or twice. We were outside on the porch, so of course she had her trusty umbrella to protect her from the sun's harmful rays (she has a new favorite, a lovely Louis Vuitton with bright pink cherry blossoms), but one of the umbrella's sharp metal end-tips kept sticking me in the head. She mouthed "Sorry," and scooted a few inches away. It was a cloudy day, and I wasn't about to tell her that she probably didn't need it. Lindsay's a dear friend and fellow Alpha Beta Delta sorority girl who's born of Canadian royalty (real royalty!), and I swear, she's never without her umbrella. Ever. She uses it to shield herself from the sun (even on cloudy days), given the untimely death of her beloved aunt, Princess Christiana of Northumberland, who sadly succumbed to melanoma. But sometimes I think Lindsay carries it too far. Just this morning at breakfast, she opened up her umbrella in the kitchen because early-morning sun was streaming in through the window. We all had to duck just to get to the coffeepot. And don't get her started on that report where scientists claim that sunshine can actually help prevent cancer (since the sun gives us Vitamin D, which guards against many types of cancer, including melanoma).

"It's a conspiracy," she told me plainly. "Doctors just want more money. The more sun we get, the sicker we get, the richer they get."

And the proof, as always, is her sadly departed Aunt Christiana. Actually, when I think about it now, that's pretty hard to argue with, though even Lindsay admits that "Auntie was a sun whore" who spent most of her time sunbathing topless on her yacht with Uncle Stephano (I've seen pictures; she had a lovely figure, as all royalty seem to have, but her skin color did remind me of a freshly baked Butterball turkey).

For her part, Shanna-Francine continued to cheerfully explain the new changes for Alpha Beta Delta. Our charity events would be increased three-fold, she told us, and they would now have "real purpose." We'd start slow. In the next few weeks, we were going to set up cookie booths outside various academic buildings.

"We'll be raising money for starving children in Cambodia," she proclaimed breathlessly. "Just like Angelina Jolie."

That got a big response from all of us. And why not? Okay, so Angelina Jolie likes to slash up her body with tribal knives and engage in really dirty S and M sex, but even Mom is impressed by her charity efforts, and Lisa is too.

"Oh my God, I like everything about her," Lisa once said. "She's this total slut ho-bag, but it doesn't matter, you know? 'Cause then she'll go off and wear some big-ass burka in Pakistan and look s-o-o-o righteous. It's like, if Mother Teresa were a skank, she'd be Angelina."

All the girls were really excited about Shanna-Francine's new ideas, but I think they were actually more excited about Shanna-Francine, to tell you the truth. She's so inspiring, and so joyful—I swear her cute, frizzy hair seems to gesture askew to help accent any point she might be making—and I can't help but marvel at how much she's changed since Meri's departure. This is the real Shanna-Francine: happy, giggly, passionately intelligent, and okay, "appropriate" and all that stuff too, but that's all right. I'm so glad she's come into her own. And I think she really will save Alpha

Beta Delta. She also mentioned that we'll be able to welcome a few new members to the house, since, given the departure of Meri and Gloria Daily, there's room for two more. My hand shot up.

"How about Patty Camp?" I eagerly asked. Shanna-Francine looked at me quizzically, but I already knew which buttons to push. "Fat people are oppressed—by the media, by society. I was in the grocery store with Patty once, and this woman had the nerve to come up to her when she was reaching for some Mallomars and say, 'Now, dear, do you really think you need those?' Can you imagine? And can you imagine enduring all the name-calling—and the flight arrangements? When she flew for a long weekend to Padre Island last month, the airline made her buy two seats, even though the plane was only half-full."

Lindsay gasped, "That's horrible."

"Besides, we all love Patty, right? And she's so smart, and she's so—"

Shanna-Francine's bubbly laughter cut me off. "Okay, okay. All those in favor of welcoming Patty Camp as a new Alpha Beta Delta sister, please raise your hand."

She raised hers, and so did I, and so did everyone else. I almost cried. One of my best friends ever is going to be in the house. And even though I know I'm not supposed to think about Meri anymore, I couldn't help but chuckle at the thought of her learning that Patty's becoming an Alpha Beta Delta sister. She'd scream. *Well, too bad, Meri, you're not here anymore.*

I was startled by a loud buzzing sound. *Whirrr.* It was coming from Lindsay. I glanced at her, or rather, I lowered my head just a bit to see her face beneath the umbrella, which she held at an angle.

"Cell phone," she whispered hastily.

The meeting continued—it's amazing how a decision regarding what kinds of cookies to sell can become so contentious—and then I heard the buzzing sound again. *Whirrr.* It was the strangest cell phone sound ever. It seemed to rev up slowly, then really let 'er rip. Lindsay had her umbrella angled even lower, and I tapped on it lightly, again leaning down to see her face. She looked panic-stricken, and beads of sweat were on her forehead.

"Cell phone," she whispered. "I'll answer it after the meeting."

Who, I wondered, was calling? And why was Lindsay so anxious about taking their call? After the meeting, I stepped up to the bathroom. Lindsay was inside, nervously scrubbing her face.

"Is everything okay?" I asked.

"Fine, fine. Everything's fine," she swiftly responded.

Then her cell phone buzzed. *Whirrr.* She froze.

"Aren't you going to answer it?" I asked.

She practically yanked me into the bathroom. Then she closed the door and whispered anxiously, "I can tell you anything, right?"

"Of course," I said, and I meant it. Lindsay and I have grown close, and I'd like to think that I'm a good friend and confidante. I may not be able to offer astute psychological insight like Patty, but still, sometimes people just need to unload.

"Okay, here's the deal," she said, nervously dry-dabbing her face with a towel. "It's not my phone that's vibrating."

"So what is it? Your pager? Your PDA?"

Then she told me. The color drained from my face. I can barely write this. Somehow, Bud Finger convinced Lindsay—sweet Lindsay!—to insert a small vibrating egg inside her vagina. It's some sort of sex toy; the girl has the egg, her partner has the remote control, and he can use the remote to turn the "vibrate" on and off from a distance of up to ten feet. But Bud jerry-rigged the remote. Now it has a reach way, way beyond ten feet. In fact, it can reach her clear across campus, and Bud, as Lindsay apprehensively explained, hits the on switch periodically throughout the day, so Lindsay will know when he's thinking about her.

I stood absolutely still as she told me this. Do not judge, I repeated to myself, just listen. But I was judging big-time. I couldn't help it. I wanted to reach out and shake her and scream, "Don't you see what he's doing to you? He's turning you into a pervert! He's corrupting you!"

And I should know. I actually grew up with Bud Finger back in Marietta, Ohio. I'll be blunt: Bud's a scrawny twerp with a very annoying hyena laugh and a greasy leer—everything for Bud is about sex. Sex-sex-sex. He somehow managed to start his freshman year at RU last August just like me, and within days of his arrival he kept begging me to be his "college bitch." Gross. Still, I try to be nice to Bud. He did come through for me (somewhat) when I was battling against Meri, and to my complete astonishment, he began dating Lindsay. I just don't get it. She's definitely a good girl, so why she's with Bud Finger is anyone's guess. Maybe it's some sort of twisted "Beauty and the Beast" thing, though calling Bud a "beast" is doing him a big favor. It's more like a "Beauty and the Perv" thing, if you ask me. Lindsay is so sweet and so pretty, she can have any guy she wants, and yet she's with Bud, a guy who's proud to tell you about all the Hollywood-inspired porno titles he's come up with, like *Plowing Miss Daisy* or *Schindler's Fist* or *Star Whores: Revenge of the Clap*. Hardy-har. Stuff like that cracks Bud up.

I didn't say anything as I stood across from Lindsay in the bathroom (what could I say?). I just listened. She turned beet red.

"Never in a million years," she said, and she didn't have to finish the sentence. But sex, she explained, was so freeing with Bud. Just being with Bud was freeing (for her).

"I mean, I've been with guys before, of course," she whispered. "But it always felt like I was on the outside looking in, you know? Like it was someone else who was having sex. But with Bud . . ." Then she covered her mouth and stifled a giggle. "We're just so dirty."

A sudden whirring sound jolted me upright. I met Lindsay's eye. She nearly yelped.

"Please don't tell anyone."

"I would never," I assured her. And I meant it. A knock at the door startled us both. I swung it open. I nearly shrieked.

"Yo, Cindy," said Bud with a greasy grin. "Aw. And there's my boo. You're lookin' sexiful, Linds."

Then he swept her into a sloppy embrace. Eeeow. I'm so lucky I have a normal boyfriend. I accompanied Keith to one of the "secret keggers" tonight. It was at the Pi Kappa Phi fraternity . . . in the basement. It was supposed to be fun, I guess, but everyone was so paranoid. Keith and a few of the other frat guys keep peeking out the basement window every ten minutes just to make sure there were no campus security around. I had a couple of beers (I'm not buzzed as I write this, though), while Keith and the frat guys and their girlfriends did shots of Jägermeister. Doreen Buchnar kept looking at me disapprovingly each time I passed up a shot and finally said, "What the fuck's up with you, Bixby? This is your fault, you know, that we're fucking hiding down here."

Ooo, that made me so angry. Yes, by exposing and bringing down Meri, I caused RU to become newly strict, but Doreen seems to forget that she was one of Meri's blackmail victims too, and so was Keith. But I just smiled kind of faintly; I really didn't want to get into it. One of the guys there was Wolfgang Rimmer, a bony German student with big bug eyes who's majoring in chemistry. Meri had once tried to eject him from campus by pulling strings to get his visa revoked, but Meri's not here anymore, so Wolfgang is back (unfortunately). He kept trying to hit on Doreen (fat chance, Wolfie), and the drunker he got, the less everyone understood him because he kept speaking in German. *"Ich habe einen sehr grossen penis!"* he screamed, laughing uproariously, and no, I didn't need a translator.

Keith is such a sweet drunk. I practically had to carry him back to Alpha Beta Delta (he hung on my shoulder; I nearly tipped over twice). I like that he needs me sometimes. He's passed out on the bed now. I'd take off his clothes, but somehow that seems wrong. Not that I would do anything, but Keith is so respectful of me, and I certainly don't want him to think I'm not respectful of him, too. I should take his shoes off, though. At least. God, he's cute! He's sleeping there all sprawled out, and Rags is resting his head on his back. How did I get so lucky? I wish Patty were awake right now, because I'd call her and tell her how good I'm feeling, even "authentic." She still doesn't know she's been invited to join Alpha Beta Delta. We're springing it on her tomorrow.

So, Diary, what more can I say? My life is actually going pretty well now. Meri's gone, Keith is with me. I really don't have any idea what to write about anymore. Maybe I should just stop journaling and start living! Ha!

So that's it. Good-bye, Diary. I'm putting you away. Maybe years from now when I look back at this entry, I'll realize that this was the day when everything in my life finally started going right.

October 20

Dear Diary:

My life is disaster! My eyes are welling up with tears as I write this. Keith and I are over. Kaput. History. Or as Shanna-Francine now says, "Her-story." I still can't believe what happened, and I definitely didn't see it coming. And the silly thing is, it all has to do with Keith's partying, or at least my not partying, though Patty claims that the whole partying thing is just a "surface issue." I really don't care if it's surface or not. All I know is that I'm in bed. Alone. On a Friday night. Without Keith.

Yesterday, Keith and his buddies decided they wanted to party (big surprise). They're kind of over gathering in the basement of Pi Kappa Phi (I can't blame them for that, it is kind of dreary down there), but no one could think of any other place to go, and they were like, forget going off campus (it's much cheaper to buy a few kegs and some bottles of Stoli and Jack than to go to a club in town and pay for drinks). I was sitting across from Keith and his friends in the cafeteria when he suddenly exclaimed, "Dudes, I got it!"

I have to admit, it was a pretty ingenious idea. His plan was simple, but seemingly foolproof: Keith and his buds would rent the largest available U-Haul they could find and outfit it with several kegs, plastic cups, bottles of hard alcohol, and a few bags of ice; in the evening, they would pick up all available partiers and drive all over campus. In other words, the U-Haul would be a movable party for the entire weekend. I was about to say that, while inventive, being in a U-Haul sounded just as dismal as being in Pi Kappa Phi's basement, but Doreen suddenly chirped up.

"Oh, my God, that's so fuckin' tasty. You're so fuckin' smart."

She was wearing a low-cut ripped T with "Bitch Kitty" stenciled across her chest, and she was obviously flirting—she held her face in her hands and pressed her elbows inward as she leaned over the table to accentuate her cleavage, which is, I admit, pretty stupendous—and I thought, oh, brother, how obvious can you get? Keith's not going to fall for that. Okay, I know, I know, I'm completely lame. I gazed at Keith and he practically looked like one of those old cartoons of a wolf whose eyes and tongue suddenly pop out when he sees a pretty girl. I had to compete. I had to do something. I suddenly squealed, "What a great idea. It's so trashtastic!"

I had heard Lisa use the word "trashtastic" before, and I thought, *I'll sound really super-cool saying it*, but I was so nervous that my voice shot up—like I'd just sucked on helium—and my attempt to mimic Doreen's cleavage-accentuating pose was kind of unfortunate. One of my elbows slipped off the lunch table, so instead of accentuating my (modest, but not bad) cleavage, my head slipped and I nearly banged my chin on the table. "Geez, looks like Bixby's already tanked," chuckled Doreen.

"Yeah, that's me," I quickly added with a smile. I wasn't going to let Bitch Kitty have the last word. "Just call me Bombed-Out Bixby. Ha ha ha. We're going to have a blast tonight. I just know it."

Then I reached across the table and possessively took Keith's hand. Did I really have to compete with the likes of Doreen Buchnar? Keith liked me because I was different from the other girls, because I was smart. But in that moment in the cafeteria, I had a small epiphany. Guys will be guys, and there will always be girls (like Doreen) in low-cut T's with stupendous racks. The trick, I realized, was to stick by Keith's side and make sure he wasn't too distracted. That's how I found myself in downtown Rumson with Keith at the U-Haul rental depot. I was trying so hard to be helpful. I'd put together a list of everything that needed to be done to get the party going: rent the U-Haul, go to Costco for the cups, the alcohol, the coolers, then drive to Pi Kappa Phi to pick up some sort of tricked-out iPod and speaker system and load up the kegs. I'd even printed out a map of the campus and used a red Sharpie to mark who would be picked up where. Keith had his arm around me when I filled out all the paperwork for the U-Haul. It felt like we were a young married couple renting a truck to move our stuff into our first new home together. He smelled good too. And he kissed me on the cheek. Doreen who?

Unfortunately, I soon found myself all alone at the depot. I don't blame Keith. He can be so scattered sometimes. He forgot that he had an afternoon graphic design class.

"I know it's a pain," he said sheepishly. "But you think you could finish up here?"

I couldn't believe it. Was he really going to stick me with driving the U-Haul off the lot? Did he honestly think I was going to pick up all the liquor and ice and everything all by myself? Was the word "doormat" carved into my forehead?

"I gave Doreen your cell phone number," he continued. "She said she'll take care of everything if you don't have time. Or she'll swing by and help you out if you want her to."

I felt a dull pang at the bottom of my stomach. Doreen? Help me? Pul-lease. Yes, Doreen was aggressive—in terms of her rack and her attempts to shove me aside to impress Keith—but I wasn't going to roll over.

"I don't need help," I said with a slightly fakey smile. "Besides, I want to do it. It'll be fun."

"You sure? Doreen said you might not know what kind of vodka to buy."

"Stoli," I happily responded, having observed Keith's blow-outs on many occasions. "Regular, vanilla, and cranberry. Large size."

"You're awesome."

"Really? You think so?"

Okay, I was fishing for a compliment. I blushed, I looked away. I knew I would feel his lips pressed to mine in the next moment.

"Call Doreen if there's a problem," he said, bounding out to catch a bus back to campus.

A few minutes later, when the nice U-Haul man was leading me to the truck, my cell phone rang. I checked the caller ID: "Doreen." I let it go to voice mail. I wasn't too terribly worried about Doreen (compared to Meri, she was child's play). Still, I must have been distracted thinking about her, because I didn't even hear what the nice U-Haul man was saying when he handed me the keys to the truck. It was only when I turned the ignition that I realized that maybe, just maybe, I was in over my head.

I was behind the wheel of a twenty-six-foot-long U-Haul Super Mover with an estimated weight of eleven thousand pounds. And it wasn't even an automatic. But I figured, how hard can a stick shift be? (I remember Dad once taught me how to operate the stick shift on his car; just press the clutch down gently as you switch gears. Simple.) Still, Dad has a small car, and this was a colossus. I was ready to give up when my cell phone rang again. The caller ID said: "Doreen." I bristled. What would Doreen do? She'd learn how to drive a freakin' stick-shifting U-Haul, that's what she'd do. And fast. I slammed down the clutch, hit the gas—and shot like a rocket out of the lot. Really, I thought I was airborne. This wasn't a U-Haul, it was a supernova. *Ka-boom!* I hit the street hard—and I shrieked, because it almost felt like the whole truck was going to tip over on its side. I could hear car horns blasting around me. In the rearview mirror, I saw the nice U-Haul man looking not so nice and chasing after me. I freaked. If he took the keys away from me, I'd have to call Doreen (and somehow I figured that Doreen would know her way around a stick shift). I had no choice. I had to do this. I hit the gas and blasted down the street. I may have run a red light. Luckily I didn't hit anyone (though I did hear a few bloodcurdling screams as I barreled through a pedestrian walkway). In an odd way, I felt exhilarated, I felt powerful. There I was—me, little Cindy Bixby—driving a huge-ass hunk of metal. I was transformed. I wasn't Cindy Bixby anymore, I was Big Mama Trucker! I honked the horn a few times, just for fun.

Somehow I managed to park in the Costco lot, and once inside, I worked fast, tossing bottles of liquor and large jumbo containers of cups and napkins into my cart. My cell phone rang. The caller ID said "Doreen." I had to give her points for persistence. I flipped the phone open.

"Hello?"

"Hey, it's me. I'm in the frozen food aisle. They have some fuckin' awesome cocktail weenies here. Think we should get some?"

"You're here at Costco?!" I yelped.

"Fuck yeah," she enthused. "I figured you'd need some help."

I was about to say, "You figured wrong, Bitch Kitty," but instead I said, "Huh? What? Gosh, I think my phone battery is fritzing." Then I clicked off the phone, gripped my cart handle, and ran to the checkout area. Luckily, it wasn't the weekend. Back home, I'd gone to Costco on the weekend with Mom and Lisa on many occasions, and it was always jam-packed (with "The Great Unwashed," as Lisa liked to say. "This is fun for them. It's actually the highlight of their weekend"), but here I was through checkout and back in the parking lot in record time. *To heck with Doreen*, I thought. *She can stuff those weenies. Keith is mine. And Big Mama Trucker has places to go.*

I leaped back into the U-Haul, hit the gas, then barreled down the streets of Rumson until I found myself on campus. First stop, Pi Kappa Phi. I whipped the wheel and came to a screeching halt in front of their house. Bounding out was Doreen, who must have raced to the parking lot after I hung up on her. She was all smiles, and she'd changed into another low-cut ripped T with "Gr8 Trick" scrawled across her chest. Jeez, maybe it should have just said "Big Slut," but I guess that would have been too obvious, even for Doreen.

"Hey, Bixby," she snorted. "You look very manly behind the wheel of that truck."

Then she gave a horse whistle, and a whole bunch of guys from Pi Kappa Phi barreled out carrying kegs, throw rugs, stereo speakers, beanbag chairs, a disco ball. Opening the back of the truck, they arranged everything inside, and I have to say, it was all pretty impressive. This really was going to be a movable party.

A few hours later, the sun had set and the party was going full blast. And yes, yours truly was stuck behind the wheel driving the entire night. I hate Doreen. She played me like a patsy. When Keith asked who was going to drive, she practically flung herself on him and said, "I will, Keith. I can handle a big-wheeler."

But I quickly intervened. I don't really drink, I said, and it made more sense to have someone straight driving. Keith agreed, and behind him, Doreen stifled a snort. She really didn't want to drive at all. I'm such a ding-dong. Why didn't I see that coming? As I drove slowly around the campus, I could see everyone in back because Keith had hooked-up his Powerbook with an iSight camera in the trailer. All the fun was being broadcast to anyone on campus with a a Internet connection. It also broadcast to a twelve-inch Powerbook sitting right next to me on the passenger seat in the cab. Why? Because I was told by one of the frat brothers that I would need to monitor the image to make sure I wasn't driving too fast or making turns that were too sharp (God forbid I should cause one of the drunken revelers to loose their footing). I could see everything: Keith and his frat buds and their girlfriends were drinking and dancing, and the music was blaring. At one point, Doreen pounced on the iPod and flipped on the dance remix of Brandy's "The Boy Is Mine."

You need to give it up, had about enough.
It's not hard to see, the boy is mine.

The beat was fast, and Doreen was mouthing the lyrics, rhythmically booty-bumping Keith—and glaring in triumph right at me through the iSight lens. Nice try, Doreen. She seemed to have forgotten that Big Mama Trucker was behind the wheel. As Brandy says to Shaunta, "Gurl, your game is slow." I made a quick sharp turn and ignored the yelps and screams behind me. All I could see was Doreen—flying through the air, arms and legs flailing, her eyes popped open. She landed safely, but gawkily, on top of a canary yellow beanbag. It's funny, but as I'm writing this, I'm thinking about Meri. Yes, Meri was evil, there's no doubt about that, but I guess I've learned quite a few important survival skills from her. Or to put it another way, I "pulled a Meri" on Doreen.

Unfortunately, things went from good to bad to worse. It was just so awful. I'm getting a lump in my throat as I'm writing this. When I made my big herky-jerky turn that sent Doreen flying, I sort of remember hearing a small tinkling crash. I assumed someone broke a beer bottle. But that wasn't it. A few minutes later, everyone in the U-Haul could hear it: police sirens! Frozen with fear, I carefully pulled the U-Haul to the side of the road, and behind me, I could hear everyone shushing each other. The music was silenced, and when I looked over at the iSight image, I nearly screamed. Doreen was crouched down next to Keith, pressing herself against his chest. Then she pushed her face right into the iSight lens and loudly whispered, "Don't blow it, Bixby. Just play it cool."

I guess I didn't play it cool enough. After instinctively slapping the Powerbook's screen shut, I rolled down my window. The officer told me that my left taillight was broken (it must have slammed against something when I made my big turn). I was sweating profusely, and I guess I must have looked suspicious, because the officer asked me if I was nervous about something, and then he asked me if I had been drinking.

"Of course not, officer," I responded. "I hardly ever drink. Ask anyone. Most people think I'm a real bore at a party."

In back, I could hear snickering laughter (I swear it was Doreen), and the officer must have heard it.

"Whatcha got in the truck, ma'am?"

"Um, just my furniture. For my dorm room. I'm moving. My beanbag. And my disco ball."

Then he asked me to open the back of the truck—and the jig was up. It's all a blur to me now. We were brought downtown to the police station, and since a lot of us were under twenty-one, we were charged with alcohol possession. I was hit with an additional charge of reckless driving, and my first thought was, *This is not going to look good for Alpha Beta Delta*. I was furious with Keith.

"I've had enough of your dumb partying!" I shrieked. "Now look what's happened. And after all I've done for you. I saved you from Meri."

"Yeah, and you'll never let me forget that, will you?" he snapped back.

He was really drunk, and I probably shouldn't have gotten into it with him right then, but I was so angry about everything—about being taken for granted, about the partying, and most of all about that stupid slutty Doreen. I told him things had to change; I'd reached my limit. But I guess he'd reached his limit too.

"I thought you were my girlfriend," he bellowed, "not a nun." And then he dropped a bombshell. "Maybe we need a break."

I was shocked. I could barely move. A few minutes later I was like a zombie as we were all processed and released, and I stood gape-mouthed in the parking lot, watching as Keith stepped into the backseat of one of his frat buddies' cars—and sat right next to Doreen, who was thoughtful enough to blow me a kiss as they drove away.

"Tch. Boys. They don't like to stay too long in one place, do they?"

I turned around. It was Officer Roberta Woods, a nice, slightly frumpy-looking middle-aged policewoman I'd met during my misadventures with Meri. She put her arm consolingly around me. She must have seen what happened between me and Keith in the police station.

"Don't worry, sweetie. There's a sea of men out there."

"Not like him," I sniffled, and I meant it. I was trying so hard not to cry.

"Oh, but you're young. Not like me," she chuckled. "All I got is gray hair, liver spots, and a hey-nonny-nonny that forgot how to sing."

"I think you're very pretty. And I bet your husband does, too."

She smiled sweetly. "He married me for my meatballs. My famous meatballs. That and my baba au rhum. He must be really teed off he can't get it in Heaven."

I suddenly felt so stupid—and so indulgent. Here I was whining about Keith, and Officer Wood had lost her husband.

"Do you still make baba au rhum?" I asked.

"Naw, not anymore," she said. "See? There's a downside to widowhood. That and there's no one around to kill the really big

30

bugs. Damn him. And you. Tch. Running around with bad boys and booze. You're a regular hellcat."

"I know." I hung my head. I felt so ashamed.

"C'mon, I'm giving you a ride home."

She not only gave me a ride, she gave me a lecture. Bad boys might be fun, she said, but they're trouble with a capital T. The trick, she advised, was to find a good boy, and then teach him how to be a bad boy "when the lights are low." It sounded like straightforward advice at the time, but now everything just seems so bunched up and complicated and confusing. I'm still in love with Keith. But here I am in my bedroom. Alone. In an odd way it's comforting. Feeling miserable is so familiar. And luckily, there's a bright spot. Things can't possibly get any worse.

October 21

Dear Diary:

I woke up to an earsplitting scream this morning. And it wasn't mine. It's Saturday. I had no responsibilities. Nothing. Before the scream, I woke up at eight and my heart was racing—but I wasn't thinking about Keith, I was thinking about Meri. I must have had another nightmare about her, but I can't for the life of me remember what it was about. I guess my repressed anxieties were acting up again, with the added fuel of losing Keith. I had a quick image; my head is normal looking on the outside, but on the inside it's a terrifying bonfire. I decided to go back to sleep, but an hour or so later, Lindsay's earsplitting scream woke me up. I whipped my covers aside, raced down the stairs. Was someone hurt? Did someone fall?

"It's here!" Lindsay screamed.

At the bottom of the stairs, the front door was flung wide before a handsome UPS man (they always wear the cutest brown shorts), and Lindsay was joyously jumping up and down in front of him, clutching a medium-size cardboard box. She was so overjoyed, in fact, that she had to be calmed down by Shanna-Francine, who elbowed forth and reminded her that she had to sign for the package or the handsome UPS man couldn't leave.

In the living room, me and Shanna-Francine and a few of the

other sorority girls gathered around Lindsay as she carefully and very slowly opened her package. She was quivering with anticipation.

"I found it on eBay," she breathlessly informed us. "I can't believe it's here. I can't believe I have it."

Then she paused. The top box flaps were open, and inside, there was a fluffy pile of Styrofoam peanuts. All she had to do was reach inside.

"I can't," she stuttered, her eyes welling with tears. She thrust the box into my hands. "Would you? Please?"

I didn't know whether to feel honored or afraid. What on earth was inside this box? And was it, perhaps, a gift from Bud Finger? And if that was the case, should I put on plastic dishwashing gloves to protect myself?

"The suspense is killing me," squealed Shanna-Francine.

What the heck, I thought. I plunged my hand in, grabbed at something hard and cold, and pulled it out. My eyes widened; I had to fight for breath. It was dazzling, it was beautiful.

"It belonged to my Aunt Christiana," whispered Lindsay softly.

I gingerly placed it into her hands. Light streaming in from the bay window refracted off of it, causing it to shimmer and sparkle. Lindsay was holding a diamond-and-ruby-encrusted tiara that had belonged to her beloved aunt, the late Princess Christiana of Northumberland. It was beyond spectacular, and we all just stood there for a few moments gazing at it in awe, as if it were a magical object from some fairy tale that had popped out from the pages of an ancient tome—*ka-boink!*—and landed in Lindsay's hands.

"It was on eBay all night," Lindsay explained. "Someone named 'GoPepperGo' kept bidding against me."

"eBay's awesome," said Shanna-Francine. "One time I tried to get Brad Pitt's cowboy hat from *Thelma & Louise*."

"Ooo, I'd love to have that," I said.

"I'd rather have Brad," added Lindsay with a wink. Then she carefully handed the tiara back to me and asked if I'd do the honors. How could I refuse? It was like a coronation ceremony. For emotional support, Lindsay gripped Shanna-Francine's hand, then bent her head before me. I could hear birds chirping from outside. I swear their chirping seemed musical. They were singing "Hi-Lili, Hi-Lo." I'll never forget that song. It's so pretty. I first heard it when I was a kid and Mom and Lisa and I were watching *Lili* on TV, this absolutely enchanting movie-musical from the 1950s with Leslie Caron, who plays a sweet orphan girl who falls in love with a cute wooden puppet, having no idea that a sad, crippled puppeteer is high above her pulling the strings.

"This is retarded!" snapped Lisa. "No, she's retarded—she's gotta be. Who the hell falls in love with a puppet?"

Mom yanked on her ear.

"Ow!" screamed Lisa.

"Watch your language," scolded Mom.

"Whatever. I'm right. What's she gonna do? Make out with a puppet? Get splinters in her tongue?"

But I loved the movie. And of course Lisa never stopped teasing me about it. One morning she all but mauled me with my little blue parrot puppet that I'd gotten as a Christmas present.

"Polly's got a woody!" she screamed. "You and Leslie can get jiggy with him."

I guess some people just don't understand magic. But Shanna-Francine and Lindsay do. I placed the tiara on her head, and when she leaned back up, I swear she seemed even more beautiful than before; her white skin seemed to glow from within, her eyes twinkled. Then I heard a soft whirring sound.

"Is that your cell phone?" asked Shanna-Francine.

For the briefest second, Lindsay caught my eye—I thought

she was going to scream—then she rushed to the front door, and swiped her umbrella.

"I've got to show Bud," she nervously chattered, then whipped around to face us. "Do you think I look strange? Can I walk across campus to his dorm room wearing it?"

I was about to say that wearing a tiara wouldn't look any stranger than holding up an open umbrella on a very overcast day, but I am so not a killjoy.

"It'll be just this once," she added. "And then I'll put it away."

"You look beautiful," I said, and I really meant it. She popped open her umbrella, adjusted her tiara, and swept outside, with another soft whirring sound following in her wake. I turned to Shanna-Francine and we shared a smile. Then she placed her hand on my shoulder.

"Cindy, we have to talk."

Oh, no. Now I was in for it. No doubt she'd heard about my escapade with Keith and was about to tell me how this would reflect badly on the new Alpha Beta Delta. December isn't really that far away, and everyone wants the house to have a spotless record when we go before the intersorority governing council, including me.

"It's about Patty," she continued, and that really caught me off guard.

Patty has already moved into Alpha Beta Delta. She was so thrilled when I invited her to join, and though she was quick to point out that sororities are "breeding grounds for nonpathological dependent disorders and possible atypical cognitive conflicts," she was touched by Shanna-Francine's determination to make the new Alpha Beta Delta all-inclusive and socially nonjudgmental. It was a happy day, even though it started out with a bit of difficulty. I had to help Patty pack up all of her belongings in her dorm room, and that presented a special challenge, since the room was jam-packed with huge stacks of crumpled newspapers, half-eaten take-out containers, scattered piles of dirty clothes, candy wrappers, mashed-up bags of chips, and empty tins of cake icing, along with clumps of half-filled garbage bags which, I realized, were the remnants of her many aborted attempts to clean up. Patty's always had, as she says, "undifferentiated manic and dissociative tenden-cies," which manifest in her chronic inability to clean up her room, but we both realized that this was about to change for the better when we arrived at Alpha Beta Delta. I swung open the door to her new and spotlessly clean room. She actually shed a tear.

"A fresh start," she said with a slight quiver.

And it was. I helped her organize. I even took her to Stacks 'n' Stuff, where we bought three large plastic bins and placed them in her closet. I carefully labeled each of them with a Sharpie pen; on the first I wrote "Newspapers and Recyclables," the second, "Clothing," and the third, "Garbage."

"You're enabling me," she whispered, shedding a tear.

"No, I'm helping you," I countered.

That night we had a welcome dinner for Patty, and she was wide-eyed the entire time. I think a small part of her just couldn't believe that she was completely welcome, and that we didn't care about her immense size (or worse, judge her for it). But it's true, we don't. And that's why I was really startled when Shanna-Francine wanted to talk about her. Something was wrong, and I had no idea what it might be.

"It's the smell," said Shanna-Francine guardedly.

She explained further. Yes, everyone had accepted Patty's ongo-ing problems with cleanliness, and Shanna-Francine was quick to say that Patty was neat and clean in the kitchen and other common areas of the house. But her room was another story. Already it was a complete disaster. I'm not on the same floor as Patty—and I've been too consumed with my ongoing issues with Keith to pay attention—but apparently some of the girls, while again mindful of Patty's right to maintain her living space as she sees fit, were now reluctantly complaining about the smell coming from her room: a turgid odor of fermenting garbage, rotting food, and body odor that's seeped into the hallway and into some of the girls' rooms.

"You two are s-o-o-o-o close," said Shanna-Francine, and then she scrunched up her face. I knew what she was going to say.

"Don't worry, I'll talk to her," I assured her. And I did. Sort of. When I took the stairs to Patty's room, I have to admit I could smell what everyone was talking about. The odor grew stronger as I arrived at her door and gently knocked. She swung it open—and I nearly dropped to the floor. The smell hit me like a truck, my eyes welled with tears; I swear I almost felt like retching. But I didn't want to offend Patty, and she seemed to be in such a good mood. She led me inside, pushed aside a clump of dirty clothes that were piled on a chair, and immediately addressed the issue.

"I know. I've heard. And I'll take responsibility. I swear. In fact, I already have."

Then she triumphantly whipped out a SavOn bag, which was filled with recently purchased Glade Plug-Ins room deodorizers.

"Smell this one," she offered excitedly. "It's Lilac. So pretty. Oh, and this one's Orange Blossom. And I just love the Cinnamon Stick."

"That's just going to mask the smell," I told her, surprising myself with my firmness. "You're going to have to clean up. And I'll help you. We'll do it together. Right now."

Patty sighed and nodded her head (she's still concerned about being "enabled"). Then she began recounting her ongoing issues with her mother, whose cruelly dismissive treatment of her as a child is the "core cause" of her many "fascinating" disorders, which she's now taken to charting on graph paper—the ups and downs of each line corresponding to each specific disorder, and how strong or weak they may be on any given day. But I was only half-listening. I was looking around, and when I opened the closet, I saw the three bins: "Newspapers & Recyclables," "Clothing," and "Garbage." They were all empty. I burst into tears.

"I'm so sorry," exclaimed Patty, who raced up and swiftly closed the closet door.

But that's not what I was crying about. It was Keith. I burst like a dam. I told Patty everything. She was so sympathetic, and as usual, she had illuminating things to say about the situation.

"Once the projection ends, the reality sets in," she sagely observed.

"Meaning what?"

"Well, new love is a verifiable chemical state, akin to dementia and mild psychosis. Neuroscientists have actually plotted so-called 'hot spot' areas in the caudate nucleus area of the brain that change and alter when we first fall in love."

"What does that have to do with 'projecting'?" I asked, thinking she was talking about a projector in a movie theater. I have so much to learn. Patty is so smart.

"Well, when we first fall in love, we psychologically 'project' all our hopes and desires for our new relationship onto our loved one," she patiently explained. "Which means that we don't always see what's right in front of us. We're too busy see-ing what we want to see, or what we're imagining might be there in the future. In your case, you saw Keith as your ideal-ized love, as someone way different from your average frat boy. But in actuality, Keith has many characteristics of the average frat boy, a lot of them heavily pronounced, including his propensity for partying, which your overactive caudate nucleus caused you to overlook, at least initially."

"But I told him to stop," I protested. "I said I was over it."

"Yes, and that's when his own idealized projection of you ended.

That's when he saw you as you really are."

"But that's terrible!" I cried, burying my face in my hands.

"No, Cindy, that's good."

"I just wanted him to listen to me," I added in vain. "That's all. I just wanted to be heard." Patty tsked.

"Poor Keith. He's probably suffering from alexithymia."

"What's that? Keith is sick?"

"Don't worry. A lot of guys suffer from alexithymia—and it's a condition specific to men."

"What is it?"

"In layman's terms, alexithymia is the inability to process emotional information or listen to information of an emotional nature. Think of it as a pronounced deficit in expressivity."

"What?! So guys have a chemical excuse for not listening to women?!" I shrieked. Patty shrugged.

"Sucks, huh?"

She offered me a hanky to wipe my tears, but I kindly declined (it looked like it had dried day-old salsa on it). We spent the rest of the day thoroughly cleaning her room, and I was happy to hear that her relationship with Pigboy was progressing nicely.

"We recognize our growing mutuality," she happily informed me. And then she sighed. "Plus he's dynamite in the sack."

And yet, there are signs of potential trouble. Pigboy refuses to come into Patty's room (no surprise there), and he's growing weary of her Karl Lagerfeld diet, which limits their options when they go out to eat. Patty admitted that she's ready to make changes and finally give up on the diet.

"Besides, I don't think it really works," she said. Then she tore open a package of pink Hostess Sno Balls with her teeth. And threw the wrapper on the floor.

I took a stroll around campus late this afternoon, just to clear my head. Everyone was rushing about, no doubt readying for their big Saturday night dates and parties. When I walked past the Great Lawn, I saw a small crowd gathered. It was Lindsay, happily showing off her aunt Christiana's tiara. Bud Finger was by her side, gallantly holding her umbrella above her head. Bud has a date tonight. And I don't. Something is wrong with the world.

When I got home, I checked and rechecked my e-mail. No message from Keith. Then I checked and rechecked my cell phone. No voice or text message. Nothing. I'm all alone in the house tonight. I'm so sad. And I'm angry, too. And though Patty told me earlier that now is a good time for me to finally get in touch with my "authentic self," I think she's wrong. I think I need to get back in the saddle. I think I need a new boyfriend. Ha. That would show Keith.

Before climbing into bed—which is where I am now—I neatened my room a bit and turned on the radio, and I was about to shut down my computer when I suddenly heard you-know-what blaring from the radio speakers:

> Oh, tune it, tune it, tune it, make me purr!
> Tune my motor up! Oh, baby, yeah!

I had to laugh. Lisa's song is still getting airplay, and according to Dad, who called me yesterday, Lisa's thrilled to be in Los Angeles. She's there with both Mom and Dad so she can meet with record executives and music managers and, hopefully, get a deal for a full CD and cut a new single. My mind was still on Keith (it still is), and my own miserable state of loneliness (that too), so I decided to distract myself and send her an e-mail.

EMH:From: <cindybixby@yahoo.com >
Date: 21 October

To: <lisa@lisabixby.com >
Subject: Miss You!

Hi Lisa:

How's everything in Los Angeles? Are you staying at a fancy
hotel? Have you seen any movie stars yet? Dad said you guys
are going to Grauman's Chinese Theatre to see the stars'
foot prints. Sounds like fun!

Things are great here at Alpha Beta Delta. I don't think
I've ever been happier. Write me back when you get a
chance!

xxoo
Cindy

    I was a little bummed when I heard back from her—and in
what seemed like mere seconds:

From: <Lisa@lisabixby.com >
Date: 21 October
To: <cindybixby@yahoo.com >
Subject: Re: Miss You!

        THIS IS AN AUTOMATED RESPONSE

Dear Fan:

Get real! If I took the time to answer all my fan mail, I
wouldn't have time to burp. I'm, like, sooooo busy right now
you wouldn't believe. But it's all for you. So make sure to

buy lots and lots of copies of my current single, "Tune My Motor Up," and tell your friends to buy bunches of copies too. As you probably know, I'm in Hollywood right now. I know, I know. Calm down. I have totally resisted Hollywood for s-o-o-o-o-o long, 'cause I really feel that Hollywood is so incredibly phony. And I'm so real.

But I figure if Eminem can stay real and be in Hollywood, then so can I. I really identify with his songs. It really is hard being THIS popular, and even though I don't have a skanky crack-ho wife or a little baby I can never see 'cause I'm always out touring, I do have problems! I can't get into it, though—give me a break, I have to have SOME privacy—but I'm sure you'll be reading all about it in *People*, and *US*, and all the rags soon.

Thanks so much for writing. It means so much to me even though I NEVER have time to read ANY of my e-mails.

Keepin' it real,
Lissa

October 22

Dear Diary:

Keith is gone! That's the first thought I had when I woke up this morning. It's all I've been thinking about all day. When I stepped into the kitchen for breakfast, everyone looked up at me, and all of their faces were sad and gloomy, so they obviously knew what was going on, and yes, I appreciated their sympathy and support, but I hate pity, and that's sort of what it felt like. Shanna-Francine scrunched up her face and squealed.

"We're here for you, Cyn."

A couple of the other girls chimed in.

"It must be so hard being you right now" and "I don't know how you get out of bed in the morning" and "Do you feel like killing yourself?" and "Mild depression is to be expected at this time, along with recurrent hypomanic episodes."

The latter was said by Patty, of course, and I know she means well, but I really don't like being diagnosed in public. Then Lindsay abruptly squeezed my hand and fiercely proclaimed, "I'll hate his guts if you want me to. I will."

Oh, I love Lindsay! For some reason, that's just the sort of support I wanted. I wanted her to hate Keith. I wanted everyone to know what a big dumb mistake he made. And I wanted him to know it too, and boy, he will, especially when he sees that I have a new boyfriend, though I'm not telling anyone about my plans for that right now, especially Shanna-Francine, who wasn't too appreciative of Lindsay's brand of encouragement.

"Hate is such an inappropriate emotion," she gently, but instructively, announced. "Why hate when you can forgive?"

Everyone nodded their heads, taking in her wise words (except for Lindsay, who discreetly rolled her eyes). Shanna-Francine's right, of course (in my gut, I know she's right) but I guess I just can't get past the hate right now. And I certainly can't go to the place that she did when she quietly added, "I forgive Keith."

A few of the girls gasped. Then they followed her lead. I sat there completely bewildered, surrounded by their soft whispers.

"I forgive Keith," "Me too," "I do too," "I'm all about forgiving Keith," "I forgive Keith s-o-o-o much."

Then they turned to me expectantly. They actually expected me to say "I forgive Keith." I stuttered like a dork. I think I was even sweating. I was about to blurt out, "I don't forgive him for anything," when Lindsay boldly came to my rescue.

"I'll tell you what's inappropriate. Telling someone how to feel. And when to feel it. That's really inappropriate."

She was so firm, and so demonstrative, that her tiara nearly slipped off her head (she was going to put it away for safekeeping after wearing it all day yesterday, but I have a feeling it's never going to leave her head) (I wonder if she wears it in the shower).

"Lindsay's right," concurred Patty. "We have to allow Cindy to go on her own emotional journey in her own time."

Everyone agreed (thank God), but they looked at me with even more pity than before (no doubt wondering where I was on my "journey," and perhaps assuming that I wasn't as far along as I should be). Luckily, it was a busy day for all of us. The house is opening its first Charity Cookie Booth on campus tomorrow to raise money for starving children in Cambodia. It'll be the first real test of the new

Alpha Beta Delta. In the backyard, a few of the more mechanically inclined girls built the cookie booth with tools and wood they'd bought from Home Depot. They were having a pretty rough time of it, though, and on their first try, they constructed a booth that leaned to the left in a strangely asymmetrical fashion.

"We need lesbians," sighed Lindsay. "Lesbians know how to build things, and how to use tools. They like golfing, too. And consume only vegetables and whole grains."

"That's such a gross generalization!" exclaimed Patty, and Shanna-Francine wasn't amused either.

"It really is inappropriate."

Then they all looked at me (what? I'm supposed to have an opinion on lesbians today too?).

"Um, I've never met a real-life lesbian," I truthfully responded. "So I wouldn't know."

As it turns out, no one at Alpha Beta Delta has met a real-life lesbian—not even Shanna-Francine—though Lindsay did recall that her beloved aunt Christiana had two very tempestuous "Sapphic affairs," as she called them: one with her Guatemalan cook, and the other with Franzetta Maria Del-Rio Del-Rubio Del-Fuente, a glamorous Spanish princess whom she met one fateful day in the quaint village of Forio during Immacolata Concezione in the Basilica of Saint Maria di Loreto (sadly, the affair ended when Aunt Christiana learned that Princess Franzetta had bought her title and was not, in fact, real royalty).

In the kitchen, Patty and I were in charge of making the cookies. It was so much fun. Patty has her own recipe book, and I have to say, her recipe for Chocolate Chip Peanut Butter Chunk Cookies is out of this world. We danced, too. Lindsay blared this really cool techno dance music from her iPod (which she somehow connected to the stereo) (don't ask) (I'm really not good with technical things).

"It's from Bud," she proudly pointed out. "He ripped it from 'XTC Radio in Tahiti.'"

"Meaning what?" I asked. "He ripped it off?"

"No, no." She laughed. "He has this program called Stream-Ripper on one of his computers, and it records the songs and then organizes them in files by song and artist on his iPod. Isn't that amazing?"

Is it just me, or is all this computer music stuff a bit overwhelming? I mean, I'd love to have an iPod in one sense—they're really small, and some of them come in pink—but all this talk about "ripping" and "downloading" and "streaming" and "shoutcast" and "killabites"—none of it makes any sense to me. Who wants to learn all that when you can just buy a CD and listen to the music? Still, I had a blast making cookies and dancing with Lindsay and the gang. *This is why I'm in a sorority*, I thought. *This is why they're my new family!* I even forgot about Keith for a few hours. And then I had another thought: *Meri who?* which was a little strange. I haven't thought about Meri in days, and I haven't had any nightmares about her either, which can only mean that I'm somehow dealing with all my repressed fears and anxieties. Yes, Keith dumped me, but I guess it's made me stronger. I can go on. Why? Because I have Lindsay, and Shanna-Francine, and all the other girls at Alpha Beta Delta.

It's going to be a very busy day tomorrow. Not only are we opening our first Alpha Beta Delta Charity Cookie Booth, we'll also be having a Smoker Meeting in the morning to fill one more vacant slot for some lucky girl (Patty replaced Meri; the girl we choose tomorrow will replace Gloria Daily). Oh, but we're not allowed to call it a Smoker anymore. It's now called "Prospective Member Assessment," which is more appropriate.

I have to say, I'm feeling more hopeful than I have in a long time, which is a pretty big accomplishment considering you-know-who gave me the big heave-ho. Keith-Shmeeth. "There's a sea of men out there," according to Officer Wood, and I'll bet one of them is just as good-looking as Keith, and hopefully more mature, too. That's what I need this time. Someone who's grown up. Then I'll have everything: good friends, a solid academic career, a mature boyfriend. As I'm writing this, I'm almost tearing up. If I had been feeling this good just a few months ago, I wouldn't have trusted it. I would have thought, *Disaster is looming*.

"Sometimes good feelings stir up just as much anxiety as bad feelings do," Patty once told me. "Because we don't think we deserve to feel good about ourselves. We start to feel better, and then we neurotically assume that something bad is lurking just around the corner, ready to leap out and ruin our lives. This is called 'magical thinking.' It's actually very common."

That was me, "Common Cindy." That's how my brain worked months ago. But not anymore. I'm "Happy Cindy" now. And nothing can ruin that.

October 23

Dear Diary:

I hate myself! I hate my life! I hate everyone and everything! She's back. She's here. In Rumson. And she's free. I can barely hold my pen in my hand as I'm writing this. I've been shaking all day. It started this morning. I was barely awake. I plodded downstairs to the kitchen. I picked up the coffeepot. Reached for a cup. I noticed that everyone was staring at me. I thought, *Great, here we go again. More pity about Keith.* Oh, how I wish that was it!

"You guys, really, I'm over it," I mumbled impatiently. "And I forgive Keith, okay? How's that?"

Lindsay burst into tears. Shanna-Francine was hyperventilating. One of the girls ran out of the room. Patty, however, was an ocean of cool. She sat Buddha-like at the table, her palms open on the table.

"We have to tell her," she calmly intoned.

Something was wrong. Desperately, horribly wrong. I held my breath for a moment, and the room seemed to tilt sideways—violently, as if we were on a really big ocean liner and we'd just hit an iceberg. Then I shrieked.

"He's dead?! Oh my God. Oh my God, I love Keith. I'm not over him. Oh my God."

"No one's dead," assured Patty, who turned pointedly to Lindsay. "Show it to her."

"Not me," she yelped, passing something under the table to Shanna-Francine like it was a hot potato.

"No way, not me either," she squealed. Quivering, she nervously passed whatever it was to Patty, who met my eye and said, "Cindy, I want you to sit down."

"No. I'll stand, thank you very much. Whatever it is, I'll stand. Right here. And I'll take it."

"She's so strong," whispered Lindsay.

I held out my hand. I was ready. Oh God, if only I had known. I wouldn't have just stood there. I would have run screaming. I would have leaped back into bed and willed myself to yesterday. *Please-oh-please-oh-please, take me away to yesterday!* But yesterday was herstory. *Poof.* Today was here. In all its cold unforgiving glory. Patty retrieved a folded newspaper from beneath the table and placed it gingerly in my hands. I forcefully whipped it open. It was the *Rumson River Daily Gazette*. There was a headline. Three simple words. My eyes scanned them quickly: SUGARMAN CUTS DEAL.

I can't be sure what happened next. Or in what order. But I suddenly realized that I was bleeding. Shanna-Francine later told me that I dropped the coffeepot; it shattered on the floor, I lost my footing, slipped on hot coffee, fell to the floor, cut my thigh on shards of broken glass. And I screamed. I think I even howled. Because in those brief seconds, I took in more than just the headline. Words ignited in my head: "community service," "in lieu of jail time," "mercy from the court," "returns to Rumson River," "happy to be home." And the picture. Yes, there was a picture. A close-up of Meri. She was smiling. And her head was tilted impishly to the side. Just like Diane Sawyer does when she's interviewing someone and trying really hard to be sincere. And her hair. Her thick raven hair. She must be wearing a wig, I thought, it couldn't have grown back that fast. And her eyes. They bore right into me. And her mouth. And her lips. Her moist, moist lips. They moved. They formed words. They said, "Cindy's my little bow-wow. Bow-wow. Bow-wow. Grrrr." Pain struck. Blood flowed. I was hit. I was dying. She had won. At last. Meri had destroyed me. It was all over. I suddenly saw Whitney Houston. She wasn't skinny. She wasn't spooky. She glowed. She was an angel. She sang gospel. She sang loud and proud: "I love the Lord! He heard my cry! And pitied every groan!"

"Somebody get some bandages!" screeched Shanna-Francine.

"Don't die, Cindy," wailed Lindsay.

Oh, I didn't die. I'm still here. Barely. As I sat there on the floor, allowing the girls to carefully clean and bandage my leg, I knew; I knew that Meri was back, and I knew that she'd be coming for me. *I don't know how, and I don't know when, but it will happen,* I thought. *And I have to be ready. Alpha Beta Delta has to be ready.*

"We need to prepare," I whispered.

"For what?" asked Shanna-Francine.

Oh, brother. Am I the only one who gets it? I tried to explain, but everyone kept talking to me like I was a jittery little girl who'd just seen *Scream* and needed to be told it was just a movie (actually, I did have to be calmed down a bit when I first saw Drew Barrymore get all cut up and disemboweled, and Lisa did too, though she now claims that she was really frightened by Drew's "tragic" ribbed cardigan and blond bob wig). Meri, they insisted, would be nowhere near RU or Alpha Beta Delta. For the remainder of her senior year, according to the article, she'd be attending Chappaqua Community College in nearby Ronkonkomo County and performing countless hours of community service in order to fulfill the requirements of her plea bargain.

"I hope she's cleaning toilets," I shrieked. "With a toothbrush. No. With her tongue!"

Several girls gasped in shock.

"Shh. It's okay. We're all okay. See? Look right here," said Shanna-Francine, who gestured to the newspaper like I was blind as well as infantile. "It says 'ninety-two hours' of community service. Gosh. That's a lot. She won't have time for anything else. Don't you guys agree?"

They all nodded their heads in unison, like a row of Jack-in-the-box" dashboard bobbles. I was mashing my teeth. My anger was building. "She's coming," I warned. "We have to prepare."

In the midst of their assurances, the doorbell rang. Patty discreetly stepped away, and when she returned, she tactfully leaned in to Shanna-Francine and whispered, "The girls are here for the Smoker. Should I tell them to come another time?"

"They're here for their Prospective Member Assessment, not a Smoker," corrected Shanna-Francine. She decided not to cancel it, and softly instructed Patty to take me upstairs to my bedroom.

"No, I want to be there," I wailed. "I'm not a baby." Then I burst into tears. My anger evaporated. I was suddenly a gunky puddle of anxiety and fear. Luckily, Patty could see what I really needed. Though I was, according to her, "in the midst of maladaptive shock with schizotypal delusions," she felt that I would be better served by joining the group and proceeding with my day as if everything were normal. But will any day be normal now?

At the meeting, I sat shell-shocked in the living room while Shanna-Francine and the other girls served the small group of prospective members milk and cookies from the batch that we'd made for our cookie booth today—which turned out to be a big mistake.

"Are these cookies cruelty-free?" one of them asked. "I do *not* eat refined sugar," snapped another. "Ech. Animal products," shrieked one girl.

It suddenly dawned on me. In her efforts to create a more

appropriately diverse house, Shanna-Francine had invited an all-lesbian group of prospective members to assess, and they weren't too thrilled about being served "cruel" cookies, and God forbid, milk. Only one girl dug right in. Her name's Bobbie Sugar, and gosh, she has the broadest shoulders of any girl I've ever seen, and absolutely enormous hands and feet. She has a large pug nose, too, and a pretty scary-looking dyed-black Mohawk. She also has septum nose piercing with two black metal hornlike thingies sticking out of her nostrils, a silver ring that pierces her lower lip, and a silver tongue stud that gives her a slight lisp when she speaks—and she speaks in short, loud, gruff growls. If you didn't know any better, you might assume that she's mean and perhaps dangerous (at first I was certain she had a switchblade). But she's actually a really sweet girl (Patty was thrilled when she complimented her on her cookies), and she listened very attentively when Shanna-Francine gave everyone her spiel about the house—about all the good works we were going to do, including today's inaugural Charity Cookie Booth, and about the many benefits of joining a sorority, including the opportunity to make lifelong friends and career contacts. She was also frank about the precarious status of Alpha Beta Delta as an officially sanctioned national sorority.

"We're evolving," she explained. "For example, our symbol used to be the crown, but now it's the dove. Our official flower's also changed from the white carnation to the more appropriate blue cornflower. Our motto is 'Giving from the Heart.'"

A lot of the prospective members were snickering, which is so rude (and yes, inappropriate). And when a soft buzzing sound emanated from Lindsay and she reflexively whispered, "It's my cell phone," two of the girls looked at each other knowingly and nearly fell off the couch, they were laughing so hard.

For my part, I was preoccupied. Meri had invaded my head—and she wasn't leaving. I kept stealing glances at the newspaper, and everything I read made me angrier and angrier, and more frightened, too, such as: "The court was impressed by Ms. Sugarman's sincerity, as well as her heartfelt determination to reform and serve her community."

I felt bile building in the back of my throat. Who wrote this dreck? And then I made a not-too-shocking discovery. In small print beneath the newspaper's masthead, it read: "A Versalink Company." Of course. Meri's dad is the chairman and chief operating officer of Versalink, a huge media conglomerate that Lindsay once told me dwarfs even Viacom and Time-Warner. And that explains the ridiculously positive spin on her story, and no doubt the whole deal she cut with the court to begin with, since the Sugarman family is beyond wealthy and powerful. Each sentence was like a dagger. This section really threw me for a loop:

> WBCC, the Women's Broadcasting Cable Company, has made an impressive seven-figure offer for rights to Ms. Sugarman's story. "We feel it has all the right elements for a wonderfully uplifting TV movie or miniseries," explained WBCC's programming veep, Tatyana Boyle. "Ms. Sugarman's story is inspiring. It has redemption, self-transformation. [Ms. Sugarman] has evolved into a truly remarkable young woman whom we feel our viewers will both admire and applaud." For now, however, Ms. Sugarman is declining the many offers that are coming her way. "I just want to do good," she was noted as saying.

Saint Meri. And yes, WBCC is a Versalink-owned cable channel. Holding the newspaper, my hands were moist and clammy, and I realized I was shaking. Then I noticed a brief paragraph near the bottom. It was almost a throwaway:

> Ms. Gloria Daily, whom the court determined initiated
> most of the illegal activities that Ms. Sugarman was also
> charged with, will be serving a six-month sentence at
> the Fairfield Women's Correctional Facility.

Unbelievable. Gloria is taking the fall for Meri. No doubt there's a payoff. I had to look away from the paper, it was just too overwhelming. Anxiously folding it in my lap, I attempted to redirect my attention to the meeting. To my surprise, I realized that several of the Prospective Members had already departed (I guess "cruel" cookies and milk are a sure way to clear a roomful of lesbians). In fact, there were only two left, Bobbie Sugar and another girl, Danni Meinhart, who's very slim, tense-looking, and prefers to be called "Cricket," which I guess is her nickname (and maybe lesbian code for something, but I'm not sure). Shanna-Francine informed them that the new Alpha Beta Delta doesn't believe in hazing, but in order to be considered, they would have to perform a "selfless act," be it something for the house or something of a charitable nature. Cricket said she'd have to give this some thought, but Bobbie piped right up.

"I'll build you the best goddamn cookie booth you've ever seen," she barked, gazing directly at Shanna-Francine.

"Well, we already have one for today," she responded, and then she quickly looked away. I think she was even blushing, but I'm not sure why.

"Yeah, you do have one, and it looks like a piss-ugly piece of crap, if you'll pardon my French. I'll build you a new one. I'll do it in an hour. Right in your backyard. Right now. I got tools in my pickup. In fact, I'm doing it whether you want me to or not. You know why? 'Cause I don't want to see you selling cookies in anything that's not up to your normal high standards. And I can tell they're high. Just by looking at you."

Shanna-Francine responded with fluttering giggles. I exchanged a shrug with Lindsay; what was so funny? Then I looked at Patty, who was sort of half-smiling as if she was in on some big secret (but what?).

I like Bobbie. She may look menacing, and I'm not sure a poncho and straight-cut jeans are the best look for her, but even though I initially thought she fulfilled a lot of the clichés about lesbians that Lindsay spoke about yesterday, I was surprised when she told me who her favorite author was.

"Barbara Cartland," she gushed.

She was in the backyard with all kinds of tools that she'd retrieved from her Chevy Avalanche pickup truck. Danni had left; Shanna-Francine, Lindsay, and the rest of the girls were packing up cookies in the kitchen, and Patty was off to her first class, which left me in the backyard with Bobbie. I still couldn't get Meri out of my head, and yet I was struck by Bobbie's vehement defense of Barbara Cartland.

"She's not just a romance novelist," she growled. "I hate when people put her down that way."

"I'm not saying anything," I protested meekly.

I've never really read any of Barbara Cartland's novels, at least not all the way through, but I do remember that my Grandma Sophie was absolutely addicted to them (she was always quick to remind me that the author's full name was Dame Barbara Cartland and that she was related to Diana, the Princess of Wales, by marriage). I'm a sucker for a good romance, and I did try reading one of her novels called *The Taming of a Tigress*, but I was a little put off by the heroine . . . who spoke . . . in a . . . sort of . . . breathy . . . way with . . . ellipses . . . scattered . . . in every . . . sentence.

The sudden roar of Bobbie's circular saw bolted me upright, and for the briefest moment I saw Meri holding the saw—and gleefully using it to hack me in half on the sawhorse.

"The cookie booth's gonna be pink," screamed Bobbie over the noise of the saw. "That's Barbara's favorite color."

I was running late for class. I bid good-bye to Bobbie and wished her luck, then strolled quickly but zombielike across campus to Professor Scott's class. And I wasn't imagining things; people were pointing at me and whispering and giggling and snickering, too, because even though the *Rumson River Daily Gazette* didn't mention my name—why should Versalink give me publicity of any kind?—everyone on campus is well aware of the fact that I had brought down Meri. I guess I'm a celebrity now, which is more than strange. I held my head low, and then I thought, *Am I ashamed of something? Why not hold my head high? I didn't do anything wrong.* I straightened my shoulders. I even attempted a pleasant smile. Sudden flashes temporarily blinded me. Voices blasted rapid-fire:

"Are you happy that Meri's free? Do you want to be friends with her? Did you know that the Sistine Chapel has naked people on it? Are you scared of Meri now? Gosh, will you ever laugh again?"

The bright pops from the flash camera faded, and I could finally see Randy O. Templeton, aka ROT, and Nester Damon standing before me. Best buds since their arrival at RU, they're now a greasy-faced pimply twosome for the *Rumson River University Press*. Randy does the supposed "investigative journalism" while Nester takes the photos. I suddenly realized that I was their latest target. Meri was news, which meant I was news too. I was outraged. I felt attacked.

I shrieked, "Stay away from me!"

It all happened so fast. Nester lunged with his camera, I held my hand up, I wailed in protest. Flash-flash-flash. Then I must have pushed my hands out hard, because the next thing I knew, Randy was falling backward onto his behind, Nester was screaming, and I was running as fast as I could across the Great Lawn.

"Catch!" squealed a female voice. I looked up. It was Doreen. She was flinging a Frisbee, seemingly right at my head, and wearing a bosom-enhancing cut-off T that read "Shy at First" (she must have an inexhaustible supply of those semidirty Ts). I gasped, I ducked, then I whirled, and I saw Keith (my love, my sweet, my everything!) leaping majestically into the air, his hand reaching for the sky, his shirt trailing up, exposing his amazing six-pack and cute belly-button. The Frisbee thumped into his hand. Rags bounded forth. And so did Doreen, practically crashing into him. They tumbled to the ground. She pressed herself against him, mashing her lips to his. My heart sank violently to my knees. And right when Doreen was readying to grossly masticate on Keith's neck, he turned his head and he saw me, and even though I wanted the look in his eye to say, "This is wrong! I still love my Cindy B.," I tragically realized that it said nothing, or more to the point, "Yeah? So? You got a prob? You had me and you blew it." My jaw dropped. I wanted to scream. But I couldn't. I was demolished, emptied out. *It's official*, I thought, *I'm Keith Ryder roadkill*. I turned and walked-ran, clutching my thumping chest. Tears burst forth, but it didn't even feel like I was crying; something beyond me had flipped a switch, and the tears flowed on their own.

In Professor Scott's class, I tried to ignore the whispers and bleating little snorts around me. *Concentrate*, I told myself. Professor Scott was lecturing on Pierre de Ronsard, a French humanist known mainly for his poems about the beauty of love. Professor Scott finds Ronsard "profoundly sensuous" and "brilliantly musical."

"'You are the scent wherewith your posy's scented, bloom of its bloom,'" he quoted from Ronsard's *Sonnets for Helen*. "'The wherefore and the whence of all its sweet, that with your love acquainted suffers, like my passion's pale decadence.'" He went on and on and on, seemingly levitated by Ronsard's words. "Isn't this poem beautiful? You see, in Ronsard's work, love is where we find eternal salvation. Love, he tells us, brings true meaning to our existence."

"Oh, really?" I snapped. Then I smartly (I thought) quoted François La Rochefoucauld, a solidly cynical French counterpoint to the slop of Ronsard. "'Some people would never have been in love, had they never heard love talked about.'"

"Ms. Bixby," said Professor Scott, attempting to interrupt, but I continued bitterly, "Roland Barthes makes the point even clearer. 'No love is original. Mass culture is a machine for showing desire; here is what must interest you, it says. Men and women are incapable of finding what to desire by themselves.' You can take his position even further, I think. Like, if I'm really-really in love with someone, then poof, that someone is suddenly desired by everyone else around me."

"But wouldn't that situation also make you suddenly desirable?" asked Professor Scott. He was speaking softly, and standing right before me, and his hand was outstretched and holding a tissue. I involuntarily took it, once more realizing that my cheeks were stung by involuntary tears. I wiped them. A powerful, choking lump was building in my throat. There were more cruel whispers and titters. The class bell saved me. I sat motionless until almost everyone had left, then I stood up.

"Ms. Bixby," said Professor Scott.

I turned—and I saw his gentle eyes. The next thing I knew, I was engulfed in Professor Scott's strong arms. Not a word passed between us. He held me tight and I breathed—maybe for the first time all day. When I left his class, it felt like the blahs had lifted, just a bit. Why? Because I'm not alone! Yes, there's a storm in my heart, but someone understands. Professor Scott understands. He's a mature adult (unlike Keith). He understands love. He knows what I'm going through.

Unfortunately, the rest of the day didn't improve. In fact, it got progressively worse. Alpha Beta Delta's first Charity Cookie Booth was a complete fiasco. Later in the afternoon, Lindsay and I helped Shanna-Francine and Bobbie heft the cookie booth (yes, it's pink, just like Bobbie had promised) into the back of Bobbie's Chevy Avalanche, drove to RU's administrative building, and then set the booth up. Patty and several other Alpha Beta Delta sisters were already there waiting with the Tupperware-packed cookies. That's when I noticed the large sign. In their eagerness to be "appropriate," Shanna-Francine and Lindsay, along with an encouraging Bobbie, had decided to make a special price list. The sign read:

ALPHA BETA DELTA'S HOMEMADE COOKIES
TO BENEFIT STARVING CHILDREN IN CAMBODIA!

And in smaller lettering:

CUSTOMER PRICE LIST (PER COOKIE)
Caucasian Men: $2.25
Caucasian Women: $1.75
Asian Americans: $1.00
African Americans: $.75
Latin Americans: $.50
Lesbian/Gay/Bisexual/Transgendered: $.25
Native Americans: Free

"Is this a joke?" I asked Shanna-Francine.

"The plight of the oppressed is so no laughing matter," she cheerfully blurted.

No, I guess it's not, because in what seemed like mere moments, we were surrounded by a furious, jostling, screaming mob of students. The RU Young Republicans (who all seemed to be dressed in chinos, pleated skirts, and topsiders) pushed forth, shrieking and carrying placards that read AFFIRMATIVE

ACTION IS RACISM! and students from the RU Black Political
Action Group had large placards too, which screamed JIM CROW
COOKIES! and then a group from the RU Gay & Lesbian Caucus
ankled forth with placards that said ALPHA BETA DOWNER and
CAN GAY COOKIES GET MARRIED? With just one small (and pink)
cookie booth, Alpha Beta Delta had successfully infuriated every
student group on campus. They all hated us. Now that's equal
opportunity.

Randy and Nester were ecstatic. They were flashing pictures
and hollering out questions to me, Shanna-Francine, and all the
sisters: "Is Hate Speech a part of the new Alpha Beta Delta?" and
"Do the gay cookies taste better than the black cookies?" It was
sheer chaos. I was certain it was going to turn violent, but it was
brought to a quick and shocking halt by Bobbie, who forcefully
ripped a two-by-four loose from the bottom of the cookie booth
and waved it threateningly above her head, bellowing, "The cookie
booth is closed!"

Then we scrambled like screaming meemies, quickly hefting
the booth and ourselves into the back of Bobbie's Avalanche. She
hit the gas and we were off. Lindsay screamed. The takeoff was
sudden and her treasured cherry-blossom Louis Vuitton umbrella
went flying with the wind.

"Hold on to your tiara," wailed Shanna-Francine.

Lindsay gasped and held it down. She was so upset, but Patty,
who managed to clutch three large Tupperware bowls of cookies—
one of which she'd apparently raided—tried to calm her down by
informing her that Bottega Veneta makes a truly wonderful line of
cream-dotted off-white leatherette umbrellas.

"There's a huge waiting list for them," she enthusiastically
informed Lindsay, wiping cookie crumbs from her chin. "They're
almost impossible to get."

That seemed to mollify Lindsay, who's surely going to pull every string she can among her royal friends and family to get that umbrella, but it didn't make me feel good, because in the back of my head a horrible thought kept gnawing away: The "sudden" arrival of organized protesters was way too co-winki-dink, which could only mean one thing.

"Meri was behind this," I said. "There's no other explanation."

Oh, why don't I learn to keep my big trap shut sometimes? I was subjected to baby talk (again); poor traumatized Cindy just can't seem to get a grip. Then I asked Shanna-Francine if she had kept an eye on Bobbie while packing cookies with Lindsay.

"Did she use the phone?" I asked insistently. "Does she have a cell phone? Did you see her call anyone?"

Shanna-Francine was appalled by my suggestion that Bobbie might be a plant by Meri, and so was Lindsay. They assured me that Bobbie was visible the whole time through the large kitchen window over the sink—and then they leaped to Bobbie's defense and sang her praises, pointing out that she was, in fact, an all-out miracle worker given her efforts on the cookie booth. Bobbie could hear us in the front seat, and when we came to a stop light, she turned around and thrust her cell phone into my hand.

"Check my outgoing call list," she growled, but not unkindly. "Go on. I got nothing to hide."

I shrank back. I felt so small.

"Honest, Cindy, you so need to chill," said Shanna-Francine.

"I forgive Cindy," chimed in another sister. A chorus of "I forgive Cindy" followed.

Do I need forgiveness? In my bones I know that Meri was responsible. I just have to figure out a way to prove it. After dinner tonight, Shanna-Francine held an emergency Alpha Beta Delta meeting. We had to address the cookie booth debacle, she said; we couldn't let the protesters have the last word, and we had to let everyone know that Alpha Beta Delta respects the rights and beliefs of everyone. But how? The suggestions offered weren't very inspiring.

"Let's say we're sorry," said one girl.

"We'll just tell people we really didn't mean it," offered Lindsay.

"Maybe it'll go away," said another ridiculously hopeful girl.

But I knew it wouldn't go away. I racked my brain—and then it hit me. If you want to fight Meri, think like Meri. Just flat-out spin like a dirty politician.

"Street theater," I exclaimed. "It was intentional. Alpha Beta Delta successfully demonstrated the fragility of race and gender relations on campus. With a simple pink cookie booth, we highlighted the fear and distrust that lurks within all social groups." My words weren't sinking in at first, but I was on a roll, so I plowed ahead. "We'll send out a press release to the *University Press*. We'll send it tonight. Something like, 'Alpha Beta Delta is pleased that our street theater cookie booth was able to illuminate our campus's ongoing conflicts with diversity. We encourage all faculty and students to be a part of the conversation.' Blah-blah-blah. Something like that. Oh, and we'll throw in a few historical references. We were inspired by Harriet Blatch. She was this really cool early British suffragette who staged huge theatrical street theater protests and hunger strikes in order to get equal rights for women. See? What we did wasn't just right, it was respectable."

There was dead silence—and I have to say, I was just as surprised as anyone that such a fully formed offensive plan had come tumbling so quickly out of my mouth. Even better, it looked like everyone was pretty much certain that this was the best way to go.

Then Patty cautiously asked, "Yeah, but wouldn't that be lying?"

Oh, darn it-darn it-darn it. I was so mad at Patty in that moment (even though she was right), but we didn't have time to discuss the matter any further. The doorbell rang, and when Shanna-Francine swung open the front door, a university messenger served her papers. She ripped them open. She nearly fainted. Alpha Beta Delta was being sued by David Martinez, the vice chancellor of RU Student Affairs. Our cookie booth, according to Martinez and the university, was illegal under federal law, including the 1964 Civil Rights Act.

"Will we go to jail?" shrieked Lindsay.

I swiped the document and quickly scanned it. Unless Alpha Beta Delta admitted wrongdoing and issued a full and immediate apology, we would be subject to a lawsuit—an embarrassing lawsuit that could definitely harm our standing when we go before the national sorority governing council in December.

"Then that's it, we've got to apologize," said a persistent Patty, but I wouldn't hear of it.

"Are you kidding? We're going to let a pink cookie booth bring down Alpha Beta Delta?" I countered. "If we apologize, we admit wrongdoing. If we tell a teensy little lie and say that we meant to do it, then it's totally win-win. There'll be no lawsuit, because it was a free-speech demonstration, and we look like heroes for diversity because our plan worked and started everyone talking. But we have to send out a press release now. We have to do it tonight."

It's four o'clock in the morning now. After I wrote countless drafts of the press release, all of which were checked and rechecked by Shanna-Francine and all the sisters, we e-mailed it to the University Press. We did it on my desktop computer, and it was kind of a pain because the *S* on my wireless keyboard kept sticking, and it's never done that before. The computer's fairly new, too (Dad was nice enough to buy me a new iMac desktop; he knows how much I hate laptops, because the keyboards are so tiny, and besides, I'm not the type who likes to do assignments or writing at coffee shops, and I've always thought that people who do are just posers). Exhausted, I went down to the kitchen for a drink of water, then headed back upstairs to my room. Patty met me at the landing.

"Meri would be very proud of you," she intoned ominously.

I looked her squarely in the eye. There's no hiding from the likes of Patty; she knew exactly what inspired my fantastic energy and lickity-split quick thinking. I shrugged.

"Fight fire with fire."

"There is no fire, Cindy. There's just you."

But, oh God, how can she be so sure? I have go to sleep now. Meri is back. I have to be ready for whatever tomorrow may bring. And, boy, I'm not going to take it lying down. This time I'm going to be proactive. This time it's Meri who'd better watch out.

October 24

Dear Diary:

My eyes popped open at five a.m. I couldn't sleep; my heart was hammering out of my chest. I needed to distract myself. I turned on my computer and checked my e-mail. There were two new ones. The first was from Lisa.

From: Lisa@lisabixby.com
Date: 23 October
To: cindybixby@yahoo.com
Subject: Re: Miss You!

Hey Cindy:

What is up, my sistah! L.A. totally rawks! I've been
s-o-o-o-o incredibly busy. So much has happened. And
guess what? I have a manager now. His name's Frederick
something, and he's gay, which is so cool, 'cause the gays
really know how to handle, like, big careers (like mine).
He told Mom and Dad that I was "ready to pop." How cool
is that? Are you jealous?

And no, I don't have a deal for a full CD yet, but

Frederick's already got me hooked up so I can lay down some
tracks for my second sure-to-be-super-successful new single.
It's called "Touch My Daisy!" Isn't that a great title?
I wrote the whole thing myself. It goes like this:

My daisy knows, my daisy feels
My daisy needs love
It's, like, head over heels.
Oh, touch it touch it touch it!
Touch my daisy!
Touch it, yeah!
My daisy quivers, my daisy's shy
My daisy needs you
It says aye yi yi!
Oh, touch it touch it touch it!
Touch my daisy!
Touch it, yeah!

Isn't that good?! Mom was such a meanie when I read it to
her. She told me it was "puerile" and Dad just kind of shook
his head. They DO NOT get me. At. All. They actually expect
me to be back at the hotel and in bed every night by ten.
For reals!

But last night—oh my God, if they only knew! I had the
best night E-VER. After pretending to go to bed, I waited
for a half hour or so, then I got up, dressed in this
really cute outfit (I'm bringing back fringe), tippy-toed
downstairs, and took a cab to the Spider Club in Hollywood.
It's THE place for all the coolest celebs to hang out and
be chill—so of course I had to be there.

At first, this big muscly guy at the door pretended he didn't know who I was (nice try, dirtbag). Anyhoo, I got in and . . . are you sitting? Are you ready? Get this. I met Lindsay Lohan!!!! And she's my new best girlfriend!!!!

L. Lo knew exactly who I was (of course) (she told me to call her L. Lo, 'cause all her closest friends do) (and I'm her absolute closest now). We had the best chat ever. I told her I was really into her tan-tan look and her super-incredible-new-hair, 'cause it makes her look sooooo fucking fierce! And she said, "Thanks, I know."

Then she told me that she really loves my single, "Tune My Motor Up," and thinks I should be really proud of it 'cause it's "so rockin!" and "s-o-o-o-o-o-o fuckin' awesome!" And I said, "Thanks, I know." And then, get this, Nicole Richie (Miss Skeletor) (gross!) tried to bone her way into our conversation and I was NOT having it. NOT-NOT-NOT-NOT.

L. Lo and I snubbed her (y-e-s-s-s-s-s!) and even though she and Skeletor have hung out in the past, I could tell it was w-a-a-a-a-a-a-y over between them. 'Cause now L. Lo can hang with me, which is much better. I mean, duh! And we're so real with each other. Like, I told her, "L. Lo, what up with that Herbie shit?" And she sighed and told me all about her obligations to her fan base, and I said, "Dude, I know. My fans are unbelievable. They are s-o-o-o-o-o-o-o needy." And we were like, wow, we have so much in common.

Mom and Dad are clueless. I was back at the hotel by three a.m. and they had no idea, so now I know that I can go out and it'll be okay. And I have to go out now 'cause L. Lo

needs me, and I need her, too. No one understands us but us.
Lissa & L. Lo 4 Ever!!!!

Oh, I'm glad to hear everything's good at RU. Are people
still playing my CD? Tell them to buy more copies. And tell
them I have a new one coming out. Will you do that? And
then write me back and tell me what they say.

ttyl!
L. Lo's Homegirl

I'm happy Lisa's having fun. At least someone is. But I don't
know about "Touch My Daisy." Do all pop songs have to be so
crudely soaked in sex? Besides, it's such a rip-off of Britney's
"Touch of My Hand." I remember when that song first came out.
It made Mom so angry because Lisa was only thirteen years old,
and she was running around the house screaming and singing:
"'Cause I just discovered . . . the touch of my hand!' Woo-hoo! I
know what that means, I know what that means!" Yes, thanks to
Britney, my little sister was learning all about masturbation. I'm
sorry, but that's just wrong. Dad was furious too. He grabbed the
CD, broke it in half, and threw it in the trash. "Where it belongs,"
he said. Lisa was outraged.

"Some of the songs on that CD were produced by Moby!" she
gasped—as if that was going to make Dad apologize or run out
and buy her another copy. It didn't matter, though. Robbie Pewtis,
this quasi-hippie fourteen-year-old stoner at her school, burned
her a new copy.

I was getting tired staring at the computer screen. I had one
more e-mail to look at. It was odd, though. It had no subject line,
and it was from me—and addressed to me. Confused, I clicked it
open. It read:

From: cindybixby@yahoo.com
Date: 23 October
To: cindybixby@yahoo.com

Hi.
Why don't you just kill yourself? :(
Bye.

I stared at it a moment—and it seemed like all the air was suddenly sucked out of the room. I slowly backed away from the computer. I was shaking. Then I heard loud tapping behind me. I shrieked and whipped around. It was just a tree branch batting against the window. I was so freaked, and so were Patty, Pigboy, and Lindsay. They came rushing into my room. Pigboy was even holding a baseball bat. I nervously apologized, explained the branch tapping at my window, and gestured fearfully to my computer screen.

"Look. I just got this."

Everyone gazed at the screen. Patty gasped. "Wow. You have a cyber-stalker. Fascinating."

"It's Meri," I whimpered.

"Well, we don't know that," said Patty. "And I kind of doubt it. I mean, how would she have time to do this on her first day of freedom?"

"She's been free for two days," I pointed out. I'd already read the *Daily Gazette* article a zillion times; it was reporting on a court hearing that had already happened.

"Yeah, but why is it from you?" asked Pigboy, who saw that the e-mail was from cindybixby@yahoo.com and addressed to cindybixby@yahoo.com. I didn't have a logical answer for him, and when I started to speak but hesitated, I noticed that they were all staring at me like a big bug under glass. Oh God. I knew what they were thinking.

"You don't think I sent this to myself, do you?" I sputtered. "It's—it's some sort of computer trick. It has to be. You believe me, don't you?"

They didn't answer fast enough. Boy, that ticked me off. I suddenly wailed, "Do you really think I would tell myself to kill myself? That's sick."

"Cindy, calm down," said Patty with a yawn. "Why don't we all get some more shut-eye and deal with this in the morning? Or, you know, later this morning."

She sauntered out of the room, leaving Pigboy and Lindsay standing awkwardly before me.

Lindsay said, "I believe you, Cindy. And I bet if you show it to Bud and let him look at your e-mail he can figure it out. He's so good with electronic things."

I'm actually much too aware of how good Bud is with electronic things. But God bless Lindsay. I gave her a warm hug before she stepped back to her room. That left Pigboy, who was still clutching his baseball bat. He looked so cute standing there in his apple red Joe Boxers with his belly hanging over. I had to smile.

"You can put the bat down, Jesse."

"Right," he said, setting it down.

"Nice to see you staying over again. I guess Patty's still keeping her room clean."

"Sort of," he said. Then he shifted uncomfortably. "But she's so tired all the time. And I know why. It's all those dumb diets. She's on the Russian Air Force Cabbage Diet now."

"The what?"

"Yeah, I know. Stupid, huh? She's thinking of switching to the Power Pop Lollipop Diet next. That or the Neve Campbell Soybean Corndog Diet. I'm not sure which, I can't keep track anymore. And none of them are going to work. She cheats all the time. And she thinks I don't know."

"Well, she's not trying to fool you or anything. Maybe herself."

"Uh-huh. So if a tree falls in the forest . . ."

". . . and no one saw you eat all those Boston cream donuts, then yeah, you didn't eat them. See? Or if you're standing up and you're eating something at the sink or in front of the fridge, that doesn't count either." That last part was in reference to Mom. She's always hopscotched from one insanely strict diet to the next (even though she's always been slim), and in her mind, if she eats a piece of chocolate cake, or wolfs down half a pint of Rocky Road, and she's standing in front of the refrigerator or the sink, then that's not cheating. I guess the theory goes, if you take the trouble to sit down at the table or get comfortable on the couch— with the ice cream or the cake or whatever it is—then that's real commitment, that's cheating. In an odd way it makes sense, but I understood where Jesse was coming from when he said, "C'mon, that's dumb. And Patty's smart. I don't get it."

Then his eyes turned to the computer. And my anxiety shot right back up.

"Turn it off," he gently advised, and I did, but it didn't make me feel any better. For all I knew, Meri was watching me. I darted to the window and pulled down the shades. Jesse thought I was being paranoid (of course) (like everyone else), but what the heck, why shouldn't I be paranoid?

"The e-mail may not even be from Meri," said Pigboy. And then he told me what I've heard before. A lot of students are mad at me regarding the Meri situation, since one of the unintended consequences is a newly strict RU. "You can't even have a beer without someone coming down on you," lamented Pigboy. "And forget about having a beer bust. Not that I'm into that shit as much as Keith is, but still." Then he paused self-consciously. He had said Keith's name, but honest, while I still love-love Keith and always will (oh my God, I can't believe I wrote that, but it's true!), right then my focus was on Meri and what her next move might be, and what I might do to stay one step, or hopefully two steps, ahead of her.

"Can you leave the baseball bat?" I inquired meekly.

Pigboy laughed—and refused. He said all I had to do was call out and he'd come running. Then he gave me a big hug. Wow. What a nice hug. What a nice guy. I'm so happy for Patty. He stepped away and urged me to get some sleep. *Fat chance*, I thought, but I did try. I was in bed for about two seconds, then I swept the covers aside and grabbed my cell phone. I needed to take action. I turned on my cell phone and saw that there was a text message waiting for me. My heart fluttered. Was it from Keith? I clicked it open. It read:

TEXT MESSAGE

u r dead bitch

————————————

FR: GuessWho

OCT 23, 11:40 PM

I didn't scream. Instead I thought, *Okay, so this is Meri's first step, sending me nasty little e-mails and text messages. Fine. I can handle that.* Exhausted, I fell back into bed and shut my eyes for what seemed like two seconds. My rapid heartbeat bolted me upright. It was seven thirty in the morning now, and I had a thought: Meri had just given me the ammo to prove (finally) that she hasn't changed one iota. I swiped my cell phone and carefully saved the text message. Then I dialed.

"Wazzup," a voice answered huskily.

"Bud, I'm sorry to wake you up so early, but it's really important."

"Yo, Cindy B. Not a prob. Bud Finger's always at your cervix. And don't worry. I was already up," he said, with emphasis on the word "up." Then he chuckled dirtily. "Know what I mean? Can't help it. It's a morning thing. It's a Finger thing."

Oh, I hate Bud Finger! But I had to put those thoughts aside—along with the horrifying images of him and Lindsay together. Bud could help me in my quest to bring down Meri. I told him what had happened, and he instructed me to come to his dorm room right away with my cell phone and my computer. It was eight a.m. by then, and the sun was already rising, but dressed and ready to go, I charged outside. I had the cell phone, the computer cords, the mouse, and the keyboard in a large shopping bag, and the iMac held awkwardly in my arms. It was a bit heavy, but I didn't care. I was taking action.

The campus felt strangely motionless in the early morning light, like it was holding its breath and waiting for the day to really begin. That's when I realized I was holding *my* breath. *Breathe*, I told myself, *everything's going to be fine*. I inhaled, I exhaled. Ahhh. Relief flooded through my body. Then I tripped and fell to my knees—and nearly dropped the iMac. But I held on to it. Klutz or no klutz, I was not going to drop the computer. I stood up—and gasped. In the distance I saw what looked like the silhouetted figure of Meri; but not the real Meri, a teeny-tiny version of Meri, as if she'd somehow managed to shrink herself to convenient pocket-size. I must have been hallucinating. The figure whisked behind a tree, vanishing as quickly as it had appeared. *Great*, I thought, *Meri's become a shape-shifter*.

Figuring that the early-morning light was playing tricks with my eyes, I willed myself to move forward and arrived at Bud's dormitory. My shoes made loud *clompity-clompity* sounds as I walked down the empty hallway—or weaved, to be more accurate; the computer was beginning to strain my arms, so I deliberately leaned from one side to the other in an attempt to shift the weight. I was aware of how ridiculous I looked, but luckily no one was around or awake yet (I could hear snoring behind a few doors) (RU has some real honkers!). Finally I was in front of Bud's door. Phew. But I wasn't out of the woods yet. I'd have to knock, and how was I supposed to do that? My arms were so stressed-out and rubbery that I was afraid I'd drop the computer if I tried to lean forward and set it down, so instead I banged the door with my forehead, seeing, for the first time, why Bud had only recently decided to move two doors down from his previous dorm room. Bud was now in room number 69. *Why me?* I thought. I waited for a moment. There was no answer. My arms were beyond strained at that point, so I gave another powerful bang with my forehead. *Ouch!* It really hurt.

"I'm coming," Bud said. I could hear rustling, then a dirty laugh. "C-o-o-o-ming. Get it?"

I couldn't take it anymore. The weight of the computer was too much. I fell to my knees, and I had just managed to set the computer down when the door abruptly swung open.

"Say hello to my monkey," said Bud with a chuckle.

It took me a moment. I was, in fact, looking at a monkey. Bud was standing directly before me in his underwear; his Paul Frank underwear, with a red-lipped monkey face right on his crotch, eye level with my face. He jiggled his hips rhythmically.

"Monkey say, 'heh-wo there, Cindy.'"

I couldn't help it. It was the only logical response. In a flash I stood up—*bam!*—and kneed him in the crotch. He screeched and fell backward on his behind, gripping his monkey, writhing in pain. I stumbled into the room, pulling the computer with me.

"Bud, if you don't put some clothes on right now, I'll—"

"Okay, okay!" he wailed, backing away from me. Tears were stinging his cheeks. "Geez, Cindy. Peace out."

He dashed into the bathroom. I was beyond exhausted, and after I shook out my arms and closed the door, I was surprised by what I saw, or rather, by what I didn't see. There's practically no available space for anyone or anything in Bud's room. It's chock-full of huge computer hard drives, flat-screen monitors, stacks and stacks of whirring external drives, along with piles and piles of CDs and DVDs. The air was musty, and the windows were covered with dark, heavy blankets. It felt oppressive. I scanned a few of the DVD titles: *King Kong*, *Star Wars: Revenge of the Sith*, *Brokeback Mountain*, *Harry Potter and the Goblet of Fire*. Bud stepped out of the bathroom dressed in seriously gay-looking khaki capri pants and a wrinkly red wife-beater.

"Are you downloading and copying movies?" I asked, disbelieving. "And music?"

"Dude, I lost my scholarship."

"Don't call me dude."

"I'm serious. How else am I supposed to pay for my tuition?" he whined.

"You mean you're selling them too?"

"Hey, I deserve to be here as much as anyone else."

"Bud, you're breaking the law."

"Whatevs," he said, then he held up three fingers, which I realized was Bud's "cool" way of making a *W*. He went on to explain that the university was just as much at fault as he was for what he was doing. They're the ones who supply the students at RU with Internet2, the superfast next-generation Internet network. "You can download an entire movie in thirty seconds," he boasted.

"Oh, I get it," I said. "So if I supply you with a knife, that means you've just got to kill someone. Sure, that makes sense."

He snorted derisively and held up three fingers. "Whatevs." Then he was all business. First he examined my cell phone and the text message. "Forget this," he said. "Someone could have bought one of those pay-as-you-go thingies. You know, they send you a few texts, throw it away. Totally anonymous. Impossible to trace."

Next he picked up my computer, rifled through my bag for the keyboard and mouse (he was impressed that they were wireless), hooked everything up in what seemed like mere seconds, and brought up my e-mail in-box on the screen.

"Which one?" he asked.

I leaned forward and double-clicked the mouse, revealing the e-mail from Meri. His eyes scanned it.

"Ooo, nasty," he observed. "It says here you sent it to yourself."

"Really?" I snapped. "Is that what it says, smart guy?" I shouldn't have been so sharp, but I was so tired from not sleeping and anxious to have my proof.

"Cindy, I'm not going to help you if you keep being mean to me."

"Bud . . ."

"I'm serious. You're being a turbobitch. And you really hurt my monkey."

I caught myself before I said something I'd regret. What is it about Bud that makes me just want to wring his neck? "I'm sorry," I quickly told him, and I was, even though I really didn't appreciate being called a turbobitch, but Bud was helping me, or promising to, so for what seemed like the millionth time that morning, I inhaled, I exhaled. Bud's fingers went *clickity-clack* over the keyboard. Then he paused and went "Mmm-hmm," sounding ridiculously self-important. Then more *clickity-clack*, another "Mmm-hmm." Who knows what he was doing, if anything, but he was putting on a big show. Finally, he printed out the e-mail, which had all this extra gibberish on it:

X-Apparently-To:
cindybixby@yahoo.com via 68.142.201.64; Mon, 23 Oct: 11:43 - 0700
X-Originating-IP:
[198.31.62.21]

Return-Path:
<cindybixby@yahoo.com>
Authentication-Results:
mta287.mail.scd.yahoo.com from=email.; domainkeys=neutral
Received:
from 198.31.62.21 (cindybixby@yahoo.com) (198.31.62.21)
X-MID:
<Kilauea116170-55936-124796465-3-1007@flonetwork.com>
MIME-Version:
1.0
Content-Type:
multipart/alternative; boundary="

"What does it mean?" I asked.

He explained—in excruciating detail. It was all computer-talk to me, so it went in one ear and out the other (people who are "into computers" seem to think that you, too, want to know everything about them, when really, you just want the computer to do what it's supposed to do). I still didn't have my proof, and as he printed out even more pages, he told me all about Professor Gould, a kindly RU statistics instructor who was subjected to shocking anti-Semitic attacks years ago; the door to his classroom was spray painted with epitaphs, the books in his office were ripped apart. The university actively investigated, and yet they couldn't find the culprit. But an industrious brownnosing young student did. She arrived early for class one morning, hoping to chat the professor up and improve her standing in class—and she was stunned to discover the perpetrator once more spray painting Professor Gould's door. She couldn't believe it. She screamed. A few guards came running. They couldn't believe it either.

"It was Professor Gould," said Bud. "He was doing it all along. Isn't that majorly twisted?"

"That's an anomaly!" I blurted. "Hate crimes are serious, Bud."

"An anoma-what?"

"Bud, I didn't send it," I stated firmly.

He sighed, and then he clicked reply on the e-mail, typed "Bud Finger is sexiful!" hit send, and waited a moment. My in-box chimed. He clicked open a new e-mail. It was the one he had just sent, which meant, he explained, that I had either sent the e-mail to myself—since the reply went right back to me—or someone was using a powerful encrypted cloaking something-or-other-thinga-majig to mimic my e-mail address.

"And if they did that, can you prove it?" I asked, trying to hide my desperation.

Bud sighed and ran his fingers through his hair—a gesture intended to show me that he was thinking deep thoughts, but all it really did was make his greasy hair stick up. He was just about to answer me when there was a knock at the door. Bud hopped up and swung it open. It was Lindsay. I was so happy to see her, but semi-grossed out when she gave Bud a hug and he nibbled on her ear. Eeeow. She playfully pushed him away.

"No PDA," she cooed, then she straightened her tiara and turned to me. "You up for an early lunch?"

My eyes bugged out. Had I really been holed up in Bud's room that long? And still with no proof? Bud must have read my mind.

"Cindy, if Meri sent it to you, I'll prove it. Okay? I swear. But you gotta leave your computer here. I've got to diddle around in your hard drive."

"Well, diddle or no diddle, we're going to lunch," chimed Lindsay, taking me by the arm. Bud promised he'd return my computer in the afternoon or evening, and Lindsay led me outside. She was cheerfully chattering. It seems I'd missed the Alpha Beta Delta Blackballing session this morning (though Blackballing is now known as Prospective Member Selection).

"I voted for you in absentee," she said. "For Bobbie. I hope you don't mind."

I didn't. I like Bobbie (even though her nose ring skeeves me out), and I wasn't surprised to learn that she was chosen to join Alpha Beta Delta in a unanimous vote. When we stepped outside, I felt assaulted by the bright light and all the noise. I was still operating on practically no sleep, and I'd been hunkered down in a dark musty room for hours, but I wasn't so disoriented that I didn't hear the familiar snickers and muffled giggles. I looked up. I saw a murky haze of gawking faces and pointing index fingers. To be honest, I was surprised. I mean, what happened to my generation's famed attention deficit disorder? The *Daily Gazette* article was so yesterday's news.

"Um, there's something else you should know," said Lindsay hesitantly.

"What?" I asked wearily.

Lindsay swallowed hard. Oh God, what was it? Then she forced a smile. "Let's go to Long John's. You wanna? My treat."

Uh-oh. It couldn't be good if she wanted to take me to Long John's. Long John's Chicken Planks are my all-time absolute favorite comfort food (I'm really getting into their Pineapple Cream Cheese Pie, too), and Lindsay knows that.

"Just tell me now," I pleaded. But she refused. We walked to Long John's, and she said she wouldn't tell me anything until I finished my meal. For a few minutes we ate in silence, but then I couldn't help it. I had to be honest about something. And it wasn't about Meri.

"I just don't understand you and Bud," I said.

"As opposed to what?" she retorted defensively. "You and Keith?"

"I'm sorry, I didn't mean to . . ."

"No, I'm sorry," she sighed. "It's just that no one wants to believe me. It's so frustrating. Bud and I are really great together. And we do things I've never done with anybody. Like, just the other night—oh my God, it was too funny. He tied my hands and ankles to the bed—"

"Lindsay!"

"Wait, wait. So I'm tied to the bed, and I'm naked, and he steps away. And I'm like, oh no, is he gonna come back dressed in some sort of creepy S and M outfit or something?"

"Lindsay, this is terrible. Are you all right?"

"Wait, wait. So I'm all scared, 'cause I really don't want to be whipped or anything like that, and then he steps back into the room . . ."

"Lindsay . . ."

"And he was dressed in a maid's outfit with a wig and an apron—and he had a huge feather duster!"

"What?"

"He kept tickling me with it. Oh my God! Complete riot. We couldn't stop laughing. Then he untied me and we . . ."

"Yeah, I don't need to hear the rest."

"And afterward we made popcorn and played Parcheesi."

I was speechless. I really couldn't think of anything to say, because there's absolutely no reference point in my life for anything that Lindsay had just described—and I kind of hope there never is. But there she was, blushing and beaming, and happier than I've ever seen her, and I thought, *Is there really anything wrong with this?* There isn't, I guess, but maybe I just don't want to be told all the gritty details anymore. I still can't get the image of Bud in a wig and a maid's outfit out of my head. I kept eating, and after I'd finished my Variety Platter serving of Chicken Planks, shrimp, and a side of hush puppies (so good!), Lindsay was finally ready to tell me what was up.

"Okay. It's really not a biggie. But you should probably see it. Just don't freak."

She handed me a copy of RU's *University Press* newspaper. Today's edition. There was a picture of Meri on the front cover; her hair looked windblown, her smile was easy and carefree. The largish headline blared: "I'VE LEARNED TO START LOVING MYSELF!"

"It's just another puff piece," insisted Lindsay.

Boy, was it ever. Meri had given an "exclusive" interview to Randy, aka ROT. And she wasn't missing a trick.

"I know I'm not perfect," she was quoted as saying. "I've had to learn forgiveness. Every day I try to forgive those who've wronged me, because I know I want forgiveness for the wrongs that I've done. I want to be a forgiving person."

The article continued on the third page. More blather, including the apparently vital news that Meri had recently purchased her own Savannah, a superexpensive cat that's the offspring of the domestic cat and the African serval wild cat; they look like spotted leopards, and they grow to more than twice the size of normal housecats.

"Her name is Purrfect," she coyly informed ROT.

At the bottom of the page, in a special box, there was a smaller picture of Meri in a designer kitchen holding a spatula, with a chef's hat angled saucily on her head, and the headline: MAKE MERI'S PETIT FOURS!

"Everyone loves a comeback," tsked Lindsay. "You know, like Martha Stewart, Mariah Carey."

"Oh my God, she'll be bigger than ever!" I shrieked.

Lindsay gripped my hand. "She's not in our lives anymore, Cindy. She's gone."

I wanted to believe her. I flung the newspaper aside. *So Meri did another puff piece,* I thought. *Big whoop.*

"Um, we're not done," said Lindsay meekly.

Then she opened the paper to the center spread—and there I was. It was a horrific close-up. My face was gnarled in mid-scream, my eyes looked deranged. It was the photo that Nester had taken when he and ROT had ambushed me (and, okay, I'll be the first to admit it, my hair looked beyond tragic). Now I know why every-one's still whispering and laughing about me today. The not-very-subtle headline read: CINDY B. SCREAMING MAD ABOUT MERI! I could barely see straight. I tried to read the story, but after the first few sentences, I thought, *What's the point?* It was so slanted. Most of it went like this: "'Stay away from me!' screamed Cindy Bixby when asked if she had a message for the newly released Meri Sugarman." So much for accuracy in the college press. I had said that to Nester and ROT, not to Meri.

I was shaking involuntarily when Lindsay led me back to Alpha Beta Delta. I was in no shape to go to my next class, she told me, and I didn't disagree; both my body and my head ached horribly. Lindsay sweetly shielded me with her umbrella, and I heard a familiar buzzing sound—followed by a truly piercing car alarm from the parked Volvo next to us.

"Lindsay," I gasped. "You're not . . ."

"Setting off car alarms? Oh, no, no, no. Ha ha ha. Bud's so good with electronic things. It's just a coincidence."

We kept walking, and she tried to cheer me up by informing me that my efforts to protect Alpha Beta Delta from controversy must have worked, because there was only a small story about the Charity Cookie Booth in the paper. It was buried in the back (it even paraphrased my e-mail by saying that students and faculty should examine diversity issues on campus, which means that the paper agrees, or they're just too lazy to write something original). When we turned the corner to the tree-lined residential area of RU, I heard Lindsay's buzzing again (I tried to get the image of a hot and heavy Bud with the remote control out of my head), and simultaneously, three garage doors across the street flew open, and then closed, and then flew open again.

"Lindsay . . ."

"Okay, so maybe he should look at it."

"Just get rid of it. What if you're interfering with local air travel? Or someone's cable reception?"

She promised me she'd remove it when we got home. We continued walking in silence until we arrived at the house. I felt awful. I didn't want to embarrass her, but really.

In my bedroom, I hit the pillow hard. I was out like a light. Unfortunately, I woke up at midnight. My sleep is really screwed up. The first thing I saw when my eyes opened was my iMac—right back where it always is. That means Bud's finished "diddling" with it. That means Bud has proof! I wanted to see it, whatever it was, right away, and I nearly raced out of my bedroom and woke everyone up. But I stopped myself. Oh, my God, tomorrow's going to be great! ROT's going to get one heck of an exclusive. About Meri. From me.

October 25

Dear Diary:

Oh my God, oh my God, oh my God, oh my God! I "crossed the line" today (Mom used to say that whenever me and Lisa misbehaved). But then, "desperate times call for desperate measures" as another phrase goes (or "Extremis malis extrema remedia," if you go back to the original Latin) (I read that in the *Dictionary of Proverbs and Their Origins*, this really cool book Dad gave me on my fourteenth birthday). Or as a more current phrase goes, "I've been a bad, bad girl" (that's from Fiona Apple's "Criminal") (which Lisa memorized) (of course). If anybody finds out what I did, then that's it, it's over—then they'll really think I'm bonkers.

The first thing I did when I woke up today was check my e-mail. I wasn't too surprised to find this:

From: cindybixby@yahoo.com
Date: 24 October
To: cindybixby@yahoo.com

Hi.
Are you dead yet? :(
Kisses

* * *

Clearly Meri has too much time on her hands. Ha! That's my new attitude. Meri may think she's going to destroy me (and bring down Alpha Beta Delta, too), but she's wrong. I'm way ahead of her. Another phrase popped into my head. "If you want to have a good day, start with a good face." Mom says that a lot, and it really made sense to me this morning. *This was going to be a good day, I told myself, because Bud will have the proof I need and Meri will be exposed.* So I stepped into the bathroom, took a quick shower, and started with my face. I took extra care with my foundation (so I'd have that seemingly natural I-don't-have-a-single-pore look), dusted with a light ultra-matte translucent powder, applied neutral shimmery eye shadow, and finished off with a moist Berry-Bella shade of Shiny-Licious lip gloss. Oh my God. I. Looked. Amazing. Then I saw my hair. Ahhhhhhhh! I tried everything. Hairspray, mousse, gel. No go. My hair has a mind of its own, and of course, it makes me hyperaware of all my other flaws, like my bulbous nose, which no amount of makeup can help (yes, I know, there are "shading techniques," but unless people are standing a whole ten feet away from you they can tell). And then I thought: *Distraction!* Anything to pull attention away from my nose (and my hair). In my room, I put on this really cute Trina Turk paisley gauze dress, my rainbow beaded necklace, and some comfy aqua blue jellys. I could still see my nose (and my hair), but it felt like there was enough going on to keep the eye moving. It must have worked, because downstairs at breakfast, I got a lot of compliments (Patty said my outfit was "almost psychotically cheerful"). Everyone seemed to be in a good mood, which could only mean that they knew what Bud had found. Yippee! I couldn't wait for the subject to just pop up, so real casually, I asked, "Hey, what did Bud have to say when he returned my computer last night? About my e-mail from Meri?"

Lindsay shrugged. So did Shanna-Francine. And so did everyone else. Oh, I hate Bud Finger! Apparently, he returned the computer around seven p.m. last night, played a giggly game of Twister with Lindsay (I didn't ask for details), then went back to his dorm room. I was astounded. I couldn't believe it.

I blurted out, "He didn't say anything? You didn't ask?"

"I'm sorry, Cindy," said Lindsay meekly. "I kinda forgot."

I sat there like a dodo for a moment, and I was about to ask for Bud's cell phone number when the house suddenly became a flurry of activity. Bobbie was moving in. She'd pulled up in her Chevy Avalanche, and we all pitched in carrying her stuff upstairs to her room. There were lots of bulky boxes, and when we helped her unpack, I saw that they were jam-packed with tons of hardback Barbara Cartland novels, all of them first editions (a few of them were shrink-wrapped). They had really corny titles, too, like *We Danced All Night, A King in Love, For All Eternity, A Kiss in Rome*. Bobbie told us she'd be giving each of us our own Barbara Cartland novel soon—as soon as she gets to know us better.

"It has to match your personality," she gushed. "Dame Barbara writes for everybody. You'll see."

I couldn't quite imagine what Barbara Cartland novel might match up with a girl who has a black Mohawk and nose rings, but what the hey, I'm not familiar with Barbara's oeuvre (that's French for "life's work," which Professor Scott uses in reference to an author's collection of books) (so sophisticated!). We continued unpacking. Bobbie has an amazing assortment of knee-high leather boots and lots of jingly silver and leather wristbands. In one suitcase, I discovered a small, beautifully ornate hand-carved wooden box.

"Shake it," exclaimed Bobbie. "Kitty likes to play."

Confused, I exchanged a quick glance with Shanna-Francine, who smiled cheerfully, nodding her head. I shook the box, having no idea what I was doing.

"That's Kitty," explained Bobbie. "He was my favorite cat. I had him cremated."

I stopped mid-shake, suddenly realizing that I was shaking the remains of a dead cat.

"You can play with Kitty any time," Bobbie told me.

There was still more stuff to unpack. Bobbie hefted two large carrying cases from the back of her Avalanche, set them down in the foyer, and opened then up. Bounding out were two immensely overweight calico cats.

"Good girl, Mrs. Fields! There you go, Chunk-a-Lunk!" she cried out. Patty, who was halfway up the stairs carrying a box with her back to us, and having no idea that Bobbie was calling out to her cats, whipped around, scandalized. Her face was drained of all color.

"Wha—what did you just call me?"

It took a few moments for Shanna-Francine to clear everything up. No one was calling her names, she insisted, and then she introduced her to Bobbie's cats. Patty was relieved, but rattled. Apparently, she'd been taunted with the nickname "Mrs. Fields" throughout elementary school (that's so mean!). In the midst of this, I lost patience. I whipped out my cell phone, asked Lindsay for Bud's number, and dialed. Unfortunately, I got his outgoing message, which blared 50 Cent's "Candy Shop" in the background: "Yo yo yo, wassu-u-u-p. Thanks for calling Finger's Fun Phone. And thanks for vibrating inside my pocket. Ahhh, yeah. Feels good. Oh, yeah. O-o-o-o-o-o-o-oh, yeah."

Then he broke into high-pitched hyenalike laughter. After the beep, I told him in no uncertain terms that he had to call me back immediately about my computer. Lindsay thought I was being a little harsh, but I didn't think so.

I was barely paying attention when Shanna-Francine gathered everyone in the living room for our morning Alpha Beta Delta strategy meeting. The house, she insisted, needed to do more to encourage diversity and highlight the plight of the disenfranchised.

"What about an Hour of Silence for the LGBT community?" proposed Bobbie. LGBT, I learned, stands for the Lesbian, Gay, Bisexual, and Transgendered community.

"And a Day of Forgiveness," proposed another sister, who explained that this was a popular new celebration on many campuses. Students gather for commemorative dinners, light candles, offer forgiveness to groups and individuals whom they (or our nation) may have offended, accept forgiveness from others, and evoke the "healing power of forgiveness worldwide."

Everyone was enthralled by these ideas, and Shanna-Francine pointed out that the house could raise money for various worthwhile charities by charging admission for the Day of Forgiveness dinner at the house, and for the keepsake cards that would be handed out before the Hour of Silence for the LGBT community. Plans were quickly put in motion for both events; we'll be doing the Hour of Silence in front of the house this coming Friday, and the Day of Forgiveness dinner on Sunday night.

"What about Halloween?" I asked.

The Halloween Monster Mash is an annual Alpha Beta Delta tradition that raises thousands each year for the Rumson River Memorial Children's Hospital, and I really didn't think we should forget about it. Luckily, everyone agreed. Everyone except for Bobbie. She shook her head dejectedly.

"Is there something wrong, Bobbie?" asked Shanna-Francine. "Don't you like Halloween?"

"No," she growled. "It's mean. It makes fun of witches with derogatory stereotypes. And it's disrespectful of the Wiccan religion."

Bobbie, it turns out, is a Wiccan priestess, and she told us she couldn't in good conscience participate in a celebration that so cruelly mocked witches. We were all at a standstill for a moment, and I have to admit, I felt like blurting out, "Oh, c'mon, that's the silliest thing I've ever heard," but I didn't want to offend anyone, least of all Bobbie (I was afraid she might hurt me) (and I know that's unfair, but no matter how sweetly she behaves, she still kind of scares me). Shanna-Francine broke the silence.

"You're right, Bobbie. Halloween is inappropriate."

There was muttered agreement.

"Yeah, but we have to do something," Lindsay noted. "We can't just ignore the Children's Hospital. How's that going to look to the intersorority governing council?"

That led to a rousing discussion of what exactly we were actually doing in preparation for our meeting with the council in December (not much), and how we were going to offer proof of our many good works.

"We'll do a video!" shrieked Patty triumphantly. "A short one. Kinda like reality TV. You know, with clips of all the great things we've been doing."

Everyone loved that idea. At the same time, my mind was working: I needed to get out of this meeting; the house needed someone to deal with the video. My hand shot up.

"I'll do it. I'll be our official cameraperson. I'll talk to Bud. He can help. He's so good with electronic things. In fact, I'll go talk to him right now."

It worked. I was excused by Shanna-Francine. I bolted out of the house, whipped out my cell phone, hit redial.

"Yo, Finger here."

"Where are you?"

"I'm right here. Where are you? Are you naked? Are you touching yourself?"

"Bud, this is Cindy. Knock it off."

I met him outside the RU science building. I quickly and impatiently explained that I'd need some sort of video camera for the next month or so, and his help when it came time to cutting everything down to a short reality-TV-type segment.

"Don't worry, Cyn. I'll hook you up."

"Fine. Great. Thanks. Now what about my computer? What about my proof? I want to give it to ROT. It's my proof that Meri's been harassing me."

As I was speaking, Patty ambled up, eating a bear claw.

"Hey, what's up, guys?" she said, dribbling crumbs on her blouse.

"Bud's going to give me proof against Meri," I proudly told her, then I turned back to Bud. "Aren't you?"

He stood there for a second—like a deer caught in the headlights—and then he spoke, very quietly.

"Cindy, don't lie. Did you send that e-mail to yourself? Your hard drive says you did. From your own e-mail account."

Words can't even begin to describe how I felt in that moment. I wanted to scream, I wanted to cry out, "That's impossible! It's Meri! It has to be!" But instead I just smiled (sort of), and asked in the most sane and rational-sounding voice I could muster, "Are you sure about that?"

Then I gazed at Patty. Her mouth was hanging open.

"Oh, Cindy," she said. Then she put her arm around me. "It's okay. You know, years ago, Professor Gould . . ."

I exploded. And I'll admit, I must have looked like a total wacko. I don't even remember what I said. My whole body was electrified with outrage. The next thing I knew, I was running—and then I was running faster, faster still—then I slammed open the door to the ladies' room in the humanities building. It was empty. Everyone was in class. Which is where I should have been. I splashed water on my face and took a good hard look at myself in the mirror. My hair was even more tragic than it usually is, my face was red and blotchy, tears were staining my cheeks. *Oh my God, am I really fruitcakey?* I asked myself. I had to go to the bathroom. I stepped into a stall, set down my purse, pulled down my panties, and sat on the toilet. My thoughts were spinning—*I'm not a wacko, I'm not a wacko*—and I heard voices, too, and they were getting louder and louder. It was Meri. "Cindy's my little bow-wow. Bow-wow. Woof. Woof woof." Then my eyes widened. I really was going crazy. I had to be. Because in the next stall, I distinctly heard: "Woof woof!"

I screamed—and it all happened in a flash. A hand shot out from under the stall, grabbed my purse. Then sudden, sharp explosions! All around me in the stall, firecrackers were blasting! *Bang-bang-bang!* They were showering down on me. I wailed in horror, frantically pulled up my panties, pushed myself out of the stall. There were already several students and a security guard rushing in. I fell to my knees, wailing in horror.

"She threw firecrackers into my stall! It's Meri! She's trying to freak me out."

They all attempted to calm me down. And there were whispers. No one saw Meri in the hall. And no, she couldn't have jumped out of the bathroom window, because it's way too small.

"How do you know it was Meri?" one of the girls asked.

"Because she woofed at me!" I cried—and then I realized how totally bonkers that sounded.

Another girl meekly handed me my purse. I angrily snatched it. And a wad of unlit firecrackers tumbled out. Everyone gasped.

"She grabbed my purse first!" I protested in vain. "She put them in there."

For the next hour or so, I sat in the Office of Student Affairs quietly chatting with Victorio ("call me Vic") Vladislav, a patronizing university psychologist with a thick Russian accent and a badly dyed red goatee (*If you're going to try and cover up the gray in your goatee*, I thought, *at least try and match the same color dye you use in your hair*). I played it smart. Yes, I said, I've been under a great deal of stress lately. And yes, I really ought to go straight back to Alpha Beta Delta and lie down for the rest of the day. And, yes, of course, I really shouldn't play with firecrackers. And yes, I promised to see someone about my "hysterical" behavior.

In moments like this, my mind seeks comfort from all the books that I've read, and in this case, all the books and the plays about supposed female "hysteria," like *The Yellow Wallpaper* by Charlotte Perkins Gilman, a really wonderful (and disturbing) story from the late 1800s about a woman suffering from postpartum depression. Unfortunately, everyone else in the story thinks she's just going crazy (then she really does go nuts). And of course, there's *The Awakening* by Kate Chopin (I think I've read it at least five times!), about a woman everyone thinks is off her rocker just because she doesn't want to be a wife and a mother.

I guess if you've been lonely most of your life like I have, you read a lot of books—and boy, they sure can help you cope in times of need. I said everything Victorio ("call me Vic") wanted to hear, stepped out of his office, strolled casually in the direction of Alpha Beta Delta—then ran like a gazelle in the opposite direction. *Wheeee!* I leaped behind an overgrown pink-flowering rhododendron. And I laughed. I laughed and laughed and laughed. I think you could even say I laughed "hysterically." Because I knew what I had to do next. And I knew I'd be "crossing the line," as Mom says. I had to. If I was going to protect myself against Meri and fight back (and hopefully expose her), then I needed to know exactly what she was up to. It was time, I realized, to go into Spy Girl Barbie mode.

Lisa and I used to love playing Spy Girl Barbie when we were little. One time, we had Spy Girl Barbie embark on an elaborate mission in order to prove that Ken was cheating on her with Midge.

"Midge is a total cooz," said Lisa. "And Barbie's gonna prove it. Then she'll drown her in her Malibu Dream House pool."

"How's she going to prove it?" I asked.

"First step, recon."

"What's that?"

Lisa rolled her eyes broadly. Didn't I know *anything*? Didn't I pay attention during repeats of *Charlie's Angels* on Nick at Night? "Recon," she impatiently told me, was short for "reconnaissance," but when I asked her for a definition she got all huffy, so I knew she didn't know what it meant. I pulled the dictionary from my bookshelf and looked it up. Reconnaissance was defined as "a secret military observation to locate an enemy and ascertain strategy, from the French reconnaitre."

"Duh, that's what I said," she snapped.

Spy Girl Barbie did discover Midge and Ken together—they were supposed to be just kissing, but Lisa ripped off their clothes and had them "doing it" in Barbie's Sparkle 'n' Style Fairytopia Townhouse—and I'm proud to say that I saved Midge from drowning. I proposed an alternative punishment: Midge would be forever doomed to wear dirndls and lederhosen from Barbie's Miss Swiss clothing line.

"Nice. That's harsh," agreed Lisa.

Hiding behind the rhododendron, I'd stopped laughing, because my mind was made up: I was going on a recon mission. But first I needed supplies. Keeping my head low, I took the crosstown bus to Target (where I sometimes feel intimidated fashionwise because they have big designers, like Isaac Mizrahi, but then I see his stuff, like the cheapie "Mizrahi Frosted Polka-Dot Shower Curtain," and junky things like the "Mizrahi Lucite Toothbrush Holder," and then I don't feel so bad). I found what I was looking for: a pair of inexpensive binoculars, a huge floral floppy hat, and dark sunglasses. With my hair pulled up beneath the floppy hat, I was incognito, or at least my face was unrecognizable in case anyone was trying to look at me, because with both the hat and the glasses you couldn't even see my face.

I hopped on the bus again and rode it all the way to Chappaqua in Ronkonkomo County. Chappaqua is two towns over from Rumson River, and I don't mean to judge or anything, but it's not the sort of place I'd want to live. The streets are filthy, at least a third of the stores are all boarded up, and I swear there's a McDonald's on every other corner (no Long John's, though). It's what Lisa likes to call a WTG, or White Trash Ghetto, and I knew I was getting close to it when I saw two seedy-looking teen guys on the bus step up to another guy and Happy Slap him. Happy Slapping's when one person slaps a victim across the face and the other person captures their shocked expression real fast with a cell phone cam and then transmits it to all their friends. It's such a mean thing to do, and I've never seen anyone do it at Rumson, though once back home Lisa got into trouble when her best friend, Kristy Scanlan, talked her into Happy Slapping their homeroom teacher, Mrs. Kolar, because she'd given them detention for talking too much (Dad made Lisa give up her cell phone for a whole month for that one).

I pulled my floppy hat down low when I stepped off the bus, and I didn't have to walk too far to get to Chappaqua Community College. My first thought upon seeing it was, *Meri's here?!* The campus is basically a collection of blocky nondescript buildings— almost like airplane hangars—and the grounds were all blotchy and brown, like someone had forgotten to use fertilizer. Students were milling about, and again, I'm so not the judgmental type, but they definitely reminded me of the burnouts back home at Chesterfield High (the ones who sort of mixed an alterna-flannel look with semipunk haircuts and swore by Limp Bizkit and smoked lots and lots of pot and never went to class). A scream abruptly caught in my throat. I couldn't believe it. There she was! I leaped behind an outdoor student posting board, pulled my floppy hat down low, and took a deep breath. My recon mission had begun. Gathering my courage, I peeked from behind the board.

Meri. Beautiful, perfect Meri. The afternoon sun was harsh, the humidity was high, but Meri seemed to be encased in some sort of cool and breezy bubble. Her look was new. She was Boho chic. Lots and lots of layers. A deliberately frayed and gauzy crochet-trim cami, strings of beaded necklaces, a light brown tiered prairie skirt, two jangly low-riding hip-belt necklaces slung around her waist, delicate heirloom jeweled sandals, with everything topped like a cherry on a sundae by immense moonbeam sunglasses, and of course, by Meri's lustrous raven hair, which seemed to flutter in the wind, even though the air around her was still and sweltering. Her new style was "real," but obviously very expensive. She was surrounded by a small cluster of sweating, fawning burnouts—her new groupies. She was chatting amiably, languidly gesturing, and they hung on her every word. The fact that she was even with them was strangely incongruous; it was as if some really big star like Nicole Kidman or Julia Roberts had suddenly decided to go shopping at the local Pick 'n Save or relax for the afternoon at a monster truck rally. A car horn blasted. Startled, I ducked back behind the board.

In the parking lot, I saw this really hot-looking burnout guy in ripped jeans and a dirty white T standing by his banged-up brown Toyota. He was waving Meri over. I crouched down lower and kept watching, and with my trusty binoculars, I could see it all. Meri strolled up to the guy and ducked into his Toyota. His burnout friends were in the back. They rolled the windows up, and even though the glaring sun made it hard to see what was going on inside, I had a pretty good idea, because when they stepped out, puffs of smoke wafted out with them, and Meri's eyes, sans the moonbeam sunglasses, were glassy and heavy-lidded. So much for Meri being "good," but that was hardly a surprise.

"Did you lose your contacts or something?"

Oh my God. I was exposed. A burnout guy had stepped up behind me and I was crouched down with my binoculars like an *obvious* spy who was *obviously* on a recon mission. How would I get out of this? How would Spy Girl Barbie get out of this? She'd adapt to her surroundings, that's what she'd do. I scrunched up my face, gave the guy my best I-Am-So-Totally-Wasted look (not that I would know firsthand, but like any good spy, I've had occasion to observe), then I giggled in a half-deranged way and made sure to sound completely ding-y when I said, "No, I'm just coming down. Wow. Like wicked harsh. And I'm really into looking at these bugs on the ground with these binocs. Wanna see?"

"That's so cool. I've done that. Careful, you might burn them. You know, like a magnifying glass? 'Cause of the sun?"

"Oh."

"Yeah."

"Wow."

"Hey, want to come back to my car? We can do a bump."

I had no idea what he meant by a "bump"—was it a dance move or drug-related or sexual or what?—and at that moment I really didn't care, because from the corner of my eye I saw Meri zipping away from the campus on a snappy-looking pale green Vespa.

"Dude, I'd love to bump, but I just remembered that I lost my crib sheet for a test, and like, I have the IQ of a lunchbox. So I really need to find it. Like now. Laters."

Then I ran superfast and spotted Meri as she rode two blocks down the street to a Kroger grocery store. I was out of breath (it's not easy to chase someone and keep yourself hidden at the same time) and slightly dizzy, but when I slinked into the store, I spotted her right away. She was buying several large containers of food at the gourmet prepared foods counter. Then she turned, and I squealed—darting behind a display stack of Mountain Dew six-packs. When I dared to peek from behind it, she was gone. I crept quietly and nonchalantly (I thought) from aisle to aisle and found her at the far end of the cleaning supplies aisle holding up two oversize plastic bottles of bleach, as if she were deciding which brand to buy; one was the cheap Kroger no-name brand, the other was Clorox. Meri was comparison shopping? She put back the Clorox and seemed to have decided on the no-name brand. She held it up high, and I think she was reading the label (for what? the ingredients? Bleach is bleach), and yet it also looked like she was hoisting a holy grail, or maybe posing for someone. That's when the bottom of my stomach felt all foamy and nauseous. Was Meri posing for me? I whipped around to the other aisle. *She couldn't have seen me,* I told myself, *and besides, my hair is up, my face is practically covered, so even if she did see me there is so no way she'd know it was me.*

I kept following her for the rest of the afternoon, and luckily, her stops weren't too far apart, so I didn't have to run more than a few miles total to keep up with her on her Vespa. After the grocery store, she turned onto Salem Lane, a surprisingly leafy residential street. She parked her Vespa and strolled up to an enchanted-looking gingerbread-ish clapboard house, carrying the takeout packages she'd bought from the gourmet foods counter. After she rang the bell, a twinkly-eyed, slightly stooped, gray-haired old lady answered the door, gave Meri a big hug, and let her in. This is part of Meri's community service, I realized, delivering food to the elderly.

I dared to move in for a closer look. Quick like a bunny, I darted from behind a parked van a few houses down on the opposite side of the street and looked through my binoculars. The mailbox said, "Forbes," and when I looked down, I saw the number "8" on the curb. I wanted to see more, but I couldn't. By the time I scampered to the back to get a look through the large bay window in the kitchen, the shades were abruptly drawn shut. I was a little suspicious, but then what could Meri be doing with an old lady that could harm me or Alpha Beta Delta?

I had to scramble when I heard the Vespa starting up again. I was still in the back, so I didn't hear her walk out the front door, but by now my movements were swift and skillful. I followed her to an ice-cream shop. When she stepped out, she was lazily licking a single-scoop ice-cream cone, her eyes half open, gazing out at seemingly nothing, but then Meri's wheels are always turning, so I didn't for a second assume that this was a restful or leisurely moment. The ice cream was a pale tan color, which meant that it was probably peach. Peach, as I recalled from Meri's days at Alpha Beta Delta, was Jackie O.'s favorite ice-cream flavor, and I marveled that she was able to find it in Chappaqua.

She was off again, this time arriving at St. Eulalia's, a private Catholic school for girls. I quickly situated myself, crouching down low in a small wood that bordered the playground, and from there I was able to look through my binoculars and see Meri, since all of the classrooms in back had large picture windows that circled the playground in a horseshoe shape. Meri, it seemed, was doing more community service. She was seated in a chair and surrounded by a group of cute little eight- or ten-year-old Catholic school girls, all of them scrubby-clean and apple-cheeked and wearing adorable matching tartan uniforms. I was pretty far away, but I could still make out the title of the book, *The True Confessions of Charlotte Doyle* by Avi, a delightful novel I read years ago about a sweet young girl who battles mutinous swashbucklers on board a ship in the 1800s. It's a lovely story, but I couldn't imagine Meri having any patience for it.

Then I nearly dropped my binoculars in shock. It happened

lickity-split fast. Another book fell from Meri's hands—a smaller book that had obviously been hidden by the Avi book; this was the real book Meri was reading. She quickly snatched it, hid it with the Avi book again, and made a discreet shushing motion to the girls, some of whom stifled giggles, while others imitated her shushing motion (perfectly, I might add). Then a middle-aged teacher strolled into the room. The girls immediately perked up, smiled toothsomely, and Meri smiled too—beautifully, reassuringly.

The teacher strode back out and Meri dropped her smile like a ten-ton brick and began reading again, unconsciously running her hand through her thick raven hair and flipping it back, which started a flurry of imitation; several of the girls flipped their hair back too. My throat dried up. Meri was clearly reading these girls something she shouldn't—*The Art of War? The Encyclopedia of Serial Killers?*—but more disturbing was the fact that they were all so slavishly devoted to her. Meri has disciples. She has mini-Meris. And then, without warning, a voice whispered loudly.

"You're a peeper."

Oh my God. I froze. A figure was standing to my side. Was I dreaming?

"You're a dirty peeper. And I'm gonna tell."

I forced a swallow, turned slightly, and looked up from my crouched position. *I must be dreaming,* I thought. Standing next to me was a tiny little Catholic school girl with a shock of long, seemingly bleached-out white hair. Her skin was white too, almost fluorescent, and the pupils of her eyes were bright pink, just like a bunny rabbit's, and they darted in a skittish motion, as if they were attempting to focus or avoid indirect light from the afternoon sun.

"I know what you're doing," she whispered. "And it won't work."

I had to get a grip. This wasn't a dream. The abnormally tiny girl before me was real. And she was albino.

I stammered, "I'm just, I mean . . ."

"Don't lie," whispered Albino Girl. "We know when you lie."

I dared to ask, my voice barely above a murmur, "Who's 'we'?"

She gazed at me for what must have been only half a second, but it felt like an eternity. I was spellbound by her piercing pink eyes.

Then she abruptly cried out, "Woof woof!"

My mind shattered; I struggled for a response, but I didn't have time. She whipped out a whistle and blew! The high-pitched screech galvanized me. I was on my feet, I was running, and I had no idea where I was going as I pushed through a tangle of overhanging branches. From a distance, I heard a voice cry out.

"She's here!"

I kept running, bounding out of the wood and onto a roadway. A car horn blasted! I leaped aside in the nick of time, flinging myself to the curb. *Don't just lay here,* I screamed to myself, *keep running.* I made it to the bus, and I must have looked like a freakazoid because people were staring at me, and my elbow was scraped and bleeding. I reached into my purse and searched for a Kleenex. Instead I found a stray unlit firecracker. Then I looked further. And I gasped with delight. I almost burst into tears. I couldn't believe it. I was vindicated! *I am not a wacko,* I told myself, and when I had that thought, and knew in my gut that it was true, I wanted to jump up and down inside the bus and hurl my arms in the air and scream out loud, "I am not a wacko!" because at the very bottom of my purse, stuck to an old lemon-lime lozenge that must have been there since forever, was a single strand of white hair. And it sure as heck wasn't mine.

I pulled it carefully from the lozenge, and I swear, if I'd had tweezers and latex gloves I would have used them, because I suddenly had a giggly vision of Spy Girl Barbie starring in her very own special episode of *CSI* (a forensics expert, yes, but always in a mini) I took off my big sunglasses to make sure I was seeing what I thought I was seeing and held it up to get a closer look. I was beginning to get the picture. It wasn't Meri who attacked me with those firecrackers in the ladies' room and stuffed unlit firecrackers into my purse, it was Albino Girl. She's certainly tiny enough to fit through the small window in the ladies' room, which was wide open—but which everyone insisted Meri couldn't have fit through in order to make her escape. *I am not a wacko*, I repeated to myself. I finally found a Kleenex, and I used it to carefully wrap the strand of white hair.

It was early evening by the time I stumbled through the front door of Alpha Beta Delta. Patty audibly yelped when she saw me.

"What happened? Where were you?"

"I was, um, playing Frisbee on the Great Lawn and I fell."

"Oh, c'mon. Do I look stupid? Don't answer that. Where were you all day? Really."

"Classes. What do you mean?"

"Tch. Cindy. We have a four thirty class together on Wednesdays. Remember?"

I wasn't in the mood to be grilled, so I strode past her and stepped into the kitchen. I was hungry, and everyone had already eaten. Patty was the only one in the house. Shanna-Francine and the rest of the girls had gone out to rent an "appropriate" DVD for the night.

"Oh, Cindy, Cindy, Cindy," clucked Patty, who was following behind me. "It's me. Patty Camp. The most open-minded and understanding friend you have."

I ignored her, swinging open the fridge, searching for the ground beef I'd bought a few days ago. I needed a burger. I needed beef. But I couldn't find the ground beef anywhere, and when I asked Patty if she had used it, she calmly explained.

"We threw it out. You missed a lot today. We purged the house of inappropriate food. It was fascinating, actually. Shanna-Francine had us throw away all the cruel food—like your beef and my garlic chicken and Lindsay's frozen salmon burgers—and then we rid the house of all unnatural processed foods."

"Where's my cheese?"

"Ah-ah. Cheese contains rennet, which is the lining of a calf's stomach. Gross, huh? So no more cheese."

I made do with leftovers from Alpha Beta Delta's first appropriate dinner, a macrobiotic stew with lotus root, leeks, red cabbage, and kombu seaweed. It was awful. In theory, I'm all for eating "appropriately" and "cruelty-free," but obviously Alpha Beta Delta has a lot to learn about making these foods edible. Patty sat with me, munching from a large tin of peanut brittle.

"Peanut brittle is appropriate?" I asked.

"Of course not, silly," she said, grinning, with bits of peanut brittle and powdered sugar dribbling from her mouth and dotting her blouse. "But I'm starving. I have to eat something after that bowl of crap we were served tonight."

We shared a chuckle, and she shared the peanut brittle with me too (thank God), but she didn't give up with the inquisition. I tried my best to be evasive. I really didn't want to talk about it. I was still running everything back and forth in my mind, and I needed to formulate my own thoughts and feelings about it—along with a plan of action. In the midst of Patty's inquest, Chunk-a-Lunk, one of Bobbie's plump cats, leaped up on one of the chairs and glared at me peevishly, as if he were saying, *Well? Where is my flambé? Where is my aperitif? What, no after-dinner speaker?*

"Go away, Chunk-a-Lunk," I said.

"Ah-ah," said Patty. "They have brand-new appropriate names. Chunk-a-Lunk and Mrs. Fields are gone. They're now called Tamari and Pumpkin Seed. It was Bobbie's idea. It was very thoughtful of her, actually." Then she took my hand and quietly added, "Cindy. Do you want to talk about what happened today? About the fire-crackers?"

I guess good news travels fast. Obviously, all of Alpha Beta Delta, and likely all of RU, by now knew about the incident in the ladies' room, along with my "hysterical" accusations against Meri.

"No, I'd really rather not," I responded as airily as I could.

"Maybe you should get a medical checkup," she urged. "Path-ological delirium is sometimes caused by space-occupying lesions in the brain."

"I do not have brain lesions!" I bluntly retorted, and okay, I don't know that for sure, but really.

"I just want to rule out a few things before attributing your recent behavior to an Axis I disorder."

"And then what? You'll have me committed?" Then I laughed— a good hearty laugh—and though I could tell that Patty felt stung, I wasn't laughing at her; it just felt so good to laugh after the day I'd had. A paw suddenly swished forth, and I thought, *Who am I to deny this cat what it really wants?* I magnanimously set the bowl of macrobiotic stew on the floor.

"Knock yourself out, Tamari."

But Tamari, having more sense than anyone at Alpha Beta Delta, took one sniff, hissed loudly, and backed away. Patty con-tinued to prattle, convinced that I was in desperate need of psychoactive pharmaceuticals, while Tamari, ever on alert, hopped onto her lap and carefully licked her blouse.

"He likes me," squealed Patty.

No, he liked all those tiny bits of peanut brittle and powdered sugar on her blouse.

"Aw, he does. What a sweet cat," I said, because the last thing I wanted to be was a spoilsport.

The rest of the night was a trying experience. Everyone kept stealing glances at me in the living room. We were gathered to watch *Thelma & Louise*, which was deemed an appropriate DVD rental. Bobbie found it "empowering," and Shanna-Francine whole-heartedly agreed.

"It's just so right-on about men and women," she babbled cheerfully.

A lively discussion commenced, and eventually all eyes were on me. What was my opinion? I guess I was still frazzled from my day, because I didn't stop myself from impatiently snapping, "Please, you call that 'empowering'? They punish men by driving off a cliff and killing themselves. They're not empowered, they're dead. And Geena Davis's outfits were awful."

There were a few gasps and several quick furtive glances—*The wacko speaks*, those looks said—and then Lindsay looked up at me hopefully.

"But you thought Brad was cute, didn't you?"

I didn't hear her at first. I was caught up in a blissful vision of Meri soaring off a cliff to her death and joining Thelma and Louise (in their surely all-girl empowered heaven). But I focused, gazing at Lindsay's open and hopeful face; she wanted me to be okay so badly, to be sane, and I counted myself lucky in one sense. Should Meri ever truly drive me loco, then at least I'll have a very caring group of friends to look after me.

"Yes, Brad's a hottie," I said with a smile.

There was a huge collective sigh of relief in the room; there was hope for me, they realized, since in the darkest recesses of my unstable mind, I was still sane enough to realize that Brad Pitt was hot. And then I heard a familiar buzzing sound—and then the TV's channels began flipping real fast from one to the next. I exploded.

"I told you to take that thing out!"

Lindsay covered her mouth in shock, burst into tears, then

ran out of the room and up the stairs. Oh, what had I done? Why was I so mean? I love Lindsay.

"What's going on between you two?" asked Patty.

"You guys, something's wrong with the TV!" shrieked Shanna-Francine, who was fighting the TV's possessed behavior with the remote control.

When I stepped into my bedroom, the computer loomed like a ticking time bomb. Was I ready to check my e-mail before going to bed? But then I realized I had something more important to do. I walked down the hall and knocked on Lindsay's door.

"Lindsay. It's me. Can I come in? Please?"

There was no response. I opened the door and found her curled up on her bed, sniffling, her tiara on her bedside table.

"I'm sorry," I said.

"I know. And you were right. I got rid of—"

"No, don't. Really. I'm not in a position to cast judgment on anyone." And I meant that. I may not have found my authentic self yet, and yes, I lost Keith, but if there's one thing I've learned in the past few days it's this: Your real girlfriends will stick by you no matter what, even if they think you're completely wacko, and that includes Lindsay. Especially Lindsay. So I'll just have to adjust myself to her relationship with Bud, because even though I've never said it outright (though I've come awfully close), she knows I think Bud is pond scum, and that has to hurt. Maybe I just need to realize once and for all that if Bud makes Lindsay happy, then that's it, finito, that's all that matters.

"Are you going to be okay?" she asked tentatively. "I mean, everyone's worried. And so am I. She's not at Rumson, Cindy. Meri's not here."

Oh, Lindsay. Dear, sweet Lindsay. I wish I could feel safe like her with just an umbrella and a tiara.

"I know she's not," I said, hoping to relieve her.

Apostolina

She was thrilled, and we spent the rest of the night listening to a mix CD that Bud had made especially for her. I have to admit, it was very sweet and remarkably eclectic. It was all love songs, like Amerie's "Why Don't We Fall in Love?" and "If You Love Me" by Brownstone and "Simply Being Loved" by BT and "All the World Loves Lovers" by Prefab Sprout. I actually shed a tear when I heard the Prefab Sprout song.

> All the world loves people in love. Don't forget it.
> Love. Don't forget it. Love. Love whatever the price.

I wish I were in love. Maybe then I'd have more strength to fight off Meri. But maybe it's better that I'm alone. Meri needs to be stopped, but the last thing I want to do is create more targets for her, whether it's my friends or my boyfriend (like Keith) (my love, my sweet, my everything!) (I know, I know, I have to get over him) (but I don't want too) (I really hate Bitch Kitty). No, this is one battle I have to fight on my own.

Back in my bedroom, I flipped on the computer and checked my e-mail. Just like that. Bring it on. There was only one.

From: <elainebixby@yahoo.com>
Date: 25 October
To: <cindybixby@yahoo.com>
Subject: Your Sister

This is your mother. We have a serious family problem. Your sister is out of control. As you know, your father and I very kindly brought her to Los Angeles in order to support her dreams of become a "big-time star" (those are her words, not mine).

I'll be frank. I do not like Los Angeles and neither does your father, and I do not like these so-called industry people whom we've been forced to take meetings with. They dress tastelessly and behave impolitely (with the exception of Frederick, her manager, who's very well-mannered and doesn't let Lisa interrupt him). Still, your father and I have held our tongues, even upon hearing your sister's smutty new song, "Touch My Daisy," which she recorded this morning.

But Cindy, your sister must think your father and I are new-born chicks. We know she's been sneaking out of the hotel at night, doing God knows what with who, and we've told her to stop it immediately. She outright lies to us, claiming she stays in every night.

We have now reached our limit. And this afternoon, we told her that if she sneaks out one more time, we're taking her home. Period. She laughed at us. And she screamed, "Please, you can't do that! Look at me! I'm a star! Now go away and leave me alone! I have to get up early tomorrow morning and sparkle, I tell you, sparkle!" Then she slammed the door to her hotel room.

Cindy, maybe you can talk some sense into her. I am honestly at my wit's end. I do want what's best for your sister, and I know you do too, but if she sneaks out again or backtalks your father and me one more time, then we really will drag her back to Ohio and put a stop to this nonsense once and for all.

Your mother.

I marveled at my mother's carefully worded e-mail. Lisa was misbehaving, therefore she was referred to as "your sister" (and not just once). I was a little perturbed that I had to deal with this, given everything I have to deal with in my own life. But I fired off a quick e-mail.

From: <cindybixby@yahoo.com >
Date: 25 October
To: <lisa@lisabixby.com>
Subject: Be Nice!

Lisa:

Mom tells me you're being a major brat in LA. Knock it off! She'll take you back to Ohio if you don't straighten up, and if you think she's bluffing, remember when she cut the cable cord to the TV in your bedroom after she caught you trying to steal DuWop lipsticks at Penney's? Remember? You couldn't watch E! for two whole months!

I'll put this in terms that you can understand. If she takes you home, that's the end, your career's kaput–you're a one-hit wonder like Vanilla Ice. He works in a lousy bike shop now. Did you know that? Or maybe you want to be like Paula Abdul. Do you want to be like her? Rubbing up against teenage boys in thirty years? Acting like you're still the shit? Get it? Am I speaking your lingo?

xxoo
Cindy

I was relieved that I hadn't received any nasty e-mail from "myself," but just as I was ready to go to bed, I had a startling thought. What if the person sending me nasty e-mails is simply stealing into my room while I'm asleep and writing them on my computer then? It's possible, isn't it? I rummaged through my dresser. There it was in the bottom drawer, something I've never used before: my door key. This would come in handy. I locked my door. I'm going to bed now. And I'm putting my door key under my pillow.

October 26

Dear Diary:

The day began so peacefully. I should have known better. I woke up early to catch up on my studying, and then I checked my e-mail. Nothing. Well, well. I guess I hadn't sent myself another hostile e-mail during the night. Ha! Maybe a locked door is the best door. Then I headed downstairs. No one was awake yet except for Patty, who was in the kitchen making coffee.

"No crullers?" I asked, since Patty always has at least two or three crullers in the morning no matter what diet she's on (but maybe crullers aren't appropriate anymore).

"I don't need them," she happily informed me. "I'm on a new diet—totally new. It's from Wolfgang."

"Wolfgang Rimmer? That squirmy little German—"

"Yeah, but don't make fun. He's gonna make a billion dollars. And so am I." Then she proudly held out a small glass canister filled with white granules. "It's his special new diet sugar. He created it in chemistry class. And it really works. But he's not telling anyone about it. Not yet, anyway. See, he took some pictures of me, and once I lose tons and tons of weight, he'll take more pictures and then use them for his first before-and-after campaign and sell it to some really big company like General Mills or something. Isn't that great? He hasn't come up

110

with a name for it yet, but I think he should call it Skinny. Don't you like that? Skinny?"

"So it's like Equal. Or Splenda."

"Oh, so much better!" she enthused. "Those are just sugar substitutes. This helps you lose weight." Then she poured a cup of coffee, sprinkled a tiny bit of "Skinny" in, gave it a stir. "Voilà. See? Just a teensy amount in your—"

She didn't get to finish her sentence, because from the front of the house, where Lindsay had stepped out to retrieve the morning paper, we heard her scream, "Oh my God!"

By this time most everyone in the house was up, and we all ran outside. I ran numbly, and I was thinking, what fresh new horror has Meri created for me now? It was actually very simple. Everyone was on the front lawn. There were gasps and finger-pointing, and in what seemed like a flash, ROT had leaped forward with Nester, who was frantically taking pictures. Flash-flash-flash. Everyone was looking back and forth; at me, hoping for a reaction, and the front lawn, which had huge letters bleached out on the grass that spelled: "I hate Cindy Bixby!" I couldn't move—I think I was in shock—and when Lindsay came up to me and gently shook me, I hoarsely whispered, "Meri."

"Meri did this?!" exclaimed Lindsay. God bless Lindsay. She grimly straightened her tiara, pushed out in front of the crowd, and screamed for all to hear, "Meri did this. It was Meri Sugarman!"

There were murmurs in the crowd, snickers of disbelief ("Isn't that the firecracker girl?" I heard one guy say), a few whispery mentions of Professor Gould, and then everyone turned to Bobbie, who was barreling out the front door.

"You stickin' by that story, Bixby? Meri did this?" she bellowed. Then she held up an empty bottle of bleach. "What about this? It was under your bed. I saw it poking out when I ran past your room."

That was it. Complete bedlam. I screamed in vain, "It was Meri! I saw her buy it."

"You saw Meri?" asked Patty. "When?"

"Meri uses no-name bleach?" screeched a stunned Shanna-Francine.

"Yesterday," I yelped. "I saw her."

"You stalked her!" cried ROT.

"I saw her buy bleach," I wailed. "She's doing everything. Oh my God, you've got to believe me. She has people helping her! She has an albino!"

Oh why, oh why did I panic and open my big mouth? Everyone started laughing, campus security pushed forward. Lindsay grabbed me protectively and violently pushed back the gawkers and finger-pointers and brought me inside. I turned for a quick look before she closed the door and I saw him across the street. It was Keith! He was standing there alone with a look of stunned disbelief stamped on his face. I wanted to cry out, "I'm telling the truth!" I wanted to convince him that I wasn't crazy . . . and then I saw Bitch Kitty flounce up to him and the door slammed shut. Lindsay whisked me into my room.

"Stay here," she said.

I sputtered, "I have proof. I have the—the lemon-lime lozenge. And a single strand of albino hair. Look, look!"

"Cindy, the less you say the better. Just stay here."

Then she was gone. I flung myself against the bed, and I could hear the screaming and laughter from out front. But I didn't cry; I clutched my pillow like a life raft, bracing myself. Then I leaped off my bed and whipped up the bed skirt. There were two small dribbly white bleach stains on the wood floor. Whoever bleached the lawn and then shoved the bottle under my bed must have done it in the dead of night. I tried to think clearly: I've been sabotaged at every turn, and so has Alpha Beta Delta, which means that there must be a mole in the house. But who? What's the timeline? When did all the bad things start? It was so obvious. And it made me furious.

Bad things started with the Cookie Booth fiasco—how, I still wondered, did all those groups know to organize their protests so quickly? And guess what? That was just about the time that a certain Mohawked Dame Barbara Cartland–loving Wiccan lesbian was welcomed into the house. The mole is Bobbie! She's obviously in cahoots with Meri. It was Bobbie, after all, who "found" the bottle of no-name bleach under my bed. Oh, how I wish I had locked my door before going down to breakfast this morning. And yes, Meri must have known that I was following her yesterday when she so coyly posed for me in the cleaning supplies aisle with the bottle of bleach, which means that when I left the campus and began following her, I was already being followed by Albino Girl, since she was already on campus, given her fire-cracker attack.

I went to my classes. And I assumed that my every move was being watched. I had another realization. I now knew for certain that when I carried my iMac to Bud's dorm room the other morning and thought I was imagining a teeny-tiny version of Meri lurking in the shadows, I wasn't imagining anything. It could have been Albino Girl, or it could have been any one of Meri's devoted St. Eulalia girls. But I didn't imagine a thing. Today, though, I was watching too, and I followed Lindsay's advice. The less I say the better—to anyone. It was hard at times. I heard whispers and mocking little titters as I walked on campus, and in my classes, too, and it took all my strength to pull the blinders and just ignore it and concentrate on my studies.

Late this afternoon Alpha Beta Delta had a brief organizational meeting for the Hour of Silence for the LGBT community tomorrow. There will be no prepublicity, since Shanna-Francine wants it to unfold "organically." Tomorrow morning and throughout the day, we'll be silently selling small keepsake cards for five dollars to everyone we can. They're still being printed, but Shanna-Francine showed us a sample:

> *Please understand my reasons for not speaking. I am participating in the Hour of Silence, an Alpha Beta Delta event protesting the silence faced by lesbian, gay, bisexual, and transgender people and their allies. My deliberate silence echoes their silence, which is caused by harassment and prejudice.*
>
> *Please join Alpha Beta Delta and donate to LGBT causes by purchasing this keepsake card for $5.00, and then join us in front of Alpha Beta Delta this afternoon from five to six p.m. for our moving Hour of Silence Protest Rally.*

Throughout the entire meeting, I kept my eyes on Bobbie. I'll bet she's not even a real lesbian. Barbara Cartland. Right. That should have been a tip-off. And no, I've never had the pleasure of meeting a real live lesbian, but given the behavior of all the other lesbians who were at the Prospective Member Assessment meeting, it made sense. None of those girls took joining a sorority seriously. To them it was a joke. But not to Bobbie. I kept quiet. *The less I say the better*, I reminded myself, and I had to keep reminding myself when Bobbie sheepishly came into my room tonight after dinner. What a performance. She apologized for embarrassing me by running out with the bottle of bleach—she was caught up in the moment, she claimed. She also said that she really didn't know what was going on between me and Meri; in other words, she was keeping it deliberately vague, and not saying whether or not she believed me. Then she gazed at me with supposed compassion and handed me a book.

"Here. I picked it out for you. Especially for you. It's by Dame Barbara."

I glanced at the cover: *The Little Pretender*, by Barbara Cartland, with a picture of a gowned woman from the 1700s being clutched by a handsome paramour.

"It's one of her best," she earnestly informed me. "You'll love it. And it's a first edition."

I looked up at her; I was trying to get a read. *She really must think I'm a total numbskull,* I thought.

She couldn't take my stare. She flinched and said, "What?"

"Get out of my room," I told her as plainly as I could. Then I flung the book back at her. "And take this with you."

She was shocked; she stood there stammering for a bit. I rolled my eyes. I really was getting tired of this. Yes, I'm scared of Bobbie, but I guess my annoyance at being so easily hoodwinked was taking priority.

"Please just go," I repeated, and okay, I broke Lindsay's the-less-I-say-the-better rule, but I had studying to do and I was tired of pretending and if I had to look at Bobbie's face for one second longer I really was going to scream and I didn't want to do that. She looked at me with a pained expression, as if I'd actually hurt her feelings—nice try, you fake lesbian, you—then she turned around and walked out. I leaped from my bed and slammed the door shut. And locked it.

October 27

Dear Diary:

I pride myself on maintaining a positive and cheerful outlook no matter what the circumstances. It's probably a holdover from my elementary school years. Jordi Kane, this really nasty little boy in my second-grade glass, put a whoopee cushion on my chair one morning, and when I took my seat and the cushion exploded with a horrible farting sound and the entire class erupted in giggles, I nearly burst into tears. Even my teacher, Mrs. Brown, was laughing (I hated her for that). But instead of crying, I joined in the laughter. I laughed and laughed and said, "Wow, you really got me, Jordi. You're so funny."

It wasn't the reaction Jordi wanted, and though I cried my eyes out later at home, and wondered why so many people were so eager to pick on me, I knew I'd somehow ruined the fun for Jordi by laughing along with everyone else. In fact, the very next day, he moved on to a new target, Angie Ryan, a morose third grader who talked to herself in low, angry mutters and sported improbably cute pigtails. Jordi "pantsed" her on the playground. Wrong move, Jordi. Angie had a powerful left hook. *Bam.* She decked him, his nose started bleeding, and best of all, he started crying. Aw. What goes around comes around, Jordi, or as Mom used to say, "You get what you want, and in the form you deserve," which is what she said to Lisa years ago before putting her over her knee and spanking her for playing cat-toss in the living room with the neighbor's cat, Billy, and breaking Mom's blue and gilt porcelain Limoges vase.

Today I tried to put on a happy face, as if to say to anyone within earshot, as I'd said to Jordi years ago, "Wow, you really got me, Meri. You're so funny." I mean, I know that Meri has little helpers, including Albino Girl, and I know that Bobbie is more than likely her secret mole at Alpha Beta Delta, and no, I haven't yet formulated a plan to defend myself and the house, but what, I thought, was the point of being so down in the dumpity-doo? Why give Meri that satisfaction? I strolled chipper as could be throughout the campus today: I gave a friendly wave to Nester, who hesitated to snap a picture of me, since my face wasn't all twisted in fury or shock; I shook my head while smiling, as if to say, "Aw, shucks, that Meri's such a kidder," when a group of students on the Great Lawn snickered and pointed at me; and God help me, I even said hi and gave a wave to Doreen, aka Bitch Kitty, who was on her way to cheerleading practice (to Doreen's credit, she shrugged and waved back).

I even exhibited exquisite patience with Bud when I met him in the equipment room at RU's Film & Video wing to get a quick lesson on how to operate the videocam I'll be using to document Alpha Beta Delta's good deeds for the intersorority governing board. As Bud demonstrated all the camera's controls, I couldn't help but notice that his pants were hanging down really low—even lower than normal, and since he wasn't wearing any underwear, you could see his butt, or at least the top part of it. If this were any other day, I wouldn't have thought twice about letting Bud walk around with his "bidness" hanging out, but instead I generously told him, "Bud, maybe you ought to wear a belt today. Your butt's showing."

"I know, pretty cool, huh? Ass-cleavage is so in right now," he said with a stupid grin. Then he stuck out his behind and started jiggling. "Wanna slap it? Huh? Oooo, yeah. C'mon, give it a—"

I didn't really mean to slap Bud as hard as I did, but then, "you get what you want, and in the form you deserve," so I guess Bud deserved to be slapped so hard that he flew face-forward and banged his head on the wall opposite. To my surprise, he laughed uproariously, and for the rest of the day kept referring to me as "Mistress Cindy" and slinging his arm out as if he were cracking a whip.

At Alpha Beta Delta, Shanna-Francine paired us off in teams and sent us out to sell our Hour of Silence keepsake cards. Lindsay and I decided to be a team, and at first we followed various pairs of girls so I could document this activity for the video. I could already tell that I'll be cutting his section down to the bone; all of the girls, including Shanna-Francine and Bobbie, were so drearily silent and solemn. I mean, I know violence and oppression against LGBT people is a serious matter, but jeez, we were supposed to be raising funds and exciting people about coming to a rally, not scaring them away. Lindsay agreed with me.

"Let's go, you've got enough of this stuff," she said. She led me away, shielding us both with her new Bottega Veneta cream-dotted off-white umbrella. "C'mon, I know who can help us sell lots of these things."

Lindsay took me to meet Sebastian Plummer, a bright-eyed, exceptionally well-dressed blond freshman who's majoring in drama and speaks with a slight lisp. I don't think he was expecting us. When he arrived at his dorm room, the door was ajar, and we could see him dancing and shimmying in his tightie-whities in front of a full-length mirror and singing along to "Dreamgirls."

We're your Dreamgirls, boys! We'll make you happy!
Oh, yeah, yeah, yeah!
We're your Dreamgirls, boys! We'll always care!

Then he froze. He saw us through the mirror standing stunned in the doorway.

"Wow, I didn't know you were this hardcore," sputtered Lindsay.

Sebastian quickly put on his clothes, and Lindsay explained our situation: We needed to sell tons of keepsake cards and make sure lots and lots of people came to the rally. I stood there awkwardly until Lindsay realized she hadn't made proper introductions. Sebastian shook my hand firmly and smiled (his teeth were gleaming!).

"Sebastian Plummer—with two *m*'s. I'm a tenor."

"Pleased to meet you, Sebastian."

"Oh, and if anyone asks, I have eight by tens. Commercial and dramatic."

It took Sebastian a moment to comprehend who I was when Lindsay introduced me as "the" Cindy Bixby, but then he screamed (and I mean screamed), "Ohmygodohmygodohmygod! Shut. The. Fuck. Up."

I wasn't sure why he was so thrilled to meet me—most people run in the opposite direction—and I didn't have time to ask, because we were off.

"Perfect timing, you guys," he exclaimed. "It's Gay Day at Six Flags!"

But first things first. We followed Sebastian, who hip-swung down the hall, knocked on a dorm room door, cleared his throat, and announced with mock gravity, "Ladies and gentlemen, there is no greater star than Sheila Farr."

The door whisked open, and out stepped, well, I don't know his real name, but he was dressed in a beautiful, form-fitting, glittery, gold lamé gown, a poofy-big platinum beehive wig, impossibly high heels, white elbow-length evening gloves, and flawlessly garish makeup. He breathlessly intoned, "Shhh! Whisper thy name. And please, when you speak to me, call me Sheila. When you refer to me, then I'm Miss Farr."

Whoosh. We were off to the parking lot, passing the football field where Doreen and the cheerleaders were practicing. Sebastian tsked.

"You know what I hate about cheerleading? Floor patterns. All floor patterns. Uck."

"Uck," echoed Sheila.

Then we were off in Sebastian's Ford SynUS—or "Sin Wagon," as he gigglingly referred to it. We had the loveliest chat; Sheila and Sebastian greatly admired Lindsay's tiara (she let Sebastian try it on, and I've got to say, it looked pretty darn good on him), and Sheila regaled us with stories of her "youth." See, this wasn't just a guy in drag, he had invented an entire character. Sheila, as I was quick to learn, was a major movie star in "Old Hollywood" and had even adopted a daughter, Katrina.

"My daughter, please," she fussed, elaborately lighting a Bel-Air. "I brought her to the Academy Awards, introduced her to *all* my famous friends—she could have ridden my coattails. Even when she was a youngster, I tried to teach her humility, obligation. Sign Mommy's name at the bottom of the glossy, but no, instead, 'Best Wishes, Sheila Farr,' from the top of my forehead to the bottom of my chin. Now I ask you, a cry for help? Or just a cheap shot?"

The gays sure are funny. If ever I need to remind myself to maintain a positive and cheerful outlook, I'll just think of Sheila Farr, because I honestly don't think Sheila would ever let anyone or anything keep him (or her) down. When we arrived at Six Flags, she was off and running.

"Do you mind?" she queried. "I feel the need to mingle, to make contact with the little people. As I learned in my studio days, people work so much harder"—she paused for a wink—"if they think you care."

Then—*poof!*—she was gone in a swirl of sequins and freshly sprayed Aquanet. As for me and Lindsay, we ran out of keepsake cards. We sold all of them! I was so psyched. And I was treated like royalty. All Lindsay had to do was tell people that I was "the" Cindy Bixby, and suddenly they screamed and squealed and jumped up and down. They wanted to know all about Meri and whether or not I'd seen her recently, and whether or not we'd "bitch-slapped" each other. I was confused by this enthusiasm at first, but Sebastian explained that the gays have a thing for warring female stars—from Bette Davis and Joan Crawford, who were apparently at each other's throats in Old Hollywood, to more current cat-fights, such as the ongoing battle between Lindsay Lohan and Hilary Duff, who can't be seen at the same club or movie premiere together without one of them being furiously ejected.

Right. So I was being admired and celebrated . . . for what, exactly? I don't find my situation with Meri very funny, and I like to think that I have a good sense of humor. It all felt vaguely misogynist, or at least borderline, and it gave me the same sort of uneasy feeling I sometimes experience when I watch certain drag queens on cable—you know, the ones who make crude "pussy" jokes, or even cruder jokes about feminine hygiene; they seem to get laughs by making fun of women solely for being women, and that's just wrong. I guess it's a fine line, though, and I wouldn't want to censor anyone, and I did see a drag queen once who did a comic routine about PMS and he was absolutely dead-on and very funny. Presently, my discomfort vanished in a flash when I heard gasps and delighted giggles in the distance. I looked up. Sheila was working the crowd. She threw her arms up in triumph.

"Here I am, boys. It's me! Shining brighter than you ever imag-
ined!"

"Hey, Miss Farr," asked a young gay, who was handing her a
joint. "Have you ever been stoned?"

"Only once, my dear boy. When I played Bathsheba. Ah ha ha!"

For her part, Lindsay was anxious to ride at least one roller
coaster before we left—and it was already getting late in the afternoon. As we rushed toward the Superman roller coaster with
Sebastian, I could still hear Sheila delighting the crowd.

"So tell me, boys: teriyaki—that's just a fancy way of saying
fish piss, isn't it? Ah ha ha!"

I was nervous as we strapped ourselves into our Superman car.
I've never been all that fond of roller coasters because they remind
me of bad turbulence on airplanes—and who wants to put themselves through that?—but Sebastian and Lindsay were so excited
that I could hardly refuse. Sebastian very kindly offered to hold
Lindsay's tiara in his lap (*She'd better watch it*, I thought, *or she might
not get it back*), and cheerily informed us both that Superman is one
of the tallest roller coasters in the world and runs at a top speed
of one hundred miles an hour.

"We're going to be falling forty-one stories straight down," he
gleefully shrieked.

The car jerked forward—and I clutched the safety bar. *Just close
your eyes and it'll be over soon*, I told myself. I shut them tightly, but
a moment later I opened them. Oh my God, I wish I hadn't. I saw
her! She was leaning against an observation railing, smiling, eye-
ing me directly. It was Albino Girl!

"We have to get off this roller coaster," I gasped, and frantically
tried to push up the safety bar as we jerked closer to the first ascending hill. Sebastian chuckled.

"Wow, you really are scared of these things, aren't you?"

I couldn't speak. My throat was closing up. "Aba . . . albi . . ."

"Just hold my hand," said Lindsay with a giggle.

There was another violent jerk, and then we were finally ascending the first impossibly steep hill. The car made a loud metallic *clackity-clack, clackity-clack* sound with each yank upward. I twisted around—and she was still there. She gave a little wave, blew me a kiss. Oh, why had I let my guard down today? Why did I relax? We were getting closer to the top. Thoughts blazed through my head: Did Albino Girl do something to the roller coaster? Was I about to die? With Lindsay? And a blond tenor with eight by tens (commercial and dramatic)? *Clackity-click, clackity-click.* We were going up higher and higher; so high, in fact, that I could barely make out Albino Girl below, much less anyone else. *This is it*, I thought, *this is the end*. Sebastian screamed as we reached the top.

"Hold on!"

Then we plunged down—and stopped! I wasn't able to grasp what was happening at first. My eyes were closed, and I heard blood-curdling screams, but I didn't feel the wind whipping past my face as I knew I would, or should. I opened my eyes. *This isn't happening*, I thought. I felt a powerful gust of panic; my stomach was crushed with terror. *Oh, yes, this is happening*. The entire roller coaster was creakily suspended at the very top of the hill, with one end hanging back over the ascending side, and the other end, with me and Lindsay and Sebastian, hanging over the descending side and looking straight down (nearly forty stories straight down, if Sebastian's estimate was correct). Now even Sebastian and Lindsay were getting scared.

"Is it supposed to do this?" yelped Lindsay.

There was a sudden electrical pop, then a loud *ker-chunk*—and we inched forward and stopped again. By this time everyone on the roller coaster was panicky. Lindsay caught my eye. I stammered.

"M-M-Meri."

A gusty wind blew past. I couldn't see straight anymore, but I heard sharp sickening screams after the car—*ker-chunk*—violently inched forward again, and I could even hear Sebastian, who must have whipped out his cell phone.

"We need help! Yes, that's Plummer. With two *m's!*"

Then he started crying. Big, messy sobs. *Poor Sebastian*, I thought. I dared to look down. It was a vertiginous view, to say the least. *There's no surviving this*, I thought. And then, as if reading my mind—*ker-chunk*—the entire roller coaster lurched forward, and then—as if held by the tiniest of threads that had been pulled way too tight and was quickly unraveling—it violently snapped loose from its hold and plunged down the hill! I was in a chamber of screams. I couldn't even tell if I was in the coaster car anymore; all I knew was that I was falling and the only thing I could feel was the wind and my breath—gasping in, always in—and it felt like my nightmare was suddenly coming true. I had been pushed off a skyscraper roof by Meri.

"Have a nice trip, see you next . . ."

I've jumped into the sunlight, I thought, *and here I am, pinned down by the wind and the screams and the scorching light. So this is what it's like to die. Meri has won.* Then strong arms grabbed me under both of my armpits and yanked me up. I saw the face of Sebastian, and at first I couldn't connect his sweet face and gleaming smile with such strong arms, but then I fleetingly recalled Lindsay mentioning that the gays work out frequently, but only on their upper bodies, which gives them impressive chests and arms with rather odd and spindly-looking legs. I saw Lindsay's face too. She was sighing with relief and laughing. The ride was over. I had lived. Everyone had lived. And Sebastian, who had been bawling like a baby, was full of merry chat.

He wasn't scared, he too-forcefully insisted, because, as he was no doubt hearing from everyone who was babbling around him, sometimes roller coasters experience a momentary "block system halt" or a "switch failure," which is "completely safe" and "like, nothing to worry about," and then he rattled off everything that might have caused this "halt" or "failure," but none of the reasons satisfied me, because I knew that the real reason was Meri, and I knew that I was meant to see Albino Girl—she waved to me, didn't she?—because the entire incident was meant to demonstrate the awesome reach of Meri, a reach so powerful and so breathtaking that she could, if she wanted, pay off an operator to jerk the roller coaster to a terrifying stop at the very top of a forty-story drop just so a certain someone on board would know that she meant business.

"Let's get some water," said Lindsay, a little too lightheartedly, then she tugged me away from Sebastian and led me behind a cotton-candy stand and popped open her umbrella. Her face turned white. She stuttered, "I—I saw her. Waving to you. The albino. At least I think I did."

Oh my God, I couldn't help myself. I pulled her into a hug. Someone finally believes me about Meri! And it's Lindsay (of course it's Lindsay!). And yet that also made me feel even more terrified than before. Meri is realer-than-real now.

"We have to get back to Alpha Beta Delta," I urged.

"My tiara!" yelped Lindsay. She bolted from behind the booth and quickly scanned her surroundings. We didn't have to look too far. A gaggle of gays were gathered around Sebastian, who was demurely posing with it.

"What do you think? Does it bring out my cheekbones?"

"It's flawless."

"Thank you. Hi. I'm Sebastian Plummer. That's with two *m*'s."

Poor Sebastian. No, Lindsay would not let him "borrow" her tiara for the rest of the day, and yes, we had to get back to RU. Right away. Sebastian bid good-bye to his new tiara-admiring friends—I tell you, those gays sure know how to exchange phone numbers fast—then we were off in Sebastian's "Sin Wagon" with

Sheila Farr, who was happy to be returning as well. She dabbed at her makeup.

"Oh, look at me," she moaned. "What. A. Mess."

"I think you're perfect," said Lindsay sweetly, and I had to agree.

"Tell that to the Academy," sniffed Sheila. "I ask you, is there a sadder sight than a sweet old lady without her Oscar? I've been nominated five times. Oh, the money I've spent on dresses! Always the bridesmaid, never the bride. Shafted, I tell you—laid, relaid and parlayed. Does anyone have a tissue?"

"Hey, Cindy," chirped Sebastian. "Is it true? Is Lissa really your little sister?"

"No!" I cried too defensively, and definitely too quickly, and probably too loudly. "Same last name. Pure coincidence. People make that mistake all the time. No relation. None." I exchanged a panic-stricken glance with Lindsay, who was stifling giggles. Great. She wasn't going to help me out of this one.

"I l-o-o-o-o-ove Lissa," enthused Sebastian. "And even though you don't, you know, know her, if you did, and you could get me a copy of her new single before anyone else gets it and maybe have it autographed, I'd re-e-e-eally appreciate it, but that's only if you know her. You know? And it's totally okay if you don't."

I suddenly had an image of Sebastian in his tightie-whities shimmying and shaking in front of his full-length mirror to Lissa's "Tune My Motor Up." I must do what I can for Sebastian (even though it involves Lisa). I mean, he did help me and Lindsay sell all of our keepsake cards, and both he and Sheila promised to invite all of their friends to the Hour of Silence.

Back at Alpha Beta Delta, we had only a few hours before the rally, and Patty was running a mile a minute. Honestly, I've never seen her move so fast. Not only had she sold all of her keepsake cards, she'd also driven all the way to Camoville and picked up some beautiful pale red tulips to hand out to each person who arrives for the rally, and when Lindsay and I met up with her, she was furiously cleaning the kitchen. She'd already done the dishes and, apparently, she'd been inspired to repaper six shelves with floral laminate shelf paper. She also rearranged all of the spices in the spice rack alphabetically, and now she was energetically mopping the floor—alternating between the mop and quick sips of coffee.

"Maybe you ought to slow down on the caffeine," I cautiously advised.

"Why? What for?" she said—and very quickly. "This kitchen's a rat's nest, it's a pigsty. Don't you like a tidy kitchen? I'm just doing it once over lightly. See? Clean as a whistle. Nothing to it. Hey! Don't set that umbrella down there, I just mopped that area. Tch. Move-move-move."

Who was I to tell Patty not to clean? At the same time, Lindsay and I tried to clue her in to what was going on. I calmly explained: I wasn't imagining things, we had to prepare. Who knew what was going to happen at the rally? And now it's been confirmed by a source other than me; Meri is out to destroy Alpha Beta Delta, Bobbie may be a mole, Lindsay saw Albino Girl. Patty exploded with high-pitched laughter.

"Wait a sec, wait a sec. Back up. Let's see if I get this. You saw an albino girl? Cindy's Albino Girl? You actually saw her?"

Yes," said Lindsay, feeling accused.

Patty continued laughing, fastidiously mopping and remopping the same spot on the floor. "You're projecting. Oh, this is good. This is rich. And you're emulating Cindy's factitious disorder with physical delusions and dissociative—"

"I'm not crazy!" yelped Lindsay. "I saw what I saw."

"What did you see?" blurted Shanna-Francine, who'd just stepped in and, as usual, was beaming with good cheer.

I was about to clarify when Bobbie appeared right behind her, putting her hand possessively on Shanna-Francine's shoulder. "Who's crazy?" she gruffly asked.

"I'm crazy for this day!" squealed Shanna-Francine, who was delighted that practically every girl in the house had sold all of their keepsake cards.

For the time being, I realized, Lindsay and I would be on our own. I didn't have much time to formulate a plan, but then Lindsay reminded me about the videocam. Of course! Who can argue with video proof? We hastily plotted: Lindsay will keep an eye on the crowd during the rally, while I'll make like I'm taping it for the inter-sorority governing council, but I'll really be scanning the crowd, on the lookout for any aberration, or a certain Albino Girl, or perhaps Meri herself, and if something really big happens, good, because then everyone will know that it's Meri and not me. And I'll have the tape to prove it.

The rally unfolded without a hitch. And silently. At first. The bell tolled five o'clock from the top of the RU clock tower. It was the only sound you could hear for seemingly miles around, except for a few plumpish black birds who were perched on the rooftop, gently cawing. A soft breeze trembled past as I strode out the front door with Shanna-Francine, Bobbie, Lindsay, Patty, and all the other girls of Alpha Beta Delta and took formation in a straight line on the lawn. A large crowd was already gathered. I exchanged a glance with Lindsay, who discreetly nodded from beneath her umbrella. That was my cue. I pressed the videocam viewfinder to my eye, began taping, and slowly panned past the assembled crowd. I couldn't believe it. Everyone really was being silent. The rally was a success. I followed Patty as she stepped up to each person and sweetly handed them a tulip—first to Pigboy, of course, who gave her a quick peck, then to Bud, who started to say "thank you," only to be shushed by a tall guy next to him.

I panned the camera further and, oh my God, I didn't even realize it at first but there he was, staring right at me (with his gorgeous blue eyes) right through the camera lens—and then he shyly looked away—and he wasn't even with Bitch Kitty, and my first thought was, as always, my love, my sweet, my everything! Keith looked so unbelievably cute! Lindsay elbowed me, and, yes, she was right to do that (I guess) (but still) (and where the heck was Bitch Kitty? my heart screamed).

I continued panning. There were several professors in the crowd, including Professor Scott (who looked very stern and solemn, and kind of handsome, too, though he really does need to get a new jacket), and there was Sheila Farr, who blew a kiss at the camera (with such stylish aplomb, I might add) and there was Sebastian, who was smacking on chewing gum. He gave the camera an impish wink, pulled his gum out, and elaborately mouthed, "Watch this." Then he squinted his eyes, took careful aim, and threw the gum. I swish-panned to follow it. It took me a second. Whoa. I suddenly realized that I had quite the startling close-up. The sticky gum had landed—*plop!*—right between Bud's exposed butt cheeks. Eeeow! Double-eeeow. Confused, Bud reached around and dug his fingers into . . . I had to swish the camera away. Some things really are best left undocumented, though I did hear Bud whisper, "Motherfucker!" followed by a few insistent shushing sounds from those standing near him.

I continued panning across the gathered throng, which was getting larger and larger since more people were arriving, and I started to panic because I couldn't capture everyone on tape fast enough and I couldn't tell if there was anyone who might be associated with Meri, so I swish-panned back to Patty, who I rightly figured would be handing a tulip to each new arrival. She handed one to Doreen. Crap. Crap crap crap. Bitch Kitty herself. Though today she wore a too-tight T that read, "They're Real!" in spangly appliqué across her chest. My heart went into a spiraling nosedive when I saw her pony all bouncy-bouncy up to Keith, so I swished away and caught Sebastian stifling giggles and affixing yet another wad of gum to a piece of notebook paper. Then he pressed the paper ever so gently to the back of Bud's blue jeans, just beneath his ass-cleavage, so everyone could read, in big red letters: "Behold My Ugly Booty!" For the briefest of seconds, I felt sorry for Bud, but then I remembered that he had stuck a piece of paper on my back last year in Marietta that read, "If you want my attention, moo!" So there. There is such a thing as poetic justice. And that's when I heard the banging.

Everyone heard it. Loud, tinny, rhythmic bangs. Was this really happening? A large group of very well dressed students marched forth holding pots and pans, and they were forcefully banging them with spoons and metal spatulas. I think everyone was just plain shocked at first. I know I was. They were the Campus Evangelical Crusade, or CEC, a growing and popular campus club that holds prayer breakfasts every morning in the cafeteria. They also have an a capella singing group (I hear they're quite good), as well as a respected philanthropic group, the CEC Union, that gives to selected charitable organizations. They were handing out their own keepsake cards to anyone who would take one:

> *I am making a Joyful Noise! I believe in equal treatment for all, and not special rights for a few. I believe in loving everyone, but part of that love means not condoning dangerous personal behavior.*
>
> *I believe that by boldly making a Joyful Noise, hurts will be halted, hearts will be healed, and lives will joyously be saved!*

The first thought that leaped into my head was, *This is Meri!* But when I frantically zoomed across the faces of the CEC students, I didn't see any St. Eulalia girls or mini-Meris, much less Albino Girl. The crowd was getting restless, and you could feel it: Something awful was about to happen, and I thought, *This is really unfair. No one from Alpha Beta Delta charges into the CEC prayer breakfasts and disrupts them.* But I also thought, *The prayer breakfasts aren't public gatherings, and this is, and isn't everyone entitled to protest publicly in any way they see fit (as long as it doesn't physically harm anyone)?* I was so confused, because I honestly believe that everyone has the right to their own opinion. For example, I really would like Bitch Kitty to suddenly become flat-chested, and while that's not exactly an opinion worthy of a protest rally, it's a thought, and I should be allowed to have that thought and even express it publicly should I so choose (though I would never).

I swished back to the silent multitude, and while you could see that they were just itching to retaliate, they remained mum. And the CEC group didn't do anything to retaliate either when Patty started ripping the heads off of her tulips and merrily flicking petals at them. And everything probably would have been just fine if Bud hadn't removed one of his Triple 5 Soul Ludlow sneakers and thrown it. It made a loud smacking sound as it hit the forehead of a handsome CEC guy in pressed chinos. And then all hell broke loose when a prim-looking CEC girl (in a lovely square-neck sheath) furiously hurled back a spatula. I saw everything through my camera lens: punches flew, hair was pulled, Lindsay fended off comers with the tip of her closed umbrella, Sheila sprayed offensively with her Aquanet, Patty was knocked to the ground, and Shanna-Francine loudly screeched.

"This is so inappropriate!"

It was a riot, pure and simple, and when I swish-panned back toward the house when I heard Bobbie bellow, I was roughly knocked down—and as I tumbled, stunned, with the viewfinder still pressed to my eye and offering a skewed view of the second story, my jaw dropped in horror, because there she was gazing placidly out the window, smiling slightly, flipping back her long, luxurious raven hair.

"Meri!" I cried.

I was up and running. There wasn't a second to waste. I sped into the house and leaped up the stairs two at a time—and I held on to the videocam like a lifesaver, because there was no way anyone could argue with video proof. I could see the headlines: MERI CAUGHT ON TAPE! or maybe SUGARMAN'S SHAMEFUL TRESPASS!, and when I arrived at the second-floor threshold, I shrieked, "Where are you? I know you're here!"

"Woof woof!"

I whipped around. The voice was coming from the bathroom. I bounded forth, brought the viewfinder to my eye, and all but gasped, because Meri was there in the bathroom, smaller than I remembered, less significant, her head hanging down, her long raven hair newly stringy and obscuring her face. *Nice try*, I thought, *everyone will know it's you.* And then in a flash she ripped off her hair, and whiter-than-white locks tumbled forth, and she looked up at me with her piercing pink eyes, and that's when I knew. It was Albino Girl! She viciously flung the wig at me, pulled a small object from her pocket, threw it in the toilet, and—*oomph!*—bodychecked me as she charged out of the bathroom. I fell backward, the videocam soaring from my hands. And I panicked. I knew what was in that toilet.

"Cherry bomb!" I screamed.

I ran toward the bathroom—but at the same time a voice in the back of my head shrieked, *Wrong way, Cindy B!* and I jerked my body backward. *Ka-boom!* I have never in my life seen a toilet bowl explode. I mean really explode. All at once, the seat cover burst up, banging on the ceiling, shards of jagged porcelain blasted in all directions, the float ball ricocheted violently off the wall, the tank lid whipped in the air like a spinning whirligig, and water gushed and geysered in every possible direction. I was on the ground, and

I instinctively turned over and protectively covered my face, and I stayed that way until all I could hear was water—just a steady stream of fizzy spraying water—and when I dared to turn over and take my hands from my face, I saw Bobbie leaning over me.

"Now you've done it," she growled.

I was shaking when she pulled me up in her strong arms (but different-strong from the gays; they felt real-strong, like Dad's) and led me shaking down the stairs and outside to the front lawn. The riot was over, no doubt extinguished by the explosive *ka-boom* sound from the second story. It was deathly quiet, and I had a half-crazy thought: *Well, well, it takes an exploding toilet to keep things silent during an Hour of Silence.* But I summoned my strength.

"It's all on tape," I proclaimed hoarsely. "It—it was Meri. It wasn't me."

As if on cue, Lindsay scampered breathlessly out of the house behind me holding the battered videocam. Oh, Lindsay! I was saved.

"There's no tape in this camera, Cindy," she meekly intoned.

I gazed thunderstruck at the videocam. The cassette compartment was wide open, like a gaping mouth with a dislodged jawbone, and, of course, it was all too conspicuously empty. Another pair of strong arms pulled me away, and I saw Bitch Kitty whispering nastily into Keith's ear. Patty was speaking softly to Shanna-Francine—about my brain lesions (again)—Sheila Farr was giving me the black power salute, and I heard Sebastian dressing down a few CEC members.

"And you. Stridex Pimple Pads. Yesterday. And you. Ever hear of a bronzer? And you two. Dickies? Get real."

And I saw Professor Scott, too, gazing at me with such kind eyes. I may have been hallucinating, but I swear I saw him mouth, "I believe you." And then I found myself once again plopped in the Office of Student Affairs before Victorio ("call me Vic") Vladislav, who scratched his badly dyed red goatee thoughtfully and laid it all out for me. This time it was serious. Really serious.

I was in very big trouble. Repeat. Very. Big. Trouble.

"Rumson is not inclined to be understanding about explosives, Miss Bixby," said Vic, stating the obvious. "And you appear to be escalating in firepower."

The university was prepared to file criminal charges against me, which would most certainly result in my complete dismissal. But there was an alternative. I could agree to see Vic twice a week and "work with him" to sort through my many problems and hopefully discover the root cause of my "hysteria." That didn't leave me much choice. If I pleaded my case (meaning, if I told the truth), I'd be kicked out of RU and Mom and Dad would be horrified (I'm not sure how Lisa would react) (maybe she'd give me a job as her personal assistant) (or her driver).

It was clear now what Meri's agenda was: Not only was she intent on making it seem like I was crazy, she was also determined to make it look as if I was prone to crazy violence. Why? Maybe so I'd be doomed to community college like her (though that seems too small potatoes for Meri), or maybe so I'd end up in jail, or the loony bin. Vic admonished me for using a cherry bomb. They're illegal in North Carolina, he testily informed me (as if that would stop someone who was really psycho), and powerful enough to take off a hand (that bit of info would actually encourage a psycho, wouldn't it?).

I signed an agreement with Vic. I barely looked at it. A tear slowly escaped from my eye and dripped—*plop*—creating a bomb-like ink splatter on my freshly penned signature. I didn't even realize till that moment that I was so spent. *I'm powerless*, I thought. *All the efforts I've made to combat Meri have failed miserably, and if anything, my attempts to expose her and stay one step ahead of her have blown up in my face (pun sort of intended).* My heart began thumping. *Boom boom boom. Oh God*, I thought, *I'm dying; my heart's going to explode.* And then I realized I was having an anxiety attack, or a Meri-attack, as I now like to call them, since it was Meri who caused me to have my first anxiety attack just a few weeks ago.

Vic continued droning, but I steeled myself. I've been playing it all wrong. All. Wrong. I haven't been planning. My efforts against Meri have been too scattershot, too willy-nilly. But with the information I've gathered so far, perhaps a plan can be formulated. Maybe, just maybe, there's a way out of this.

It was dark out when I returned to Alpha Beta Delta, and no one heard me when I stepped inside. Everyone was in the living room. Shanna-Francine was on the couch sharing popcorn with Bobbie (and Tamari and Pumpkin Seed, too); Lindsay was cozied up with Bud; and Patty (who was strangely jittery) was with Pigboy on throw pillows on the floor. They were watching *The Machinist* with Christian Bale.

"Eeeow, he's so skinny," gasped Patty. "I can't believe he lost all that weight."

"And he did it all for a part in a movie," echoed a disbelieving Lindsay.

"They should have just hired Nicole Richie to play the part as a man," added Pigboy, and everyone laughed.

Lindsay was the first to spot me. I meekly smiled and said, "Hi."

Then I cleared my throat and scurried upstairs—and stopped short on the landing. Yellow police tape was strewn across the entrance to the bathroom, along with a piece of paper that stated, with admirable understatement: "Broken." In my room, I was just about ready to check my e-mail—and confront whatever new horror might have arrived electronically—when Lindsay gently knocked and let herself in.

"Okay, don't freak, but I'm your friend and I think you should know."

I gulped. What now?

"Shanna-Francine called a meeting tonight after you were

taken away," she continued. "And she called a vote. All those in favor of voting Cindy out of Alpha Beta Delta, say yes; all those in favor of letting her stay, say no."

I couldn't believe my ears. Shanna-Francine? "Why did she do that?" I gasped.

"'Cause she thinks you're losing it. She said your 'unstable behavior is creating an inappropriate atmosphere at Alpha Beta Delta.'"

I still couldn't believe it. But there it was. Stabbed in the back by Shanna-Francine. I am now officially inappropriate.

"So we took a vote," she gingerly continued, "and we decided . . ."

"Tell me who voted what. One by one," I grimly asked. Since the battle lines were being drawn, I wanted to know who was on my side, because anyone who voted against me could, in fact, be a Meri mole. After all, who's to say that Bobbie is the only one?

"Okay. But jeez, don't tell anyone I—"

"I won't. I swear."

"Patty was the first to vote," she said, taking a big breath. "She voted yes. To have you leave."

Patty! Oh my God, oh my God, oh my God, oh my God! Now there were two knives in my back.

"She had a whole theory worked out. Something about the house being the source of all your delusions and your schizo-depressive fantasies about Meri. She thinks it'll be a whole lot better for you—you know, mentally—if you're not here anymore. But she said she'll totally be there for you, and she promised she'd help you find your authentic self."

How considerate of her, I bleakly thought.

"Then she held up a black wig. It was wet. She said she found it near the bathroom."

Oh God. The wig. The Meri wig that Albino Girl had worn.

"She told us that you probably wear the wig when you're pretending to be Meri. When you have psychotic breaks."

Gee, now I have a split personality, too. Maybe next I'll be stir-frying babies.

"She was talking really-really-really fast. And Shanna-Francine kept nodding her head in agreement."

Of course she was. Just more inappropriate fuel for the fire.

"Who else?" I asked. I was ready for the worst. She went on down the list. A few voted yes, a few voted no (of course Lindsay voted no) (thank God!). Finally, it was an even split. There was only one person left to cast the deciding vote.

"Who was it?"

"Bobbie," she answered quickly.

Well, that's it, I thought, *I may as well pack my bags.* Meri had won—with the help of an albino, a cherry bomb, and a fake lesbian with a Mohawk.

"She voted no," said Lindsay, and I really didn't hear her at first. "She started crying, too. And she quoted some book by Barbara Cartland—I think it was *A Duke in Danger.* She told us about how the heroine's best friend stood by her side, even after everyone in the kingdom had turned against her. And then she said we should all be ashamed and try to help you, instead of casting you out into the cold light of loveless indifference. I think that last part was another quote."

It was too much to process. It still is. And when Lindsay said, "I really don't think Bobbie is the mole," I wanted to believe her, but who can tell anymore? Obviously Shanna-Francine's concern for the house and its survival trumps any concerns she might have for me, and Patty just thinks I'm a basket case. And Bobbie? She wants to stand by my side? None of it made any sense.

"Oh, and I found this," she whispered, and she whipped out a cassette tape. My eyes popped out of my head. There was the tape—the tape that should have been in the videocam. As if anticipating my question, Lindsay leaned in. "I saw it sticking out from under your bed when I walked past your room tonight."

"Just like the bleach bottle," I marveled, which means Albino Girl, or someone helping her, must have removed the tape from the videocam after I dropped it and then placed it under my bed before taking off. But why? We scampered quietly to Lindsay's room (since she has a TV and VCR and I don't). Lindsay hadn't watched the tape, and she hadn't told anyone about it either. God bless Lindsay! She popped the tape into her VCR, and at first it looked like everything was there—the Alpha Beta Delta girls selling keepsake cards; the trip to Six Flags; the Hour of Silence on the front lawn. But predictably, the tape went to snow right as the picture jerked up to the second-story window, which is where I first saw Albino Girl in the Meri wig (mistaking her for Meri). But that didn't stop Lindsay.

"Ask Jeeves!" she exclaimed, then opened the browser on her Sony laptop and typed a question. Almost instantly, this came up onscreen:

Q: If a videotape has been accidentally erased, can I recover the original recording?

A: No. The only organization with the technology to recover erased material is the FBI. This technology is classified and is not available to the general public.

"Know anyone with the FBI?" Lindsay asked hopefully.

No luck there. And neither of us was sure whether or not we should ask Bud if he's in possession of this forbidden technology, though Lindsay said she'd try to find out in a roundabout way.

"Is there anything else I should know?" I asked. "About the meeting?"

"Not really. You know about Halloween, right?"

"Just that it's inappropriate. And offensive to Wiccans."

"Right, so we're not throwing a Halloween Ball this year. We're throwing a Fall Harvest Ball. Kinda dumb, huh?"

"Yeah. Kinda."

"There's going to be a hayride, though. That might be fun. And we'll have candy. 'Vegan candy is dandy.'"

"What?"

"That's what Bobbie says. So we'll serve stuff like soy mints and cruelty-free Jujubes. And Caribbean tuber Dum Dums."

"What else?"

"That's it. Oh, and everything's in place for the Day of Forgiveness dinner on Sunday. A lot of people are coming. They have to pay a donation to . . ."

She stopped short. She must have seen the glazed look that was coming over me; I really didn't care about Alpha Beta Delta's latest "appropriate" maneuvers. Or, scratch that. I do care—very much—but I guess I was still smarting from the knowledge that some of the girls at Alpha Beta Delta care about me, and some of them don't. I stepped dejectedly back to my room. It was time to go to bed, but first I checked my e-mail. There was one new message.

From: <cindybixby@yahoo.com >
Date: 27 October
To: <cindybixby@yahoo.com >
Subject: Hi!

I think Christian Bale looks hot all skinny and shit.
Just think, if you were that skinny, you might die!
Kissy kiss!
:)

I wasn't scared when I read it, and I didn't wonder how Meri was pulling off this computer stunt, either. Instead, I was astonished by the shocking knowledge that it provided. The girls had been watching *The Machinist* just a few hours ago (everyone's in bed right now), which means that whoever sent this message is in this house. Right now! Which means that now I know, beyond a shadow of a doubt, that Meri has a mole at Alpha Beta Delta. Oh my God, oh my God, oh my God, oh my God! Is it Shanna-Francine? Is it Patty? Is it—and I can't believe I'm writing this— is it Lindsay? Or some other girl here? Or is it, as I've suspected all along, Bobbie?

I decided to try something. I hit respond on my e-mail and wrote back. The *s* is still sticking on my keyboard, but who the heck cares? I had to satisfy my curiosity. After checking my spelling (old habits die hard), I sent this off:

```
From: <cindybixby@yahoo.com >
Date: 27 October
To: <cindybixby@yahoo.com >
Subject: RE: Hi!


I think you're sick!! And I know you're in the house!! So
there!!
:(


Sincerely,
The Real Cindy
P.S. Everyone knows Christian Bale looks hotter as Batman.
```

After a sec, I checked my in-box. The e-mail I wrote came right back to me. No surprise there. But maybe someone else was still reading it—and writing a response. I grabbed a flashlight and tip-toed into the darkened hallway. I was engulfed by silence. I gently clicked on the flashlight, which punched pale holes before me as I tiptoed up and down the stairs and paused at each girl's closed bedroom door. I couldn't hear a thing (there are no snorers at Alpha Beta Delta). If someone was tippy-tapping on their keyboard, they were being ridiculously careful about it. For the briefest second, I began to ponder the notion that the mole—or at least the mole writing the e-mails—was somewhere else. I mean, even on a laptop you can hear someone typing from behind a closed door. Especially when everything else is so totally quiet. And there's no way some-one could have dashed into my room and sent the e-mail on my computer, because I locked my door before walking with Lindsay to her room. Frustrated, I tiptoed back upstairs, unlocked my door, and stepped inside. My computer was blinking. I had new mail! I was shaking as I clicked it open.

From: <cindybixby@yahoo.com >
Date: 27 October
To: <cindybixby@yahoo.com >
Subject: RE: RE: Hi!

Woof woof, Real Cindy!

Am I in the house? Ooo, wouldn't you like to know! Maybe I'm just an itty-bitty little alien hiding in your computer. Or maybe I'm in your head. You are crazy, aren't you? Aw. Poor Cindy B. She's crazy AND her hair is tragic. Hahahahaha!

Remember, crazy people are thirteen times more prone than normal people to have irritable bowel syndrome. Eeeow. Just

don't use the bathroom on the second floor, 'kay?
Hahahahahaha!

Die in your sleep!
:)

P.S. Please. Everyone knows Christian Bale is at his hottest
in *American Psycho*. Especially when he's all naked and cutting people up. Now that's hot!

I've placed my door key under my pillow, I double-checked the
door lock. The house is silent as I'm writing this. I know Meri has
a mole at Alpha Beta Delta. I know it.

October 28

Dear Diary:

Is everyone going nuts except me? This morning my eyes popped open at around five a.m., and I heard soft rustling and banging, and I thought, *The mole is on the move!* I leaped out of bed and unlocked my door. When I realized where the noise was coming from, I was shattered. She was the mole? I was standing right outside Patty's door. *Well, there's no time like the present,* I told myself. I boldly whipped open the door. Patty shrieked.

"Holy mother of God, Cindy! Haven't you ever heard of knocking?"

My eyes had to adjust to what I was seeing. It didn't make sense at first. Patty's room was spotless. There was no garbage, no moldy half-eaten food containers, no piles of newspapers and dirty clothes. Her closet door was open, and all of her clothes were washed and neatly hung. In one corner of the room were several large garbage bags, all of them tied up. There was an open bag near Patty, and she was standing before her desk, fastidiously polishing it.

"Jeez, Louise. What's gotten into you?"

"What's gotten into you?" I sputtered.

"Me? I'm winning the battle against my psychosomatic afflictions, that's what's gotten into me," she cheerily and very breathlessly informed me as she alternated between polishing and quick sips of what I assumed was coffee (but it was actually rose hip tea with just a dash of Skinny). "I'm losing weight, too," she enthused, rattling off her accomplishments rat-a-tat-tat. "I've lost six pounds. I look better. Bang! I feel better. See? Now I'm cleaning. This room's chaotic state was symbolic of my own inner turmoil. And now it's not. Why? Because I'm happy. Bang! A happy person has a happy room. See? See?"

I was pleased for Patty. I mean, who knows what's really prompted this momentous turnaround, but it's obviously working, and yet my happiness for her was tinged with the painful knowledge that she had betrayed me. I surprised myself with my boldness when I said, "Why did you vote to kick me out of the house?"

"Cindy," she admonished. "I did not do that. I voted in favor of your own mental stability."

"You're not a real therapist yet," I said, and I could feel a bitter lump building in my throat. "You have no right to diagnose me."

"Cindy. Sit. Here. Hey, now you can find a chair in this room," she tittered, then continued. "Okay. Listen. I'm not saying you're any crazier than Meri. Okay? I mean, please, Meri would steal her own mother's uterus if it would help her in some way. All right? I get that. But Cindy, as a friend, and not as a budding and hopefully very successful professional psychologist, I have to say that your behavior lately has been a little wack. And I admit it, yes, I voted to have you leave the house. But for your own good."

"How dare you," I whispered. Tears were streaming down my face.

"I know. Oh, Cindy, I know. I was wrong."

"You were?" I asked, not sure where this was going.

"Yes. Because I now believe that the key to overcoming your anxieties and depression is exposure therapy. That's why I think you should come with me tonight. To the football game."

I wasn't following. She knew that, so she plowed ahead.

"All anxieties and hurtful fantasies have a trigger. Take me. My mother is overbearing, my sisters think I'm annoying; ergo, I overeat. Simple. You have a boyfriend, he dumps you for a slut; ergo, you have wild fantasies about Meri. See? See?"

Yes, I saw, but I wasn't buying. For obvious reasons. She leaned into me.

"Cindy, can you look me straight in the eye and tell me you don't still think about Keith? That your heart doesn't still go pitter-patter when you see him? That you don't still think he's the super-cutest slice you've ever known? Can you do that? Can you? Can you?"

I gulped. I couldn't. She was right. I think about Keith all the time (my love, my sweet, my everything!), and just yesterday, when he came to the Hour of Silence, I wanted to run into his arms and kiss him and hold him and beg him to take me back, and though it has absolutely nothing to do with Meri—Patty's way wrong there—when she challenged me to say, "I don't care about Keith," I just couldn't. There's no way. My face flamed up with shame. And I burst into tears. Patty held me.

"Shh. There now. Remember when you first learned to drive? The more you did it, the easier it became. Ergo, the more you see Keith, the less of a hold he'll have on you, and the less depressed you'll feel. See? See? That's exposure therapy."

Okay, so it made sense. I thought about it in my classes today. I have been carrying a lot of "unresolved emotion" about Keith, as Patty would say, for quite some time, and I have been harboring fantasies of reuniting with him. It's true. I can't deny it. I thought about it during my first session with Victorio ("call me Vic"), too (he's such a bore!), and it made me think about Mom. Not because she went through any of this (that I know of), but because she'd always play this old Carly Simon CD whenever she was cleaning the house. Naturally, Lisa would get out of helping ("Pul-lease, I just—and I mean just—got a French manicure," was her favorite excuse), so it was always me and Mom, silently cleaning and scrubbing, listening to Carly. One song made me pause each time I heard it. It played in my head all day today. It felt like I was singing it directly to Keith:

> *You belong to me*
> *Tell her, tell her you were fooling*
> *You don't even know her*
> *Tell her that I love you*
> *You belong to me*

I hate Bitch Kitty.

I hate Meri, too (more). Pushing my thoughts about Keith aside (momentarily), I formulated a new plan. A smart one. And I'm sticking to it. Instead of trying to find out what Meri's doing, or publicly blaming her for stuff that she does do (that's playing right into her hands), I've decided to just find the mole. Period. That's it. It's the mole who's letting her know my every move, and every move that Alpha Beta Delta makes too. Find the mole, stop Meri.

As I strolled to the library to catch up on my studying, I caught someone waving at me from the corner of my eye. I turned, and I couldn't believe it. Briskly jogging to the street corner opposite, it was Sebastian (in a cute, maybe too-tight white jogging outfit with a rainbow headband and thick slouch socks with high-tops and tiny free weights in his hands) and his new jogging partner: Patty! They gave me a wave and a wink, running in place, then the light changed and they were off. *Everyone's changing for the better except for me*, I thought. Not too long ago I had a wonderful life with all my friends at Alpha Beta Delta, the hottest boyfriend ever (my love, my sweet, my everything!), and now? I'm loveless. I'm a loser. Oh, and I'm "crazy," too.

The RU library is a free-for-all on Saturdays; there's definitely more flirting than studying going on. It's like, why don't they just serve cocktails here and call it a day? I had research to do and several papers to write, and I needed to finish a book for Professor Scott's class, *The Romance of Tristan and Iseult* by Joseph Bedier, a classic tale of knights, magic, and, my luck, doomed romance. It's a lovely story, but it cut way too close to the bone today, so I pushed it aside.

At lunch I decided to cheer myself up by going to Long John's. Lindsay and Patty joined me. Lindsay and I ordered Chicken Plank meals, but Patty only ordered a small side of slaw. She sprinkled a bit of Skinny on it.

"You use it on food?" I asked.

"Skinny's good on anything!" she squealed, but she hardly touched her slaw. She also informed Lindsay about her exposure therapy plans. Lindsay shrugged, noncommittal.

"I guess it's a good idea."

"Boys," tsked Patty merrily. "They're a handful, huh? Just the other night, Pigboy asked me to spank him. Pigboy! A big guy like that and he wants to be spanked. Can you believe? I gave him a good whoopin'. And he loved it."

"Are you sure you should be telling us this?" I asked. I mean, it was awfully private information, and would Pigboy really want people to know that he likes to be spanked? He's a big macho football player, after all, but I guess that was Patty's point.

"You never know what anyone's like till you get them in the sack," she observed.

"Or what you're like," Lindsay quietly responded.

"What do you mean?" said Patty—almost pouncing with curiosity. Lindsay balked.

"Um, nothing."

"Oh, c'mon. It's just us girls."

Oh, no. I could tell by the expression on Lindsay's face that this was going to be a doozy. Thank God I had a normal sex life with Keith!

"You don't have to say anything," I told her.

"No, that's okay," she said sheepishly. "I think I should talk about it."

"Atta girl!" said Patty.

"It's just that whenever he . . ." She paused and winced, then guardedly continued. "See, whenever he 'finishes,' it goes everywhere. And I mean everywhere."

"What are you talking about?" I asked. Did she mean when he ejaculates? Shouldn't he be doing that in a rubber (good God, the world does not need little Bud Fingers)?

"He pulls out right before he finishes," she whispered. "That's what he likes to do. Just before he's ready to finish, he pulls out, rips off his rubber . . . and then ka-boom. He finishes. And, you know, I don't mind. Not really. But it gets everywhere. It gets all over my sheets and makes them all sticky and gunky—and I have these really comfy twelve hundred thread-count Luxury Sateen sheets. And one time a really big wad of it landed on my wall. And the other day it shot so far it spattered on my little framed picture of Auntie Christiana. Right on her face. And that's clear across on the other side of the room. I mean, that's just gross. Right? Am I right?"

As if on cue, we heard a loud squishy sound from Patty's half-empty squeeze-bottle of mayonnaise. It splattered all over Patty's slaw and onto my hand. Eeeeow! Oh my God, I nearly hurled. But I managed to say, "Beyond gross." Then I frantically wiped my hand with a napkin.

"Talk to him about it," said Patty.

"I have," Lindsay insisted. "At first he thought I was complaining about him finishing before I finish, but I wasn't. I swear, he makes sure I'm finished every time. And I mean every damn time."

"Thank God," said Patty, and imperiously advised, "Look, just talk to him again. Tell him that it really bothers you and to, I don't know, try aiming . . ."

"Excuse me, why don't you just tell him to keep the damn rubber on, for Christ's sake!" I snapped. "I mean, jeez, whatever happened to normal sex? Do you have to do every single weird thing he asks? That's so self-loathing."

"Oh, Cindy," chuckled Patty condescendingly, sprinkling more Skinny on her slaw. "What's a girl supposed to do? Go back to the Stone Age and just be satisfied with the missionary position? And that's it? Did you tell Keith, 'No, no, stop, don't go down on me. It makes me feel self-loathing'?"

I stopped short—and, oh dammit, sometimes I hate when Patty picks up on things.

She squealed, "Keith never went down on you?!"

"I . . . I . . ."

"Not once?" asked Lindsay softly.

Isn't anything private anymore?

"We never talked about it," I lamely offered.

"That's so sad," said Lindsay, and she meant it. She took my hand and gave it a squeeze.

"And unfortunately all too status quo," opined Patty. "Statistics show—"

"I really don't need statistics."

"Cindy, calm down. I'm just saying that a lot of guys, a huge majority of normal red-blooded guys, in fact, are just too damn selfish to—"

"Okay, can we change the subject? I'd really like to change the subject."

We finished our meal in silence. Outside, Lindsay straightened her tiara and popped open her umbrella. Patty tsked.

"You really need to get over that umbrella thing."

"Really? Do I? Well I think you need to clean up your room," she said, feeling attacked (as she always does when someone makes her feel self-conscious about her fear of melanoma) (which is not a nice thing to do).

"I already did," said Patty, and maybe a bit too triumphantly. "It's spotless. Ask Cindy."

"Well, goodie for you," snapped Lindsay.

"Hey. That's not being very supportive."

"Why are we arguing with each other?" I asked.

"Guys, guys. I'm just trying to help," said Patty. "I want everyone to be healthy. And, all right, I'm holding myself up as an example. But the changes I'm making are life-altering. My room's clean, I'm losing weight."

"Because you don't eat anything," screeched Lindsay. "How healthy is that? You'd better not be throwing up or anything. I knew a girl who did that back home and she ended up in the hospital. It's not healthy. Plus it's gross."

"I would never do that," she assured us, and I believed her. But at the same time, I was beginning to tire of this newly self-assured Patty. Yes, she's losing weight—you can especially tell in her face—and, yes, she's always been quick to diagnose anyone or anything, but never with such pious certainty. And she talks so fast now. It's a wonder Lindsay and I were able to get a word in edgewise throughout the entire lunch. Chatter-chatter-chatter. She never stops.

"Now, Cindy . . ."

Oh God. I knew it would come back to me. The exposure therapy. The football game. My need to get over Keith. Funny thing about that, though. All roads seem to lead right back to Meri. When I sat in the bleachers tonight with Lindsay, Patty, and Bud (eeeow! I couldn't even look him in the face now!), I watched the football game indifferently. On purpose. Keith and Pigboy were playing a rousing game for the RU team (as they always do), the crowd was going wild, and even though Patty was excitedly cheering the team and Pigboy, too, I knew she was keeping a sharp eye on me, looking for a reaction (what, exactly? pain? relief? horror?), and I really resented it. I tried to watch everything with a sort of remove. Thoughts breezed lightly through my head: *Keith is as good a quarterback as he's ever been; RU really does seem unbeatable; Bitch Kitty's cheers are a totally lame mix of crunk moves and, yes, boring floor patterns (Sebastian is right).* But like I said, all roads lead back to Meri. Before he was with me, I remembered, Keith was Meri's boyfriend. And Meri dumped him. I don't know why, but that made me smile. Just a bit.

"You're feeling good about this, aren't you?" exclaimed Patty, seizing upon my change in expression. "Exposure therapy is so helpful."

"I guess."

"Don't you feel sorry for Doreen? I mean, given what you told us—about Keith in the bedroom."

"What about Keith in the bedroom?" piped up Bud.

"Nothing," I shushed. I couldn't believe that our private, supposedly "just girls" talk was being made public.

"He doesn't eat downtown!" Patty squealed. "Get it?"

"Enough," I said, and I meant it. My heart corkscrewed. I felt a pang for Keith. A sharp one. I wanted to protect him. And Bud—who jumps onto sex talk like a puppy onto a squeeze toy—just wouldn't let go. He laughed and laughed.

"Really? No face job from Keith? No licky-licky?"

"Enough!" I cried.

"What about you? Did you slob his knob, Cyn? And he didn't return the favor? That's harsh."

"Wait a sec, we didn't ask her that," gasped Patty. "Did you? Cindy?"

Ahhhhhhhhhh! I wanted to scream and run to the field and leap into Keith's arms and hold him and kiss him and tell him, "Oh, Keith, I don't care about that stuff!" (okay, maybe I do, now that I think about it, and okay, I guess he was just looking out for numero uno in the bedroom, but right then I just wanted him back). Suddenly the entire stadium leaped to their feet and roared. Keith had scored a touchdown. He flew past the goal line, slammed down the football, then danced a little jig. So cute! *Whoosh.* Bitch Kitty blasted through the air like a large-breasted surface-to-air missile. *Oomph!* Keith caught her in his strong arms. Limbs entangled. And they kissed. And I mean really-really kissed.

"Day-um. He's gotta be goin' down on that," gaped Bud.

Ahhhhhhhhhh! This wasn't exposure therapy. This was torture! I leaped out of my seat and pushed past the cheering crowd, my arms and hands thrust in front of me. Get away, get away, get away. I could hear Lindsay calling after me. But I kept going. I couldn't breathe.

I was battered by a brisk autumn wind. I was standing outside in the stadium parking lot. I was okay. I was safe.

"Woof woof!"

Oh, my God! I whipped around. A middle-aged woman was walking her dog and making coy little *woof-woof* sounds at him. She jerked her head up. Apparently mortified by my mere presence, she protectively pulled the dog's leash and quickly headed in the other direction. What? Did I look like a crazy person or something (or was it my hair)? I began walking. I just wanted to go back to the house, jump into bed, and pull the covers up. Why can't I get over Keith? Why does it hurt so much? Oh, but he was so immature. "Let's get tra-a-a-a-shed." Please. No wonder Meri dumped him. And now I know why. Ha. If you don't return the favor for Meri, then that's it, I'll bet.

"Walking all alone?"

I turned, snagged in the moonlight. Professor Scott had pulled up alongside me in his apple red Honda Civic. His voice was so soothing.

"You've been crying."

"No I haven't," I snapped. I was still a bundle of nerves. I felt so exposed, so vulnerable. "I—I have allergies. And I like to walk alone."

"Why don't I give you a ride?"

"Sure you want to do that? I'm a little crazy, you know. I'm Firecracker Girl. Haven't you heard?"

"Hmm, no, I haven't heard that one. I heard Boom-Boom Bixby."

I laughed. I couldn't help it. And he laughed too. But not like Keith. Or Bud. Not all jerky and immature. It was an adult laugh, a thoughtful laugh (it had so many different colors and deep shadings). The inside of his car was warm. It was so strange seeing Professor Scott out of class. *He's a real person*, I thought, *and so relaxed*.

"Where are you off to?" he asked.

"Home," I said.

"Aw, on a Saturday night? That's no good."

"Whatever," I proclaimed. "I don't buy into all that pressure to 'have a good time' on a Friday or Saturday night, you know? Or New Year's, for that matter."

I. Am. A. Total. Spazz. I wanted to sound adult and sophisticated, but I could hear myself, and I sounded like some snot-nosed little second grader suddenly declaring, "Teeter-totters are s-o-o-o déclassé." But he laughed. A nice laugh. And he patted my hand. Gently (it was warm) (and just slightly calloused).

"You're right. Let's just go for a drink."

"Oh, I'd love a drink, Professor Scott." I was gushing. Oh my God, I really needed to get a hold of myself. Fast.

"Please. Call me Scotty."

"But I thought your name was Charles . . ."

"Charles Scott. That's right. But all my good friends call me Scotty."

All his good friends call him Scotty! That's so cool. We didn't go to Swingles (where all the jerky immature college students go) (like Keith). We went to Blarney Stone, a dark corner bar with a pool table and old-fashioned red leatherette booths—oh, and Dervil, this broad-shouldered, wrinkly-faced, sort of mean-looking waitress who wore a frayed skirt (with hand-embroidered Celtic designs), a green lace-up vest over an off-white peasant blouse, and a cute green sequined headpiece. She had a lit cigarette dangling from her lower lip, and she snickered when she first saw me—why, I don't know—then she turned to Professor Scott and said, "Bourbon? Straight up?"

"Thanks, Dervil. And the lady will have an Irish Candy."

"Of course she will," she snorted. Then she waddled off. An Irish Candy, I learned, is a really tasty cocktail with Bailey's Irish Cream, chocolate raspberry liqueur, and white crème de cacao. S-o-o-o-o-o good! When I took my first sip, I thought, *Keith never ordered drinks for me. Not once.* In fact, I was always the one who had to go to the bar to get us our next round whenever we went out. But this was different. Why? Because Professor Scott is a gentleman. He's an adult.

"Cheers," he said, raising his glass with a wink. "Let's pretend it's a Tuesday night and really cut loose."

I guess I did cut loose. I had four Irish Candys (he kept ordering them for me, which was so thoughtful). And I was astounded to learn that Professor Scott is a real writer. He's not just a professor. And no, he's not published or anything, but that's no surprise, because he's been working very hard on his book for at least the last eleven or twelve years.

"It's the journey, not the result," he said. "I'd love to show it to you sometime."

I couldn't believe it. I was speechless. He wanted to show his book to me. Me. I felt so honored. I sputtered, "What's it about?"

"It's about a girl. Kind of like you, actually. She's beautiful. And she's pure. But headstrong, defiant. She's at a crossroads in her life. Should she or shouldn't she? She's thirsty. For real life, real knowledge. Real experience."

Okay, maybe I was drunk, but from what he was saying, it kind of sounded like he was reading from one of Bobbie's Barbara Cartland novels. She's "thirsty"? Give me a break. Let me guess: Do her bosoms heave tremulously beneath her bodice? Do her lips part like two welcoming moist petals? Was I being unfair? Was I rushing to judgment?

"But it's about more than that," he insisted. "It's about the slipperiness of truth, the complexity of human emotions. It also a damning indictment of society's unquenchable appetite for violence, both domestic and foreign."

Maybe I was really-really drunk, because I didn't understand what the heck he was talking about. From what he was saying, his novel sounded like it was trashy, and also a little pretentious. Trashy's so hard to pull off. I'm convinced that the only one who can do it with any real pizzazz is Jackie Collins (Lisa read an old copy of *Hollywood Wives* five times, and though I only read it once, I understood why). Professor Scott downed his third bourbon, then gazed at me silently; there was a resigned sadness in his half-lidded eyes, and a sort of faint, flickering hopefulness, too.

"It's my birthday next week. I'm becoming an old man."

"Oh, Professor Scott . . ."

"Scotty."

"Please. You're not old. Geez."

"I'm not?" he asked, visibly brightening.

Poor Professor Scott. And poor me. I knew what was going on. Here was a professor looking to score with a "thirsty" young student (even though teacher-student "liaisons" are now included in the long list of no-no's among RU's new policies). And there I was. Boom-Boom Bixby. I was gushing. And I was flirting. And, okay, I admit it, I was sort of flattered that someone—anyone—was flirting back. So who was more pathetic?

"Who is Cindy Bixby?" he softly asked.

She's Keith's girlfriend, I thought, and I winced, remembering that I'd once secretly scribbled that as the winning answer to the question, "My Authentic Self Is" during one of Professor Scott's classes. All right, so what's the answer now? Who is Cindy Bixby? A voice ripped through my body: *She's Meri's roadkill, that's what she is!*

I sat up with a gasp.

"Everything okay?" asked Professor Scott.

Dervil waddled up and smirked.

"Last call, lovebirds."

"I've really got to go," I yelped to no one in particular. Professor Scott followed me, confused, as I made a beeline for the street.

"Cindy, wait. I'll drive you."

I really do allow myself to get distracted too easily. That's what I was thinking while riding shotgun in Professor Scott's Honda. Why was I so stupid? Flirting and drinking with a professor? If Victorio ("call me Vic") found out, then that would surely be the last straw: blowing up toilets, making goo-goo eyes with professors in dimly lit bars—good-bye Alpha Beta Delta, toddle-oo RU, hello community college. I won't give Meri that satisfaction. I won't. Professor Scott steered up to the house.

"I hope I didn't do anything to offend you," he asked.

"Oh, Professor, you didn't . . ."

I never finished my sentence. His lips were pressed to mine, his hands ran through my hair. I wanted it to stop. And then, Oh God, tongue! But I couldn't. I couldn't stop, because (and here's the real kicker) Professor Scott is a really good kisser. He kissed my mouth, my lips, my neck. And I felt bathed in salty sweat, controlled by him . . . at the mercy of his . . . desire . . . and, oh, oh . . . I started . . . to feel . . . all . . . breathy . . . like I was in a . . . Barbara . . . Cartland . . . novel. And that was definitely a buzzkill because it made me feel self-conscious and depressed— like there was me, floating outside of me, making fun of me—so I pushed him back.

"I'm sorry," he said, catching his breath. "You're just so . . . oh, Cindy."

He was on me again. He reached for my breast. And I thought, *I'm just so* what? *Easy? Available?* The spell was broken. I gently but firmly yanked his hand away and reached for the door.

"Really nice seeing you tonight, Professor Scott."

"Please, Scotty. Oh, I'm throwing myself a birthday party Monday night," he said, and then, as if to calm my suspicions, he added, "A lot of my really good friends will be there. Students, too. I'd love it if you came."

I smiled. "Maybe."

"Good night, Cindy."

"Good night, Professor Scott."

I stepped into the house. I heard muffled voices coming from the kitchen:

"Exposure therapy . . . no, it really is good for her, I swear . . . cognitive isn't enough . . . as long as you don't think she'll freak . . ."

I rolled my eyes. They were no doubt discussing my quick and embarrassing exit from the football stadium. Whatever. Or as Bud says, "Whatevs." Let them. All I wanted was a nice cool Coke before bed. I strode in, swung open the refrigerator. And I sighed.

"Let me guess. Diet Coke is inappropriate."

"The Coca-Cola bottling company stands accused of causing environmental damage in India," said Shanna-Francine perkily. She was sitting at the table sharing tofu chips and kumquat-soy soda with Bobbie, Lindsay, and Patty (who sprinkled Skinny on her chips).

"And they don't pay their workers in poor countries the American minimum wage," added Bobbie.

"So the alternative is what?" I snapped. "No jobs at all? And they stay unemployed? And they starve? Boy, somebody really thought that one through, didn't they?"

Crickets. They looked at me like I'd just clubbed a baby seal. Except for Lindsay, who forced a nervous, toothy smile and straightened her tiara. Keep it together, she was telling me, so I took a breath.

"Good night," I intoned. I strode upstairs and took a long hot shower. That felt good. *Keep the focus*, I told myself. Just find the mole, stop the flow of information. Then Meri can be stopped. I dried off, unlocked my bedroom door, and turned on my computer. I had two new e-mails. The first one didn't surprise me.

From: <lisa@lisabixby.com >
Date: 28 October
To: <cindybixby@yahoo.com>
Subject: RE: Be Nice!

Hey, Cindy!

It's your sistah in the hizzy! Woo-hoo! Like, your concern for me is s-o-o-o-o-o o touching. Hehe. But really, don't

worry. I have it all under control. I had a long-ass talk
with Mom and Dad and promised them I would never-ever-
ever-ever-ever sneak out of the hotel at night again.
And they believed me. Ha! Then I flipped some dub to the
night-time desk manager and told him to cover for me.
Score! Now whenever I take off at night, he forwards calls
from my room to my cell phone—and I can see when it's Mom
calling on the ID, and whenever she calls I pretend to
get all p.o.'d and stuff like she just woke me up. It's
s-o-o-o-o perfect!!

Meanwhile, me and L. Lo are mega-tight. She said she'd intro-
duce me to Meryl Streep 'cause they did a movie together, and
I'm like, "Who the fuck is that?" and she's like, "Dude, Meryl
does s-o-o-o many accents," and I'm like, "Okay." I mean, guys
who do lots of accents are cool. I guess.

We hit the Spider last night and it was totally jammin'. And
get this. I met Henry Garza!! I know, right? And I'm thinking, guuuurl, you so gotta tap that hot cholo now. Hehe. And
his hair! Oh my God, it's s-o-o-o-o long. Mega-mega-mega
hot. He was there with his brothers, and I stepped up and
I'm like, "Yo yo yo, LLB, wassuuuuuup!" And they looked at
me like I was a freak or something, and I'm like, oh,
please, get real, you know who I am.

I told them we should so lay some tracks together—Lissa
Mashes Los Lonely Boys! And they were still doing this
who-are-you trip, so I busted out, "Tune my motor up, make
me purr!" and they laughed. That was cool. Then I pulled
Henry aside and told him we should totally hang sometime.

And get this. He asked to see my ID. WTF? But whatever,
I know he's into me. And Lissa WILL mash with LLB. You'll
see!! And then I saw Jamie Lynn Spears and talked to her
about her new single and said, "Girl, it's tired." That's
it. I didn't need to say anything else to her.

Then L. Lo says, "This place is busted," and I'm like, "So
busted," so we went to her house, which is w-a-a-a-a-a-ay up
in the Hollywood Hills and so cool 'cause she has the most
awesome collection of Beanie Babies E-VER and then Tara Reid
shows up and we decided to pig out!! We ordered pizza and
had some chocolate mousse cake (I ate most of it) and I told
them all about "Touch My Daisy," 'cause it's gonna drop,
like, any second, and Tara was like, "Lisa, you are just so,
oh my God, I don't know, but you just so are," and I totally
knew what she meant.

I like Tara. But L. Lo will ALWAYS be my main homie. ALWAYS-
ALWAYS-ALWAYS. I don't think I could be famous without her.
You DON'T know how HARD it is to be WORSHIPPED! You don't.
Thank God I have L. Lo!!!!! So don't worry about anything,
okay?

Peace Out!
Me

I hit reply and sent this:

From: <cindybixby@yahoo.com >
Date: 28 October
To: <lisa@lisabixby.com>
Subject: RE: RE: Be Nice!

160

Meri Strikes Back

Lisa:

Do me a favor. Autograph a copy of your new CD single and
FedEx it to Sebastian Plummer, c/o Wright Dorm, South
Residence, here at RU. Do it right away. Please don't forget!

I'm glad you have nice girlfriends in Los Angeles. But I
really don't think you should be going out behind Mom's
back. Reread my last e-mail. Vanilla Ice performs in high
school cafeterias!

xxoo
Cindy

I was about to check my second e-mail when I was startled by a
loud door slam and heavy pounding down the stairs. Instinctively,
I backed away from the door. It's probably nothing, I thought, but
then who knows? I swiped my flashlight and opened my door. Just
a crack. There didn't seem to be anyone there, so I opened it all the
way and tiptoed down the darkened hallway. Nothing again. More
silence. I figured it was probably just someone going to the bathroom, and I gave a little chuckle—Meri sure does have me on edge
these days—then I turned to go back, and I gasped in horror! I
dropped the flashlight. There was a hulking figure, and I was about
to scream when a hand clamped over my mouth!

"Cindy, it's me."

Oh God. I really am a ridiculous bundle of nerves. It was Pigboy.
But he wasn't in his cute Joe Boxers. He was all dressed, and he
had his bookbag with him too. Something was wrong. I followed
him down the stairs as we talked. It's not good. Pigboy has had it
with the "new" Patty. She hardly ever sleeps, he told me, she talks
a mile a minute.

"It's like she's got diarrhea of the mouth," he said, then he turned to me sheepishly. "Sorry."

He didn't need to apologize. Everyone's begun to notice Patty's endless talkee-talkee.

"And now she's a big expert on everything. Including football." Patty, it seems, thinks Pigboy needs to emulate Reggie White, a pro defensive player who set records for the most sacks ever made while playing for the University of Tennessee (or something like that). "Oh, and she told me I need to lose some weight and firm up."

"You guys aren't breaking up, are you?" I asked.

Pigboy sighed. "We're taking a breather."

My eyes welled with tears. Instantly. And it's not like Pigboy's *my* boyfriend or anything, but for some reason it hit me really hard. I guess I just sort of assumed that they'd always be together—and in some weird way, maybe I took as much comfort in that belief as Patty did. It's like, since their relationship was so solid, then my relationship, or my next relationship, would be just as solid too.

"I gave him a good whoopin'!" I recalled Patty saying, and I really didn't want to remember that as I gazed into Pigboy's proud, but obviously pained, face.

"Not a big deal," he said, then he walked out the front door and into the night. I flew upstairs to Patty's room. I had to console her. Whatever else the "new" Patty may be, she's always been there for me. I swung her door open. The lights were on, the room was now even more spotless than before (if that's possible), but no Patty. Then I heard a rhythmic metallic *ker-chunk* and a thumping sound. Over and over. It was coming from outside. I stepped to the window, and I could see Patty, or rather, I saw her and then I didn't see her; her face and lower body bounced up—*boing!*—and then down from behind the paling fence that surrounds our backyard. As Lisa would say, WTF?

I stepped outside, pulling my nightgown close. I don't think

I've ever seen anything quite as strange. There was Patty, smiling to beat the band, on a large pogo stick, bouncing up and down: *boing, boing, boing, boing!*

"Patty?" I whispered to myself.

As if she had supersonic hearing, her head whipped around—though she maintained her speedy bouncing on the stick—and she smiled, her eyes widening with glee.

"Cindy! Oh, Cindy-Cindy-Cindy. Isn't it a beautiful night?"

"What are you doing?" I gaped.

"Exercise!" she squealed—still going up-down up-down up-down. "Cardio-shmardio. Most people jog. I say, phooey. Why jog when you can pogo-stick. See? See?"

"What about Pigboy?" I couldn't believe she wasn't upset.

"Pigboy? Oh, Pigboy. We're experiencing a lack of mutuality. See? See? I'm getting better. And then what happens? Bang! People get jealous. I'm losing weight. More every day. I mean, c'mon. C'mon. Look at me. I. Am. Bomb!"

"Don't you think it's a little late to be doing cardio?" I timidly asked.

She snapped, "Sour grapes! Green-eyed Cindy. Don't be jealous. Oh, look. My lights. In my bedroom. They're on. Be a pally and turn them off. Will you? Will you?"

And off she went—up-down up-down up-down. In her bedroom, I turned off her overhead light, reached for her desk lamp. And I stopped, gazing at the large open glass canister of Skinny. I suddenly had a terrible thought: cocaine! I was terror-stricken for the briefest moment, but I just as quickly pushed that thought aside. Cocaine, as I know from watching countless episodes of *NYPD Blue* (I cried when Jimmy Smits died!), is quite expensive, so it was unlikely that this largish canister that was almost full of Skinny was incognito cocaine. Then I remembered that Skinny was created by Wolfgang Rimmer, of all people, who's perpetually broke. And it's not like he's selling this stuff to Patty. He's giving it to her for free to help him with Skinny product testing (Wolfgang doesn't have the cash to buy drugs, and even if he did, he'd definitely sell the drugs to make money). No, this wasn't some illegal substance like cocaine, I reasoned, but then what was it? And why were my hand and forefinger shaking as I started to dip my hand in for a little taste test?

I fearfully yanked it back and swiped an empty cup from the bedside table and dipped it in the canister, taking a healthy scoop of the sugarlike crystals. I'm sure Bud will be dumb enough to taste-test this, since he prides himself on having tried all kinds of illegal substances (he says that he smoked "lots of pot" in high school—though I never saw it—and he seems especially proud that he can fashion a "pipe," he says, with just a teensy bit of tinfoil and the cardboard from an empty roll of toilet paper. This is something to be proud of?).

I hid the cup of Skinny on the top shelf in my closet, and I was ready to hit the hay when I realized that I still had one more e-mail to check. I clicked it open:

From: <cindybixby@yahoo.com >
Date: 28 October
To: <cindybixby@yahoo.com>
Subject: RE: Be Nice!

Hey:

Why don't you just drink Pepsi? Or better yet, swallow some Drano. :)

This one threw me for a loop, and not because of its content (I've grown used to their nastiness). The mystery of the mole is now close to being solved. I just had an argument in the kitchen about Coke, which means that I've now narrowed down my mole suspects to four people: Bobbie, Shanna-Francine, Patty, and Lindsay.

I'm feeling pretty confident as I write this. And sad, too, because I really hope the mole isn't Lindsay (it can't be), and yet, I'd be just as sad to learn that the mole is the "new" Patty, or Shanna-Francine, who really does seem to be trying to make the house better, no matter how misguided her "appropriate" efforts may seem to me (they certainly aren't hurting anyone). It has to be Bobbie. It just has to be. But I'm not jumping to conclusions. All I have to do is figure out a way to narrow it down. To one.

October 29

Dear Diary:

Oh my God, oh my God, oh my God! If Meri wants, she can send me to jail! Okay, I'll back up. Today was Sunday. The word "Sunday" is pagan in origin. Ka-billions of years ago, pagans used to gather and pray to the sun. Why do I know all this? Because Meri told me! Oh my God, oh my God, oh my God, oh my God! Oh, and October 29 is Frankenstein Day, in honor of Mary Shelley, who wrote *Frankenstein* in 1818. It's also the day that NOW, The National Organization for Women, was founded in 1966.

"Coincidence?" asked Meri airily. "You tell me. But remember, it's also Winona Ryder's birthday."

I can't think straight. Can I write a coherent sentence? I don't want to go to jail. Before going to bed tonight, I checked my e-mail:

From: <cindybixby@yahoo.com>
Date: 29 October
To: <cindybixby@yahoo.com>
Subject: The Pokey!

Hey:

Can't you see it? You. In prison. With Squeaky Fromme.

Braiding each other's hair! Hahahahaha. Did you know? She
attacked a fellow inmate with a claw hammer. Oucha magowcha!

:)
Mwah

I had to Google Squeaky Fromme. Lynette "Squeaky" Fromme
was a follower of Charles Manson, a super sicko killer in the 1960s,
and she was imprisoned in the 1970s for attempting to assassinate
President Gerald Ford. Oh please, God, I really don't want to share
a prison cell with Squeaky Fromme. Or anyone.

Everyone was at the Day of Forgiveness Charity Dinner tonight.
Lots of students and teachers—even Professor Scott showed up—
along with a few administrators, and yes, Victorio ("call me
Vic"), who chatted amiably with Patty. I could barely hear them
over the din.

"Exposure therapy . . . oh, that's a very good idea . . . why did-
n't I think of that?"

The buffet was elaborate and unappetizing (to me). Curried
rice salad with seaweed strips and shelled hempseed nuts, Tofurky
slices with Caribbean pink bean spread, fried tempeh with screw-
pine leaves in apricot sauce (and again, I'm all for eating cruelty-
free, but really, someone's got to teach Shanna-Francine and Bobbie
how to cook). I swear, all I wanted was a Coke. Still, the house
was raising a lot of money for the "Stop Jennifer Lopez PETA
Fundraiser," which Bobbie insisted was a worthy charity, and I
guess it is, since there's really no reason why Jennifer Lopez can't
start wearing faux fur instead of all those icky dead animal pelts
she keeps throwing on herself.

"Drew Barrymore wears faux fur," squealed a cheery Shanna-
Francine to the assembled group of guests. "And like, oh my God,
who'd you rather hang out with? Jennifer or Drew?"

The answer was unanimous (and obvious, I thought; I mean, even if Jennifer Lopez does go faux someday, I'd still rather hang out with Drew) (I mean, duh). Still, I've got to hand it to Shanna-Francine. She walked the talk; she wore a very pretty pink faux-fur tippet with a cute red ribbon, and she had on these surprisingly stylish-looking vegan Blake Black Moo Shoe high heels (if only she could cook as well as she dressed, I thought).

"Are we ready to forgive?" hollered Bobbie.

The time had come. Everyone was supposed to step forward with a sheaf of rosemary (supplied by the house) (of course), place it in a large oversize silver bowl, and then publicly ask forgiveness for one thing (if the person that you seek forgiveness from happens to be in the room, then that person may, if they choose, say, "You're forgiven"). Then, before stepping away, you're supposed to forgive someone or something (such as an organization or a state or a country), for one thing that they've done (and that presumably they want forgiveness for). I readied my videocam, because even I had to admit, this would look good for the intersorority governing board. Bobbie was first. She solemnly lay the sheath of rosemary in the bowl.

"I ask for your forgiveness!" she bellowed, and then she turned to Patty, her head bowed shamefully. "I shouldn't have named my cats Chunk-a-Lunk and Mrs. Fields. That was really inappropriate."

"Oh, please, you're forgiven," said Patty with a smile, raising her teacup in salute (a cup no doubt spiked with Skinny). There were a few scattered murmurs of "aw" and clapping.

"I offer my forgiveness," continued Bobbie (and louder than necessary) (like always). "To Cindy."

Oh my God. You could hear a sharp simultaneous sucked-back gasp from everyone in the living room. I smiled faintly. I guess I'm used to the spotlight now, for better or for worse. *Just smile,* I thought.

". . . for blowing up the toilet on the second floor. But I really don't mind walking up to the third floor to pee. I swear. I don't."

All eyes turned to me. What the heck was I supposed to do? I didn't blow up anything. The silence was unbearable. I found Lindsay in the crowd; she helplessly shrugged.

"Thank you for your forgiveness, Bobbie," I heard myself whispering. There was a shattering explosion of people saying "aw" and way, way more clapping than Patty got. My back was slapped a few times too. And I saw Patty exchanging an aw-shucks-our-girl's-coming-along-just-fine glance with Victorio ("call me Vic"). I felt my stomach turning. But then I reminded myself, *That's it, it's over, this is as bad as this night gets.* Bud was up next.

"Hey, you guys, how you was," he goofily exclaimed, giving a "live long and prosper" *Star Trek* hand wave. Then he laughed—with that high-pitched hyena laugh that he has. No one was laughing with him (and I couldn't help but notice a small booger dangling from his left nostril) (eeeow!) (why do I notice these things?!). "I ask for your forgiveness," he abruptly bleated, clearing his throat. "Lindsay. I'm so sorry I was caught sniffing your panties at Toys "R" Us when we were buying a birthday gift for your nephew. I just had them. They were in my pocket. I swear I don't know how they got there. And I know it was really major embarrassing when you had to tell the police that they were your panties, 'cause at first they thought, you know, that maybe they belonged to some little girl I was finger-banging in the store or something. Which is so fucked up. And which I would never do. To a little girl." He was getting all choked up, but he kept going. "I just wanted a whiff. Just a quick one. I mean, Lindsay, you smell s-o-o-o good down—"

"I forgive you, Bud!" shrieked Lindsay, cutting him off. And geez, not a moment too soon. Bud moved on to offer his forgiveness.

"I offer my forgiveness to Metallica for being such total ass-holes and trying to sue everyone for sharing their lame-ass music. Oh, and I forgive James Hetfield for cutting his hair and finally looking like the dork-ass he is. Metallica sucks ass!"

Bud was quickly shunted aside (thank God) (and Lindsay pulled him aside and used a tissue to pluck the booger from his nose) (eeeow!). More people continued offering their rosemary sheafs, including Patty, who burst into tears when she offered forgiveness to her mother.

"Mom, I forgive you for calling me your cute little baby hippo when I was six. And for saying that boys don't kiss girls with chunky trunks when I was sixteen. And for telling me not to laugh too much, because that's what fat girls do. Well, Mom, guess what? I'm laugh-ing now. Ha ha ha ha. But I still forgive you—I still forgive you. I do. You'll see. Soon I'll be wearing Spandex. Ha ha ha ha. How do you like that, Mom? Huh? Huh?"

Professor Scott forgave John Irving for writing *Until I Find You*, Shanna-Francine asked to be forgiven for hating the French because they invented really high heels and mayonnaise and stole away Johnny Depp, and Lindsay forgave Patty for making fun of her umbrella the other day (and pointed out, kind of sharply, I thought, that it was Patty who recommended her new Bottega Veneta cream-dotted umbrella when she lost her cherry-blossom Louis Vuitton).

I knew that I'd have to go eventually, but I was stalling. I thought, *I forgive the world for not realizing that Meri Sugarman is a psychopath. Ha. That'll go over well.* But then I shook my head angrily, trying to push all those stinky thoughts out of my head. Meri was turning me into a cynic. And I've never been a cynic. Ever. And it's not like I haven't been given good reason on more than a few occasions. I could have turned into a major sourball when I lost out on the part of Anne Frank in the junior high school play. Lisa said it was because I was too "buttly" and "like, everyone knows Anne Frank was fuckin' hot." And I guess I could have become really negative when I went to get a new haircut at this fancy salon in Chesterfield Mall and the haircutter said, "Mmm. Too bad we can't do anything about your forehead." You're damn stinking right you can't do anything about my forehead. It's way too high and it's shiny. So what? I've been the smiling butt of every joke my entire life, and I've learned to deal with it by realizing, correctly, I think, that there are good and nice things about everyone, even if I can't see them, but Meri is testing that. What's good about Meri? What's good about nuclear waste? See? That's what she's doing to me. And I don't like it.

"I hope I'll see you tomorrow night," murmured a voice in my ear. It was Professor Scott, who was reminding me about his birthday party.

"I'll try," I offered weakly, and before allowing him a response, I realized that this was as good a time as any to grab a rosemary sheaf and get my forgiveness over with. But when I stepped up to the bowl, Shanna-Francine blocked me. Then she smiled winsomely. Too winsomely (even for her).

"Why don't you wait a few minutes?"

"For what?" I asked.

The doorbell rang. Shanna-Francine's eyes widened—and I could sense an electric surge whipping through the room. What it meant, I didn't know. Shanna-Francine stepped away to the foyer, and I walked to the dining room. I was hungry, which took precedence over my confusion, but I still couldn't find anything at the buffet I wanted to eat. But I did hear the door open and a startling roar—like the roar from a mountain lion or a jaguar. I assumed someone had turned on the TV in the living room to Animal

Planet, but then I heard Bobbie say, "Maybe you can put him out back on the porch."

I also heard whispers; the lively din had swiftly dissolved to a troubling flimsy hush. I began trembling. Then I heard:

"Exposure therapy . . . oh, yes, I've heard of that . . . systematic desensitization . . . avoidance only keeps the neurosis going . . ."

My shoulders dropped with relief. It was just more talk about Keith, about my embarrassing departure from the stadium. That I could handle. I stepped back into the living room—just as someone else swept back in from the porch. And that's. When. Time. Stopped.

Oh my God, oh my God, oh my God, oh my God!

It couldn't be. But it was. A delicately French-manicured hand reached out for mine. And a chillingly familiar breathy voice said, "Hello, Cindy."

I was standing directly across from Meri Sugarman. It didn't compute. Meri's been banished from Alpha Beta Delta.

"She's not at Rumson anymore," I recalled Lindsay reassuring me. "Meri's not here."

But there she was. Crisply dressed in a fiery red, gold-buttoned Chanel blazer with knife-pleat Versace wool pants. A Miu Miu handbag was slung over her shoulder, and a (no doubt one-of-a-kind) gold and silver opal bracelet jangled on her outstretched hand, which she extended further. Further still.

"Please," she insisted softly.

For the briefest second, I realized that Meri's "casual," yet very expensive Boho-chic look, which I had spied before, was solely for the benefit of her new community college chums; her version of "dressing down." Here was the real Meri. Her every stitch of clothing said, *Envy me*, but quietly, discreetly. Then she grasped my hand and shook it, and the entire room erupted with applause and giddy laughter and sighs of relief and then I knew: This was my real exposure therapy! I didn't realize that her hand was still clasped to mine, but I suddenly felt myself pulled forward into a hug. Oh my God, oh my God, oh my God! Meri held me gently. She smelled of lavender, bergamot, and vanilla. It was "Fleurissimo," a perfume created for Princess Grace of Monaco by the Creed family perfumery in Paris, and later adopted by Jackie O. She whispered delicately into my ear.

"Don't blow it, bow-wow."

Then she stepped back and joined the applauding throng, smiling graciously for all to see, as if she were a benevolent queen well-disposed toward mingling with the great unwashed—but just for show, and only on brief occasions. *This is completely out of control*, I thought. I gazed at the crowd. "Everyone loves a comeback," Lindsay told me not too long ago, and here was startling, jaw-dropping, horrific proof. I whipped around. Where was Lindsay? She was cowering in a corner. She caught my eye, then disgracefully looked away. *Oh, poor Lindsay*, I thought. She had obviously been sworn to secrecy about this event—but then she could have confided in me. Right? Couldn't she have? Unless she's the mole. Oh my God. My legs felt rubbery, and my vision was momentarily sprayed with sparkly black dots. Was I going to faint? Hands reached out and settled me in a chair. It was Victorio ("call me Vic").

"You have friends who love you very much," he cooed.

I looked up at his face; his simpering smile, his high-hatty condescending gaze. I wanted to spit. I looked away. I saw Shanna-Francine, who gaped at me with utterly sincere concern and compassion, and Patty, who looked lickity-split back and forth between me and Meri; first me, then Meri—me, Meri, me, Meri, me, Meri—and there was Bobbie, whose Mohawk and piercings must have inwardly horrified Meri when she handed her a rosemary sheaf.

"Thank you," she uttered gracefully. Then she smelled the sheaf, and it seemed to satisfy her, because she smiled. Just slightly. Then she strode toward the large silver bowl. The crowd silenced as she took her place before it and raised her sheaf to drop it. Then she stopped.

"Before I begin," she cooed, "I'd just like to thank Alpha Beta Delta, and Dean Pointer, too, for inviting me to return to Rumson. For just one night. This wonderful night."

The crowd hung on her words, and they were just about to applaud when Meri paused, cocked her head, and gazed anew at the sheaf. She seemed momentarily transported. She whispered. And everyone strained to hear.

"I had a small herbaceous garden just outside my window when I was five. It was tended to with loving care by Tuptim, our Japanese gardener."

Then she giggled girlishly—abruptly, out of nowhere—while running her hand through her thick raven hair. Then she flipped it back, turned to the bowl, dropped the sheaf in, and turned right back around. To face me.

"I ask for your forgiveness, Cindy."

I suddenly realized that my jaw was hanging open. I clamped it shut and tried to swallow, but the biggest lump ever was in my throat. I willed myself not to faint. I wasn't about to give Meri the pleasure. The room was quiet, but cymbal crashes and booming drumbeats were exploding inside my head. I couldn't look her in the eye. Instead, I looked at her smooth neck, her aquiline nose, then her mouth (in full pout as always), which barely moved as she spoke with her deceptively dainty and whispery voice:

"Earlier this year, I caused Cindy Bixby such stress, such unnecessary pain. And Cindy—oh, Cindy—please believe me, I am truly and deeply sorry for that. More than sorry, actually. I'm shamed. And I carry that shame with me every day. So when I got the call from Alpha Beta Delta to participate in this wonderful gathering, I knew I had to come. I—I . . ."

She stopped. She was trembling. Her eyes fluttered. Tears welled. She caught a gasp—a tiny one, nearly imperceptible—and then, tremulously, urgently:

"I want the healing to begin. But not just for me. You see, my journey is only beginning. Life is simple for me now. But it's good. And it's decent. And yet it won't be truly good until Cindy Bixby heals. And that's why I'm here. I guess I'm just hoping against hope that by admitting my faults, and my grave mistakes—here, publicly, on this wonderful occasion—that Cindy Bixby will finally be able to continue with her journey, too. Her wonderful journey. Cindy? I ask for your forgiveness."

The crowd was in sudden momentary conflict—a few people started to applaud, but they were urgently shushed. Why? Because everyone was waiting for me. And so was Meri. I was supposed to say, "I accept your forgiveness," but instead, I was looking at my hands folded in my lap. I could feel their gaze, and especially Meri's, burning right through my head. *I can do this*, I thought. *Just look up, face her, and say the words, then this will all go away.*

Then I felt an invisible string connected to my spine. It extended all the way up to my head. It gently tugged, straightening my back, forcing me to look up—and oh my God, I saw her face; a terrifying symphony of pseudosympathy—and suddenly the string violently yanked forward and I flew from my seat and I felt a wail escape from my mouth and my hands reached out and Meri ducked and then the string yanked harder and my body was propelled—*whoosh*—out of the room and onto the back porch, and then I doubled over and held my stomach. An earsplitting roar shook me from my trance. A jungle cat leaped toward me, only to be held back by a tied-off leash. *Oh my God, get a hold of yourself*, I thought, *that's not a jungle cat, that's Purrfect, Meri's Savannah, one of those super expensive crossbred cats; a little domestic, a little African serval.* It really did look like a spotted leopard. And it was huge. Quivering, I took a seat on one of Alpha Beta Delta's new hemp-covered porch chairs—one far away from Purrfect. I could hear the chattering from inside the living room. Everyone's well-intentioned plans, ruined. By my inability to say four simple words: I accept your forgiveness. The porch door swung open. Meri sashayed out. She giggled.

"Think they bought it?"

She fired up a joint and took a deep drag, then extended it to me.

"You want? Looks like you could use some. It's good shit."

I shook my head. And I looked away. I was beyond speechless.

"I told them I'd come out here. And calm you down."

I was barely able to speak. But I did. I croakily told her, "Go away."

She laughed; lightly, flutteringly. "Aw. No can do, Cindy B. You're my little bow-wow. Remember? And you're in my way."

"Sure you should be saying that out loud?" I dared to ask. "Is the house bugged again? Like before?"

"Tch. Cindy. Simple Cindy. Why don't you call in the experts? Have it checked out? I'll even pay for it. But really, you should know by now that I don't repeat myself. That's just gauche." She smiled, amused with herself, then she scratched Purrfect's head and once more extended the joint. "Sure you don't want? It's ganja. I pay my maid to go to this really fucked-up section of town to get it."

"Mamacita?" I asked.

"That's right," she happily responded. "You remember her? She can barely stand up straight these days, poor thing. But no one does handsies-kneesies better than Mamacita. And that's so important. Don't you think?"

Stay alert, I screamed to myself. *Meri still doesn't know the real Mamacita—and how she unwillingly helped me bring Meri down the first time.* I tried to clear my head. I had to use this opportunity wisely. Psychopaths are arrogant. They slip up. I needed to stay sharp. Meri bent forward and gave Purrfect a kiss on the nose.

"Isn't he the cutest? I keep his claws extra sharp. I think wild things should be allowed to be wild."

I gathered my courage. *Start slow*, I thought.

"So, uh, what are you really reading to those little girls at St. Eulalia's?" I blurted out. Meri's eyes narrowed. She took another toke from her joint, slowly, thoughtfully. And then she said:

"*The 48 Laws of Power* by Robert Greene. Honestly, I wish someone had read it to me when I was a little girl. The laws might be simple, but they're very helpful. 'Pose as a Friend, Work as a Spy,' 'How to Use Selective Honesty,' and my absolute personal favorite, 'How to Crush Your Enemy Totally and Completely.' Not that I need any pointers on that, but it's nice to have your own strategies confirmed. I'd love to meet the author someday. Actually, he'd probably love to meet me. I'm sure I'd inspire a whole new chapter. It's such a boy's club—you know, Machiavelli, Mao, Kissinger—and boys tend to be messy." She took another small toke, then carefully stubbed out the joint in an ashtray. "Personally, I've always preferred the clean kill."

My mind was gyrating and spinning in a zillion different directions at once. I had so many questions—but how would I ask them? Pretty lamely, now that I look back on it, but I was so nervous.

"Who's the mole at Alpha Beta Delta?" I awkwardly blurted. Meri gazed at me—a laugh was threatening to emerge—then she casually retrieved her Chanel compact mirror and Infrarouge Whisperlight lipstick from her Miu Miu and began lightly reapplying, pursing her lips as she breathily whispered, "Mole? What mole? Do you think I need one?"

"You have one," I responded apprehensively. And then I got a little brave. "I mean, even you're kind of obvious sometimes. There's no way those student protesters at the Charity Cookie Booth could have been ready so quickly unless they were tipped off."

She snapped her compact shut, retrieved a tissue, neatly blotted, while airily chattering to no one in particular, "If only all women would make a habit of moisturizing regularly. After showering, I use rosewater and glycerin. That's it. I keep it simple. And, of course, I pay special attention to my knees, and my elbows, too. You can't see your own elbows, but other people can."

I kept asking questions. Some of them were straightforward, like, "How do you send the e-mails to me so they look like they're from me?" and "What's the Albino Girl's name?" while others were more cagey in my attempt to trip her up, like, "Do you really think Christian Bale's at his hottest in *American Psycho?*" Unfortunately, Meri responded with mostly half-amused silence, and more unrelated daintily hushed decrees, such as:

"I can't stand makeup that stops at the chinline. Your neck is part of your face. Makeup should be narrowed subtly down the neckline to wherever your blouse begins," and, "If I wake up and it's raining outside, I apply my makeup under cold, hard light, never yellow, because your blues can turn a different shade."

I was beginning to get frustrated, but one thing I said perked her up: "Mrs. Forbes really seems to like you."

"You think?" she responded, visibly cheering. "Nancy's a doll. I always try to bring her the finest and freshest meals I can find. She's partial to brandy pie for dessert, but I introduced her to mousse au Champagne and chocolate amaretto balls. She loved them both." Then she beamed inwardly. "We have so much to learn from the elderly. Nancy's taught me so many wonderful things. Useful things. Oh, and it's Miss Forbes, not Mrs."

What, I wondered, could a nice old lady teach Meri? She was obviously bluffing on that one. I sat there stymied for a moment. And deeply frustrated. But then I thought, *Wait a minute, I have some power here, don't I? I'm not the one who had to cut a deal with the DA's office.* I gulped, gathering my nerve, and then I asked a very specific, slightly nasty question, hoping that it would provoke her, or at the very least reveal a chink in her armor.

I said: "Are you enjoying your time at Chappaqua Community College?"

It worked! She flinched, almost invisibly, but I could see it. Then her face darkened, her teeth clenched. She stalked toward me. Oh my God, oh my God, oh my God. My heart was pounding. She took a seat right next to mine.

"Today's October twenty-ninth. A day when Jackie could relax. The Cuban Missile Crisis was over."

Then she told me about Frankenstein's Day, Winona Ryder's birthday, and NOW, and as she did, she removed a gold-plated lighter from her Miu Miu, and a tiny two by three photo. I gasped. It was me. I don't know how she got it, but it was my high school graduation picture; my forehead was greasy, my hair tragic, my smile goofily forced, with my eyes slightly crossed.

"Why don't you leave Rumson, Cindy? Hmm? It really is best for everyone. Especially you."

Flick! She ignited the lighter and brought it to the picture. Flames consumed it. I don't believe in voodoo, but I swear it felt like I was on fire, like my heart had suddenly been tossed onto a blistering hot pan. She spoke in a subtly cruel undertone.

"I like to watch things burn. And then I like to do this."

She gave a delicate but forceful puff. My picture, now reduced to embers, scattered in tiny darkened particles. I was frozen to my seat. I thought, *What now? What now?* My emotions were unraveling.

"Why don't you just do what you want to do?" I wailed. "Instead of playing stupid games?!"

She fixed me with a glare. "Careful, Cindy. People will hear you. Your friends will be concerned. And you do like your friends, don't you?"

"I love my friends," I said, catching a sob. "More than anything."

She smiled. Just slightly. "I know." Then she patted my hand. "And you love your family, too. Don't you?"

My heart stopped. What was going on? What was she saying?

She continued, hushed, just above a whisper, "Pity about you and your mom, though. Hmm? Oh, I know, you two have come to some sort of understanding these days, right? But a new awareness can't really heal old wounds. Can it? It's a sad fact of life, Cindy. Mothers take better care of pretty children than they do ugly ones. It's instinctive. We're like animals that way. We parcel out our means on the basis of value. And children feel it. Deeply. I know you did. Isn't that right? You must have been so lonely as a child. It weakened you. It still does. And the sad thing is, you'll carry those feelings with you forever. They'll always be just beneath the surface. 'I'm the ugly one, I'm the one who wasn't held enough, I'm the one who isn't valued.' And here's the kicker: You're absolutely right. That's why it hurts so much. That's why you're damaged goods. That's why Lisa gets all the attention. Still. That's why Keith dumped you. And that's why you and I need to end this. Now. Leave Alpha Beta Delta, Cindy. Leave Rumson. Go home."

Then she stood up, smiled with satisfaction, and smoothed her blouse.

"Should we head back in now? We can hold hands if you like. Let's not ruin this night for everyone. C'mon. We'll go to the kitchen. I need to get Purrfect some water."

I suddenly realized that tears were streaming down my face. Oh, I hate Meri Sugarman! More than I ever thought it possible to hate anyone. I quivered, stood up. I felt slightly dizzy, as if I'd been physically pummeled. But then I had a thought. Several, in fact. Thoughts and questions. And all of them in mere seconds. *I am, in fact, still standing. I am not destroyed. And why does Meri really want me to leave? Because this is a turf war, because this is where she reigned. And I dared to cast her out. And if I fail to stand up to her now, I'll fail at everything. And then everything she just said will be true. Horribly, horribly true.*

"Why don't you go on ahead of me? And smile." She dug into her purse and pulled out tissues and her compact. "Here. Freshen up. You know, there's no better treatment than a good mask. Cook makes mine. He uses oatmeal, a few crushed almonds . . ."

"Oh, shut up!" I screamed. I can't believe I did that. I can't believe I screamed. I could hear the chattering from inside drop to an edgy silence. Oh, no! Meri lunged her face into mine, fuming.

"Watch it. They think you're unstable, remember?" Then she called out lightly. "Everything's fine. We're doing fine." She turned back to me. I could smell her fury. I was complicating her night. But I didn't care. Not anymore. I could feel a newly freed sense of courageousness bubbling up inside myself. I looked her straight in the eye.

"I'm not going anywhere. See? I'm standing right here. Maybe you'd better get used to that."

She smiled. Just slightly. Then she deliberately took one small step back from me. Then another. Then she violently flung her head back and shook out her hair—and slapped herself several times. Hard. I didn't understand what I was seeing. It was all happening so fast. She clawed at her face, deeply, savagely raking the skin, digging in with her fingernails. Then she fell to her knees, screamed at the top of her lungs—writhing in pain like a howling banshee—jumped back up, kicked over a hemp-covered chair, and bounded toward the house, but not before whirling around, her face and hair in grisly disarray. She stormily seethed.

"You're fucked."

She ran inside and I could hear her high-pitched, hysterical screams and shrieks—joined by other screams and shocked gasps from the guests. Oh my God, oh my God, oh my God. I stumbled backward, desperate for a handhold. Bobbie raced out onto the porch.

"Cindy?" she gasped.

I stood there dumbstruck, at a complete loss for words, watching as Bobbie nervously untied Purrfect's leash and led him quickly inside. I don't want to go to jail. Please, no. I had to give a statement to the police after they were alerted. Meri had already given her statement and was whisked to the Rumson River Memorial Hospital. She was brutally attacked and beaten, she claimed. Witnesses at the gathering recalled me screaming. "Shut up," I had cried. And they saw me seemingly lunge at her before that, when I had refused to accept her forgiveness.

"She's lying," I stammered to Officer Hanson, but I was so nervously high-strung and jumpy I can't be sure if he believed me. "Can't you do tests? Like, to prove that maybe the skin or blood under her fingernails is hers?"

Officer Hanson chuckled. They only do that for serious crimes. Like murder. However, this was serious enough, I later learned, that should Meri choose, she can file criminal and civil charges against me, and civil charges against the university as well, for failing to provide for her safety in the presence of a student they had known to be "unstable" and "prone to violence." *That's it*, I thought. *I'm gone from Rumson, I'm headed to jail.*

After giving my statement, I ran upstairs, closed my door, and locked it. I stood in the center of the room, frozen with indecision. What's going to happen to me now? Will I be kicked out of Alpha Beta Delta and RU? And if that does happen, which seems likely, how does that bring Meri any closer to her goal of returning here?

Lindsay knocked on the door, but I gently told her that I wasn't up for talking. I don't know what I'm up for anymore. Meri is winning—in a big way—and I'm no closer to finding the mole. I checked my e-mail, discovering the one about Squeaky, and after scaring myself silly by learning about who she was, I was ready to go to bed when I remembered Meri's fond opinion of Nancy Forbes: "We have so much to learn from the elderly," she had said.

Curious, I opened my browser to Google and typed, "Nancy Forbes." *Probably not enough*, I thought. Then I remembered the leafy residential street, the gingerbreadish clapboard house—and the number "8" on the mailbox. I continued typing, adding "8 Salem Avenue," and hit return. Oh my God, I wish I hadn't done that. I should have just turned off the lights and gone to bed. The top link read: "Forbes Released from Prison." A chill ran up and down my spine, but I double-clicked it. It was a newspaper article from six months ago from the *Ronkonkomo Daily News*. My eyes scanned it hungrily:

Nancy Forbes, convicted nineteen years ago of murdering her fourth husband, Benjamin "Binks" Von Huffling, was released from Ronkonkomo Women's Correctional Facility today after her conviction was overturned by Judge . . .

I jumped up from the computer. I may have even screamed. There was a knock on my door, and I reflexively snapped, "I'm fine.

Just stubbed my toe." I stepped timidly back to the computer.

Apparently, Nancy's murder trial nearly two decades ago was quite the scandal. She had been a trusted and much-beloved nurse at the local Ronkonkomo County Home for the Aged, and the prosecution claimed that she had killed her husband, a wealthy yet ailing man who was many years her senior, by injecting him with a lethal dose of morphine while caring for him at their home. Rumors swirled. Her three previous husbands, who were also wealthy, aging, and sickly, had died under her care as well. The prosecution tried to gain permission to exhume their bodies, but the judge refused. There were two trials, the first resulting in a hung jury, the second sending Nancy to prison for life.

"I have little doubt that your husband thanked you as he submitted to your deadly injection," the prosecution claimed in open court. "Yours was not the healing touch."

But Nancy lucked out—eventually. After numerous appeals, and with her lawyers pointing out all the inconsistencies and technical gaffes in the second trial, a judge commuted her sentence, threw out the conviction, and set her free, though he noted that the State could retry her case in the future. That seems pretty doubtful. Nancy's in her mid-sixties now, her victim (or victims!) long forgotten.

"Nancy's taught me so many wonderful things," Meri had said with a smile. "Useful things."

I was shaking. Can I trust my own eyes anymore? When I was spying on Meri, I had seen a sweet, twinkly-eyed old lady. I'm in bed now. I may never get out. Meri is consorting with a killer! And what about me? I may go to prison, I'll certainly be booted from Alpha Beta Delta and RU. And yet it's Meri's painful words that keep pounding in my head.

"You must have been so lonely as a child. You'll carry those feelings with you forever. They'll always be just beneath the surface.

'I'm the ugly one, I'm the one who wasn't held enough, I'm the one who isn't valued.'"

Oh my God, is she right? It feels like she is, and I hate that. I *was* lonely as a child, and I *was* the loser in the family. Is that my authentic self?

October 30

Dear Diary:

Everyone stayed far away from me today—and I stayed away from them, too. All the girls at Alpha Beta Delta were busy preparing for the Fall Harvest Ball tomorrow night, and even though I wanted to contribute and help, I was afraid. Everyone has to be assuming that I'm completely gaga bananas (except for Lindsay!), and when I heard everyone going up the stairs to gather in Shanna-Francine's room for an early morning meeting, I waited until I heard her door close before daring to open mine. *Just go to class*, I thought, *and enjoy yourself, because you may not get to go to classes at RU much longer.*

I tried to think the impossible throughout the day: *What if I'm not kicked out? And if that's the case, shouldn't I be concentrating on how to find and stop Meri's mole?* It hit me in Orientation to Science and Technology (a core curriculum class that I hate). We were discussing the techniques for analyzing and interpreting data, and I realized that, yes, I do have some data, and yes, there might be a way to successfully interpret it in order to find and isolate the mole. It's actually pretty simple. I've already narrowed down my mole possibilities to four: Bobbie, Shanna-Francine, Patty, and Lindsay. How did I do this? That's simple too. When I had an argument about the inappropriateness of Diet Coke the other night, I almost immediately received an e-mail (from myself) (ha!) telling me to drink Drano instead. The only four people who heard that conversation were Bobbie, Shanna-Francine, Patty, and Lindsay. One of them responded to the argument and sent the e-mail. One of them is the mole. For the sake of this argument, I've decided to take Meri at her word; the house is not bugged like it was before (and for some reason, I actually do believe her on that).

So this is what I have to do. To find the mole, I'll casually (and separately) say four different, and hopefully very provocative things about Meri to Bobbie, Shanna-Francine, Patty, and Lindsay. Then I'll see who responds by e-mail. In other words, let's say I tell Bobbie, "I think Meri has a big problem with blackheads," and then ask Shanna-Francine, "Did you know that Meri once dry-humped Kevin Spederline? In the back of his Chevy TopKick? Isn't that gross?" If I later get an e-mail expressing outrage about Meri's blackheads, then eureka, I'll know the mole is Bobbie!

It was late afternoon by the time I'd finished with my classes and I was feeling okay. Not great, but okay. I decided to sit under a shady Empress tree on the Great Lawn. I love its fresh jasmine-like aroma, and as I sat there gazing out at the students tossing footballs and Frisbees, along with the inevitable couple or two making out in public in order to show everyone, or maybe me specifically, that yes, they have boyfriends and I don't, I thought, go on, kick me out of RU, kick me out of Alpha Beta Delta, but before I go, I give this parting gift to the house: I give you the mole. That will be my legacy. My personal legacy. Meri is wrong and I'm right. And I'm not a loser, and my authentic self is . . . I'm not sure yet, but it's not what Meri says it is. And it's probably not what Patty will say it is either, or at least I hope not, because she really is out of control these days (I was woken up briefly at five this morning because I heard her pogo-sticking outside again). I guess I fell asleep beneath the tree, because the next thing I knew, I heard a voice whispering, "Hullo, my dear.

I've arrived. And I'm here to lend my support in any way I can."

I opened my eyes. Was I hallucinating? I swear, for just a sec I thought I was in an old-time black-and-white Hollywood movie— and a glamour queen was right in front of me in gauzy close-up. She was wearing an enormous hat, its brim cutting diagonally across her face. She tittered.

"I'm a woman of a certain age. I'm allowed hats."

Then she tipped the brim up and gave a wink. I wasn't dreaming. I could smell the Aquanet! It was Sheila Farr (looking as sensational as ever, too). She took my hand in hers.

"Like it or not, you have my blessing—whatever dark path that may lead you down," she said with a gentle smile. "Just remember, the only certainty in life is this: There is no greater star than Sheila Farr. Ah ha ha!"

Sheila strolled with me back to Alpha Beta Delta. I was happy she did, too, because the sight of Sheila Farr, towering forth in all her glorious finery, including an elegantly flowing velveteen coat with ermine trim, sure as heck trumped me (which meant that no one snickered and pointed at me) (like they usually do).

"Would you like to come in?" I tentatively asked when we reached the door. It seemed like the only polite thing to do. After all, she is a movie star. No one was home yet from classes; we had the house to ourselves. Sheila swept in behind me into the kitchen and very majestically shrugged off her velveteen coat, allowing it to drop to the floor. Then she spoke, her voice deeply resonant.

"Somebody should have been there to catch that."

"Would you like a coffee, Sheila?" I asked. "Or maybe some tea?"

"No, my dear, I'd like bourbon. It's in my coat. Over there. On the floor."

I dutifully retrieved Sheila's flask from her coat, and we sat chatting amiably at the table. I drank ice water, even though she merrily invited me to "take a swig." Then she gazed at me, concerned.

"Why the sourpuss, puss?"

I sighed heavily. I didn't know how much Sheila knew, but then I figured the whole campus probably knew about me and Meri's confrontation last night by now. And I was right.

"Meri," tsked Sheila disapprovingly. "The little engine that couldn't. She's a heathen. Shower scum. Cheap store-bought pretzels. Chin up, dear. Sheila Farr is never ever on the side of losers, and you can't possibly be one. Why? Because you know me—that's why. Ah ha ha."

She laughed, and I laughed with her. What is it about Sheila Farr that makes everything seem okay? And then I wondered, Who is the guy who's buried underneath all that glitzy makeup and hair? Was he a loser when he was growing up, too? Was he made fun of? And what the heck is his authentic self (there's a million-dollar question)? Unfortunately, it was time for Sheila to go. She had a premiere to attend, she said, and she never disappoints her fans.

"Sheila, have you ever been on any crazy diets?" I hastily asked. I had a sudden thought: Maybe Sheila would know what Skinny was and if it was okay for Patty to be using it. I was right. Sheila told me that she was put through all kinds of "nutso" diets in her Hollywood days and considers herself something of an expert. I led her to my room and pulled down the small cup of Skinny I had hidden on the top shelf in my closet.

"I haven't tasted it," I told her. "I'm kind of scared to."

"Allow me," she said, then she elaborately moistened her forefinger, dipped it in the Skinny and took a taste. Almost instantly, her eyes bulged—and it almost seemed like her whole face dropped too, as if the mask of Sheila Farr had, for the briefest instant, fallen to the floor, because when she spoke, it was a guy's voice, and it emphatically boomed, "Where the hell did you get this?!"

I was stunned for a moment, but I explained that one of the sisters had a large canister of it.

"Where? Show me!"

Nervous, I led Sheila into Patty's room—and when she spotted the canister of Skinny, she lunged forth, grabbed it, then swiped the small cup of Skinny from me and commanded, "Where's the crapper?"

I led her to the (working) bathroom and she ankled ahead of me, flipped up the toilet seat, and dumped all of the Skinny inside.

"Sheila," I gasped.

She ignored me. She flushed it—and she kept her eye on the toilet until she was sure every granule of Skinny was gone. Then she turned to me, and again, I don't think it was Sheila talking to me, I think it was him (or, you know, the guy who is Sheila), and he wasn't amused.

"The next time you see this stuff in the house, you do exactly what I just did," he said sharply. "You flush it. Get rid of it. Keep it as far away from you and everyone else here as you can. You understand?"

I stammered, "Sheila—what—"

"Do. You. Understand?"

I gulped, "Yes. But what is it?"

I followed him down the stairs as he hastily explained. "It's tina. It's tweak. And it's bad. The worst."

I didn't understand what the heck he was saying. I tried to explain about Wolfgang, but he whirled, admonishing me.

"And the next time you see it in the house, you'll do what?"

"Um. Flush it? Right?"

And in that instant, the curtain was drawn shut. Sheila reappeared. As if by magic.

"Good girl," she cooed, giving my cheek a sweetly delicate pat.

"And now, I'm afraid I really must be off. Oh, and do the old girl a favor. Don't worry about Meri. Be brave, take risks. You see, that's how I, Sheila Farr, have remained on top"—she paused for a wink—"that and my divine recipe for coleslaw. Ah ha ha." Then *poof!* She was gone in a swirl of sequins and freshly sprayed Aquanet. Was she really just here? I wondered. I saw it in color, but I'm remembering it in black-and-white. I was still in a daze when I heard my cell phone ring. I clicked it open.

"Hello?"

"Cindy? Are you coming? We're already serving cocktails."

I rolled my eyes. It was Professor Scott. Oh, darn it, darn it, darn it. I was newly strengthened by Sheila Farr's encouragement, I was ready to find the mole (everyone would be home soon), and yet I had forgotten completely about Professor Scott's birthday.

"Sure, I'll be right over," I droned. I mean, I did say I'd go.

Professor Scott's house is only a few blocks away from campus. It looks like a small, drab, beat-up cottage on the outside, but on the inside, it's what you might call Boho chic, like Meri's clothes at community college, but from a very long-ago era. In the living room, there were four lava lamps (really, one is enough), a huge Led Zeppelin "Stairway to Heaven" poster with a psychedelic blimp, a plasma ball in the shape of a skull that was light-activated by music from the stereo (which had a turntable!), heavy blocky wood furniture that I heard was "sustainable" (though I'm not sure what that means), and of course, several floor-to-ceiling bookcases. I wasn't struck one way or another by the house or the guests who were gathered because my mind was elsewhere. What questions would I individually ask my mole suspects? I wondered, but after a few minutes it suddenly hit me. I don't know why I didn't notice it at first. Professor Scott was the only man at the party.

"Cindy," he cried, and then he coughed, having just taken a

huge hit from a large ceramic bong in the shape of Einstein's head. Everyone giggled. All of Professor Scott's guests were women. All of them. And all different ages, too. The oldest woman, Barbara O'Brian, a cheerfully expansive woman in a stunning and shimmery silk-sequined blue cocktail dress, had to be at least forty (at least), and when she saw me, she threw her arms out, pulled me into a warm hug, and exclaimed, "So you're the latest! Oh, look at you. Turn around, turn around. Everyone, this is Cindy. Isn't she just darling?"

Everyone tittered and applauded, and I have to admit, I was a little confused. I'm the latest? The latest what? The youngest one there besides me was Susan Milstein, a squeaky-voiced girl in an emerald green geisha girl dress, who looked like she maybe graduated from college about five years ago.

"Now, don't you dare call Charles an old hippie, don't you dare," she playfully scolded. "He's an Ancient Bong Master."

Then she laughed uproariously (and squeakily) and everyone laughed with her. Cocktails were flowing. Joints were passed. I declined both. And I still wasn't sure what was going on until I met Jazel and Jazlyn, the Crawford twins, two lovely thirtyish African-American sisters in matching tangerine strapless dresses.

"We were in his Victorian Poets and Poetics class," explained Jazlyn.

"Oh, he made Wordsworth come alive," enthused Jazel.

All of the women at the party, I realized, were former Professor Scott students. Professor Scott sidled up, pulled me close (a little too close, actually) and gave a moist kiss to my cheek.

"Cindy's mind is brilliant," he swooned. "And Dervil approves."

That prompted a near chorus of gleeful recollections. All the women apparently knew Dervil from the Blarney Stone. It still felt like I was missing something, but the party was in full swing, so I wasn't able to ask any questions, though at one point, after

Professor Scott blew out a forest fire of candles and the cake was served (a surprisingly yummy flourless chocolate cake), I remembered Sheila Farr's strange reaction to Skinny and how it confused me, so I tossed out a question to see what kind of reaction I would get.

"Does anybody have any tina?" I asked.

Several heads craned and whipped around. Voices murmured: "And she looks so innocent," "There's always something new," "Yes, but I wonder if there's anything we can do about her hair." Then Barbara leaned in close to me.

"Sorry, sweetie. It's not that kind of party. More cake?"

I gladly accepted, and as she served me another slice, I noticed the large blotchy heap of blown-out candles on the side of the serving platter.

"Weren't there too many of those?" I asked.

Barbara chuckled. "Not unless he's got a time machine. But he does look pretty robust for forty-eight, doesn't he?"

I stopped mid-bite (which was really something because the cake was that good). Forty-eight? Oh my God, I was tongued by a forty-eight-year-old. And I mean really tongued. Forty-eight. That's older than Dad! I honest-to-God thought Professor Scott was in his thirties, and that's definitely way too old already—and now he's almost fifty? Gross! What was I thinking? What was he thinking? I suddenly felt all greasy and soiled, but I didn't want to ruin the party or anyone's good time (or embarrass Professor Scott) (I mean, he obviously just forgot himself or was too drunk and didn't mean to do it). And then the professor suddenly cried out, "Can I have everyone's attention please? I have a poem to read. And I wrote it for all of you."

Everyone delightedly hushed and a few of the women applauded, and I have to say, I thought it was so sweet that he wrote a poem for everyone, and I was anxious to hear it (because Professor Scott is a serious writer, after all, in addition to being a professor). Everyone settled, and the smoky haze of pot, incense, and cigarette smoke cleared slightly as the professor proudly stood up, cleared his throat, unfurled a piece of notebook paper, and softly announced, "It's called, 'I Have a Jar of Cherries.'"

This prompted more applause (which was a bit unnecessary, I thought). The professor kindly waved them silent, and then began to very tenderly read his poem.

> *"I have a jar of cherries,*
> *I've kept them through the years*
> *They're each a meadow clary,*
> *How I've calmed their timid fears.*
>
> *Oh, cherry sweet, oh, cherry wine,*
> *Oh, cherry yes, oh, cherry mine.*
> *I pluck one yearly, so succulent*
> *So sweet. I bend her slowly,*
> *Slowly, and try to be discreet.*
>
> *Oh, sing my cherry, oh, tremble nigh,*
> *And know that I'll remember you*
> *With every wake and sigh, for*
> *You have giveth to me your*
> *Most precious gift, and I giveth to*
> *You my crested swift which soars*
> *And plumps and rushes and rises*
>
> *And then I plucketh your cherry like*
> *A greedy Czar and*
> *I put you here, right here*
> *In my precious jar.*

> Come to me, new cherry, as I strum my guitar
> And know that I'll be grateful
> When I put you here, right here
> In my precious jar."

There was instantaneous and thunderous applause and girlishly gushing compliments from all of the women. Except for me. I sat there with my mouth hanging open. Because now everything was clear. W-a-a-a-a-y too clear. These women weren't just former students of Professor Scott's. They were each, to be blunt, a cherry that he had pluckethed when they attended RU. I was beyond appalled, beyond repelled. And then I heard tinkly metallic strumming. I looked up. Professor Scott met my eye and gave me a wink. He was on the couch, gently strumming a zither, his lips forming a sickeningly sweet smile.

"Come to me, New Cherry," he called out with a musical lilt. "Come. Sit right next to me."

Ahhhhhhhhhhhhhhhh! All of the women clucked and fawned and encouraged me to sit next to him—a few even gently prodded, pushing my shoulders—and all I could think was, *Who the heck are these freaks? And did he get two cherries for the price of one with the Crawford Twins? And I much prefer the indignity of being called Boom-Boom instead of New Cherry* (oh my God, too gross!). I bolted up from my seat, confidently stalked the length of the room, and walked right past the professor and right out the front door. I didn't run back to Alpha Beta Delta, I walked, and I wasn't crying, either. I didn't even have a lump in my throat. I just felt stupid. Stupid-stupid-stupid. Why didn't I see that coming? (Could I have seen it coming?) The sun was setting as I strolled onto the campus; the sky turned from a shrill red to a blotchy bluish purple to a troubled darkness punctured by the usual snickers and giggles in my wake, including the occasional, "Hey, Boom-Boom, wassup?" I shrugged it all off. *You won't have Cindy B. to kick around much longer*, I thought, *but you'll know who the mole is.*

When I arrived at the house, I was just about to turn the knob to the front door when I heard a fiendishly high-pitched scream: "Who took my Skinne-e-e-e-e-e-y?!"

Oh, no. Patty's noticed that her Skinny, or twink (or tina, or whatever it is), is missing. When I stepped inside, the house looked like a tornado had blown through. Furniture in the living room was upended, cushions were strewn, and in the kitchen, every cabinet was flung open and boxes of (appropriate) dried goods were scattered on the floor. What the heck was going on? Bobbie ran into the kitchen, breathless.

"There you are," she boomed. "Have you seen it? Patty's Skinny?"

It seems that Patty, after returning home for the day, had planned on having a cup of chamomile tea with a light dash of Skinny, and upon realizing that it was gone, she became unhinged—literally ripping the house apart and tearing through everyone's room in her desperate search. I was about to tell Bobbie about Sheila Farr and her dire warning, but something inside me screamed, *Don't say a word, not yet!* and I'm not exactly sure why.

Upstairs, I saw Patty blast down the hall screaming. Her hair was like a fright wig, sticking up electroshock high, and her eyes, oh my God, they were huge and puffed-out and slashed with jagged red lines that looked like tiny throbbing lightning bolts, and her mouth was wide open, in the shape of a crazy eight, shrieking for all to hear.

"Who took my motherfucking goddamn fucking Skinn-e-e-e-e-e-e-y?!"

Whoosh. She blew past, nearly colliding into Lindsay, who grasped her tiara and allowed Bud to put his arm around her protectively. Then we heard violent booming and crashing. Patty was ripping apart another room in her desperate search. Lindsay meekly yelped.

"I mean, I get kind of pissed when people take my Equal, but jeez."

Then Patty staggered out. She looked like a crushed beer can. Her fantastic energy had vaporized. She wavered unsteadily, her eyes were half-lidded. She whispered faintly, "Feel funny. You're all fading away. Mommy? Where's Daddy? Is somebody playing with a dimmer? More Parks Sausages, Mom. Please? Look, just beyond the church, I can see the ghetto. Huh? Wha? Mommy made Shake 'n Bake. And I hey-yulped. I love you, tomorrow, you're only a day a . . ."

Boom. She crumpled to the floor in a dead heap. But not before gasping, "Tara!" and then her eyes closed. Minutes later we were all in Patty's room, having carried her to her bed, and we were all freaking big-time, especially Shanna-Francine, who squealed.

"I called 911. They said they won't come unless she's stopped breathing."

Then we stood there, caught off guard. Patty's eyes had opened. She weakly whispered, "Plop-plop, fizz-fizz, oh, what a relief it is. Ah, oui. Avoirdupois. Avoirdupois." Then her eyes shut and she was out once more.

"We'll take turns sitting with her," commanded Bobbie. "All through the night."

I volunteered to be first. I sat at Patty's bedside in her fantastically scrubby-clean room from seven to nine p.m., and I'll admit I had an ulterior motive. In my gut, I knew that Patty would get through this, and I knew that there was a possibility, however small, that she was the mole (despite her problems with Skinny). I was determined to plant the seeds with inflammatory questions to each of my four mole suspects tonight, and Patty was one of them. Finally she stirred, groggily mumbling.

"My core. My core is damaged. Must fix my core."

"Patty," I gently asked. "Can you hear me?"

"I hate being fat. I can admit that now. My problems are fascinating. But I don't need therapy. Need Skinny. More Skinny." Then her eyes widened, just a bit, and she finally noticed me. "Cindy? Oh, Cindy. Did you take my Skinny? I hate being fat. I can admit that now."

I had to tread carefully here. I didn't want to lie, but then I realized that no, I hadn't taken her Skinny, it was Sheila, so even though it was morally dicey, I said, "No, I didn't do anything with it."

"I'll have to get more," she responded weakly. Then she fixed me with a glare, her eyes narrowing. "Why did you attack Meri? That's the last thing you should have done."

Here was my opening. This was my chance to ask her a specific and provocative Meri-question—and see if I got a response to it in my e-mail.

"Did you know that Meri has scabies?" I blurted out. "She told me. Isn't that terrible?"

Patty gazed at me, confused, and then she laughed. "How awful for her. I wouldn't wish that on anyone one. Hmm. Okay. Maybe her."

I insistently repeated myself, "Meri has scabies."

And again she looked at me, utterly perplexed. I was relieved of my duties a few minutes later, and I almost flew to Lindsay's room. In fairness, I had to ask Lindsay a Meri-specific question too, but for Patty's sake, I had to tell both her and Bud about Sheila and hopefully get some answers. I swung open her door without knocking. They gasped. They were in the midst of Strip Scrabble; Bud was pouting in his Paul Frank underwear and socks, Lindsay was fully clothed, though she had removed several pieces of jewelry (but not her tiara) (I had a feeling that would be the last to go, no matter what the circumstance) (but then she always beats Bud by using tiny little *q* words, like "qi" and "qat" and "qin"). Without even catching my breath, I told them Sheila Farr had dumped all of Patty's Skinny in the toilet.

"She called it something like trick," I said, searching my memory. "No, wait, tina. That's it. She called it tina."

Right when I said that, Bud burst out laughing—but it wasn't an "I'm-laughing-at-Patty's-expense" type of laugh, it was an "Oh-my-God-that's-so-unbelievably-upsetting-that-the-only-thing-I-can-do-is-laugh" laugh, and Lindsay and I gazed at him, confounded, because we had no idea what could be so horrific. Once he calmed down, he explained. Skinny isn't a new diet sugar, it's exactly what Sheila said it was. It's "tina," which is drug-talk for crystal methamphetamine, and from what Bud was telling us, it's every bit as horrible as Sheila claimed it was.

"I thought it was cocaine," I sputtered, still reeling. "But I figured that would be too expensive."

I was right on that. Cocaine is expensive—way too expensive to have such a heaping jar of it. But crystal meth, Bud made clear, is almost ridiculously cheap to make. It's also obscenely addictive, and chronic use can lead to seizures and heart attacks, even death.

"It totally fucks people's lives up," said Bud with a shocking degree of solemnity (for him). And then, to our astonishment, he went on to tell us about his youthful and lively Aunt Tracy, who years ago had been under enormous pressure at work as a corporate accountant. She started using tina in order to help her meet deadlines, only to be fired after she began to exhibit bizarre mood swings and really scary bouts of hyperactivity. She lost her job, she lost her apartment—and all the while she couldn't stop doing tina. She lied, she stole money from her family; no one could stop her. Then she vanished. Months later her family received a call from a hospital two towns over. Aunt Tracy had been rushed there from a homeless shelter where she was staying after experiencing heart palpitations and seizures.

"She was bone thin," said Bud, who was obviously still shaken by the memory.

"So it does help you lose weight," I responded numbly.

"Oh, yeah," he said with a cutting chuckle. "She was totally Kate Moss-ed out."

I swallowed. This was all way, way beyond me. Lindsay had tears running down her face.

"Who gave it to her?" asked Bud.

Just as he asked that, I could see Lindsay about to say Wolfgang Rimmer, which was the right answer, of course, but I involuntarily beat her to the punch and shrieked, "Meri!"

"I love my friends," I had told her last night. "More than anything."

She smiled—just slightly—then she cryptically murmured, "I know."

Oh my God, oh my God, oh my God, oh my God. Meri isn't just out to destroy me, she's out to destroy all of my friends, too! That's part of her master plan. I knew it; in that moment I just knew it. The hows and the whys and the whens weren't coming to me, but really, is it such a stretch to imagine Meri forcing Wolfgang to give Patty tina? She certainly has the power to do that; if she was able to threaten Wolfgang before by revoking his Visa, it follows that she could play that card again. Wolfgang may have been my pawn before in my battle against Meri, but now he's Meri's pawn. It was Wolfgang who introduced Patty to his new "magical" diet sugar—and that has the mark of Meri all over it. Only Meri would be diabolical enough to take advantage of Patty's most glaring frailty, her anxiety about her weight, in order to get her hooked on a dangerous drug.

"I'll take her to the RU Rehab Center tomorrow," said Lindsay dazedly, ignoring my Meri outburst. "Poor Patty." Then she looked up at me. "What were you saying about Meri?"

I looked down at her on the bed. She was gazing up at me so innocently (I could see her letters, too; she had "qat" lined up and ready to go), and I thought, it's not Lindsay, it can't be. But then, if I was going to analyze and interpret my data properly, I realized, I had to cover all bases. I abruptly pulled her out into the hallway and shut the door to her room.

"What?" she asked, disturbed by my sudden jumpiness.

I awkwardly burst out with, "In junior high, Meri had sex with a retard. His name was Rupert. Everyone knew him. And Meri boned him."

"What are you talking about?" exclaimed Lindsay.

I nervously repeated myself, "Meri had sex with a retard."

Lindsay's jaw dropped; she just couldn't compute what I was saying. I got pretty much the same reaction when I cornered Bobbie in the kitchen, where she was preparing appropriate snacks for the Fall Harvest Ball. I charged right in and told her, "Meri has the worst split ends. Ever. And breakage. Did you know that? Bad split ends and breakage."

"Um, uh," she muttered helplessly, then she forced a smile and handed me a small lumpy blob. "Cruelty-free Jujube?"

When I charged into Shanna-Francine's room, she was on her bed in a pink nightie with hand-embroidered bunnies, and engrossed in several master lists as part of her organizational tasks for tomorrow's ball.

"The Children's Hospital is unsure about the appropriateness of our Halloween celebration," she merrily informed me. "But they'll see. We're creating, like, a totally new tradition. We're gonna raise tons of money for them. Don't you think?"

I had no response at first, because in this case I sort of understood the hospital's concerns, and secondly, I was wondering why Shanna-Francine was wearing such an infantile nightie (though to be fair, I have one with a bluebird pattern) (but it's not as childish-looking). "I'm sorry I haven't been much help these past few days," I limply offered, "But I'll be sure to video-tape everything. You know, for the intersorority governing council."

Shanna-Francine sighed heavily and seemed genuinely apolo-getic when she informed me, "I'm having one of the other girls do that. Okay? I think it's for the best." Uh-oh. Maybe she knew something I didn't, but before I could ask anything, she wearily informed me, "I've been on the phone practically all day with Dean Pointer, and no, RU hasn't been served with papers by Meri's lawyers, and obviously you haven't either, but everyone's talking."

"No one's talked to me," I nervously responded, and that only made Shanna-Francine sigh even more heavily.

"Right, I know. Look, I think you should also know that every-one is trying really-really hard to protect you. Meri could file criminal charges—and she has every right to. And Cindy, I'll be completely honest here. I just don't get you anymore. I mean, you're one of the coolest, most super-fabulous girls I know, but lately, um, you know, I don't know, do you really want to be here? At Alpha Beta Delta?" Then she admitted that the house took a secret vote regarding my status after the toilet bowl explosion, and she even told me that she voted to have me removed from the house. "It's one of the ugliest things I've ever done," she said, and I believed she felt that way. She seemed so nervously plaintive, and the merry high pitch was gone from her voice. "It felt like I was stabbing you in the back or something, and that's so not appro-priate," she continued. "But Cindy, I just don't feel equipped to help you with whatever it is you're going through right now. No one does. Not even Patty."

Yeah, because she's flying on tina, I thought grimly. But I blurted out with, "Meri's the criminal. I wish you could see that. She's the criminal. Not me." Hmm, not bad, I thought; that can serve as my provocative Meri-question for Shanna-Francine. I even repeated myself. "Meri is the real criminal."

Shanna-Francine looked at me with a wounded expression; she didn't know what to say. She was obviously thinking, *This girl's lost it and I don't know how to handle it*, but instead she cautiously intoned, "There won't be any more votes, okay? I promise. No one's kicking anyone out of the house. But for the good of the house, I just, I think . . ."

Oh my God, she wanted me to leave Alpha Beta Delta voluntarily. I felt my eyes welling up with tears. She quickly handed me a tissue.

"Just think about it. Okay? Think about what's best for you. Will you do that?"

I choked back a sob. "Meri's the real criminal," I repeated, and then I walked out of her room. *Feel absolutely nothing*, I told myself, *because Meri wants all of this to hurt. Badly. Just concentrate. Keep the focus.* I had done everything I needed to do. I had asked the possible moles their individual questions. Everything was in place. If I get an e-mail about scabies, the mole is Patty; if I get an e-mail about Rupert the Retard, it's Lindsay; if I get one about split ends, then Bobbie's the one; and if I get an e-mail discussing Meri's criminal status, then I know the mole is Shanna-Francine.

It's three thirty in the morning now. I still haven't received any e-mail. Nothing! Oh my God, maybe Meri's onto me. Maybe she can read my mind.

October 31

Dear Diary:

I tumbled through a crack in reality today! Oh, how come nothing in my life unfolds the way I want it to? Or think it will? I woke up late this morning—I must have pushed away my alarm clock, because I found it on the floor—and when I groggily padded downstairs and into the kitchen for an appropriate cup of coffee, all the girls were eagerly bustling around, carrying huge trays and covered bowls of cruelty-free snacks, along with several gargantuan bolts of woven bunting and other party supplies for the Fall Harvest Ball tonight. Was I imagining things? No one was looking at me or acknowledging my presence. When I saw Shanna-Francine, she quickly looked away, then hustled past.

"Sorry, Cindy. Kind of in a rush."

"Where's Patty?" I yelped to no one in particular as I stepped toward the living room. "And Lindsay?"

"Patty's at the RU Rehab Clinic," boomed Bobbie, who was manfully (I hate to use that adjective, but it really is the most appropriate one) hefting three long metal tables, their legs folded, toward the front door. "Lindsay took her there. I think she's out front with the truck right now."

"Is everything okay?" I asked.

"Everything's fine," she said in a voice I recognized as politely forced. "You know. With Patty. She'll be fine."

And then she was out the door before I had time to ask her if everything was all right . . . with me. Because the look in her eye told me that she knew something else. Something awful. Had Meri filed charges? Had Boom-Boom Bixby finally reached the end of the line? Oh, I hate being treated like a child. No, scratch that. I hate being treated like an unstable psycho who can't be told the truth. I rushed upstairs to change out of my robe and into my clothes. I figured I might as well help load up all the supplies and that way convince someone—anyone—to spill the beans. Then I saw my e-mail blinking. I had a new message. I stood there motionless for a moment, chilled to the bone, because the e-mail was from me. Now I would know. The mole would be revealed! The wiring in my brain began fritzing, as if I were a big klunky robot and someone had flipped my destruct-o switch. But my hand moved independently, snaking slowly toward the keyboard. I hit a few keys. And read my new mail.

From: cindybixby@yahoo.com
Date: 31 October
To: cindybixby@yahoo.com

Very funny.
Do you really think your retard rumor will stick?
How sad. Maybe YOU'RE the retard. Ha! That's it.
You're a big fucking retard! Hahahahahaha!

Kisses,
:)

I read and reread the e-mail several times— and each time it felt like a daggar was being stabbed into my heart. No! It couldn't be! I was flooded with emotions—outrage, disbelief, harrowing sadness. Lindsay is the mole. N-o-o-o-o-o-o-o! It can't be. I read the e-mail again. And again. And then I grew angry. How could I have been so foolish? Something terrible was building up inside of me. The sadness was pushed aside. Now all I felt was cold, throbbing fury. I was a robot again. Robo-Cindy. My kill switch had been activated. I wailed with anguish and bolted out of my room, and then I ran down the stairs and I pushed open the front door and then I saw her, standing behind Bobbie's Chevy Avalanche, her umbrella raised, the jewels from her tiara glinting in the sunlight—and her face, the face of my betrayer! I must have still been screaming. I flew toward her, my hands and arms outstretched. And she ran! She shot like the wind across the street, yelping with fear. I was right behind her, my legs pumping furiously, tears streaking my cheeks, my heart shattering into a billion pieces. My closest friend! My betrayer!

Car horns blasted. I kept running. We were on the Great Lawn. She was desperately fleeing, zigzagging past the students playing Frisbee and Hacky Sack, her umbrella by now roughly upended. And then I leaped into the air—howling in outrage, craving revenge—and I fell on top of her and her tiara tumbled herky-jerky to the ground and her umbrella went flying and that's when I saw it! Oh my God, oh my God, oh my God, I couldn't believe it, but there it was—and in that instant, I violently clamped my hand across her mouth, because she was just about to scream. I made a fierce shushing motion with my other hand. Her eyes widened in confusion. I pointed. Terror-stricken, she turned her head. She saw it too! She struggled against my hold, wailing frantically, though my hand successfully kept her stifled. Now we knew. We both knew. Lindsay was not the mole. There was no mole. But there was the tiara. When it fell to the ground, one of its large, sparkling, encrusted rubies had popped loose, revealing a small black mini-mic weighing less than an ounce, carefully glued against the metal setting. Meri hadn't lied. There were no mics hidden in Alpha Beta Delta. I forced a smile, because I wanted to sound as casual as possible.

"It's so nice to get in a good jog before the day starts. Don't you think?" Then I nodded to her, imploring her to play along, and she anxiously nodded back. Cautiously, I released my hand from her mouth.

"I'd love to get some new Pumas," she said, her voice trembling slightly. Then she mouthed, "What the fuck?"

"Keep talking," I mouthed, and she did, chattering nervously, but not too nervously, about the virtues of New Balance, and Mythos Racers, and Reeboks, and as she did, I picked up the loose ruby and pressed it carefully back into place. We would need a more permanent solution—maybe superglue would work—but for now it would have to do. We both stood up, and I placed the tiara gently in her hands. Sadly, her Bottega Veneta was pretty mangled; its wiring now tore through the leatherette material, giving it the look of a slightly disfigured crème-dotted little alien whose guts had been split open. We kept up our conversation about running shoes, but she shed a tear when she tossed the umbrella into a trash can as we headed back to Alpha Beta Delta, and I knew what she was thinking, because when we stepped out from beneath the relative safety of the overhanging trees that outlined the Great Lawn, the sun bore down harshly. Luckily, I was wearing a light jacket against the autumn breeze, and I quickly took it off and gave it to her. She held it in a position above her head, giving herself at least some protection. *Poor Lindsay*, I thought. As we kept up our fakey conversation, I mouthed, "I'm so sorry." She made a shushing motion, smiled sweetly, and mouthed, "I know."

We continued onward—and I sensed Meri's passage through the air. Her fragrance filled the outlying area. *Impossible*, I thought.

Meri? Here? Now? A startling roar jolted through me. I knew that roar. It was Purrfect! Lindsay and I were still talking aimlessly about running shoes, but I gave her my best please-tell-me-I'm-not-totally-crazy look, and she must have known what it meant, because she stopped talking about running shoes and lightly segued into:

"Oh, I have some news. I was going to wake you up this morning, but Shanna-Francine said to let you sleep."

"What n-news?" I stuttered.

"Meri's not suing or filing criminal charges against RU. Or Alpha Beta Delta. Or you. Isn't that great? The Sugarman lawyers and RU reached a compromise. See, Meri's been doing so well with her community work—I think the *Rumson River Daily Gazette* is doing another article about her."

She continued babbling. But I didn't need to listen. It was all too clear. Meri had taken stunning tactical advantage of her invitation to the Forgiveness Day Dinner. Under the threat of a lawsuit, and the embarrassing publicity it would surely generate, RU had pathetically caved. Meri was welcomed back. No more community college. No more Boho chic. Good-bye, Ronkonkomo. She was here. And closer than ever—to me, and to Alpha Beta Delta.

"Everyone loves a comeback," I half-mumbled. Then I saw her. She was strolling past the Polk Academic Building in a breezy short-skirted Prada ensemble with sharp spiky knee-high Jimmy Choos, her lustrous raven hair flung back with a cashmere headband, a gold Panthère de Cartier necklace gleaming around her neck. In one hand, her Miu Miu, in the other, a thin black leather leash that she gently tugged to keep Purrfect in line. Already a small crowd of adoring fans were gathered around her; a few professors, equally stylish students (though none possessed Meri's singular flair), and of course, Nester and ROT, who were furiously flashing pictures and peppering her with questions. Quite a step up from the burnouts at Chappaqua. Her head turned toward me. She smiled and waved. I was bewildered. Was she looking past me? Lindsay and I turned around. Keith was crossing the street with Bitch Kitty, who wore a low-cut T with "Good Girl!" spangled across her ample bosom. More like Dead Girl if Meri has anything to do with it.

"She wants him back," I said out loud. Lindsay made an insistent shushing motion, then gestured to her tiara, but I didn't think stating the obvious would do any harm. Meri wants everything back that she had before. Everything. And that includes Keith. He waved back at her and almost seemed to smile. Rags was with him, and I wondered how Purrfect and Rags might get along. It didn't feel hurtful when Keith and Meri waved to each other. Not at all. What hurt was that Keith didn't even seem to notice me. I was in eighth grade again. I was the invisible ugly ducking. I was nothing. And for a second, I remembered my eighth grade Valentine's Day. I didn't receive a single card from anyone that day (except from Mr. Dee, my social studies teacher, who wrote on my card, "To Cindy, one of my most well-behaved students. Best, Mr. Dee") (but then Mr. Dee gave a Valentine card to all of his students) (and that "Best" was like a bullet) (Lisa, of course, came home with a grocery bag full of cards) (of course). There's an old Alfred, Lord Tennyson poem, "In Memoriam," with a quote that goes "'Tis better to have loved and lost, than never to have loved at all." I tried to seek comfort from that as it popped into my head—I loved Keith, I lost him, but I had, in fact, loved him. Unfortunately, it didn't work, because I knew "In Memoriam" wasn't a poem about an ill-fated love affair (as many people assume from the quote), it's a eulogy for Arthur Hallam, Tennyson's deceased best friend (and besides, Tennyson ended up marrying Emily Sellwood, the pretty daughter of a wealthy solicitor, so what the heck did he know about lost love anyway?). Yes, my mind frequently seeks comfort from all the books that I've read, but this time, it felt like they were biting back at me and saying, "Comfort? So sorry. We're clean out. Please come again. Buh-bye." Keith. My love, my sweet, my everything. How hollow those words sound now.

"I'm hungry for Long John's," said Lindsay with a forced smile, tugging at my arm. "Aren't you?"

I didn't answer, because Meri, turning her gaze away from Keith, briefly caught my eye and smiled—just slightly—with a smoothness that could have been mistaken for sincerity, but which really seemed to be saying, *Destroying you is such fun.*

"Am I being kicked out of RU?" I suddenly yelped, and again Lindsay forced a smile.

"C'mon. Long John's. Chicken Planks. Mmmm."

Lindsay's so smart! At Long John's we stood in line and made small talk for the tiara while we got our meals, and then, when we passed the soda dispensers, she stopped short and deliberately said, "Let's sit here. At this booth." I looked at her, perplexed, but she was way ahead of me. She wrapped the tiara in my jacket, gently stuffed it behind the dispenser, and added, "God, I'm so hungry. Let's just sit here and eat." Then she took my hand, rushed me to a booth on the opposite side of the restaurant, and whispered, "Does this—does this mean Auntie Christiana never even had a tiara?" She was ready to burst into tears. I felt so bad for her.

"I don't know," I fumbled. "I'm sure you can . . ."

"Damn her. Oh, now I really hate her. Meri knows I'm fucking addicted to eBay," she snapped, her anger rising. "I just can't figure it out. The only person bidding against me was 'GoPepperGo,' and that doesn't make any sense."

"Go pepper what?" I asked, and I guess I was a little too loud, because she shushed me. Then she told me all about Patty. She's not doing well. She's in the midst of a painful medical detox, and she's refusing to meet with rehab counselors and psychologists because she's handling her "core issues" on her own and "doesn't need therapy." She even bit the hand of one of the nurses and screamed at Pigboy to get out of her room. She just wants Skinny. More Skinny. Campus security stormed Wolfgang Rimmer's dorm room, but they didn't find any pseudoephedrine or iodine crystals or any of the other stuff you apparently need to make crystal meth, and Wolfgang himself has mysteriously vanished.

"Meri's protecting him," I said. Thanks to the tiara, Wolfgang must have had ample warning in terms of clearing out his room and skipping town for a few days. I told Lindsay everything I knew, including the murderous truth about Nancy Forbes and my own theory that Meri's out to destroy all my friends at Alpha Beta Delta, and not just me.

At the same time, I couldn't stop thinking about "GoPepperGo." I ran it back and forth in my head several times. "GoPepperGo." "GoPepperGo." Then I froze. All the little crumbs in the forest led right back to Jackie O. Starting with Pepper. Sergeant Suzanne "Pepper" Anderson. The lead character on the old *Police Woman* TV series (Lisa and I used to watch it on Nick at Night; she thought it was "like, more real" than *Charlie's Angels*). Pepper was played by Angie Dickinson, a now aging Hollywood beauty who's best known for that TV series, along with her scandalous affairs with Frank Sinatra . . . and President John F. Kennedy, who was married to Jackie O. And then I remembered a certain movie night at Alpha Beta Delta. When Meri was president. And Gloria Daily was vice president. We were watching *Dressed to Kill*, this really scary movie in which Angie Dickinson plays an oversexed middle-aged housewife who picks up some hot guy in a museum and then lets him go down on her in a cab. Gloria was screaming with laughter during that scene.

"Okay, if you're Jackie, then I'm Angie," she had said.

"Deal," cooed Meri. They sealed their pact with a just-us-girls high five.

"Where's Gloria?" I blurted out. I already knew the answer in the back of my head, but Lindsay reminded me. Gloria had been arrested with Meri after they fled Alpha Beta Delta and tried to evade capture in Vegas. The *Rumson River Daily Gazette* had reported: "Ms. Gloria Daily, whom the court determined initiated most of the illegal activities that Ms. Sugarman was also charged with, will be serving a six-month sentence at the Fairfield Women's Correctional Facility." My mind burst with questions. Does Gloria have access to the Internet in prison? Was she "GoPepperGo"? She had to be. And if so, is she somehow skilled enough to send e-mails to me (that look like they're from me) from a prison computer? And where, exactly, does the tiara's mic send its signal? To Meri? Gloria? Albino Girl? Nancy Forbes? All of them?

"Oh, and get ready for Friday," Lindsay abruptly warned me. Safely away from the tiara, she could now tell me about whether or not I was being kicked out of RU. She didn't know exactly, she informed me, but when Shanna-Francine heard the news about Meri this morning, and the deal Meri cut with Rumson, she also received a call from Dean Pointer. Since I was still asleep, he instructed Shanna-Francine to tell me that I'm to report to his office this coming Friday. At noon. Just me. And the dean. And my parents on speakerphone.

"So Friday's it," I gasped. "I'm out."

"We don't know that," implored Lindsay, but even she wasn't able to put a positive spin on this. I thought, *Unless I can expose Meri by this Friday at noon, then that's it, I'm out. And Meri's won.*

"I've got to talk to Gloria," I murmured, mostly to myself. Finishing our meal, we tiptoed back to the soda dispenser, where

Lindsay carefully retrieved the tiara and broadly announced, "Gosh, I'm stuffed. Aren't you?"

I didn't answer. I was still thinking about Gloria as we stepped out of the restaurant. I thought, *What does Gloria know and what, exactly, is she doing to help Meri? And is there some way that I can get her to talk, or at least slip up and reveal something?*

Out of nowhere, a high-pitched, squealing voice called out, "There you are!"

A trendy-looking BMX Mongoose Mischief bicycle skillfully swerved in front of us and—*boing*—off hopped Sebastian Plummer, smiling to beat the band, thrusting his iPod speaker buds at me. "I've been listening to it nonstop a-a-a-a-all day," he gushed. I placed the buds in my ears. Why did I do that? I really wasn't in the mood to hear:

> *Oh, touch it, touch it, touch it!*
> *Touch my daisy*
> *Touch it, yeah!*

"It's her best ever," shrieked Sebastian, who was obviously more than thrilled to have received his own Lissa-autographed "Touch My Daisy" CD single (along with a stern letter telling him that she'll "s-o-o-o sue his ass" if he makes copies of it). "If there's anything I can do to repay you," he continued, "just name it." In that instant, I realized that there was.

"Let me borrow your bike," I commanded. Sebastian balked; he had just bought the bike (he's training for the upcoming Icicle Bicycle Festival in Chicago) (which includes the Gay Icicle Bicycle Winter Parade and the Icicle Bicycle Bar-Hopping Gala in "Boystown"), but I wasn't in the mood to negotiate. I grabbed the handlebars and bellowed (loud enough for the tiara to pick up),

"Meri's doing community service today. I'm following her," then I gave Lindsay a broad wink. She wasn't following, and I didn't care. I hopped on the bike and took off. Sebastian cried out, "Be careful with the mag wheels!"

I tore down the street, and no, I wasn't headed to St. Eulalia's, or Nancy Forbes's house. I was on my way to the Fairfield Women's Correctional Facility to see Gloria, and I trusted my pedal power to get me there faster than any crosstown bus. I have only four days to expose Meri and save not just myself, but everyone at Alpha Beta Delta, too—which probably explains the fantastic speeds I reached on Sebastian's bike (I had to be going at least twenty miles an hour) (or more), as well as my skillful maneuvering through traffic. When I swerved down a main thoroughfare, however, I heard what sounded like hard plastic slapping on cement. I turned around—and I couldn't believe what I saw. Soaring straight up into the air over the center divider on ghetto-fabulous Hello Kitty skateboards were Albino Girl and three other St. Eulalia girls, all of them in their tartan plaid school uniforms, their faces grimly determined, blasting right toward me. I screamed—and pedaled a whole lot faster.

But, oh darn it, they were gaining. And then ka-pow! A bone-crushing explosion of water smacked me in the back of my head. I was nearly knocked off my bike. I whipped around. All four of the girls were aiming Super-Shooter Aquapack squirt guns at me; you know, the type that can shoot up to thirty-five feet? And they hurt! Another blast streamed past—I ducked just in time. Then I jerked my wheel and daringly cut across the lane. Car horns were blasting. I flew over the center divider and into the opposite lane, narrowly evading an oncoming truck as it slammed its brakes.

Holy crap, I thought, I've gotta lose these psycho schoolgirls. I sped desperately down a side street, only to find it jammed with street construction. *Ka-pow!* I was blasted in the head by another shot from a Super-Shooter. I tipped violently on my bike—and my leg stuck out just in time, stopping my fall. Then I whipped around and pedaled with all my strength, zooming right past the girls, who were whizzing forth in the opposite direction. Ha! So there! But I didn't have the advantage for long, because as I turned the corner, I looked back and saw all four of the girls zooming right for a bulldozer—and then, one by one, they powerfully launched off its huge curved blade, using it as a ramp. *Whoosh!* They soared into the air, executed perfect board flips, then hit the ground and sped right back toward me.

Ka-pow! Another blast beamed me in the head. Ouch! Then another. And another. *Ka-pow! Ka-pow!* Could my head take much more? I was beginning to get dizzy, but I pedaled faster. They were still gaining. Then Albino Girl swerved right up to my side, screaming in triumph, and reached out and grabbed my hair—and she pulled hard, nearly yanking me off the bike. I violently kicked my leg out and struck her in the midsection. Down she went— *boom!*—hitting the ground hard. I didn't wait for the other three to catch up. I hiked my front wheel up over the curb and into Fairfield Park, cycling frantically across a very bumpy, grassy surface that even St. Eulalia girls couldn't skateboard across. *Ka-pow!* I was beamed in the back by another Super-Shooter blast. But I was getting away. I looked back quickly. They were at the edge of the park, clutching their skateboards, aiming their Super-Shooters, their blasts now failing to reach me.

The Fairfield Women's Correctional Facility is at the end of a long gravel road that runs straight through a wheat field, one that seems to stretch to the horizon no matter which way you look. I slowed down a bit on my bike, catching my breath. It was quiet— almost too quiet. All I could hear was my breathing, the sound of my bicycle wheels crunching against the gravel, and the eerily rustling stalks of wheat (which had a sound similar to rain, but like rain that was far, far away). I was nearing the facility, and oddly enough, it looked similar to Chappaqua Community College. It had the same cluster of blocky nondescript buildings, but with a much different feel, mostly because of the super-creepy barbed-wire fencing that surrounded it. *Can I really do this?* I asked myself. I felt a soft nudge of anxiety after I parked my bike and stepped into the main building, but to my relief, everything was a snap. I simply told the unsmiling (but not unfriendly) lady at the front desk that I was here to see Gloria Daily, and she gestured to the visitors' room at the end of the hall. Gloria would meet with me shortly, I was told, if she was available.

The visitors' room continued the facility's nondescript design scheme; it was like a cafeteria with tables and chairs, but with no soda pop or mystery meat. A few visitors and prisoners were gathered at various tables, murmuring softly, some of them clutching each other's hands (you could tell who the prisoners were, because they all wore a light blue blouse and blue pants). The door at the other end of the room creaked open—and I held my breath. There she was. Gloria Daily. She looked hardened and impatient. Different somehow. Her eyes scanned the room. I smiled faintly to catch her attention (like a ding-dong) (but at least I didn't wave). She rolled her eyes, walked up to the table, plopped into a seat and snapped, "Got a cigarette?"

"Sorry, I don't smoke," I nervously responded.

"Yeah? Well then, fuck you." She stood up to walk away.

"Gloria, please, it's me," I stammered. That stopped her short for some reason. She turned around slowly, grinning strangely from ear to ear. *Oh my God*, I thought, *do I even know Gloria anymore?* This was definitely a different Gloria, and it was beginning to freak me out. She sat back down, lazily retrieved a cigarette from a pack she had rolled up in her blouse sleeve, torched it with a match, and took a deep drag.

"Okay. So who the fuck are you? And what do you want?"

"Gloria, it's me," I whispered. "Cindy Bixby." Her eyes widened.

"Well well. The little bow-wow," she chuckled.

"That's right," I said, and I attempted to chuckle along with her. Then I thought, *Hurry, find out what you can and then get the heck out of here*. So I plunged right in, asking her, "Do you guys have access to the Internet here?"

"Why? You wanna be my pen pal? Wanna get married after I'm released?"

"Um, no, not that . . ."

"Aw, too bad," she snickered. "But no, no Internet. Damn shame, too. I miss my Page Six. Hey, wanna mail me some *New York Posts*?'"

I didn't have any idea what she was talking about, but if she didn't have access to the Internet, then how was she sending me e-mails (from me), and how did "GoPepperGo" bid against Lindsay on eBay in order to get her excited about the tiara? I was so confused.

"But you're 'GoPepperGo,' aren't you?" I vainly asked. "Or is that Meri? I mean, you're the one who's into Angie Dickinson, right?"

She gazed at me blankly. Then she took a deep drag from her cigarette and blew smoke in my face.

"Your hair's tragic."

"Gloria . . ."

"You didn't bring me shit. Not even a lousy cigarette. That sucks. No wonder everyone hates you."

"How much is Meri paying you?" I blurted out. That got a response. She angrily gritted her teeth.

"Not enough."

217

"I'll bet," I continued, anxious to trip her up. "And after every-thing you did for her. And everything you're doing now. That must make you really mad."

Uh-oh. She snapped. She pushed her face into mine, her nos-trils flared, her brown eyes narrowed. "Look. Why don't you do me a favor? Okay? Why don't you tell Meri and Gloria that I'd at least appreciate some goddamn fucking cigarettes. All right? Think you can handle that?"

I stammered for a response, I was so shocked. "Why don't you tell Meri and Gloria?" What did that mean? Oh my God, oh my God, oh my God! I wasn't sitting across from Gloria at all. I was sitting across from . . . what? Her imposter? Her doppelgänger? In literature, doppelgängers, or doubles, often appear as a warn-ing sign of some terrible disaster that's about to happen (Edgar Allan Poe uses them extensively in "The Tell-Tale Heart" and "The Fall of the House of Usher"). Was something awful about to happen to me? Was the prison going to explode? Was I going to explode? Gloria's doppelgänger reached out and fingered my hair, sneering.

"Try a better conditioner. Or maybe shave it all off and start over." Then she laughed, cruelly, and blew more smoke in my face.

"Who are you?" I gasped. She snickered.

"You can go now. Go on. Get the hell out of here before I scratch your eyes out. Or maybe just one. One-Eyed Cindy. That could be fun. What do you think? Do you want to wear an eye patch?"

I was cycling way faster than I needed to as I sped away from the Correctional Facility. Night had fallen, and I could barely see, so I trusted my ears—knowing that my wheels were on the path when I heard the hard crunch of gravel, and straying when I heard quickly shifting dirt. *All that anger*, I thought, *under the flat brown sur-face of her eyes.* And then I thought, *Gloria has blue eyes, not brown!*

There was my proof. It couldn't have been Gloria I was talking to in prison. Now I knew for certain.

"Why don't you tell Meri and Gloria that I'd at least appreciate some goddamn fucking cigarettes."

I tried reasoning with myself. Doppelgängers are in literature, not real life. I had just seen Gloria—and yes, admittedly, she was a newly hardened Gloria, but who wouldn't be after spending time in prison (minimum security or not)? Maybe she wore blue contact lenses while at Alpha Beta Delta (that's certainly possible). But why had she referred to "Gloria" when she demanded cigarettes? My reasoning didn't work. There was no way around it. There was no way that could have been Gloria in prison. So who the heck was it? As I sped nervously through the outlying town near RU, I could see clusters of preschool-aged trick-or-treaters with their parents; ghosts, witches, Paris Hiltons, and boys who looked like they wore no costume at all, save for the telltale little lightning bolts on their foreheads. I was racking my brain. What had I learned? Not much, or at least nothing I hadn't already guessed when I first read in the *Rumson River Daily Gazette* that Gloria was going to serve time. I figured there had to be a pretty decent payoff waiting for her, since she was taking the fall and doing the time, but obviously "not enough" of a payoff, and if I believed anything that "Gloria" had just said to me, it was that. That and the fact that she had no way of accessing the Internet.

When I arrived back at Alpha Beta Delta, the house was swarming with activity. The Fall Harvest Ball was set to start in two hours at RU's auditorium. Lindsay raced up to me and grabbed my arm.

"Hurry, I'm in the shower."

Then she yanked me upstairs to her room, explaining that she had left her tiara in the (working) bathroom.

"How long has it been in there?" I asked.

"Little over an hour," she said, firmly closing her door.

"That long?"

"I know, I know, but maybe I'm masturbating. Oh, and I bought some glue. Everything's put back together. Quick, look at this. Anyone look familiar?"

She thrust a thick pile of printouts into my hand. The top sheet had a picture of Albino Girl from the *Ronkonkomo Daily News*. But Lindsay didn't wait for me to read it.

"Her name's Eileen. Eileen Forbes. Get it?"

I gasped. So Albino Girl had a name. I quickly scanned the article. Eileen is the granddaughter of Nancy Forbes; the article detailed Eileen's arrest, subsequent indictment, and brief stay at Juvenile Hall just one year ago for setting off three cherry bombs in the girls' room toilets at Ronkonkomo Elementary School. Criminal behavior seems to run in Nancy's family. I grimaced, trying to put the pieces together.

"Wait a minute, Albino Girl goes to St. Eulalia's," I said out loud.

"Now she does," added Lindsay. "And it costs a pretty penny, too. Look." She flipped to the next printout ,from the St. Eulalia's Web site. "Fourteen thousand dollars a year. Think it pays for the uniform? Oh, and look at this." She impatiently flipped to another printout. It was a student picture from the Shirley Central High School yearbook in Shirley, Long Island. And I knew who it was.

"It's Gloria," I said.

"Very good," said Lindsay. "I didn't recognize her at first with all that teased hair. And let's not even talk about her eye shadow. What is it with those Long Island girls? Now look at this." She flipped to another picture from the yearbook. And my heart stopped.

"That's Gilda," said Lindsay. "She's—"

"I know who she is," I gulped. "I just met her." I breathlessly explained everything to Lindsay about my visit to the Fairfield

Women's Correctional Facility, and as I did, it all started to make sense. Of course Gloria seemed "different." Why? Because I didn't meet Gloria—and I didn't meet her doppelgänger, either. I met Gilda, her twin sister (with brown eyes) (and a nasty cigarette habit).

"What does it all mean?" asked Lindsay.

Boom boom boom! There was pounding on the door. Lindsay shrieked, grabbed the printouts, and stuffed them under her comforter. Bobbie's voice boomed.

"Everyone to the auditorium! Now!"

Lindsay and I scrambled. I raced with her to the bathroom and she swung open the door, gave me a wink, then carefully closed the door so the tiara's mic wouldn't pick up a door slam. I waited. And waited. And I was just about to open the door when I heard an extravagant gasping moan from inside.

"Ayiiiiiiiyahhhhhhh!"

Bobbie was striding past—and she stopped, obviously startled.

"It's nothing," I said, attempting to cover. "She's um, she's just . . ."

"She bop-a-we bop," said Bobbie with a wink. "Ain't no law against it."

"Yeah, whatever," I snapped.

"Oh, c'mon," she scoffed, then she leaned in close, whispering lewdly. "I mean, you're the one listening by the door, not me." Then she chuckled and headed down the stairs. And I turned twelve billion shades of red. And then:

"Ayiiiiiiiyahhhhhhh!"

Oh, for Pete's sake, I thought, *whoever's listening on the other end of that mic is going to think Lindsay's doing a circus act or something.* And then:

"Ayiiiiiiiyahhhhhhh!"

Okay, enough (I mean, really)! I reached for the doorknob—then the shower sound extinguished and the door swung open, revealing Lindsay, delightedly smiling, giving me a playful wink, the (repaired) tiara planted firmly on her head. She was obviously so proud of herself.

"Hi, Cindy," she squealed. "Are you headed to the auditorium? Gosh, that's where I'm going."

I rolled my eyes. It's nice to know that I'm not the only bad actress in our little group. We walked together to the auditorium, passing several RU students dressed up in Halloween costumes. Who knew where they were going—maybe there were a few secret Halloween beer busts somewhere—but all those witches and goblins weren't likely to be allowed into the Harvest Ball. When we arrived, Melissa Etheridge's "I Really Like You" was blasting from the speakers, and I have to admit, I was initially awed by the festive decorations. The first thing that stood out was the gargantuan netting on the ceiling that held what looked like hundreds of red, yellow, and orange balloons for the Balloon Drop (each balloon contained a prize); and then there were the small conversation tables with orange flat paper and cute little tissue pumpkins; large bales of hay, cornstalks, and uncarved pumpkins spray painted gold and wrapped with bows made of raffia; olive, orange, and green crepe paper and bunting that had been artfully twirled and hung to create small archways and semiprivate areas; long tables with all the (appropriate) snacks and cider and other refreshments; along with two truly wonderful disco balls over the dance floor that had alternating silver and gold mirrored facets, creating a uniquely flashy lightning scheme. Shanna-Francine was at the front selling tickets, with a large sign above her that read, HELP THE CHILDREN'S HOSPITAL! and parked out front was a large tractor-pull hayride ready for all comers.

But there was a problem. There were no comers. In fact, there was no one there at all except for the girls of Alpha Beta Delta (minus Patty). Poor Bobbie. She was manning the videocamera that had been taken away from me, all too eagerly taping, and probably hoping against hope that she'd soon have something more to shoot than Shanna-Francine smiling nervously in front, or me and Lindsay standing awkwardly before the refreshment tables.

"I don't get it," said Lindsay. "We publicized the crap out of this thing."

I "got it." Meri's back. And Meri had to have put the kibosh on this (and probably all future) Alpha Beta Delta events. I turned to Lindsay and mouthed, "Meri," and she sighed nervously, nodding her head in agreement. Then the most astounding thing happened. I heard Shanna-Francine shriek, "Of course you can! You can buy as many tickets as you like!"

I whipped around. There she was. Seemingly blown forth by a soft autumn breeze. She was dressed in a stunning (and I'll wager Zen-influenced) Jil Sander ensemble with soft brown and burgundy earth tones. Around her neck hung a glittery five-diamond necklace (with the diamonds in the shapes of hearts, clubs, and spades). Her thick raven hair seemed to flutter gracefully all on its own, as if a model shoot wind machine was being kept hidden just out of eyesight (and presumably following her wherever she chose to go). Lindsay couldn't help herself.

"Jesus Christ, does she have a fucking stylist or something?"

There were several groupies with Meri, all of whom bought tickets from a beaming Shanna-Francine. A hand abruptly grasped my arm, yanked me aside.

"Okay, if you feel like freakin', then go," bellowed Bobbie. "I mean, I think you should stay. I think it's, you know, good, uh . . ."

"Exposure therapy?" I said, inwardly chuckling. For some reason, I wasn't afraid of Meri here, because I knew that if I kept myself a safe distance from her, and in the eyeline of witnesses, she couldn't do anything. And that's not all. *My head may be on the chopping block this coming Friday with the dean, but maybe*, I thought, *I can use this night as an example of my newly chilled-out attitude toward Meri.* "I'm fine," I assured Bobbie. "And if I feel I'm not, or if you think I'm not, then I'll go. I promise."

"Atta girl," she said, giving my shoulder a (kind of painful) punch. It was then that I noticed her Mohawk. Why didn't I see it before? She had dyed it bright orange for the occasion.

"I like your Mohawk," I said.

"You do?" she asked, and then she blushed. "It was Shanna-Francine's idea." She looked over my shoulder and gave a little wave to Shanna-Francine. I turned around. Shanna-Francine coyly waved back. I tell you, if I didn't know any better (but I put those thoughts out of my head) (and not because it's gross) (though it sort of is) (to me).

"Where's the candy corn?" screeched a familiar snot-nosed voice. Bud had arrived. And he saw me. He waved.

"Dude."

"Don't call me dude," I snapped. Then I forced a smile as he snaked his grubby paw around Lindsay's waist, and I thought, *Holy moly, that tiara mic must have picked up lots of super-scuzzo stuff in Lindsay's bedroom and Bud's dorm room. What a violation!* But there were other things racing through my mind, and I knew Lindsay and I had to talk, so I pulled Bud away from her and discreetly whispered in his ear, giving him his instructions. He didn't understand the urgency, so I was more insistent. He sighed and held up three fingers ("whatevs"), but to his credit he went through with it. Le Tigre's "TKO" blasted as he took Lindsay's hand and swept her to the dance floor, and they really-really danced, and fast (Bud sort of looked like a spastic piece of vibrating spaghetti), and just as I'd hoped, he goofily grabbed both of her arms and twirled her around, and her tiara nearly flew off her head. I heard him scream over the music, "Maybe we oughta set that down."

Good job, Bud, I thought. He led her off the dance floor and

Lindsay set her tiara on a bale of hay right next to one of the speakers. Perfect. I didn't want to be too obvious (and run right over to her), but I didn't have to worry because Bud, who had no idea what was going on, led her right back to the dance floor. I glanced around. Had Meri seen anything? No, she hadn't—but I was momentarily caught off guard by what I did see. The auditorium was beginning to fill up, and a line was forming out front for tickets.

I scrutinized the situation further. Practically everyone who was stepping inside strolled right toward Meri, as if she were a great planet and all her moons were desperate to orbit around her. Meri's mere presence had obviously made it "okay" to attend, and I almost immediately felt a flutter of unease, because helping Alpha Beta Delta, I knew, couldn't possibly be on Meri's agenda. Which means she had to have something up her (earth-toned) sleeves. But what? My throat was drying up. My heart began thumping. Was I getting dizzy? I didn't trust my surroundings. And I didn't trust the sight of all those happy, beaming faces that were gathering around Meri either, including Nester and ROT, who were screaming questions and flashing pictures (as usual). No matter what she was doing or who she was talking to, Meri managed to tilt her head toward Nester's camera and run the gamut of quick facial expressions for each and every flash—shock, concern, laughter, even an impish wink. Then Nester aimed his camera toward me.

Oh, no you don't, I thought. I turned right back around—and crashed into Pigboy's (admittedly huge and magnificent) chest. Tears were streaming down his face.

"Have you seen Patty?" he cried out. Then he told me everything. Patty's gone AWOL! Her rehab bed is empty. All anyone could find was a note on her pillow that said, "Gone for Skinny, be back soon!"

"Where's Wolfgang?" I yelped, knowing that this would likely be the first place Patty would go in search of more trick (or tina) (or tweak) (or whatever the heck it is). But no go. Pigboy went to Wolfgang's dorm room—and found the door busted clear open and the room itself savagely ransacked, along with another note from Patty that screamed, "Where ARE you??? Need more Skinny NOW!!!!"

"She went to my dorm room too," continued Pigboy, and to his horror, his room was also completely torn apart, and a stash of emergency cash he keeps hidden in his old junior high school football helmet was gone. There was no note.

"I'll help you look for her," I gasped.

But Pigboy told me to stay at the ball. He figured she might come looking for me, and everyone knew the ball was tonight. Then he choked back a sob, pushed through the crowd, and ran into the night. I covered my mouth in shock. Patty is out there, half-crazed (or completely crazed), desperate for Skinny. Who knows where her search will lead her? Fluttering laughter cut right through me. It was Meri, responding to something, or someone, but when I looked in her direction, her eyes narrowed and her smile widened, and she kept on laughing. And I knew what she was really laughing about. I stared at her, and I thought, *If anything happens to Patty, I'll kill you.* I guess I must have looked really gnarly, and I had no idea (at first) that my hands were tightening into fists, or that I was charging toward her, because Bobbie suddenly leaped up in front of me.

"Whoa, horsie. Is it time to go?"

"No, she just needs some cider," chirped Lindsay, who'd raced up and pulled me toward the refreshment tables. "Don't give her what she wants," she whispered.

"Patty's gone AWOL," I sputtered.

She ignored me, smiling brightly (maybe a little too brightly). She poured us both a cup of cider, led me beneath one of the hanging twirling crepe decorations, and leaned in close, still smiling. "Here's the way I figure it," she whispered conspiratorially. "She's finished. She can't do anything more because she won't be picking up anything else she can use from the tiara."

"That's pretty optimistic," I said. "And it still doesn't explain how I'm getting the e-mails, where Gloria . . ."

I didn't get to finish. A new song was now blaring (extra loud) from the speakers:

> *Oh, touch it, touch it, touch it!*
> *Touch my daisy*
> *Touch it, yeah!*

And just at that moment, I was (involuntarily) whisked to the dance floor by a bouncing, smiling, happy-happy Sebastian, who screamed, "Touch it, touch it, touch it!"

I had to laugh, and I thought, *Does Sebastian carry that CD with him wherever he goes?* I gamely danced with him—and his friend, too, a plain but nice-looking guy who kept staring at me and smiling.

"Do you like my Halloween costume?" he asked.

Huh? Who was this guy? Then he smiled broadly, threw his head back, and laughed. "Ah ha ha!"

Oh my God. It was Sheila Farr. In costume. Or not. Or something. I laughed along with him. And really, what could I say except, "Great costume, Sheila."

Then I nearly stumbled and fell flat on my face when I saw someone else—just a few feet away with Bitch Kitty (who wore a too-tight orange T with "Like Candy!" strewn across her vibrating, shimmy-shaking chest) (and I'm so not jealous, but hasn't she ever heard of a bra?). I could barely breathe. Keith was dancing barechested, and he was a little sweaty, and his T-shirt was hanging out of his jeans. So cute! But also too cute. He caught my glance, and I saw his face, and I swear I wasn't imagining things when he very sweetly mouthed, "Hi."

No no no no no! I wanted to scream out, no way, we cannot be friends who say "Hi," okay? It's so not fair. You cannot just say "Hi" and then stand there shaking your (awesome) six-pack in front of Bitch Kitty and expect me to be okay with it, because I'm not, because no matter how grown-up and mature and all laid back and chill I think I am, you're still my love, my sweet, my everything! Oh, I hate you, Keith Ryder, I hate you, I hate you, I hate you (and die, Bitch Kitty, just die) (and put on a bra)!

I ran off the dance floor—and I didn't care who saw me or what they thought. My hands reached out. I steadied myself on a large painted gourd. Then I wiped my cheeks. *Who was looking at me?* I thought. I scanned my surroundings. No one. Not even Meri, who was whispering unobtrusively to one of her fashion-challenged followers (her handbag said "Prado," not "Prada") (nice try, hon) (uch, I have to watch my new bitchy tongue) (but it's Meri's fault) (I'm so not bitchy) (normally). Apparently following Meri's orders, Miss Fashion-Challenged hip-swung her way to the DJ, whispered in his ear, and then all too abruptly, "Touch My Daisy" was cut off and replaced by another Melissa Etheridge song. I could hear Sebastian's yelp of outrage, but I was looking at Meri, who was gazing off into the distance at no one in particular and smiling in triumph, just slightly.

My anger rose. *Two can play that game,* I thought. I mean, I may find my sister totally annoying and her music outrageously trite (at best), but she's my sister, no one else's (not that anyone would take her) (except for Sebastian), and no one, not even Meri, is going to insult her (and me) by cutting off her latest filthy pop song. I stalked right up to the DJ and calmly (I thought) gave him my orders, and when he balked, I reminded him that I was a member of Alpha Beta Delta, the house that was throwing this little shindig, and Fashion-Challenged Girl was not. Reluctantly, he cut off Melissa Etheridge, and then "Lissa," in all her glory, was once more blaring from the speakers.

I coolly returned to the painted gourd—and that's when I realized that something was wrong. Really wrong. With the exception of Sebastian and (the disguised) Sheila, most of the people on the dance floor had stopped dancing, or they were stepping away, and practically everyone in the auditorium was now craning their necks, stifling giggles, eager to see how Meri would react. Oh my God, what had I done? Were they expecting a standoff? A fight? Was Meri about to attack me? She wasn't, of course, and my heart plunged, because I suddenly realized that she must have been waiting for just such an opportunity. She had lingered inconspicuously, like a snake, and then she pounced.

Or rather, she merely turned to her entourage, scrunched up her nose (just a bit, as if she'd suddenly caught a whiff of something really foul), and shook her head. Then she breezily strode out of the auditorium—just like that—her head held high, her lustrous raven hair scenting her departure. The Pied Piper has nothing on Meri. Only twenty minutes or so after she had arrived, she left, and like lemmings, just about everyone in the auditorium followed suit, much to Shanna-Francine's screaming horror.

"But you'll miss the Balloon Drop!" she wailed desperately. "Oh, c'mon, you guys. What about the hayride?"

All of the Alpha Beta Delta girls were trying to help, but it was no use—Meri had slashed, and the wound could not be healed. And still blasting from the speakers:

Oh, touch it, touch it, touch it!

How could I have been so dumb? Shouldn't I have recognized by now the power of Meri's celebrity? Everyone loves a comeback.

And though everyone loves an underdog, too, it was obviously Meri, and not me, who was perceived as the real underdog now; she was, after all, the beautiful girl who had, yes, "made a few mistakes," but like a phoenix rising up from its ashes, she was now selflessly, even heroically, paying her debt to society, and to everyone's gasping delight, she was even more beautiful than before, and golly gee, even sweetly repentant. Aw. Then there was Boom-Boom. The bitter girl who couldn't forgive. The fruitcake who rigged up fake attacks with exploding toilets and who (seemingly), in front of everyone, attacked our poor, sweet underdog with her hands and nails. And now she was the flaming nutcase who couldn't even deal with a minor change in music. Meri was the victim. She was the injured party.

"Why did you do that?" bellowed Bobbie, and thrust her face into mine. "Think that was smart? Huh? Huh? Now we'll never sell enough tickets."

I fumbled for a response. But what could I say? From the corner of my eye, I saw Lindsay retrieving her tiara—*No, not yet!* I wanted to scream—and Bitch Kitty yelling at Keith. Oh, my God. Was I seeing straight? It looked like they were arguing. It looked like Bitch Kitty wanted to go . . . and Keith wanted to stay. Then she slapped back his hand and huffily stalked out of the auditorium, abandoning him on the near-empty dance floor. He dropped his head, dejected, and several thoughts ricocheted through my head, the first being *Poor Keith*, but then I thought, *So there, you've learned your lesson: Eventually a Bitch Kitty will stop being a Kitty, and then all you're left with is a big (braless) Bitch.* And yet, when he turned around and softly gazed at me, an all-new thought screamed in my head: *Run!*

And that's exactly what I did. Oh, I'm such a wimp! I heard Lindsay call after me, but I kept running and running, because I couldn't face Keith—I cannot be his "friend," I cannot play the role of the "nice" dorky girl who's there to console him whenever his hot (braless) girlfriend has a temper tantrum, because that would break my heart, and it already feels like it's been broken and stomped on a zillion trillion times. I glanced over my shoulder; he was actually chasing after me. I nearly shrieked, and when I was finally outside and saw the empty tractor-pull hayride in front of me, I took a flying leap and jumped into the pile and screamed at the top of my lungs to the student driver hired for the night: "Go!"

And we were off. *Phew.* I sunk into the soft piles of hay and realized, to my surprise, that this was a pretty humongous tractor bed. There was a heck of a lot of hay, too, and I wondered for a moment if I'd get lost in it. The whole thing was large enough, I knew, to hold at least fifteen people, but thanks to me (and Meri), there was only one rider on board tonight. And then there were two.

"Cindy . . ."

What? Was I hearing right? I looked around. A small clump of hay began rustling before me.

"Cindy? Where are you?"

Up popped Keith. He was obviously startled. Little hay stalks were sticking out of his tousled hair, and his bare chest was lightly sprinkled with hay dust.

"Put your shirt on," I snapped, though now that I really think about it, I was actually saying, "How dare you look this good when I look like crap. Cover yourself up, go away, and (maybe) come back after I've had a facial, a dye and a cut, a manicure, a bikini wax, a boob job, liposuction, and enough money to afford as many cute Marc Jacobs dresses and blouses as I want (and maybe a nice Dooney & Bourke purse, too) (but that's optional)."

He began pulling his shirt over his shoulders, and then we hit a huge pothole—*ka-boom!*—and I flew back and he flew forward and, oh my God, he landed right on top of me, and I screamed and pushed him back, and then all I could see were his flailing legs sticking out of the hay and his hands helplessly thrashing at his shirt, which was still covering his head. *Let him struggle*, I thought, but then I rolled my eyes and yanked his shirt off, freeing his arms, and watched him spit some hay out of his mouth.

"Cindy . . ."

"Keith," I calmly retorted. Then I looked into his (twinkling) blue eyes and felt a lump build in my throat and quickly looked away. And I crossed my arms. I didn't say, "Harrumph," but I may as well have, because he said, "Cindy, you have every right to be mad at me."

"Do I? Do I really? Well, what do you know. I didn't get the memo, but thank you. I'll keep that in mind." I thought I was being very cool and sophisticated. I gestured nonchalantly with my hand. "Shouldn't you be off somewhere? With Doreen? Getting tra-a-a-ashed?"

He had no response at first, and I continued looking away, and I thanked my lucky stars that the driver was far enough ahead of the pull so that he couldn't see us, or likely hear us either (thank God). The night air was crisp. I shuddered. On one hand, I wanted Keith to hold me in his strong arms and keep me warm, but on the other, I wanted the trailer to hit another pothole; hopefully one big enough to send him—*boing!*—flying off the tractor and onto the ground.

"Cindy, I'm really sorry I hurt you," he whispered.

I should have just responded, "Okay, fine, I forgive you," and then we could have been "friends," which means we could have just forgotten about the whole thing, but instead, remembering my conversation with Patty and Lindsay, I suddenly blurted out, "You never went down on me."

"What?" he responded. I still wasn't looking at him, but I knew his eyes were popping out of his head. Good. Let them pop.

"You heard me. You never went down on me. You were selfish in bed. But no biggie. You know, statistics show that a huge majority of guys are just too selfish to—"

"But Cindy," he gaped. "You're a good girl."

"Ohhhhhh, I see. So you'll play with the bad girls, maybe marry a good girl—and never go down on her? And you think that's enough? Well, let me tell you, mister, some of us good girls want the whole enchilada. And not just in bed. We want a guy who's fun, and handsome, too, and smart, and God forbid, let's hope he's grown-up enough to know that drinking and partying isn't a full-time occupation. Oh, and P.S., we want a guy who won't dump us for some braless wonder after the first stupid little argument they have, and if he says, 'I love you,' we'd like that to last for at least a semester, because one month isn't long enough, and it's not fair to say those words to a nice girl because she'll think you really mean them, and then she'll expect more. She'll expect way more than a guy who's really cute, but really immature, and yeah, you heard me, she'll expect him to go down on her."

I looked up at him. His jaw was dropped. Mine was too. I didn't just shock Keith, I shocked myself. Completely. I thought, *Oh my God, did I really just say what I think I said?* And then I thought, *Wow, I've officially blown it*, but then I thought, *Blown what? We aren't together now, we aren't a couple anymore.* And that was okay (it really was). I felt satisfied (sort of) (mostly), because I'd said what I wanted to say, and okay, maybe (way) too bluntly, but so what? Keith clamped his mouth shut. He cleared his throat and leaned in close, gently whispering.

"Okay. So let's say there's this guy and he wants to start seeing this nice girl again. What should he do? I mean, he knows being trashed all the time is really dumb. Or at least now he does. See, he found out that when he wasn't partying and shit when he was with this other girl, he didn't have anything to say to her—and everything she said to him sounded kinda lame. And then he remembered this nice girl and how they used to talk all the time, sometimes till three in the morning, which was amazing. And then he remembered how sexy she was. And fun. And smart. But he blew it. He was a dick. But he really wants to be with her again— for way more than a semester. What if he wanted to get back together with her? Do you think she'd say yes? Oh, and yeah, he's totally into going down on her, like, all the time."

My heart was doing backflips. I mean, I'd had my say, I was out of words. But before I could even think of responding, he quickly added, "Oh, and his dog really misses her. That's what Rags said. Rags definitely likes the nice girl better."

Rags! That wasn't playing fair. I love Rags.

"Um, tell Rags that the nice girl misses him, too."

I couldn't think of anything else to say, and I guess Keith was tired of speaking in the third person, because he leaned in closer and said, very plainly, and with heartbreaking sincerity, "Cindy, I've really missed you."

Then he swept me into his arms and we fell back into the hay and—oh my God—he kissed my lips and then my neck, and my thoughts raced back to my list, and the question, "What is my Authentic Self?" I had picked Number 3, "Being Keith's girlfriend." And so there I was, in Keith's arms, being all authentic, I guess. But something wasn't right. I thought, *Is this really who I am? Keith's girlfriend? And that's it? What if he dumps me again? Or I dump him? Will I suddenly be inauthentic? And will I have to rush out and get another boyfriend in order to be authentic?* Patty once told me that being in a relationship is "healthy," because it forces all of your "issues" to come to the surface, enabling you to "resolve" them once and for all. That's probably true, but I think it's also true that being in a relationship can sometimes make you disappear. I could feel it happening with each gentle kiss. I was vanishing. I wasn't Cindy anymore. I was Keith's girlfriend. Just Keith's girlfriend.

"Keith, wait," I mumbled, and I gently pushed him back.

"Sorry. What? Did I do something wrong?"

I gazed into his eyes. How could I explain what I was feeling? He's perfect in every way (mostly) (for the sake of argument I'm forgetting about Bitch Kitty), and yet, now I knew: When I'm with Keith, there's no room for me. And that's my fault. Which probably means that I need to be with me—and just me (at least for a while). A shivery wind blew past. The tractor pull was headed back to the auditorium.

I finally told him, "I don't think I should be rushing into anything right now," which is the understatement of the year. My eyes welled with tears. Oh, I wish Patty was around so I could talk to her (the real Patty, not the scary Skinny-addicted Patty). And then I thought about Meri. Not too long ago, Patty had told me, "Remember, Cyn, Meri's gone. The high alert is over." Okay, so Patty was wrong there, and yes, Meri may think she's destroyed her, but I won't let that happen. Somehow I'll help Patty. I've got to. When the hayride came to a stop, Keith reached out for me, but I pulled back. I was trembling, and I think he was too.

"I'm sorry," I said, and I hopped off the hayride and ran around the corner and slammed myself against the wall and tried to catch my breath. I still don't know if I did the right thing. Will anyone as perfect as Keith ever want to be with me again?

"There you are," said Lindsay, who rushed up, breathless.

"How did you know your aunt's tiara was on eBay?" I blurted out. My mind was back on Meri. I had to at least try to stay a step or two ahead of her.

"I told you, didn't I? I got an e-mail with a link to the site page. From you. Or I thought it was you."

No, she hadn't told me, but things were happening so fast, and even though we now knew to keep our mouths shut around the tiara, I had to assume we were also being watched. After all, Albino Girl (or Eileen) and the St. Eulalia girls knew I was headed in the direction of Fairfield today, and more importantly, they wanted to stop me to make sure I didn't find out about Gloria.

"The Harvest Ball's a total bust," added Lindsay. "Meri trumped us." How? I wondered. I mean, I knew she had left, but apparently there was more. It turns out that the Campus Evangelical Crusade, or CEC, was also holding a party tonight—a real Halloween party, with witches and goblins and carved pumpkins and lots of cruel candy. After Meri left the Harvest Ball, she breezed right over to the CEC party, and of course, brought a huge crowd with her (several times larger, it seems, than the crowd she brought to the Harvest Ball). Meri told the CEC to start charging admission—triple what we were charging— and to give the proceeds to the Children's Hospital, the exact same charity that Alpha Beta Delta was trying to raise money for. And then things got even worse. Someone had alerted the fire department; they stormed into the Harvest Ball, found several code violations, and shut the whole thing down. Shanna-Francine tried to negotiate with them, and when she did, she stepped away from the cash box. When she returned to it, it was empty.

"We're in there cleaning up now," said Lindsay. "Shanna-Francine's hysterical. And she's blaming you. Everybody is. Even Bobbie."

"Where's your tiara?" I asked. She said it was still on top of the speaker, and I told her to run back in and put it on; I thought it might start to look suspicious (to whoever was listening on the other end) that she hadn't been wearing it for so long. "Go," I said. "I'll meet you back at the house." She scampered back to the auditorium and I walked—and walked and walked. A light, icy rain began to fall, giving the campus and the grounds a slick, sparkly sheen, but I barely noticed. I could feel fear snaking through my veins, infecting my body, and I thought, *I can't do this by myself any-more, I can't. I need help. I need Mom. She helped me last time. She knows how diabolical Meri can be.* And even though Meri tried to put poison in my head about the new relationship me and Mom are trying to have, I know she'll want to help. I only hope she can. Maybe I'll call her in the morning.

By the time I made it back to Alpha Beta Delta, all the lights were out. Thank goodness for small favors. I didn't feel like facing anyone. I walked up to the stairs, stepped into my room, and glanced at my computer. No e-mail. Good. I didn't bother to turn on the light. I was too tired. I closed my door, took off my clothes, climbed beneath the covers, and closed my eyes. I knew I would sleep well. I had survived the day, and the night, too. Meri was active, yes, but she hadn't won yet. I thought, *Now I can relax and get some much-needed rest and be prepared for whatever she might have in store for me tomorrow.* I was still a little wet (I should have dried off with a towel), and I felt a small pattering moistness on my leg, as if water were trickling down it. But then I realized that it was actu-ally trickling up my leg, which didn't make any sense. I felt a sim-ilar trickling going up my other leg. And then more trickling. Lots more. Trickle trickle trickle. What the—? I groggily turned on my nightstand lamp, flung my covers aside—and screamed! Oh my God, oh my God, oh my God! My legs and my thighs were cov-ered with hundreds of big fat wriggling cockroaches! I jumped up out of bed; they were everywhere, crawling up my legs and my chest. Ahhhhhhhhhh! The next thing I knew I was desperately wailing and dancing around and screaming, trying to shake them off, but they were all over me; I could feel their tiny little cock-roach legs all over my body. *This isn't happening,* I thought, *this in insanity.* I wailed, "He-e-e-e-e-elp m-e-e-e-e-e-e!"

Ka-boom. My door was kicked open. Then I heard more screams—besides my own, I mean—because Shanna-Francine and Bobbie and Lindsay couldn't believe what they were seeing. The cockroaches were everyplace now; I was batting them out of my hair, off my face. Bud burst forth holding a broom and—*whack!*—he slapped it against my body, over and over. Cock-roaches were flying this way and that. *Whack, whack, whack!* He kept slapping the broom against me, and I started to scream and a cockroach flew inside. Ahhhhhhhhhhh! Inside my mouth! I could feel it! I spit it out, and then Bud grabbed me and—*oomph*—he flung me down and I could feel hard porcelain. Water gushed on top of me. I was in the bathroom in the tub, and cold water was blasting down from the shower head above. I shuddered and dared to open my eyes. Cockroaches were trailing down toward the drain, some of them on their backs, violently wriggling their legs, desperate to save themselves from drowning. I screamed again.

"Shh. It's okay, Cindy," said Bud. "Chill. You're okay."

Oh, really? You wanna bet on that (*and since when is Bud so brave,* I thought)? I heard insistent hissing sounds from outside the bathroom. I found out later that Bobbie and several of the other girls started spraying the cockroaches in my room with bug spray, while a few of them ran out to get more. By the time I was coherent, I was in the kitchen trembling in my robe, sitting at the table and sipping tea.

"Thank you, Bud," I managed to say, and I meant it. He smiled goofily (and even managed a blush). Bud seems to be so many things these days—sex maniac (God help Lindsay), computer wonk, and now my brave rescuer. How confusing is that? I want to hug him and slap him, all at the same time.

"Is there anything you want to tell us?" bellowed Bobbie, who was sitting at the table with Shanna-Francine, Lindsay, and several other startled girls.

Like what? I thought. I looked up from my teacup: Lindsay was forcing a smile, Bobbie was gazing at me intently, and Shanna-Francine was impatiently rolling her eyes.

"You mean about the cockroaches?" I asked. Bobbie nodded. But what could I say? Obviously, while everyone in the house was out, Meri, or more likely Gloria, had pulled my covers down, dumped a clump of cockroaches at the foot of my bed, then pulled the covers back up. I started to answer when Shanna-Francine impatiently asked, "Where were you tonight? After you left the ball?"

I gulped, "I went on a hayride with Keith. And then I saw Lindsay."

"I can vouch for that," said Lindsay meekly.

"Then I went for a walk," I said. "A long walk."

"A long walk?" snapped Shanna-Francine. "In the freezing rain?"

Oh my God. Did they actually believe that I ran to the house and somehow put cockroaches in my bed myself? That's ridiculous. I started to say, "Meri . . ."

Shanna-Francine exploded. "Oh, I've had it with this Meri stuff! You're ruining the house! You ruined the ball! Why don't you just leave?" Bobbie tried to calm her down, but Shanna-Francine was out of control. Angry tears were stinging her face. "I can't take it anymore! Leave! Just leave!"

Then she bolted out of the kitchen and ran up the stairs. I sat stiffly at the table. It felt like no one was breathing. Shanna-Francine had dared to say what every Alpha Beta Delta girl (except Lindsay) has been itching to say to me for quite some time: Just leave. I was now w-a-a-a-y beyond inappropriate. I'm on the sofa in the living room right now. There's no way I'm sleeping in my bed tonight. Tamari's curled up in a ball at my feet (and snoring slightly) (who knew cats could snore?). Pumpkin Seed's on the top rail of the sofa, and he keeps reaching out and batting my head with his paw. I half-expect him to say, "I think your hair's tragic too."

Bobbie offered to let me stay in her room. She said she could sleep in Shanna-Francine's room, since she has a larger room and a pull-out couch given that she's president of the sorority, but I didn't want to inconvenience or anger Shanna-Francine any more than I already have. Her words are still rumbling in the bottom of my stomach. "Leave! Just leave!" I wish I could tell her to wait just a few more days. Come Friday, I'll either be kicked out of RU or I'll have found a way to stop Meri. There has to be a way. There just has to be.

It's four o'clock in the morning right now. I was woken up about an hour ago by a strange rumbling sound that I thought was coming from the basement. Confused, I stepped from the living room, walked to the basement door, and listened. Nothing. No sound. I reached for the doorknob and turned it. It was locked. I heard the noise again—but this time I realized that it was coming from outside. And it was familiar; a kind of rhythmic metallic *ker-chunk. Ker-chunk, ker-chunk, ker-chunk.*

"Patty!" I exclaimed.

I put on my nightgown and flew out the front door—and slipped and fell on my butt. Ouch! The icy rain had stopped, and it left behind a thin coating of ice on the front walkway, and on everything else, too; even the lampposts and the telephone wires were glistening with what looked like a light dusting of sugar. I picked myself up and ran around to the back of the house. There she was. I held back a gasp. She was on her large pogo stick bouncing up and down—*boing-boing, boing-boing.* She had lost a significant amount of weight. Her face was violently ravaged and ghostly white, her eyes wide and bloodshot, and she was gleefully giggling, gazing up at the sky.

"Patty," I yelped. "Don't you want to come inside?"

"Most people jog," she squealed. "I say, phooey. Why jog when you can pogo-stick? Pogo-pogo-pogo. Wheeeeee!"

Oh, boy. I knew that I'd have to play this carefully. I had to get her off the pogo stick and into the house, and then, hopefully, back to the rehab center in the morning.

"They can't make fun of me anymore," she shrieked. "No more, 'Eeeow, look at Patty. She's got more rolls than a bakery, she's got more chins than a Chinese phone book.' Ha ha ha ha." *Boing-boing, boing-boing.* "But, hey, I don't blame them. I blame France."

"Patty . . ."

"Oh, sure, my friends didn't mind. 'We don't care that you're fat.' Sure, sure. But then my friends never wanted to fuck me, did they? Ha ha ha ha." *Boing-boing, boing-boing.* "My mom. Please. The rankest cow that ever pissed. Well, look at me now, Ma! Ha ha ha ha."

"Patty, Pigboy's been looking for you everywhere. He loves you. Remember? Don't you want to come inside?"

"Skinny-skinny-skinny."

"Patty, listen to me. . . ."

"Oh, Cindy. Cindy Cindy Cindy." *Boing-boing, boing-boing.*

"Meri did this to you," I wailed. "Oh, Patty, please come inside. Please!"

"Meri?" *Boing-boing, boing-boing.* "Meri, Meri, quite contrary. She's learned to start loving herself."

"Patty, Skinny's a drug. A bad one. Meri told Wolfgang to give it to you." I was trying to get through to her—but could I?

"Meri's here. Meri's there. Meri's everywhere." *Boing-boing, boing-boing.* "Wheeeee!"

"Did you hear me? Meri told Wolfgang—"

"Wolfgang-Shmulfgang. I have better Skinny now. Oh, it's s-o-o-o-o-o much better." *Boing-boing, boing-boing.* "Better-better-better."

Okay, I am so not a violent person, but I knew I had to take action. I mean, it was obvious I wasn't going to talk her down off the pogo stick (and who knows where she's been buying more trick) (with Pigboy's emergency stash, probably). Patty squealed, singing out, "Hey, look me over, try and feel me up, roll me in clover . . ."

Bam! I slammed into her and knocked her to the ground, then I forcefully pinned her arms down. She struggled at first, but then she went limp. And she started sobbing.

"Oh, Patty," I cried. "Please. Come inside."

The icy rain was falling again, dotting her forehead. Her eyes seemed to be glazing over—then she snapped to attention and stared right at me. And whispered, "Haze the bitch. Make her cry."

Then—*oomph!*—she kneed me in the stomach. I doubled over, howling in pain. And she was gone. She scampered around to the front of the house, screaming with giggles. I ran after her, but by the time I got to the front, she was far ahead of me down the street, lost in a swirl of icy rain.

"Patty!" I screamed. But it was no use.

"I love my friends," I said to Meri. "More than anything."

And she smiled. Just slightly. "I know."

I'm shivering on the couch now. I can't sleep. And Pumpkin Seed won't stop playing with my hair.

November 1

Dear Diary:

I had a discouraging thought when my eyes opened this morning—which was pretty early, because I didn't pull the shades in the living room last night and it felt like the sun was rising right in front of me on the couch. I thought, *My life (and everyone else's) might be a lot easier if I just gave up the ghost and left Alpha Beta Delta (and RU). Then Meri would stop; no more sabotaging the house, no more ruining everyone's life.* Then I thought back to my eighth-grade science class. Locusts only swarm when their population density is high. If there are fewer locusts in any given area, they behave as (relatively) harmless individuals (more like grasshoppers) (which they're related to). My presence is making the population density too high. Maybe if I leave, I'll stop the swarm. "Yo, what up, Cindy?" said Bud, grinning goofily as he plodded down the stairs in his Paul Frank underwear and into the kitchen, then he stepped back in with a glass of water. "Don't look. Morning wood."

"Bud, it's five o'clock in the morning. Go back to bed," I said, looking away from his stiffie (eeeow!) (which he made no attempt to cover up) (of course). I thanked him again for saving me from the cockroaches last night. He smiled warmly. For the briefest (and I mean briefest) second, I saw the softer side of Bud. I let my guard down. As always, that was a mistake.

"Heard you hooked up with Keith last night," he said with a lewd wink. "Very cool."

"We didn't 'hook up,'" I insisted. "We talked. That's it."

"Really? You didn't make out?"

"No. Not really."

He chuckled dirtily. "'Not really.' Sweet."

"We kissed. Okay? That was it. And we're not together."

"He didn't feel you up?"

"Bud . . ."

He leaned in close. "Did you blow him?"

"No! Jeez."

"Okay, okay. Chill." Then he gazed out philosophically, sighing heavily. "Makes you wonder, though, doesn't it? I mean, whatever happened to casual head?"

"Bud, go back upstairs."

"Hey, I'm seriously thinking of eye shadow. And pink nail polish. And I might shave my chest. And my armpits. What do you think?"

"What do I think? I think you and David Beckham will make a very nice couple."

"He's my idol!" he sloppily enthused. That I should have seen coming. I've always wondered, Who in this world is David Beckham trying to impress with his pink nail polish and his shaved armpits? Now I know. Bud Finger. I turned over on the couch. "Bud, go back upstairs."

"His nickname's 'Goldenballs,'" he chuckled as he bounded happily back up the stairs. "That's so cool."

It felt like I closed my eyes for just a few seconds, but it was over an hour later when I heard a muffled scream and a door slam from upstairs. *Oh my God,* I thought, *what now? Can't Meri wait till I've had my morning coffee?* Then I heard *boom-boom-boom.* Someone was quickly stomping down the stairs. It was Lindsay. She flew down to the front landing, then turned around to face me, her face knotted with anger. I quickly sat up.

"Lindsay, what's wrong?"

She held back a sob, and with great difficulty she said, "Bud and I are breaking up."

Then she burst into tears and ran into the kitchen. It took two cups of coffee and several Kleenex tissues (one after another) at the kitchen table to calm her down.

"What did he do to you?" I gently asked. Since this was Bud we were talking about, I braced myself. She blew her nose, then attempted to compose herself.

"Okay. Maybe it's not a big deal."

"Lindsay, what did he do?"

"Well, all right," she said, taking a breath. "Bud likes morning sex. And so do I."

"Okay," I said, hesitating. Did I really want to hear this?

"And this morning, he decided to, you know, do what he did before."

"What?"

She rolled her eyes and whispered in my ear. Oh, not that again. Why on earth can't Bud "finish" in a rubber like everyone else?

"So what happened?" I asked.

"We did it. And it was great."

Okay, now I was confused. They did it. He "finished." So what's the problem (I can't believe how cavalier I'm becoming about things like this)?

"He was real considerate, too," she continued. "He went to the bathroom and got four wet washcloths and wiped it all up."

This was definitely more than I needed to know. But I wanted to be supportive, so I kept listening.

"We went back to sleep. And I woke up a few minutes later. I was thirsty. He'd brought a glass of water up earlier. He had just taken a sip. I wanted some too. So I reached over to the night-stand, I took a sip, and then I . . ." She suddenly became flustered. "Oh, I can't. I can't."

"What?"

She began hyperventilating. She was trying to get it out.

"I laid my head down on the pillow. And I didn't see it. There was, like, this totally huge sticky puddle of it on my pillowcase—and when I lay down it got all over my cheek and the whole side of my face!"

Eeeeeeoooowwwww! We both squealed in horror. Bud spunk all over her face! That's (way) beyond disgusting.

Then she cried out, "I'm a good girl, aren't I?"

"Of course you are!"

"And he's . . ."

"A slob? A bad aim?"

"I'm breaking up with him. We're finished. It's over. I never want to see him again. Oh, I hate Bud Finger, I hate him."

As she sat there sobbing and wiping her nose, I have to admit I was inwardly laughing. And maybe I really am becoming cavalier about certain things, because even though I would never (never-never-never) let a guy do to me half of what Bud does to Lindsay (but I don't judge her for it) (or not too much), and even though I'm not Miss Sexually Experienced (hardly), I do know enough to realize that sex isn't necessarily neat and tidy. Still, Lindsay is Canadian royalty, and maybe royal people (and famous people too) are just more squeaky clean than common folk (like me). But then I remembered how I totally used to idolize Beverly Cleary when I was a little girl. I was addicted to the Ramona the Pest series, and the Ralph Mouse series too. In fact, I held her in such high esteem that I cut her picture out of a magazine, glued glitter stars around her face, and put it up on my wall. Dad must have thought I was going a little too far, because he sat me down and explained that all famous people, even Beverly Cleary, put their shoes on one at a time. I guess that goes for royalty as well (and Lindsay), and though I bet Beverly Clearly never had to deal with yucky, sticky spunk on her pillowcase (good God, I hope not!), I'm sure she had her share of life's messes, just like we all do. Including Lindsay.

"He apologized, didn't he?" I asked.

"Yes. I don't care. It's over."

"But you're in love with Bud. That's what you said." I couldn't believe I was encouraging forgiveness for Bud, but I wanted to see Lindsay happy, and though I'm loath to admit it, I've never known her to be happier than when she's with Bud. She sniffled.

"So maybe I wasn't in love. Maybe I just thought I was. I hate him. It's over. I'm—I'm a good girl. And he's . . ."

Just then, Bud meekly padded into the kitchen, poured himself a cup of coffee, and sort of hung by the counter, gazing at his feet. It looked like he was going to cry. The silence was excruciating.

"Lindsay . . ."

"I'm not talking to you, Bud Finger," she snapped.

More silence. I suddenly had a terrible thought, and I started to ask, "Where did you put the—"

"It's in my closet, and I put a towel over it," she quickly responded. Thank God. I mean, there has to be some privacy with that tiara. There was more silence. No one was saying a word. Bud finally looked up, facing the back of Lindsay's head. His lower jaw was trembling.

He whispered, "I love you, Lindsay."

She refused to turn around or answer him. Her jaw was set. She blew her nose again.

"Cindy, will you please tell Bud Finger that I can't hear him? Oh, and when he leaves, tell him he can take his toothbrush. And the handcuffs. And the riding crop. And the massage oil. And the maid's uniform. And the Strip Chocolate Checkers. And that stupid dolphin. I want it all gone."

Bud's eyes were tearing up as she said this.

"I think he heard you," I said quietly.

"Good. I'm glad."

Bud was a silent blubbering mess (he kind of reminded me of the Cowardly Lion when he cried in *The Wizard of Oz*; it was just all sloppy and gooey), and he was about to say something when we all heard a loud, startling *klunk*. Coming from somewhere. We froze. One second. Two seconds. Then we heard the *klunk* again. My heart began thumping.

Bud whispered, "The basement."

My eyes widened. The basement. Where I only thought I'd heard noise coming from last night. We quickly tippy-toed to the basement door. We heard another loud *klunk*. Bud gulped, carefully reached for the doorknob, gently tried to turn it. I mouthed, "Locked." Lindsay and I were quivering with fright. What on earth was down there? Oblivious, Bud suddenly banged on the door with his fists—*bam-bam-bam*—and we heard a fierce rustling below, and I screamed (I don't know why). *Ka-bam!* Bud slammed his shoulder against the door and it crashed open.

"Shit!" a voice screamed from downstairs.

Bud barreled down the stairs, vanishing in the inky darkness, while Lindsay and I stood terrified at the top. She frantically flipped the light switch on and off, but it didn't work. Then we heard more loud violent klunking, and the sound of glass shattering.

"Bud, no!" screamed Lindsay.

Then silence. Nothing.

"Bud, are you okay?" I wailed.

Oh my God. Did we dare go downstairs?

"You first," yelped Lindsay, who leaped behind me.

"Bud?" I called out.

We heard a rustling. And a moan. "I'm fine," he said, but he actually didn't sound fine. "Bring a flashlight down here."

I was angry more than scared by the time Lindsay and I were downstairs with the flashlight. We'd found a switch for an overhead light, and when we turned it on, we saw everything: the broken basement window where a quick escape had just been made, the ratty sleeping bag in the corner, the empty cereal bar packets and Juicy Juice cartons, the retrofitted iMac wireless keyboard, the no-name monitor, the incoming signal antenna, the headphones. We pulled a metal folding chair off of Bud, who sat up, a little worse for wear, but okay, and obviously confused.

"Who was down here?" asked Lindsay.

"I think—naw, it can't be. She's in jail."

I was fuming. So this was Gloria's base of operations. Which meant that not too long ago, when I discovered that the s on my wireless keyboard was suddenly sticking, it actually wasn't my keyboard at all. Gloria had pulled a switch. Bud explained, and it was all pretty technical sounding—she had copied and matched the Bluetooth signal from my keyboard to another keyboard, hotwired into the Internet2 network in order to infiltrate my hard drive and send the fake e-mails—but the upshot was that Gloria had been here. In the basement. All along. And with the headphones and the signal antenna, she could hear everything within earshot of Lindsay's tiara.

"But where's the tape?" asked Lindsay.

There was no tape. I guess Meri and Gloria learned from last time that keeping a record of what they were doing wasn't such a hot idea. Besides, all Gloria had to do was listen. And then report back to Meri. Or take action on her own.

"Gross. Look at this long white hair," said Bud, who plucked it off the keyboard.

Or report back to Meri and Albino Girl.

"You look like you're about to punch someone's lights out," said Lindsay, who obviously saw my rage building. Boy, if Meri was there right in front of me, I might have done it, I might have taken a swing. Meri is the one who's making the population dense. She's causing the swarm. She's the one who has to go. Not me. We'd all be harmless individuals (like grasshoppers) if it weren't for her. Me? Leave? No way. Not now.

"Let's call the police," suggested Lindsay. "Or campus security."

"No," I commanded. "They'll just think I put this stuff down here."

"Yeah, but we know you didn't," said Bud. "We're witnesses."

"No. We say nothing," I retorted impatiently. "We're not going to tell anybody about this—not even Shanna-Francine or Bobbie. Meri already knows that we know. Or she will in about an hour. That's all that matters." Then I smiled. Just slightly. Sort of like Meri does. Because the playing field was even now. I had a chance. And I had to be smart about it. I turned to Bud. "Can you hook up a tape recorder to that incoming signal thingie?"

He shrugged. "Sure."

I breathed a sigh of relief. I was about to do something that even Meri couldn't anticipate. But I had to do it fast. I ran up the stairs, swung open Lindsay's closet door, pushed aside the towels and the box of Strip Chocolate Checkers. And grabbed the tiara.

November 2

Dear Diary:

It's amazing how stupid people can be. And how easy they are to manipulate. I have Meri to thank for those lessons. This morning I called Dean Pointer's office to confirm my meeting on Friday at noon.

And then I asked, "Would it be possible for him to see me today, too? It's really important." His secretary was confused.

"But you're seeing him tomorrow," she said.

I knew that, I told her, but I wanted to see him today as well. I was very insistent, and I even tried sounding slightly hysterical (since I am the campus cuckoo, after all). It worked. She said she could squeeze me in after lunch at two. Perfect.

After lunch I strode happily toward the administration building clutching a large grocery bag. I was smiling. Just slightly. I thought, *This is going to be fun.* And it was. It was delicious fun.

"The dean will see you now, Miss Bixby," said Mrs. Juergens, the dean's pleasant, if harried, secretary.

I strode confidently into the dean's office, closed the door, and took a seat facing his desk. He was on the phone. He held up his hand and mouthed, "One second." *Oh, no problem, Dean,* I thought acidly, *I can wait. I can wait as l-o-o-o-o-ng as you want.* Finally he hung up and smiled at me snootily. I suppose I should have taken offense, but then I'll bet after thirty or so odd years behind that desk, he smiles that way to everyone. Well, I was about to wipe that smirky smile right off his face.

"Now then, Miss Bixby."

"That's Ms. Bixby," I corrected.

"Yes. So what's the big emergency?"

"Well, first, I heard you called my parents. Is that true?"

"Yes, it is." Then he added for emphasis, "Mzzzz. Bixby. I left a message instructing them to be available by phone. For tomorrow. At noon. I'm afraid we all have some very unfortunate matters to discuss."

Excellent, I thought. He obviously didn't know that Mom and Dad were in L.A. with Lisa (and he certainly didn't have Mom's super-private cell phone number), so chances are Mom hasn't even heard the message yet.

"I see," I responded, doing my best to be cagey. "You might want to call them back and cancel. It might be best." The dean sighed huffily.

"Mzzzz. Bixby. I really am sorry that Rumson—"

I ignored him. I whipped a small tape recorder out of the grocery bag and plopped it on the desk. "I've got a tape, Dean."

He chuckled condescendingly. "Mzzz. Bixby. Please. We've all heard those tapes. And that's all in the past. The time has come to forgive and forget."

"Actually, this is a brand-new tape, Dean," I said. Without waiting for him to respond, I pressed play. And with each passing second, his face turned whiter. And whiter. It was a recording, and it was very clear. It began with rustling sounds and a ringing bell. Students were leaving a just-concluded class.

"That's a very pretty tiara you're wearing," said the unmistakable voice of Professor Scott.

I shyly thanked him, and I apologized for leaving his birthday party so quickly the other night. I said I was just a bit startled when he called me his new—gosh, what was it he called me?

"My new cherry," cooed the professor.

Yes, that was it. His new cherry. And, gee, were all of the women at his party that night students of his? Or former students? They were all once "new cherries" too, weren't they? I just wanted to confirm that. And, boy, did he confirm it.

"It's my own special tradition," he cheerfully informed me. Then his voice lowered to a lewd whisper. "Each year I pick a very special girl. A freshman girl. Like you. And I teach them all about life. About love. And literature, too."

"Really," I said. "And when you say 'love,' do you mean, I mean . . ."

"What do you think I mean?" he playfully added. I laughed coquettishly (really) (I can do that), and I asked, "Wow. You mean, you had sex? With all of those freshman girls? All of those under-twenty-one freshman girls?"

"Cindy, please. That's so crude. We didn't 'have sex.' We made love."

Oh, brother. I hadn't listened to the whole tape yet—I figured I'd already nailed him with that "new cherry" gobbledygook—but this was too good. I just sat there, letting it play, and I watched the dean, who grew increasingly uncomfortable (there was even a little bead of sweat trickling down his forehead).

"Does the dean know about all this?" I asked the professor.

"Oh, the dean and I go way back. He came to my party last year."

"Did he? Imagine that." I didn't have to imagine, actually. The dean was right in front of me. He swallowed hard. I think he was having trouble breathing.

"Your poem was wonderful," I gushed.

"Did you like it? Oh, I'm so glad. Would you like to hear it

again?" I must have nodded, because the professor's voice suddenly boomed. "I have a jar of cherries, I've kept them through
the years . . ."

I figured that was enough of that (and I really didn't need to hear
that icky poem again). I clicked off the tape player. The dean was
stunned silent. Time to play poker. And I wasn't about to fold.

"Okay, so here's the deal. You've got a professor at RU who's
been banging freshman girls for the past ten or fifteen years. Not
good. Looks bad. And gee, seems like you knew about it. Oh, and
they were all under twenty-one. Statutory rape? Gosh. Could be.
Have your legal people look into that."

The dean sneered. "You little—"

"Watch it. And be grateful. Because I'm giving you this tape,
okay? I have the original, and I'll give that to you too. All you have
to do is call my parents, cancel our little meeting, and agree to let
me stay at RU and Alpha Beta Delta. For the next four years. Oh,
and no more meetings with Dr. Vladislav, all right? He really is a
bore." The dean was reeling. Obviously, this isn't a man who likes
to be cornered. He cleared his throat.

"But I—"

"You what? Already made a deal with the Sugarmans to have
me kicked out? 'Cause I'm psycho? 'Cause I'm violent?" His silence
answered my questions. I chuckled. "Toughie-wuffie. That's your
problem." The dean flared with anger.

"Mzzz. Bixby . . ."

I snapped, "Excuse me, but I think you'd better keep something
in mind. I can look pretty pathetic as the sobbing little freshman
girl. Look at me. My hair is tragic. I know how I come off. Think
about it. National press. An in-depth NBC report. New Cherry
speaks. I'll run this right into the ground. And you with it."

"Are you recording me now, Mzzz. Bixby?"

"No, I'm not. Or maybe I am. Either way, you have two hours.

You can call my cell. If I hear you've canceled our meeting with my parents, then I know we have an agreement, and every tape gets delivered to your office within minutes. If not, then everything goes to the police. And the press. Gosh, think of the embarrassment. To you. To the college. And just when things have been going so well."

"I don't appreciate being blackmailed, Mzzz. Bixby."

"Really? Well, New Cherry doesn't care." I glanced at my watch. "It's two thirty now. You have till four thirty."

I strode out of his office, said a pleasant good-bye to Mrs. Juergens, and stepped into the afternoon sun. Holy moly, what did I just do? I wanted to jump up and down and scream with joy, "I did it, I did it, I did it!" But I played it cool. Oh so cool. I simply strode to my next class, Orientation to Science and Technology. The entrance to the building was crowded, and the stairwell was jammed.

I decided to take the elevator, which was a bit crowded as well, and to my frustration, it stopped on every floor. The first stop was the second floor. *Ping.* The door opened . . . and in stepped Meri with her fawning entourage. I held back a gasp. She looked perfect (of course) in a soft Agnona sweater blouse, a kilt-patterned Brooks Brothers skirt, and demure Ferragamo slingbacks. I could smell the Fleurissimo; it was infecting my nostrils. My heart was racing. Was she following me? Did she know about the basement yet? Had Gloria reached her? Had she heard about me and the dean?

Pull it together, I screamed to myself. Then I realized I was facing her back, and I was crushed toward the very back of the elevator, so chances were she didn't even know I was there. *Ping.* We stopped at the third floor. More students crowded in. Meri stepped back—closer to me. A handsome senior guy in a gray muscle T and Perry Ellis sharkskin herringbone pants whispered in her ear.

"Oh, really?" she delicately responded.

The guy turned back to me—and he winked. I guess my jaw must have dropped, because he turned back to Meri and whispered in her ear again. She giggled, and then she began lightly humming. I recognized the tune. But what was it? The guy began singing along, and soon, her entire entourage impishly joined in:

> *La cucaracha, la cucaracha,*
> *ya no puede caminar,*
> *La cucaracha, la cucaracha . . .*

Ha-ha. Very funny. A cell phone rang; Kelis's "Milkshake." Meri pulled her Treo 650 PDA phone from her Miu Miu and pressed it to her ear.

"Hello?" she murmured breathily. She listened silently. Then she seethed with sudden force, "That's fucked up!" Uh-oh. The Cucaracha Singers immediately became silent—and so did everyone else in the elevator. Oh my God, could it be? Was it Gloria? For the second time in what had to have been only ten minutes, I wanted to jump up and down and scream with joy, "I did it, I did it, I did it!" But I played it cool. Oh so cool. Meri fussily clicked off her Treo, dropped it into her Miu Miu. *Ping.* The elevator doors opened.

"'Scuse me," I said in a singsongy fashion. "Coming through-hoo." I carefully stepped past, giving a slight elbow jab to Mr. Sharkskin Pants, and yes, that was totally gratuitous (and I'm not that way), but I was feeling so wonderfully triumphant. The tip of a Ferragamo slingback jutted out, blocking my path.

Meri leaned in and very quickly whispered, "Did you know? If I worked your face over with a toilet plunger it wouldn't leave any marks." Then she stepped aside and smiled. Before I could respond, the elevator doors were closing. I rushed out, whipped around, and there she was, smiling complacently, flipping back her thick raven hair, giving me a cold little wink. I have to admit, I shuddered. How could she be so confident with Gloria's basement lair exposed?

I sat numbly in Orientation to Science and Technology. I had my cell phone on vibrate so I'd know if I was receiving a call, but I kept checking it and rechecking it. Why hadn't the dean called? Was he calling my bluff? Would I really have to step into the public spotlight as "New Cherry"? What would Mom think? And Dad? Or Lisa? (Who am I kidding? She'd write a dirty pop song about it.) It was already three forty-five. I could barely concentrate on the lecture. Two minutes later, the most wonderful thing happened. My cell phone began vibrating. My eyes frantically scanned the screen: "Incoming Call: Private Number." Then the vibrating stopped and the call went to voice mail. I couldn't wait. I had to know. I shot my arm up.

"Have to go to the bathroom," I yelped.

I ran out of the class, tore down the hall (everyone probably assumed I had the runs) (and I really don't care). In the ladies' room, I rushed into a stall, closed the door, scrambled for my phone, hit voice mail, and listened breathlessly. The voice was clearly identifiable:

"Mzzz. Bixby. I've decided to agree to your terms. And I'll expect your"—he paused here—"materials in my office within the next ten minutes. Or less. However, given the circumstances, I'll have to insist that you keep seeing Dr. Vladislav. This is non-negotiable."

Click. That was it. I sat there astonished. I couldn't believe I was capable of "pulling a Meri," but I'd done it. *But wait*, I screamed

to myself, *don't blow it, think it through!* And I did. Why, I wondered, did he want me to keep seeing Victorio ("call me Vic")? Because, I figured, he's got to throw the Sugarman attorneys a bone—and prove, somehow, that the university was still intent on keeping me under close watch. Fine. I could live with that (sort of) (there's got to be a way to wriggle out of that one) (but I'll figure it out later). Another question popped up. Had the dean really followed through? Or was he laying a trap? That was easy to confirm. I called home to Marietta, waited for the outgoing message to play, then hit 999 to play back any messages. There were several calls for "Lissa"—from fans who'd discovered our new number—and then I heard the dean's voice:

"Hello. This is Robert B. Pointer, the dean at Rumson River University. I'm afraid I have a rather unfortunate matter to discuss with you regarding your daughter, Cindy. . . ."

And on he went, setting a time for their discussion tomorrow at noon, where I would be present, and instructing them to please call him in the meantime should they wish to discuss the topic in advance. I fumbled with the phone and quickly pressed 3, deleting it. Then I listened to more messages—all of them for "Lissa" (of course) (including some psycho fourteen-year-old girl with a lisp who just *had* to talk to her and just *had* to have her come to her school—immediately—so she could prove to her girlfriends that they were, like, the bestest and closest friends e-ver) (fat chance of that happening) (and people call me cuckoo). And then, once more, a familiar snooty voice:

"Hello. This is Robert B. Pointer, the dean at Rumson River University. I'm afraid my office staff made a regrettable error. Your daughter Cindy remains in good standing at our . . ."

And on he babbled, supercilious as ever, canceling the phone meeting and again blaming his office staff for the "unfortunate snafu." There was no reason for anyone to hear this message, either,

I realized, and I quickly deleted it. I clicked my phone shut and sat there, thinking. Was it time to call Lindsay and Bud? Was New Cherry really ready to retreat into the shadows? I laughed. Why hadn't I just called the home machine and deleted that first message days ago? I shook my head. It wouldn't have made any difference. The wheels were already in motion for me to be booted out of the university, so whether my parents had heard that specific message or not wasn't important. But I'm still glad they didn't. Thank God for Lisa and all her new friends who're keeping her busy (like L. Lo and Tara).

I clicked open my phone again and called Bud.

"Hey, it's me."

"Yo, Cyn. Where are you? There's an echo."

"I'm in the ladies' room."

"N-i-i-i-ce. That's hot."

I nearly screamed—but I calmed myself (in record time) and told him to put Lindsay on the line. Right away.

"New Cherry stays in the jar," I said with a smile. She screamed and giggled. She also assured me that she had everything all sealed up in a manila envelope and ready to go. I glanced at my watch.

"Go now. Hurry."

She tittered. "Meri sucks eggs." Then she hung up. I almost cried. I have the best friends ("e-ver," as that psycho fourteen-year-old would say). I didn't return to class. Instead I strolled back to Alpha Beta Delta, knowing that Lindsay, or perhaps both Lindsay and Bud, were already on their way to deliver a special package to the office of the dean. I felt a sudden, crushing fatigue. "Pulling a Meri" is mentally exhausting (and to think I came this close to being "New Cherry" in public). I looked up at the sky. It had a yawning bleached-out emptiness, and against it, fall leaves tumbled lazily to the ground. Then I saw the house. Alpha Beta Delta! I nearly cried again. Everything would be okay now. Somehow. I just need to find and save poor Patty, and then that's it, there's nothing else Meri can do. Shanna-Francine was in the front yard, raking leaves with Bobbie.

"Hi," I said. Shanna-Francine hesitated. "Everything's going to be fine now," I assured her. "I promise." She looked at me oddly— then I felt a hard manly smack on my back from Bobbie (who'd dyed her Mohawk back to black).

"Good for you," she bellowed happily.

Shanna-Francine abruptly blurted, "I'd like Bobbie to be vice president instead of you." Then she nervously looked away and continued to rake. My shoulders sank. Shanna-Francine and I used to be such good friends, and now she can't even look me in the face. Maybe as time passes, and after she sees everything returning to normal, we can strike up our friendship again. I'd like that. In the meantime, I decided to do what was best, at least for Shanna-Francine.

"That's a great idea," I said softly. "I think Bobbie will make a very appropriate vice president."

I strolled past them and into the house. My room still smells like bug spray. But I feel safe. There were no nasty e-mails waiting for me, and I think I'll sleep better than I have in weeks, knowing that the basement is empty and Gloria is gone. Maybe she's off licking her wounds with Albino Girl and the other girls from St. Eulalia's. Maybe they're all holed up with Meri at Nancy Forbes's house.

Poor Lindsay. She called her mom this afternoon and found out that her beloved Auntie Christiana's tiara has long been locked in a safe, and no, it cannot be taken out so she can wear it. She was devastated—she even said to me, "I'm devastated"—but she consoled herself by whipping out her daddy's black Amex and buying a lovely limited-edition poppy-flower-patterned Kate

Spade umbrella. And no, she hasn't made up with Bud yet. She's still furious with him—she even said to me, "I'm furious with him"—and then she kept wailing, "I'm a good girl, aren't I?" and then, "Oh my God, if he calls, I'm so not here," and then, "How the hell am I supposed to sleep tonight?" and then, "Do you have any Sarah McLachlan? I really need to listen to Sarah McLachlan," and then, "Should I call him? And hang up? And not pick up when he calls back?" and then, before she left my room for bed, "It's over. I'm over him. Here. Do you want this maid's uniform?"

NoVember 3

Dear Diary:

Oh my God, oh my God, oh my God! I hate it when planes shake! I've never been in a small private plane before, and boy, they definitely wobble and vibrate a whole lot more than big planes do. The pilot told us we'll be experiencing "minor turbulence." Minor! Yeah, right! I nearly screamed when we hit the last pocket of bumpy clouds, and a hand reached out and slapped my shoulder.

"No grita usted! No es un bebé!"

I'm not sure what that means. I'm not sure about anything anymore. Early this morning, Lindsay leaped on my bed and frantically shook me awake.

"The TV!" she exclaimed. "Hurry."

I blindly put on my robe and followed her as she raced down the stairs to the living room. What could it be? Was Meri on the morning news? Was she exchanging makeup tips with Diane Sawyer? Lindsay swiped the remote and flipped to MTV.

"The news is coming back in a sec. You're not going to believe it."

"Why won't you tell me what it is?" I asked, preparing for the worst.

She didn't have to. The news—or what passes for "news" on MTV—began, and up came a picture of Lisa, or "Lissa," and there was SuChin Pak, looking particularly grim-faced (even for her).

Pak had a "breaking" story that was "still developing," and I thought, oh God, what did Lisa do now?

"MTV News has learned that pop tartlet Lissa may be spending a lot more time in court these days than in the recording studio," reported Pak. "The one-hit wonder has been formally charged with stalking and slapped with a restraining order by the Los Angeles district attorney's office, acting on complaints from Hollywood actress Lindsay Lohan. The filing—obtained exclusively by MTV—reports that the 'Tune My Motor Up' singer has been 'aggressively and willfully stalking' the Hollywood actress, and even appeared outside her Hollywood Hills home, begging to be let inside. . . ."

I couldn't believe what I was hearing. What happened to "Lissa and L. Lo 4 ever?" Was it all in her head? Was her "tight" friendship with L. Lo just an imaginary one (and what about Tara Reid)? It sure looked that way. I scrambled for my cell phone and frantically dialed Mom. Then I dialed again. And again. Unfortunately, I was switched over to voice mail each time. I left a message, promising to help in any way I could, but really, what can I do?

"Lissa's your sister?" bellowed a shocked Bobbie, who had stepped up behind Lindsay and me without either of us noticing. I sheepishly nodded. "Wow. That's so cool," said Bobbie. "Your sister's hot."

"She's fourteen years old," I cried.

"Yeah, but still, in a few years."

Eeeeow! Double eeeow! The report continued. Apparently, "Touch My Daisy" was slated to be released in two weeks, but it's being rushed into stores today, and her manager, Frederick, claimed in a statement that the timing has absolutely nothing to do with "Lissa's" current headline-grabbing situation. Oh, please. Who's he trying to kid? Still, I felt sorry for Lisa, and I realized that we may have more in common than she'd like to admit. She wants so badly to fit in with all the Hollywood stars (but Tara Reid?), and

I guess that's gotten the better of her. I can certainly identify with that. I felt bad for Mom, too, who must be going bonkers. And I know what she's thinking. A Bixby? In court? It's unthinkable. It's shameful. And poor Dad, who didn't even want to go to L.A. to begin with.

If the news about Lisa had been the absolute worst news report of the day, then I would have been okay (really). But it wasn't. I had let my guard down last night. I had grown too confident. Meri and Gloria and their friends weren't licking their wounds. Far from it.

It started with a scream. Lindsay, Bobbie, a few other girls, and I were finishing our appropriate breakfast when Shanna-Francine ran wailing into the kitchen. She slapped the latest edition of the *Rumson River University Press* on the table. The headline blared: ALPHA BETA BOMBS! It was an in-depth report by ROT (or more like an attack). And it wasn't pretty. Basically, it used the Fall Harvest Ball fiasco as a jumping-off point to explore how all recent Alpha Beta Delta events have been "catastrophic," "frivolous," and "embarrassing to RU." Even worse, it laid the blame on one person, Shanna-Francine, "who has steered one of RU's finest charitable fund-raising institutions into the ground." It called for Shanna-Francine to step down and for Alpha Beta Delta to relinquish the house and turn it over to the CEC, "a new and enthusiastic evangelical group that has already demonstrated its fund-raising savvy by making Alpha Beta Delta's efforts on Halloween night seem flatly irrelevant."

"It's just a dumb report," I said to Shanna-Francine, trying to calm her down. "The paper doesn't have any power. They can't do anything." But she was inconsolable, especially when she read the end of the article. RU, prompted by the newspaper's investigation, has already begun discussions with Sigma Gamma Lambada's president, Sister Nellie Oliverez, of the intersorority governing council in Florida, about the feasibility of a new evangelical CEC sorority. Shanna-Francine flung the newspaper aside, ran crying up the stairs, and slammed her bedroom door shut. She won't let anyone in. Not even Bobbie.

"What are we going to do?" gasped Lindsay.

"Stop Meri," I cried. "Once and for all." That went over like a lead balloon, especially with Bobbie, who put her arm around me and smiled tensely.

"I'd like you to keep chillin', okay? Think you can do that?"

"You know this is all Meri," I said to Lindsay as we walked to class together beneath the cover of her new Kate Spade umbrella. She agreed with me. The tip-off, to her, was the bit about Rose Kennedy, Jackie O.'s mother-in-law, who gave selflessly to Catholic charities and mental retardation causes, and whom several CEC members revere (supposedly) (according to the article).

"So Meri's joining the evangelicals?" I stammered. It didn't make sense. Meri finds religion?

"Please," scoffed Lindsay. "Meri is Meri's religion. Period." Then I heard a soft buzzing sound. My eyes widened. Lindsay sighed, "It's just my cell phone, I swear." And it was. She took it out of her purse and looked at the caller ID: "FingerFone." Then she sucked back a gasp and tossed it back in. "He won't leave me alone," she wearily groaned. "He called me, like, seventeen times last night. Seventeen."

I was listening to her, but my mind was elsewhere. Now I knew for sure. One by one, Meri was picking off my friends at Alpha Beta Delta. First me, then Patty, now Shanna-Francine. I suddenly felt a blazing wave of horror.

"Lindsay," I shrieked. "You're next. You have to go home to Canada—for a week, maybe more. Lie low."

"What are you talking about?" she cried.

I explained—as best I could—and she nodded her head, taking it all in, but she didn't panic. Not at all. In fact, when I finished babbling, she smiled and said, "Oh, Cindy, don't worry. There's nothing Meri can do to me. Okay, so she got me with that damned tiara thing, but that's it. I mean, if she tries to get me kicked out of RU, Daddy's lawyers will so eat her lawyers for lunch." She had a point. Does Meri really think she can one-up Canadian royalty? "And besides," she continued. "Look at you. You're still standing. You weren't kicked out. Right?"

She was right again. I gave her a wave as she headed off to her class. I strode toward the Polk Academic Building. I was late handing in an assignment for Professor Scott's class, so I wanted to drop it by his office. But he wasn't there. In fact, nothing was there. It was completely empty. All the bookshelves were empty, and the filing cabinets were open and barren. I stood there, confused, and then Lainie Richards, the perpetually gum-chewing head of RU's Human Resources, strode in with a small cardboard box and began packing up the few items that remained on his desk: a few pencils and pens and a small gold plaque with a quote by Henry James: "Live all you can; it's a mistake not to."

"Where's Professor Scott?" I asked.

"Gone, sweetie," said Lainie between gum smacks. "Professor Arrick's taking over his classes. Be a dear, hand me those Sharpies?"

"What do you mean he's gone? Did he quit?" She fixed me with a withering stare. And she chuckled.

"Sure, sweetie. He 'quit.'" Then she snatched the Sharpies out of my hand, tossed them in the box, and strode out, her gum smacking seemingly timed to the swing of her hips. "Close the door on your way out, would ya? Thanks, cookie."

I was in total shock as I sat through my next few classes. What did it mean that Professor Scott 'quit'? And was he really fired, as Lainie seemed to not-so-subtly imply? And was I the cause? Oh God, I felt horrible. I mean, sure, Professor Scott's a total sleazepot, but he's also a great teacher (even inspiring at times) (I never would have given much thought to Charles Baudelaire's poetry if it weren't for him). And yet I'd used him for my own purposes, for my own survival. And he was fired. I suddenly felt very small. And horribly responsible. And dirty. Yes, I'd "pulled a Meri," and just like Meri, I didn't give a hoot about the consequences or even think about who I might hurt. I thought only of myself. My stomach suddenly tightened. Oh my God, Professor Scott is gone, so what does that mean for me?

My phone rang when I was on my way to Long John's for lunch. I flipped it open.

"Is there something you want to tell me?" snapped a voice on the other end.

"Mom?"

"I have enough on my agenda without—"

"Mom," I gasped. "How's Lisa?"

"Cindy, please, let's keep on topic. Would you mind telling me why I received a message from your college dean on our home phone this morning?"

"You what?"

"I think you heard me. He wants your father and I to call him today at five. Is there something you want to tell me?"

I stammered for a response. What the heck was happening? I pulled a Meri, I erased the dean's old messages—and now Professor Scott's been fired, the dean's left another message. What? I was trembling, and I thought, *I have to tell Mom everything about Meri. She has to help me.*

"Cindy, your father and I are overwhelmed here," she continued, and I could hear a sniffle; her voice was cracking with emotion.

"The last thing I need is for both of my daughters . . ."

"Everything's fine, Mom," I hastily told her. "I'll find out what's up with the dean and call you back. I promise." I clicked off and quickly dialed Lindsay. I just couldn't bother Mom with this right now—she has her own crisis to deal with, which means I'm officially on my own.

"Hey, what's up," answered Lindsay cheerfully.

"Where are you?" I cried.

She was at the house making lunch. Forgoing Long John's, I ran to Alpha Beta Delta and into the kitchen. It was empty.

"Lindsay?" I wailed.

"I'm upstairs," she called out from above, and I soon found out why. She'd had a hankering all day for a big, fat, sloppily inappropriate McDonald's cheeseburger and didn't want anyone to catch her, especially since the house is so tense right now. Shanna-Francine still hasn't come out of her room, and when Bobbie tried to call her on her cell phone, she picked up, sobbed incoherently, then hung up. I told Lindsay everything (in between stealing a few of her fries), and I could tell by the look on her face that it wasn't good. Yes, she explained, I "pulled a Meri," but Meri pulled one back, and unfortunately, Lindsay, Bud, and I didn't think things through beforehand. With the damning tiara tape in the dean's hands, and now Professor Scott fired, all obstacles that the dean might have had in terms of concluding his deal with the Sugarman attorneys are now gone. Now he's free to kick me out of RU, given my "violent" and "unstable behavior," not to mention my "attack" on Meri at the Day of Forgiveness Dinner.

"Why am I so stupid?" I wailed.

"You're not stupid," assured Lindsay. "You're just not evil. That's a good thing. And we have till five. We'll think of something."

I burst into tears. How could she be so optimistic? Then I heard music in the distance from a passing car. Faintly. But I recognized it almost immediately.

> *Oh, touch it, touch it, touch it!*
> *Touch my daisy*
> *Touch it, yeah!*

I laughed through my tears. I guess Lisa's manager was right. Cheap publicity sells singles. Lindsay's phone began vibrating. Her lips tightened.

"It's him again." Then she pouted—for about two seconds—and flipped it open.

"What? Quickly. I'm eating McDonald's."

Then the most wondrous thing happened. She listened—and who knows what Bud was saying, but her face transformed, unfolding like a flower. Her cheeks flushed, her breath became fluttery and unsteady, her eyes welled with tears. And she smiled.

"Where are you?" Then she exclaimed, "You're what?" She flung her phone aside, leaped off the bed, and ran out of the room. What was happening? I followed anxiously, and I saw her fly down the stairs, like some sort of winged angel of love, and I thought, *Wow, Dame Barbara has nothing on Bud and Lindsay.* The front door kicked open, and there he was, Bud Finger, in all his dorky splendor, his lower lip trembling, his cheeks streaked with tears. Lindsay jumped into his arms, her legs wrapping around his waist, and they kissed, oh my God, how they kissed, and it was such a wonderful romantic moment—but it was marred by the fact that Bud's not so strong, and his spindly little legs (which you could see since he was wearing those ridiculous capri pants again) unfortunately gave way. They toppled clumsily to the floor. But they didn't care. They were laughing and kissing. Then they ran up the stairs to Lindsay's room.

Lindsay paused before me and shyly asked, "Hey. You know that maid's uniform I gave you? You still got it?"

I did. I dashed into my room to find it, and I realized that I had a tear running down my cheek, but it wasn't just for Bud and Lindsay (or just Lindsay), it was for me, too. Will I ever have a love affair to equal theirs? And no, I don't want the dirty stuff that goes along with their relationship (at least not all of it) (some of it sounds fun) (like the Strip Chocolate Checkers), and I certainly can't imagine myself falling for a cheeseball like Bud (God help me), but is there someone out there for me? Somewhere? I found the maid's uniform (it has ridiculous pouffy sleeves) and when I stepped back into the hallway, I suddenly heard thunderous banging and loud thumping and I thought, *Wow, what the heck are they doing?* but then I looked down and I realized that the front door had been kicked open again and a group of men with guns and holsters were racing up the stairs—and then they violently knocked past me and one of them grabbed me.

"Bud Finger! Where is he?"

Terrified, I pointed to Lindsay's room. *Ka-boom!* They kicked open her door. I heard bloodcurdling screams from Lindsay and Bud. I could finally see straight—all the men had jackets with three big letters on them: FBI. Bud was pulled roughly out of Lindsay's room and dragged down the stairs. Screaming with horror, Lindsay followed, and so did I. On the front lawn, they threw him down, handcuffed him, and read him his rights. Bud was being arrested on multiple felony charges for copying and selling copyrighted material—all those movies, all those CDs.

"Don't say anything!" Lindsay wailed to Bud. "I'll call Daddy. Don't say anything!"

By now, students and other gawkers were gathering around. I stood there numbly. And through the haze of the crowd, it appeared—slowly at first, and just like the Cheshire Cat, all I could see was a gleaming smile, and perfect pearly teeth, and glossy-glossy lips. Then she came into focus. All of her. Meri. She was laughing. Lightly. Breathily. Flipping back her thick raven hair. Voices were building. Students were muttering and squealing:

"Just for copying stupid movies? . . . Dude, he sold them too, tons of them. . . . Oh my God, is he wearing pink nail polish? . . . Whoa, he's going to jail. . . . I want one of those FBI jackets. . . . He's so gonna be a butt-bitch."

I felt like I was drowning. Lindsay kept screaming. It was an open secret on campus that Bud copied and sold movies and CDs to pay for his tuition, but how did Meri know? The tiara! Lindsay never took it off, even in Bud's dorm room. Lightning fast, the FBI pushed a shell-shocked Bud into their van and took off, and just as quickly, the crowd dispersed—the fun was over—leaving Lindsay on the lawn, on her knees, her head in her hands, rocking back and forth, sobbing and wailing. A delicate hand brushed through her hair. Sheila Farr was kneeling before her. She gently kissed Lindsay's cheek.

"Come, my dear. We'll make tea."

Sheila led her trembling into the house. I turned back around—and shrieked. She stood there right before me, smiling contentedly.

"Give yet?"

"Wha-what?" I stuttered.

"Or not? If not, then fair warning," Meri whispered breathily. "I'm just beginning. The fun's just starting."

"I know Nancy Forbes is a killer," I blurted out, and I'm not sure why that thought occurred to me at that moment.

"Yes, she is," cooed Meri. "But we all need forgiveness, don't we? Even killers." Then she pulled a joint from her Miu Miu. "Light?"

A hand reached up from below. A lighter flicked. It was Albino
Girl! Meri took a deep hit and looked me in the eye. "You're fun.
Really." Then she strolled off, followed by Albino Girl and three
St. Eulalia girls, all of them giggling and happily spinning around
her on their Hello Kitty skateboards. My heart was thumping as I
stepped back inside. Sheila met me at the door.

"She's in her room. She won't come out. Poor dear. I made
chamomile. Why don't you have it?"

"Thank you, Miss Farr."

"Please, call me Sheila. And remember, everyone has a heart.
Except some people." And then—poof!—she was off in a swirl
of sequins and freshly sprayed Aquanet. I stepped slowly into the
kitchen. The house felt dead; and it was a big, screaming, horrible
deadness. My cell phone rang. I numbly flipped it open.

"Hello?"

"Cindy!" exclaimed Mom. Oh, no. I glanced at my watch. It
was only four o'clock. "Has Lisa called you?" she stammered. "Do
you know where she is?"

For the umpteenth time today, my jaw dropped clear past my
knees and hit the floor. Lisa has "gone missing." She's not at her
manager's office, she's not at the hotel, and one of the hotel bell-
boys vaguely remembers her asking how much it would cost to
take a cab to the airport.

"No, Mom, I'm sorry, I haven't heard from her." Mom started
crying. Oh God, where the heck is Lisa? I told her I was sure she
was around somewhere—maybe she's planning to hit the Spider
tonight—and that I'd keep trying to reach Lisa on her cell phone,
though Mom said she's already tried and it goes straight to voice
mail. I walked to my bedroom and thought, *What now?* Meri's
picked off Shanna-Francine, whose reputation is ruined; Patty,
who's addicted to trick; and Lindsay, who's lost her great love, and
me, since I'll be booted from the university within the hour. And

now Lisa's missing? *One thing at a time,* I thought. I desperately flipped on my computer and went through all my old e-mails from Lisa, frantic for a clue. I stopped breathing. The clue was right there in front of me.

The turbulence on this private plane is making it hard to write. I'm on my way to Corpus Christi, Texas. Mamacita is falling asleep next to me (one too many shots of Cuervo Gold, I guess). The sky outside is darkening, and so is my mind. It's polluted with anger and thoughts of revenge. Meri had better watch out. Why? Because I've finally found my authentic self. Ha. Really, I think I have. And it's not Cindy anymore. Please. Forget her. Cindy doesn't exist. From now on, I'm Dark Cindy. From now on, I'm going to fight fire with fire.

My cell phone just rang. It was Mom. I didn't want to worry her, so of course I didn't tell her I was on a private plane, but she could tell something was wrong. I was shocked by that, actually. Lisa is missing, after all, and I guess I'm still taking Meri's words seriously: "You're damaged goods. That's why Lisa gets all the attention." But Mom really and truly wanted to know what was wrong with me.

"Nothing," I offered limply.

"Tch. Cindy. It's me. I have eyes in the back of my head, remember? And Mommy-Radar." I laughed. When we were little, Lisa and I were convinced she had a built-in Mommy-Radar chip in her head (just behind her left ear). She always seemed to know when we stole extra sugar cookies (which she would try and hide in the dryer in the laundry room), and no matter how quiet we thought we were, she always knew when we snuck downstairs after midnight on a Saturday to watch a Creature Feature double feature. And now her radar was honed in on me. Just me. And she wasn't going to take "nothing" for an answer.

"I'm not hanging up until you're honest with me," she said impatiently.

I didn't tell her everything. In fact, all I told her was, "Meri's back at RU." There was a long, hollow pause after I said that.

Then she whispered, "That's not good."

I still didn't want to worry her, so I told her everything was going to be okay, because I'd made a big decision. From now on, I was going to "fight fire with fire." I thought she'd be proud of me for that. But she wasn't.

"Tch, Cindy. No, no, no. People who fight fire with fire usually end up in ashes. Dear Abby wrote that. And I think it's very sound advice. Don't you?"

I said yes, but did I mean it? We chatted a bit more (about Dad, mostly, who really has reached his limit with Lisa's show-bizzy shenanigans). Then I realized that I had to get her off the phone—and fast—when she mentioned that she and Dad would be talking with me and the dean in about a half hour. Oh my God, she's going to totally flip out when she realizes that I'm not there (I guess Mommy-Radar can't pick up everything) (and I'm sure as heck not going to pick up my cell phone when she calls back screaming). Instead, I'm right here, white-knuckling the turbulence and periodically pushing back Mamacita, whose head keeps dropping to my shoulder (at least she doesn't snore). I'm also questioning the wisdom of Dear Abby. Yes, I've managed to fight Meri, but at what cost? And if I keep fighting, how can I win if I don't sink to her level?

The handsome steward just announced that we're approaching Corpus Christi International Airport. Should I wake up Mamacita? I'm actually a bit frightened, and not about the turbulence or the landing (okay, maybe a little). I mean, Mamacita said she had everything under control, but really, it's pretty hard to pull a fast one on Meri.

"Pfff. What's one little plane," scoffed Mamacita at the private airstrip before take-off. Apparently, Mamacita frequently requests the use of a plane to visit her ailing Aunt Bertha in Texas (though Aunt Bertha, she told me, is really quite robust), and no one blinks an eye. Oh God, I just hope Meri isn't waiting for us at the arrivals gate. I can almost hear her breathy voice now.

"There you are. There's my little bow-wow. So tell me. Is there a reason you're using one of Daddy's private jets?"

Okay, we're landing now. I have to put my tray up and stop writing.